THE VAMPIRE AFFAIR

THE VAMPIRE AFFAIR

De Re Strigis

RAY GLEASON

Erinach LLC, Culver, Indiana

THE GAIUS MARIUS CHRONICLE
The Vampire Affair
De Re Strigis

ISBN PRINT: 978-0-578-32499-9
ISBN EBOOK: 978-0-578-32500-2
Library of Congress Control Number: 2021923262

Cover Design:
Rachel Lopez
www.r2cdesign.com

This book has been published by Erinach, LLC, Culver, Indiana

First Printing, 2022

To My Brothers
1st Platoon, Company A, 2nd Battalion, 35th Infantry
"Cacti Blue"
Especially Those "Still On Patrol":

Doc Joe Ambrosio
Richie Jones
Mark Barnes
Bobby Knoll
David Chahoc
Derris Brown

"Old age hath yet his honor and his toil.
Death closes all; but something ere the end,
Some work of noble note, may yet be done,
Not unbecoming men that strove with gods."
Tennyson, "Ulysses"

Dramatis Personae

Gaius Marius Insubrecus Tertius, our hero, known variously as

- *Arth Uthr*, "Fearsome Bear," by his Gallic comrades after a few tankards of mead
- *Pagane*, "The Hick," by his Roman army mates
- Gai by Caesar, Labienus, his family, close friends, and his few girlfriends
- Insubrecus by his army colleagues and casual associates
- *Prime*, "Top Soldier," but that's much later in his military career

Gaius Iulius Caesar – *Imperator* and commander of the Roman legions in Gaul; Proconsul of Cisalpine Gaul, Transalpine Gaul and Illyricum; ex-Consul of the Roman Republic and *Triumvir* with Gnaeus Pompeius and Marcus Licinius Crassus; *patronus,* Patron of our hero, Gaius Marius Insubrecus

Romani
The Romans

Caesar's Legates in Gaul:

Titus Labienus - a professional soldier and Caesar's right-hand man; in command of the Roman army during Caesar's absence.

Gaius Valerius Troucillus – a Roman citizen and member of the order of knights; a prince of the Helvi, a Gallic tribe in the Roman *Provincia*; Caesar's *Legatus ad Manus* and personal envoy to Duuhruhda mab Clethguuhno – or Diviciacus as he's known to the Romans – king of the Aedui.

Caesar's Military Tribunes:
Lucius Vipsanius Agrippa - an Italian from Asisium; an equestrian, a social and political nobody, but a good officer, serving as Caesar's quartermaster; he's off building roads in the *Provincia;* his younger brother, Marcus, makes it big.

The Centurions:
Tertius Piscius Malleus, "The Hammer" - *Centurio Primus Pilus* of the Tenth Legion.
Decius Minatius Gemellus - *Praefectus Castrorum*, Prefect of Caesar's army.
Cossus Lollius Strabo - "Squinty"; Insubrecus' former training officer; a *centurio prior pilus* of the second line, leading centurion of the Sixth Cohort of the Tenth Legion

Other Roman Officers, Soldiers and Slaves:
Spina – a military *medicus* in the Tenth legion and Caesar's personal physician; an aficionado of wines-fine or otherwise.
Dionysius – a *famulus,* household slave of the consul, Aulus Gabinius; originally hails from Athens; acquired by Caesar and sent to Gaul to tutor Insubrecus in the *koine*, Alexandrian Greek.
Ebrius, "The Drunk" - Caesar's head military clerk and self-appointed taster of Caesar's wine and *posca* collection.
Tullius Norbanus - "Tulli"; formerly the assistant squad leader of Insubrecus' training unit; Strabo's *optio*, his Number One.
Hirsutus – "Scruffy"; *decurio* in command of a *turma* of Roman cavalry from the Eleventh Legion.
Piscis – "The Fish"; *decurio* in the cavalry; Hirsutus' Number One.
Murmurus – "Mumbles"; the third *decurio* in Hirsutus' *turma*.
Anoulos – a Romanized Gah'el serving in Hirsutus' cavalry *turma*.
Calenos – another Gah'el serving in the Roman cavalry
Crispus – "Curly"; an *immunis,* special duty soldier, exempt from fatigues; serves as the *augur* of the Tenth Legion

Tutor – a "trustee" slave in the Tenth Legion; in charge of the *stabula*, the barracks of the praetorium slaves.

Bretos Scriba – a slave in the Tenth Legion assigned as a clerk in the supply section.

Cocus – "Cookie"; a slave in the Tenth Legion; head cook in the headquarters section.

Calo – "Orderly"; a slave of the Tenth Legion; orderly for the officers of the praetorian guard.

And Finally:

Marcus Metius – a Roman spy who claims to be a merchant, and who has had dealings, shady and otherwise, all over Gaul; living among the Remi, a Belgian tribe, as Caesar's spy.

Clamriu – a horse, of course.

Beorn – another horse who, as his German name suggests, may be in cahoots with the enemy

Galli
The Gauls

Aedui, the *Aineduai* - the "Dark Moon" people:

Duuhruhda mab Clethguuhno - *Uucharix*, tribal king of the Aedui, and *Pobl'rix*, clan leader of the *Wuhr Blath*, the Wolf clan of the *Aineduai*; known to the Romans as Diviciacus

Druce mab Cadmanos - "*Mair Duhn Mawr*," the "Big Guy"; Duuhruhda's uncle and chief of intelligence, the *eminence grise* of the Aedui. Often referred to by his Roman name, Decius Aeduorum.

Anionos mab Kamehros - Duuhruhda's *barnuchel*, the senior justice of the Aineduai.

Deluuhnu mab Clethguuhno - brother of Duuhruhda; former *pendefig*, "crown prince," of the Aedui and commander of the garrison of Bibracte; now an outlaw and exile at Caesar's orders; known to the Romans as Dumnorix.

Cuhnetha mab Cluhweluhno - *Buch'rix*, "Cattle King," of a small settlement east of Bibracte; *Pobl'rix*, clan leader of the *Wuhr Tuurch*, the Boar Clan of the Aedui; a pretender to the throne of the Aedui.

Morcant mab Cuhnetha - oldest son of Cuhnetha and Leader of Ten in the Aedui cavalry; *pendefig*, prince of the Boar Clan.

Rhonwen merc Gwen - niece of Cuhnetha; a sassy redhead, who caught Insubrecus' eye in a previous tale, and whose memory clearly lingers in his mind.

Brida merc Ronos – Cuhnetha's wife and Morcant's mom.

Ula merc Tigos – Morcant's wife and soon to be the mother of his daughter; she has the "sight."

Gouenhouhvar merc Morcant – "The White Fey"; newly born daughter of Morcant.

Tegid mab Gwen – Morcant's shield bearer and cousin; brother of Rhonwen

Trahernos mab Nelos - a warrior of five seasons in Morcant's *fintai*, warband.

Arwuhnos mab Iforos – Cuhnetha's household *meduhg*, physician.

Malouuhnos mab Dermuhtos - *Pobl'rix*, clan leader of the Bear Clan and no friend of Rome.

Malgounos mab Owenos - nephew of Malouuhnos, a warrior of five seasons, leader of a hundred, and putative suitor of Rhonwen.

Bruhchamos mab Euhdulf - Pobl'rix, clan leader of the Badger Clan; an ally of Malouuhnos.

Karadogos mab Toutoualos - or Primus Caratagus Aeduanus as he prefers to be called, the leader of the Fox Clan, fond of Roman luxuries.

Eogahnos mab Gwitheri – Duuhruhda's nephew, a nebbish whom Duuhruhda nominates as his *pendefig*.

Gourach merc Fetroda – Morna before her transformation; a messenger sent by the gods or a complete nutcase ... pays yer money, takes yer choice.

Catouallaunos mab Dubnogenos - "Clou"; one of Druce's "field agents."

Pruhderos – "Pruhde"; Clou's companion.

Ludnert – one of Clou's "sources"; runs a tavern northwest of Bibracte.

Modrona merc Cardros – a ten-year old girl snatched by the Nightwalker and intended as a sacrifice to dark god, Afalanos.

Tahernos mab Malagronos - an officer in the *fintai* of Malouuhnos mab Dermuhtos

Sheridos – a scout.

Bledigos mab Eurig - interim commander of Duuhruhda's *fintai* and the garrison of Bibracte

Sequani, the *Soucana* - the people of the river goddess Soucana:

Athauhnu mab Hergest – *Pencefhul*, "Leader of a Hundred," commander in the Auxiliary Sequani Cavalry; known as *Adonus Dux* to the Romans

Comites et Conscii Insubreci
Insubrecus' Companions and Confidants

Quintus Macro – our hero's first mentor and long-time friend; served as a *Centurio ad Manum* to both Caesar and Octavius; during this tale, he's managing the Roman military port in Massalia.

Rufia – Mrs. Quintus Macro, madame of the blue-door *lupinarium* and queen of the Mediolanum underworld.

Quintus Macro, Iunior – their adopted son, just turned twenty-one; Macro brought Junior back as a teenager from Octavius' final campaigns against Antonius; Rufia is training him to take over the family business; what his adoptive parents don't know about Junior could get them both killed; his story is told in Insubrecus' police journal, *The Murdered Centurion*.

Athvoowin merc Gwili – "Cynthia" is her professional name; she succeeded Rufia as the madame of the blue-door lupinarium and was Insubrecus' "first wife"; she and Rhonwen can never be in the same room together or the Gallic wars will recommence.

Dramatis Personae Aliae,
Other Players

Aderuhn mab Enit – part of Troucillus' household; *Barnuchel*, a senior justice and investigator of the Helvi, whose Roman name is Gnaeus Curtius Helvius.

Trahernos mab Adair – *Derwuhd*, a priest and theologian of the Helvi, whose Roman name is Spurius Fulvius.

Belimawros Golba - Belimor the Fat, an *oberkunig* of the Belgae, who rules a coalition of tribes both in the lands of the Belgians and in Britain.

Aulus Gabinius, Senior - a senatorial mid-bencher who does well and is elected consul; he wants Insubrecus dead.

Gabinia Pulchra - "Gabi"; the daughter of Aulus Gabinius and our hero's putative "one-and-only"; she also wants Insubrecus dead ... must run in the family.

Grennadios the Trader - a Greek merchant from Massalia, who seems to lead at least a double life

Evra - Grennadios' woman, from a mysterious island west of Britannia; not a redhead, but formidable nonetheless

Cleopatra VII Philopator – *The* Cleopatra, whom Gai refers to as the "Macedonian" and Caesar as *catula*, "kitten"; appearing in this story only as part of Gai's guilty conscience.

Gnaeus Pompeius Magnus - a *triumvir*, a political partner of Caesar, and the *eminence grise* in Roman politics.

Marcus Licinius Crassus – the other *triumvir*, a political partner of Caesar; too intent on going off to conquer Parthia to pay much attention to what Caesar's doing in Gaul.

Mordros mab Milour – the leader of the gang that runs the Gallic section of Mediolanum, 'Medhlán'; they do not welcome Romans into their neighborhood; he also has a secret that will complicate Insubrecus' life; his story is told in Insubrecus' police journal, *The Murdered Centurion*.

Thraex – 'The Thracian,' or more formally, Livius Drusus Thracius; a retired gladiator, which means he was good – very, very good

– and a major celebrity-jock in the Roman world of blood sport; his story is told in Insubrecus' police journal, *The Murdered Centurion*.

Liber IV
De Re Strigis
Book Four – The Vampire Affair

Mediliolani Anno Consulium Imp Caesaris Divi f
Augusti VIII et T Statilii Tauri II.
AUC DCCXXVIII
Praefatio
Mediolanum, during the consulships of the Impera-
tor, Caesar, Son of the God, the Exalted One, 8th
Term, and Titus Statilius Taurus, 2nd Term
26 BCE
Preface

Gallia in terris Aeduorum Anno Consulium L.
Calpurnii Pisonis Caesonini et A Gabinii.
AUC DCXCVI
Gaul, in Aeduan Territory, during the Consulships
of Lucius Calpurnius Piso Caesoninus and Aulus
Gabinius, 58 BCE

Praefatio
Mediolani
Anno Consulium Imp Caesaris Divi F Augusti VIII et T Statilii Tauri II
Mensis Iulii
AUC DCCXXVIII

Preface

Milan
During the consulships of the Imperator, Caesar, Son of the God, the Exalted
One, 8th Term, and Titus Statilius Taurus, 2nd Term
July, 26 BCE

Things now seem reasonably under control in the wake of the Thraex debacle. So, I'm closing my personal journal on what I call "The Mystery of the Murdered Centurion" in the fervent hope that no other eyes except mine ever see it.

I put Thraex in the frame for murdering the former centurion, Opilio, and for betraying Livia, the *Augusta*. I pray Thraex' *lars*, his vengeful wraith, is safely tucked away in the lands of *Dis*. Unless the gods allow it to pass over the River Lethe with its memories intact, it will not trouble me when darkness embraces the middle world, a time when we mortals are most haunted by our fears and guilt.

It's the living that concern me now, particularly my patron down in Rome, Augustus, our "Exalted One," and his consort, Livia.

I pray that my secret concerning the identity of Macro and Rufia's adopted son, Macro *Iunior*, is safe. Certainly, from his parents, but more importantly from Livia's spies, the *Frumentarii*. Still, every time a packet of official correspondence arrives from Rome, and I see a piece of folded papyrus sealed with the stamp of Octavius, I freeze for a heartbeat fearing it's a summons for me to appear in Rome.

Of course, I know there would be no summons.

If our "Exalted One" were ever to find out about Macro *Iunior*, a *sica* would be slipped quietly into my back in some dark alley and that would be the end of it. Octavius would bury that secret with my silent corpse.

To make matters more troubling, *Iunior* is becoming active around town running his mother's "business."

Since Rufia took over Opilio's money-lending racket, her organization has expanded, what with security, collections, and the like. She has outsourced most of the "heavy" work to Aquila, one of Antonius' ex-centurions.

But, *Iunior* has taken over the day-to-day running of the operation.

Iunior has also started a little sideline of his own. In collaboration with my newly discovered son, Mordros, he provides "security" to the warehouses and the factories down in Medhlán, the Gallic section of town. *Iunior's* job is to provide the muscle. And Mordros, for a modest percentage of the take, ignores a "Roman" incursion onto what he considers "his turf."

If the situation weren't so dangerous, I could laugh at Mordros considering Macro *Iunior* a "Roman."

My cousin, Naso, who inherited Opilio's importing business and a huge warehouse off the *Via Decumena*, was *Iunior's* first "client." *Iunior* keeps an office in Naso's warehouse, where he's set up his head *percussor*, an enforcer called Truncus, the "Tree Truck." Truncus is a former legionary of Antony and an associate of Aquila. For reasons known only to the gods, Truncus has decided the world would be a better place without me in it.

Recently, *Iunior* has started referring to himself as "*Il' Patrone*," the "God Father." He claims that the title, "*Iunior*," the "Younger," doesn't have adequate *gravitas*, the dignity needed to maintain his "new position of leadership in the community"; it would only encourage his "competitors" to question his authority, so he says.

I really don't care what *Iunior* calls himself, as long as it's not the name his birth-mother gave him. That would be an immediate death warrant for him and for me. I just wish he'd keep a lower profile. Everywhere I go recently, I hear him described as "that new guy ... the one with the singsong, Eastern accent."

When I try to explain the problem to the newly minted "*Il' Patrone*," he just laughs it off and tells me not to worry ... "Everything's under control, uncle!" he assures me.

Everything's under control! Everything's under control until a squad of Octavius' praetorians show up from Rome in the middle of the night to clean up this mess I'm hiding.

Laus omnibus dis ... thank the gods ... my darlin' wife, Rhonwen, doesn't seem to be suffering too many ill effects from the kidnapping of our son, Gaiulus, and her experience with Thraex.

I have caught her gazing at the boy with a far-away look in her eyes as he plays or while his head's down studying some scroll Dion assigned him for homework. Also, if she hasn't laid eyes on the boy for more than a quarter hour, she gets anxious and looks for him.

I'm afraid Rhonwen has discovered a hard lesson about life. Our ability to maintain peace of mind is quite frail, at best, an illusion. It depends very much on the welfare of others in our lives, a welfare over which we have little or no control.

We are not aware of our vulnerabilities until those necessary to our happiness are threatened, or worse, lost. If we do lose someone dear to us, a loved one, we spend our dark moments blaming ourselves and wondering ... no, wishing we had done things differently.

If we are fortunate enough to escape tragedy, as was Rhonwen with our son, we never forget what almost happened and become hyper-vigilant to prevent a recurrence.

My friend, Spina, the doctor who now specializes in "women's ailments," tells me not to worry. He claims Rhonwen's physical symptoms are the result of an imbalance in her bodily humors caused by the shock of what happened. A surfeit of the earth element, the "cold and dry," has produced a "black bile," a *melaina chole* according to the Greeks, or *morosus* in Latin.

"Huh conscious mind, huh *animus*, is tryin' to push da bad memories down into huh unconscious, huh *anima*," Spina advises. "It'll take cayah of itself ovah time. Just make shuwah she stays busy ... busy's good fowah dese dings ... when da humors ah back in balance, she'll be right as rain."

Gaiulus, our son, seems totally unfazed.

To him, it was a grand adventure. Wicked, ruthless brigands led by a blood-thirsty bandit-king; a daring rescue by Gallic warriors led by a golden hero; a triumphant return to his home to be welcomed by weeping women who feared him dead.

A veritable Greek romance!

Gaiulus' "golden hero" is my newly discovered son, Mordros.

His mother, Athvoowin mec Gwili, and I spent two nights together many years ago, before I joined the legions. When I met Athvoowin, I was sixteen; she wasn't much older. But she was working in Rufia's *lupinarium* under the name "Cynthia."

The first time we were together was on my sixteenth birthday; she was a "gift" from my friend, Macro. I was inexperienced and dreadfully nervous, so Athvoowin pronounced a Gallic marriage of the eighth degree between us, a "soldier's marriage," partially to calm me down and partially to tease me for my sixteen-year-old-Gallic-hick-from-the-boondocks panic.

The last time we were together was after her employer, Rufia, pulled my chestnuts out of the fire. A couple of Roman *sicarii*, hitters, had arrived in Mediolanum to remove my chestnuts and deliver them to the daughter of a Roman Senator, Gabinia Pulchra, because, ironically, I had *not* slept with her.

Rufia had me roughed up to fool the *sicarii* into thinking she was on their side. The night with Athvoowin in one of the *lupinarium*'s private rooms was a bit of compensation for the bruising I had taken.

Athvoowin's gift to me was Mordros, a son whom I did not discover until recently.

This, of course, was another shock to add to Rhonwen's recent load. To be fair, Rhonwen is grateful to Mordros for bringing Gaiulus home to her. In fact, it was she who encouraged me to formally recognize Mordros as my son before the urban praetor. And, surprisingly, she and Athvoowin seemed to have bonded.

Instead of constantly worrying about what might be in the next courier packet from Rome, I've decided to bury myself in the day-to-day routine of functioning as the urban prefect of Mediolanum - running the fire brigades, the street watch, and urban cohort of the town. When I run out of memos to read, budgets to review, reports to write, and directives to seal, I work on my memoirs of Caesar's campaigns in *Gallia Comata,* "Gaul of the Long Hairs."

Reviewing my notes, I see that my last entry was describing our pursuit of Ariovistus and the Swabian survivors of the battle on the River of Lilies near the Vosges.

CASTRUM HIBERNUM

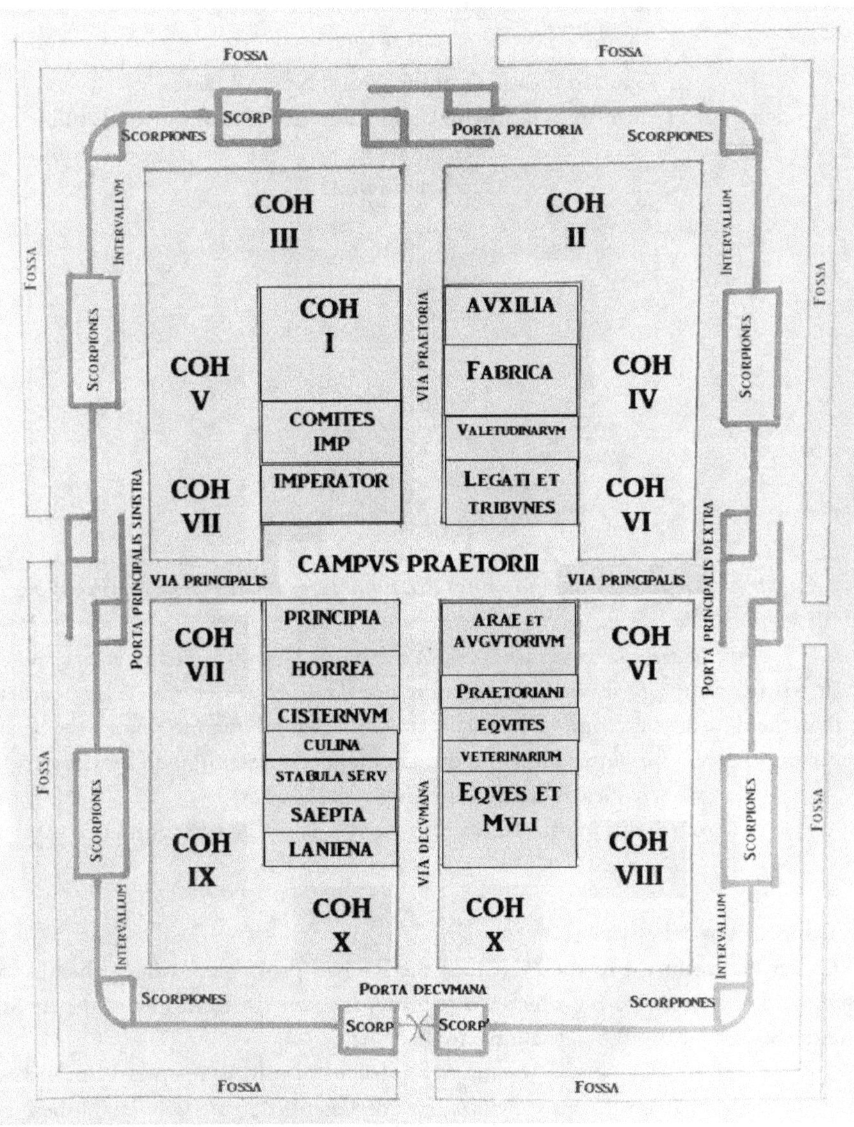

Winter Camp of the Tenth Legion Vicinity of the Aeduan Town of Bibracte 58 BCE

I

Caput I. In Castris Hiberniis
Chapter 1. In Winter Camp

Caesar una aestate duobus maximis bellis confectis maturius paulo quam tempus
anni postulabat in hiberna in Sequanos exercitum deduxit hibernis Labienum praepo-
suit ipse in citeriorem Galliam ad conventus agendos profectus est
In a single campaign season, Caesar had achieved two great victories. A little earlier
than the time of year required, he led his army into winter quarters among the Sequani, where he appointed Labienus the commander. Caesar himself returned to
Nearer Gaul to administer the district.
(From Gaius Marius Insubrecus' notebook of Caesar's journal)

Labienus was at his wits' end.

Caesar had returned to the *Provincia*, the Roman province, leaving Labienus in
command of a Roman army which was spread out across the territories of the Aedui
and the Sequani, from Bibracte almost to the Rhenus.

Two of our six legions, the veteran Seventh and Ninth, were spread out across
Sequani territory from *Castrum Bellum*, east of Vesantio, to a newly established legionary *castrum* overlooking the crossings of the Arar, which separates the lands of the
Sequani from those of the Aedui. The Eighth Legion, another veteran formation, was
sitting on the Sequani fortress city of Lugdunum, which controlled the strategically
important bridge at the confluence of the Arar and Rhodanus.

The Twelfth Legion, one of Caesar's newly recruited Gallic formations, was in the *Provincia* with Lucius Vipsanius Agrippa, Caesar's recently appointed quartermaster. Their job was to build logistics routes from the Roman docks in Massalia all the way to Lugdunum of the Sequani.

Agrippa's immediate task was converting a native dirt road, a *via terrena*, that followed the Rhodanus from Avennione, a Gallic back-water town northwest of Massalia, to Lugdunum of the Sequani, into a a gravel road, a *via glareata*, that could accommodate army supply wagons in the worst weather conditions Gaul had to offer. At Lugdunum, Caesar had established a logistics center capable of supporting army operations along the Rhondaus, Arar, and Dubis rivers, and up into the Rhenus valley.

The Eleventh Legion, the other Gallic formation, was building a road from Bibracte, the fortress-town of Duuhruhda mab Clethguuhno, the tribal king of the Aedui, to the fords of the Arar near the Aeduan town of Ventum Cavillonum. There they'd hopefully link up with elements of the Eighth in their *castrum* overlooking the River Arar and with the Seventh who were tasked with building a road up from Lugdunum.

My legion, the Tenth, was encamped outside Bibracte. Our primary job was to sit on Duuhruhda, an on-again, off-again ally at best, and remind him constantly of what a bad idea it would be to betray Caesar's trust. Our other mission was to act as the army's immediate reaction force. If anything went unexpectedly and horribly wrong, we were to fix it.

That was the theory anyway.

Communications were a nightmare for Labienus.

Since our native cavalry detachments had returned to their homelands for the winter, Labienus had created a mounted security and courier force out of Caesar's praetorian cavalry and cavalry detachments from each of the legions. Since the Twelfth was assigned road construction in a secure province, Labienus had taken their entire cavalry *ala*, about two-hundred fifty troopers – much to the relief of the troopers themselves.

Other than combat and forced marches, road construction is the worst assignment a legion can draw. No one is immune. The work is backbreaking, the workdays are long, and the work goes on regardless of the weather. No self-respecting cavalryman, who is usually immune from fatigue details, wants to mix it up in the mud with the *muli*, the infantry grunts.

Labienus drew an additional three to four cavalry *turmae* from each of the other legions creating an *ala* of Roman cavalry of almost nine hundred troopers under his personal command. Most of these troopers conducted security screening missions beyond the army's perimeter, north into the lands of the Senones and Parisii, and up into the valley of the Rhenus toward the lands of the Belgae. He also sent detachments west toward the tribes of the Aquitani. The rest "carried the mail," – status reports, demands for intelligence, logistical details, orders, strength reports – all the papyrus needed to feed a perpetually hungry army administration.

Labienus understood that the system he had created would work only until the winter shut it down. Once the temperatures dropped and the snow fell, all army activity would cease. The legions would retreat into their winter camps and hopefully they would still be there when communications resumed sometime next March.

Fortunately, it was just past the *Nones* of October, and the weather had cooperated with Labienus' plans. The breath of the *Venti*, the gods of the winds, was not harsh, and the fiery chariot of *Helios Magnus* remained close enough to the middle lands to melt away the morning frosts.

But the daylight hours were becoming shorter and soon the night of the *Samon'win* would be upon us, the Gallic feast marking the day when the hours of light and the hours of darkness were equal. For the Gah'el, this is the dividing line between the "Time of Light" and the "Time of Darkness"; it is the night on which the Gah'el surrender the middle lands to the *Uh Thloo uth uh Doo T'wil*, the People of the Dark God, Dana.

The Romans have no equivalent for the *Samon'win*. For them, the day is merely *pridie calendae Novembris*, the day before the Calends of November, a day that is for them *fas*, propitious and auspicious for all public business.

The closest the Romans have to our *Samon'win* is their *Lemuria* in May. This is the day when the *lemures*, the restless and malevolent spirits of the dead – those who went unburied, murder victims, abandoned infants, those whose bodies were lost in water – roam the earth seeking justice and afflicting the living who can still feel the warmth of the sun while they, the *lemures*, are imprisoned in the cold, black caverns of the underworld.

For reasons I cannot even begin to understand, these fearful and noisome Roman apparitions can be exorcised with beans!

The Roman *paterfamilias*, the head of the family, rises at midnight, and needs only to walk around the house nine times in bare feet throwing black beans over his shoulder while intoning "*Haec ego mitto; his redimo meque meosque fabis!* I throw these beans! I ransom myself and my household with these beans!" Then, his entire household beat on bronze pots shouting, "Ghosts of my fathers and ancestors, be gone!"

I don't know how the *lemures* react to this racket, but I have seen Roman dogs run away howling at the noise!

The "Dark Ones" of the Gah'el cannot be gotten rid of that easily. These are not ghosts, but the remnant of the people who ruled the middle lands when the Gah'el first descended from the high places. After decades of bloody conflict, we agreed to "share" the land in order to end the wars between our peoples. The Gah'el would rule the middle lands from May to November and the Dark Ones from November to May.

On the night of the *Samon'win*, the Dark Ones emerge from the shadowy places below the middle lands where they dwell during the Time of Light. The old animosities toward the Gah'el have not left them. On the night of their release, they roam the darkness playing spiteful tricks on the any of the Gah'el who are foolish enough to be caught outside after sundown or not to have secured their homes.

Somewhat like the Romans with their brass pots and black beans, the Gah'el try to ward off the malevolence of the Dark Ones. At sundown, bowls of cream and sweet-cakes are left on the doorstep of the house as offerings. Then, all the doors and windows are secured tightly, and a wreath of holly is placed on the entry way.

I remember my grandmother, once our house was secured for the night during the Dark Season, would open the door for no one. Once my gran'pa stayed out too late drinking with his buddies. When he finally got home, he found the doors locked against him. He pounded on the boards and yelled for nanna to let him in, but she would not. I remember her telling me that it would be just like the Dark Ones to pretend they were my gran'pa to fool her into opening the door. So, gran'pa spent a cold night in one of the sheds.

The next morning at sunrise, when nanna finally unlocked the house and let gran'pa warm himself at the breakfast fire, he complained to her about her locking him out. There were no sprights or monsters lurking about the neighborhood, he grumbled. Nanna just sniffed at him and said that in the condition he came home, Hannibal the Carthaginian and all his elephants could have marched down the road past our farm and he wouldn't have heard them.

That was the last time gran'pa missed curfew, which was probably nanna's point from the start.

The Aedui in Bibracte were preparing for the *Samon'win*. The fields around the Roman *castrum* had been cleared and the farm animals returned to the barns and sheds. Anything left out under the sky during the Dark Season by rights belonged to the Dark Ones. Also, fuel was being collected and piled on the three peaks enclosed within the fortress-town, the north, south and west, for the great fires, which are lit at full dark on the *Samon'win*.

The Gah'el call these fires, *uh tanau o esguhrnou*, "the fires of the bones."

Gran'pa told me that in the old days on *Samon'win* our people would burn war-captives in the great fires as an offering to the Dark Ones. When the fires cooled, there would be piles of human bones visible among the ashes. Gran'pa didn't know whether our people did this as a sacrifice to appease the malice of the Dark Ones or to demonstrate to our traditional enemies that we were still a fierce and merciless people.

Regardless, the tale's effect on me was to crawl off into the darkest corner of our sleeping loft and hide beneath my blankets, haunted by dreams of black-eyed, human skulls staring at me from piles smoking ash.

The Gah'el do not practice human sacrifice any longer ... at least not in this part of Gaul. The bone-fires are merely part of our celebration of the ending of the year. The people dance, sing, and drink the traditional red mead, while the flames launch showers of sparks into the night skies to rival the stars flickering in the firmament. It is a night of mischief, practical jokes, gifts, and feasting; young couples slipping away into dark corners to consummate a "marriage for the night." When the celebration is over, however, no one walks home alone, lest the Dark Ones are indeed lurking in the deep shadows to avenge themselves on their tormentors.

Of course, none of this Gallic lore seeps through into Labienus' Roman consciousness. Things that go bump in the night are irrelevant to the operation and welfare of the Roman army in Gaul, unless those things are carrying stabbing spears and are trying to infiltrate the *castrum*. On most days, Labienus sits in the *principia*, his headquarters, sorting through stacks of *tabulae* – logistics reports, strength reports, disciplinary reports – all the vital indicators of the readiness of the legions.

For him, seasonal change means switching summer candles to winter candles to measure the hours and the night watches; filling the granaries and the storage tents with enough grain and sundries to get the army through the winter; dispatching the *venatores*, the hunters, into the hills to harvest fresh meat for the smokers.

Darkness means longer watches at night; heightened vigilance against enemy infiltration; and spotting snuffies sleeping on guard duty.

The autumn rains slow things down – a messages from the Ninth at Vesantio takes two days longer to arrive; riders claim they can't conduct security sweeps because the wet roads are bad for the horses' hooves; the *muli* try to avoid outside fatigues by crowding morning sick-call.

The colder days means fuel is needed to keep the troops warm; the men need long sleeves, *bracae* - Gallic trousers, woolen socks, hooded cloaks and gloves; the coughing sickness spreads through the compounds; the *muli* try to avoid outside fatigues by crowding morning sick-call.

When winter arrives, squad tents need to be converted to huts of logs and earthen walls; fire watches are detailed to prevent fires and the mysterious deaths caused by the demons that are awakened by the heat of burning charcoal; men are forced together, living in tight spaces; old grudges are stirred up ... fights and stabbings; the *muli* try to avoid outside fatigues by crowding morning sick-call.

Snow! Operations shut down for the winter – if it hasn't been done yet, it'll have to wait for spring; still; the *muli* try to avoid outside fatigues by crowding morning sick-call.

So, all critical tasks need to be completed before the snow begins to fall in November.

With all that going on in the head-shed, I'm surprised when Labienus summoned me to his *cubiculum* in the *principia* during the seventh hour of an otherwise sunny and pleasant day.

Since Caesar had left the army and gone south to administer his provinces, I was being ignored to work on the old man's journals. Although technically I was a *decurio*, a junior officer in Caesar's praetorian cavalry, I wasn't assigned to take out any of the scouting missions. Labienus never mentioned it, but I'm sure one of the reasons was that the men still considered me an upstart, a fuzz-faced *tiro* who owed his rank to influence and not service.

My officer's sash and golden five-strand torc might impress my Sequani cavalry troopers, but the Roman boys in the regular cavalry squadrons weren't buying any of it.

I arrived on time at the headquarters tent in full rig, my helmet clamped tightly under my left arm. When Ebrius spotted me, he nodded, "Go straight through, *decurio*. The boss is expecting you."

Ebrius looked a bit pale. Since Caesar returned to the *provincia*, Ebrius' "other job" as Caesar's "wine taster" had been severely curtailed. Labienus was happy with *posca*, and a steady diet of that soldiers' swill would make anyone pale.

I marched into Labienus' *cubiculum* and immediately spotted his shock of dark, thick, curly hair hovering over a pile of *tabulae*. I assumed the position in front of his field desk, and started, "*Legate! Gaius Marius Insubrecus, decurio praetorianus ...*"

The head didn't move, but a hand came up to silence me. After a few heartbeats, Labienus lifted his head, refocused his eyes, and said, "*Bene ...* Gai ... right on time. Please ... *laxa*! Stand at ease."

Labienus began to search through the wooden slates piled on his desk. Finally, he found one that still had a shred of purple ribbon clinging to it from a wad of brownish-red wax; correspondence from the proconsul, Caesar.

"Ah ... *bene* ... here it is," Labienus muttered to no one in particular.

Then, to me with an inscrutable smirk, "The *imperator* has sent you a gift."

Then, "Ebri!"

"*Tib'a'sum, legate!*" Ebrius' voice from outside. "Yes, sir!"

"Bring in the slave!" Labienus ordered. "The one for Insubrecus here!"

The slave, I wondered. *'The one for Insubrecus'? What in the name of Cerberus' three heads is going on?*

"*A'mperi'tu, legate!*" from Ebrius. "Yes, sir!"

I noted how much Ebrius' military courtesy had improved since he got sober.

After a few heartbeats, the curtain opened and Ebrius put one foot into the room. He gestured to someone standing outside. "In you go, boy! Come on! Get a move on and get in here!"

A thin, dark-haired man in an undyed slave tunic entered the room. He quickly glanced around, then dropped his eyes to avoid making eye-contact with me and Labienus. He looked vaguely familiar.

"I believe you two are already acquainted," Labienus was saying. "*Serve!* Slave. Look up so we can see your face!"

The slave looked up and fixed his eyes at a spot somewhere above our heads.

Then, Labienus, "Caesar has sent you this slave ... he is from the household of the consul, Aulus Gabinius, in Insubria ... I believe you two have met before ..."

Then I recognized the slave. Dion! My tutor who taught me my "Ah, Bay, Cay's" back in my other life before I joined the army.

"Dion?" I sputtered.

Dion dropped his eyes. Labienus continued, "Caesar wants ... what'd you say his name is ... Dion? Caesar wants this 'Dion' here to teach you Greek ... the *koine* ... the *imperator* thinks it may be useful ... don't know why ... but there it is ... Caesar also says you may want to know how that Trojan poem ends."

Dion continued to stare at the ground.

Labienus, "Dion is still the property of the consul, but he's yours for as long as you need him. No idea why Caesar wants you learning Greek," Labienus shrugged. "But that's between you and him. Caesar sent you this message ... maybe he explains it better than I can."

Labienus handed me the *tabula*, the one with the brown wax and purple ribbon.

Labienus continued, "You're still bunked in with the praetorians, aren't you, Gai ... this ... uh ... 'Dion' of yours can't stay there ... find a place for him is one of the slave *stabula* behind the granaries ... have Ebrius write him an internal pass, so the guards don't mess with him ... you might want to stop by supply and get him fitted up with some winter clothes ... and see if the cooks have anything hot left over from chow ... he looks like he could use some meat on those bones."

I didn't respond, so Labienus asked, "*'Abesne questiones, decurio?* Any questions, decurio?"

"*N'abeo, legate,*" I snapped out of my shock, "No, sir!"

"*Bene,*" Labienus said, "Then, get your arse out of here! I got work to do!"

"*A'mperi'tu, legate!*" I stammered. "Yes, sir!"

I was trying to stuff Caesar's missive under my left arm alongside my helmet and guide Dion out of the tent by his elbow, when Labienus started, "Gai! Almost forgot ..."

"What? I mean, yes, sir!"

Labienus ignored my violation of proper military decorum. "I have a meeting here with Troucillus, Caesar's emissary to Diviciacus ... tenth hour ... Troucillus asked that you attend ... uniform's informal, so don't wear your iron."

Labienus didn't wait for my response but nosed back down into his stack of reports. I guided Dion out into Ebrius' area. Without asking, Ebrius handed me a round pendant of lead tied with a leather thong.

"Have your slave wear this at all times, sir" he said to me although Dion was standing right there. "Have him keep the lead pendant outside his tunic so the guards and the other *muli* can see it. That way they'll be no trouble as long as he behaves and keeps his mouth shut. Tell him not to go near any of the gates and stay off the parapets unless he wants a *pilum* in his back."

Ebrius' little speech reminded me that I'd have to give Dion a quick orientation to the life of a slave in a Roman military camp, or he would wind up with a "*pilum* in his back." The meeting with Troucillus was a surprise. But first I'd have to get Dion kitted out, fed, and bunked into one of the slave stables.

The *stabula servorum*, the quarters of the army slaves in most legionary *castra*, are located in the rear of the *quaestoria*, the logistics and supply section of the camp, well away from the parapets and gates for reasons of security. Not that there is much risk of any of our slaves trying to escape. First, when the army's in foreign territory, as were we, there's nowhere to run. Most of the slaves fear the barbarians more than they hate their status as slaves.

Second, army slaves for the most part do not hate their lives. None were prisoners of war or criminals sentenced to slavery. They were volunteers who sold themselves into slavery, many to escape a life of backbreaking labor, starvation, and living on the rough. Army slaves had *pacta*, "contracts" specifying a twenty-year tenure, after which they were manumitted, their purchase price was paid out to them, and they were given the franchise as Roman citizens.

Nor were their lives any harsher than those of the *muli* with whom they served. The tasks they performed – teamsters; pitching and packing the *papiliones*, the squad tents; assisting in the stables; working in the mess tents and the *fabrica*, the workshops for metal, leather, and wood; organizing the quartermaster tents and storage areas; clerking in the *praetorium* – were in many ways easier than those of the troops themselves who were entrenching, building the fortifications, standing guard, and serving in the line of battle.

Army slaves ate the same food, slept under the same leather, and took the same risks as the legionaries with whom they served. And, like the *muli*, they were bound to the legions until their "contracts" ran out. Even the punishments for desertion were roughly equivalent: for the *mulus*, a beating by his centurion for the first offense and being beaten to death by his *conturbernales*, his tent-mates, for the second; for the slave, branding for the first offense and crucifixion for the second.

The slaves were as much a part of their units as the soldiers. The *muli* respected the work the slaves performed and tended to be protective of *their* slaves, the ones assigned to their units. On "retirement," many slaves stayed with their legions as *liberti*, freedmen, setting up shop in the *vicus* or becoming civilian contractors within the camp. The sons of former slaves, when they came of age, often joined their father's legion as soldiers.

But Dion was no army slave; he was a *famulus*, a household slave. I doubt Dion had ever had to sleep under leather and his only calluses were from holding a *stylus*. His forebears were brought to *Italia* as war booty from Sulla's sack of Athens. He was born a slave and could expect to die a slave unless Aulus Gabinius, his master, should see fit to free him.

As we walked down the *Via Praetoria* toward the supply tents, I noticed Dion kept his head down looking a bit confused, almost shocky. So, I asked, "What happened?"

He muttered something ending in the word *domine*, "master."

"Okay," I answered, "Time for your first lesson in army life. First, you don't address soldiers as "master"; they hate that. Address them by their rank ... broad purple stripe, that's a legate or a senior tribune ... just call broad stripers, "legate" ... narrow stripers, "tribune" ... a hardcase carrying a club, that's a centurion ... avoid those bastards as best you can ... anybody else, "soldier." You with me so far?"

Dion looked up, nodded and said, "*Compre'endo* ... I understand ... uh ... soldier!"

"Close enough," I told him. "See this narrow, yellow sash around my waist? That means I'm a *decurio*; that's a cavalry rank. The purple sash means I'm part of the praetorian detail. You'll have time to figure all this stuff out. In the meantime, stick with 'legate,' 'tribune,' 'centurion,' and 'soldier.' Besides, you and I are still mates, so call me 'Gai,' like you did back on Gabinius' estate. When some of the guys get to know you, they'll call you 'Dion' and tell you to address them by their names, too. That's not a trick ... that's the way things are done here in the army. Other than that, keep your head down, speak when spoken to ... and that reminds me ... when a soldier addresses you, don't do that "eyes-down-mumbling-shuffle" thing you *famuli* do with your masters. Stand up straight, look the man directly in the eye, and pop off ... you got that?"

"Got it ... uh ... Gai," Dion managed.

We had arrived at the clothing supply tent. I opened the flap and entered; Dion followed. When my eyes adjusted to the dimness, I spotted a supply clerk sitting at a desk bent over a *tabula*, one of our legionary slaves.

"*Scriba*!" I commanded.

The man looked up and saw me. He got to his feet, "*Ti'a'sum, decurio* ... at your service, sir!"

"I need to fit this man up for the winter," I said. "Far as I know, all's he got is what's on his back ... that right, Dion?"

"*Vere, decurio*!" Dion passed his first test. "Right, sir!"

Scriba gave Dion a fast once over and asked, "Who's paying, sir?"

"The man's ... uh ... the man's *familia imperatoris* ... part of the general's household ... so, fit him out accordingly."

Scriba nodded, "The boss' man, eh? Good! Deep pockets ... let's see what we got here."

Scriba started from Dion's feet and worked up, "Those sandals gotta go ... good pair of army boots ... wool socks ... two pair, I think ... trousers ... wool ... heavy tunic ... two of those ... sleeves, of course, already October ... wool cloak with a hood ... gloves ... wool cap ... a bag to put his stuff in. Where's he staying, sir? Down in the *stabula*?"

"Yeah," I agreed. "I'll put him in with the *praetorium* people."

"*Bene*," Scriba thought it through. "They already got their cots set up ... just, a couple of blankets then ... and a mess kit ... just a spoon ... slaves don't get knives ... he know about that, sir?"

"He does now," I nodded. "I'll go over it with him when we get out of here."

Scriba nodded. Then to Dion, "Come on back here ... uh ... what you say your name was?"

"Dion," my friend answered.

"Dion, huh?" Scriba said, leading Dion back into the tent. "Sounds Greek. My name's Bretos. I'm called "*Scriba*" cause that's what I do around here. Whatta you do?"

"I teach ..." Dion started.

"Teach, huh?" Scriba-Bretos interrupted. "Then, we'll just call you *Doctor* ... "Doc," for short ... come on back here with me, Doc, and we'll see if we can find you a pair a boots that'll fit ... I'd say you're a medium ... narrow ..."

Then to me, "I'll have the Doc here fitted out in no time, sir! Then I'll need your mark on the chit!"

As I was walking out of the tent, I heard Scriba say to Dion, "Where you in from? You don't look local."

It took Scriba less than half a winter hour to fit Dion out. I put my mark on Scriba's chit and we were back on our way. With his heavy boots, *bracae* and undyed military tunic, Dion looked every inch an army slave. Since everything he was wearing was new, he also looked every inch a *tiro*, a rookie.

Since the Tenth was in a semi-permanent *castrum hibernum*, a winter camp, the quaestor had moved mess operations up to the camp level. No *muli* wants to be plowing through a few feet of snow to get to his morning gruel and warm posca, but the army didn't want squad cooking fires burning down the camp. I knew the mess hall was operating down in the *quaestoria*; at this time of day only the clerks and *tabula*-stackers would be lingering over their meal.

The sides of the mess tent were up, and I spotted the slave who ran the kitchen. "Hey! *Coce*! Cookie! Can you scrape something together quick for a new guy?" I called.

The cook, a ten-year man by the look of him, gave me the fisheye. Then, he spotted Dion with his shiny, new outfit balancing his kit bag in his arms, and the brass coins I dropped on the mess table.

"Sure thing, *decurio*," he answered sweeping up the coins. "Got some *posca* and stew left over."

Cocus brought Dion back into the kitchen area and served up the food and drink. Then he plopped down across the table from Dion. "Where ya in from, son," I heard him ask. "Be careful with that *posca* … it takes some getting used to."

Our last stop was the *stabula*, the slave encampment. Dion's sinuses had finally cleared from the posca, but his eyes were still a bit red and watery from choaking it down.

The *stabula* were at the back of the *quaestoria* surrounded by the bivouac areas assigned to the eighth and tenth cohorts; the legionary cavalry was camped directly across the *Via Decumana*. By army Standing Operating Procedure, security of the *stabula* was assigned to the first cohort, which handled internal security for the entire camp except for the *praetorium*. In practice, the *stabula* were self-regulating, security and accountability being handled by "trustees," slaves who were in the last few years of their contract.

No one challenged us when we entered.

The tent assigned to *praetorium* slaves was on the edge of the compound facing the *Via Decumana*. As we approached, a tall man with graying hair stepped out to meet us.

"*Salve, decurio*," he greeted me. Then his eyes glanced over to Dion. "What's this? You bringing me a newbie?"

I noticed the man wore a soldier's belt, a privilege granted only to the trustee-slaves. This was a sign of his rank; it allowed him free access within the camp and the privilege of visiting the *vicus*, the civilian settlement just outside the *Porta Decumana*, the rear gate. No one expected a short-timer – a slave with less than five years left in his contract - to take a runner.

I wanted to ask him how much time he had left, but I imagined such a question was considered *infelissime*, most unlucky. The question was ill-omened when asked of a *mulus* nearing the end of his enlistment. It might remind *Domina Fortuna* that she allowed one to escape. I imagined the same prohibition applied to a short-timer slave.

So, I simply introduced Dion. "*Tutor*! Custodian! This man is Dion, a member of the general's household. He needs a bunk."

Tutor gazed at Dion for a heartbeat. "General's household, huh? General's out a here down south. Why's this one still here?"

"He's a teacher," I said, wondering why I had to explain Caesar's intentions to a slave - albeit a senior one. Then, I remembered that, in the hierarchy of the legion, this man in many ways had more *dignitas*, prestige, than a seventeen-year-old, fuzz-faced, first-campaign, junior cavalry officer.

"A teacher, huh?" Tutor continued examining Dion. "What's your name, boy?"

"Dion ..." he started.

"Alright, Dion," Tutor interrupted. "I am *tutor servorum praetorianorum legionis decem*, the custodian of the headquarters slaves of the Tenth Legion. Address me as 'Tutor'. This tent behind me is your home while you're with us. You don't leave it unless you have my permission. Is that clear?"

"Uh ... yes ... that's clear ... uh ... *Tutor*," Dion started.

"*Bene*!" Tutor continued. "When you're away from this area, you go *directly* to your assigned workstation ... and *only* to your assigned workstation! The *praetorium* is up the main road behind you to the left ... you come to an intersection with the assembly area where you'll see our legionary Eagle displayed ... the *principia* is the large tent to the left. When you're dismissed from work, you come *directly* back here and report to me. Still with me, boy?"

"*Man'festum, Tutor*," Dion answered. "Clear, boss!"

"*Bene*! No dawdling around the camp ... directly to work and then right back here ... check with me when you leave and as soon as you get back. And this is most important! Stay away from the gates and the walls! There's a cleared area between the encampments and the walls; it's called the *intervallum*. You never enter it ... never ... not one pace! Is that clear?"

"*Man'festum, Tutor*," Dion snapped, getting into the role of a military slave. "Clear, boss!"

"*Bene*," Tutor nodded. "Once you get settled in, I'll brief you on what else you need to know."

Then to me, "Are you this man's supervisor, *decurio*

"I am ..." I started.

Tutor interrupted, "Then, I'll need to get some information from you. Please wait here."

Then to Dion, "Come with me ... uh ... Dion."

Tutor led Dion into the tent.

After a few moments, Tutor returned with a large *tabula* and stylus. "I have to fill out my manning roster," he announced. "Your full name ... both of them ... all three, if you got 'em ... rank and unit ..."

When I got back to the *praetorium*, it was almost time for my meeting with Labienus and Troucillus. I decided to head over to my quarters and "drop my iron."

The praetorian bivouac was located behind a cluster of sites which constitute the ceremonial heart of the legionary camp: the *tribuna*, an elevated podium from which the commander reviewed the troops and harangued them before battle; the *auguratorium*, where the auguries were taken and the chicken entrails interpreted; and the *arae*, the smoking altars where the patron gods of the legion were honored.

Among the altars of the Tenth Legion were the expected ones - Iove, the all-conqueror, and Mars, the warrior-god. However, since the Tenth had become "Caesar's legion," an altar to Venus had also been erected in honor of the *imperator*'s reputed ancestor.

According to myth, Mars and Venus were once engaged in a wildly dysfunctional affair – one in which Venus cheated on her husband, Vulcan, the gnome-like god of artificers. The wronged husband caught them at it and hung them up in a magic net, exposing them to the ridicule of the other gods. I often wondered how Venus and Mars' new living arrangements next to each other in the *praetorium* of the Tenth Legion, was working out for them. Priests have always been strangely immune to irony when it comes to the gods.

I found my quarters, a tent I shared with the junior officers of the guard. Our orderly, a slave whom we referred to as Calo, "Orderly," was there scraping rust off someone's *lorica*.

While he was helping me out of my chainmail, I asked, "So, Calo. How long's it been? Over ten years, right?"

"I've been with the legion a good while, *decurio*," he answered while lifting my lorica off my shoulders, "A good while now ... since the time of Pompeius, *Imperator*."

Calo placed my *lorica* on his table and began untying my padded *subarmalis* jacket. "You want me to give your iron a good scrape and oil before I put it away?" he asked.

I gave Calo an affirmative grunt. He helped me out of my *subarmalis*, then gave my tunic a quick scan and sniff. "Perhaps a clean tunic before you meet with the legate?" he suggested.

I had no idea how Calo knew I had a meeting with Labienus. But, as we said in the legion, if you want to know what's going on, ask one of the headquarters slaves.

Calo was saying, "The washing just got back from the *quaestorium* laundry, *decurio*. Let me pull a fresh tunic out for you and we can put the one you're wearing out of its misery."

I sat down on my cot and picked up Caesar's still sealed *tabula* that Labienus had given me earlier. "You sound like a 'Spani,'" I called over to Calo.

"My people are from what you Romans call *Hispania Citerior*," Calo agreed walking over with a fresh tunic. "A small village up the coast from Cartadasht. You Romans call the place Carthago Nova. Ever been there?"

I shook my head and took the tunic from Calo. "No ... never been. But that's home for you, right?"

"Home?" Calo repeated. "The Tenth's my home. Cartadasht's a sorry place unless you like weaving baskets out of esparto grass."

Calo helped me out of my tunic and continued. "Romans seem to like the place ... produces some of the best garum in the *imperium* ... then there's always the silver mines in the hills ..."

Calo broke off, rolled my soiled tunic into a ball and carried it over to the laundry pile.

"Silver mines have something to do with why you're here?" I guessed.

Calo came back and straightened the clean tunic on my shoulders. "You could say that," he agreed. "Me and a couple of my mates had a ... uh ... little enterprise going. When the carts carried the silver ore down from the mines to the smelters in town, bits and pieces of ore fell off onto the road. We'd collect the stuff up and sell it back to the owners. One day, this owner, a Roman ... they were the only ones who could own anything of value ... this Roman decides he wants to cut out the middlemen ... that was us. So, he has some soldiers round us up and he drags us in front of the Roman *praetor* in Cartadasht, who just happens to be one of his business partners. So, this *praetor* finds us guilty of theft from a citizen, but he gives us a choice ... ten years in the mines or twenty in the legions. I took the twenty."

"Why the twenty?" I challenged. "If you took the ten, you'd be free by now."

"Ten years in the mines!" Calo snorted. "That's a joke! No one survives ten years in the mines ... backbreaking work ... starvation rations ... beatings! The air in those pits is poisonous; it catches fire ... explodes if there's as much as a spark off one of the picks. Ten years! A man would be lucky to survive a year!"

I was silent for a few heartbeats, not knowing how to respond. Finally, I asked, "So, your mates? Are they with the legion?"

"They're dead!" Calo stated flatly.

"Dead?" I asked. "How do you know?"

"They took the ten."

Calo went back to his work, but the signal for the tenth hour had yet to sound. So, I decided to read Caesar's letter. I broke the wax seal, opened the tabula and began,

> *Gaius Iulius Caesar, Imperator, Proconsul for Cisalpine Gaul, Transalpine Gaul, and Illyricum, to Gaius Marius Insubrecus, Decurio, Sends Greetings.*

By now you have met my other birthday gift to you, the rhetor, Dion, slave from the household of Aulus Gabinius, your almost father-in-law.

Some things never fail to amaze me.

When my agents first approached Gabinius about his slave, he couldn't recall owning him. However, once Gabinius realized that I desired to obtain him, Dion became one of his prized possessions.

Fortunately, Gabinius needs my support in the senate for obtaining a posting he desires after his term as consul, proconsul of Syria. With Mithridates long gone and my colleague, Crassus, in the east shielding Syria from the Parthians, Gabinius believes Syria will be rich in plunder and poor in peril.

So, a deal was made. Dion is yours for as long as you need him. Besides, I have reason to want Gabinius away in Syria and indebted to me.

I have given Dion instructions that he is to tutor you in the koine, the Greek spoken in Alexandria. Once I have created a strong alliance of tribes north of the Rhodanus and secured the northern borders of the imperium, I believe we may visit that city.

Aegyptus is fabulously wealthy and offers the opportunity of a weak ruler, Ptolemy Neos Dionysus Theos Philopator Theos Philadelphos, known as Auletes, the "Flute Player," for reasons I do not want to know. Currently, Ptolemy is exiled in Rome with one of his regal brats, a daughter named Cleopatra – just about every other Ptolemaic she-brat is named Cleopatra. Ptolemy is nestling under the protective wing of my colleague and son-in-law, Pompeius.

Which reminds me! I have spoken to your friend, Grennadios. I did not have to summon him. He presented himself to me at the villa outside Massalia where I have established my principia.

His purpose was to assure me that he had had no part in the attempt on my life by that sicarius, Bulla. He did deliver the payment for the hit, but he was only following the instructions of his master, Ptolemy, and had no idea what the payment was for.

Or so he says.

Grennadios claimed he had no idea why Ptolemy wanted me dead. He did intimate, however, that Ptolemy may have been trying to curry favor with certain elements in the Roman senate in order to gain their support for his restoration to the throne of Aegyptus.

What is most troubling about this revelation is not that there are some in the senate that wish me dead. Ptolemy depends heavily on the favor of Pompeius to maintain his position in Rome. I doubt that Ptolemy would make a move, such as having me killed, without the knowledge and even the concurrence of my beloved son-in-law, Pompeius.

> *Be that as it may, I have pardoned Grennadios for his involvement in that affair under the condition that he will now also work for me. Grennadios has a wide network of contacts among the Gallic tribes and is privy to information from and about his master, the 'Flute Player', as well as my dear colleague and esteemed son-in-law, Pompeius.*
>
> *Grennadios has a most interesting companion, the woman Evra. She claims to have come from a remote land, an island in Oceanus, west of the islands of the Pretani. Evra claims that she herself has seen the misty islands west of her homeland where the dead dwell. She claims further that sailors from her land claim there are more wonders out across Oceanus, an island of fire mountains, huge fish that blow fountains of water from their heads, vast lands of endless forests inhabited by feathered red peoples, rivers whose banks are littered with boulders of pure gold.*
>
> *All to the west, out across Oceanus.*
>
> *Perhaps someday we will visit those places and see those wonders.*
>
> *But your immediate tasks are to complete my journals of the Ariovistus campaign – I want the plebs in the forum to see my victory as our greatest triumph over the grunni since Marius and the Cimbrian war - and next, to learn to speak Greek like an Alexandrian.*
>
> *Evra has asked me to forward a message from her. "Hold fast the white stone," whatever that's supposed to mean.*
>
> *Vale!*

By the time I had finished reading Caesar's letter, I could hear the signal being sounded from the *praetorium* announcing the start of the tenth hour.

The *principia* was just a short walk from my quarters. As I reached the intersection of the *Via Praetoria* and the *Via Principia*, I could see to my right the sanctuary where the legionary standards were enshrined. This was also the legion's treasury, where locked chests of ready cash were kept. The sanctuary was heavily guarded by *muli* from the first cohort, which by tradition is granted the privilege of protecting Iove's Eagle.

To my left was the *tribuna*, the raised platform from which the commander addresses the troops, pronounces judgment on delinquents, and announces the auguries - in other words, assures the *muli* that the gods still favor them and will grant them victory over their enemies. I've had enough conversations with Crispus, a tenth-cohort trooper who is the legion's designated augur, to know that it doesn't matter which way the chicken's intestines are twisted or what's the color of the black ram's liver.

According to Crispus, the first step in a successful augury is to understand clearly what the commander wants to hear. Then, delivering it.

The *principia*, our headquarters tent, was to the left along the *Via Praetoria* immediately behind the *tribuna*. I passed the praetorian sentries at the entry with a nod. In the tent, I immediately spotted Ebrius and noticed a bit of color in his cheeks. He must have thoroughly tested Labienus' wine to ensure no mad, Parthian assassins had poisoned it.

He nodded to me and slurred, "In ya go, decurio ... bosh'expectin' you."

Ebrius didn't try to stand as military protocol demands, I was glad of it; someone could have gotten hurt.

In the *cubiculum*, I spotted Labienus and Troucillus sitting at a field table, a reddish, ceramic pitcher between them, wine cups in their hands.

"Ah! Here's the lad!" Labienus greeted me. "Pour yourself a cup and have a seat. There's water on the sideboard if you need it."

My friend, Troucillus, held up his cup to me, "Gai! Good to see you! Sit! We have much to discuss."

I noticed Troucillus was dressed like a Roman this afternoon, bare legs and a white tunic with the narrow purple stripe of the *Ordo Equestris*, the Order of Knights. This honor had been granted by Marius, *Dictator*, to Troucillus' family, the rulers of a Gallic tribe the Romans call the Helvi, for their loyalty to Rome during the Cimbrian wars.

Troucillus caught my look. "Bare legs in October," he shook his head, brushing the bottom of his tunic with the fingers of his left hand. "Had to! Our friend here," a nod in Labienus' direction, "Has this place locked up tighter than a virgin's knees. If I had shown up in my plaid *bracae* and tartan, I'd still be cooling my heels outside the *Porta Praetoria*, waiting for some junior officer to decide whether I was a "good wog" or a "bad wog." This way it's give the password, the sentry nods at my purple stripe, and in I go."

Labienus chuckled and said something like, "Can't be too careful."

I filled my cup, *mixtum*, half wine, half water, and took a seat. I noticed some cheese and olives on the table. I wondered briefly where Labienus had gotten his hands on olives in Gaul during October, but then my stomach reminded me I hadn't eaten since breakfast. So, I grabbed a handful and settled in.

"I was just telling Labienus here," Troucillus continued, "That we have a potential problem with the Aedui ..."

"Always something going on with these shaggin' wogs," Labienus muttered as he took a drink. By the color in his cheeks, he wasn't working on his first cup.

Troucillus ignored Labienus, "Seems that Dumnorix ..."

"Deluuhnu mab Clethguuhno!" I interrupted, calling Dumnorix by his Gallic name. "That snake is back! I thought he had taken a runner north ..."

Troucillus held up his hand. "The problem is not that Dumnorix is *back*; the problem is Dumnorix is *gone*."

Troucillus waited a few heartbeats to let that settle in, then continued, "If you remember, Gai, Dumnorix was Diviciacus' *pendefig* ... his "Number One," ... his "heir apparent" so to speak. That honor was bestowed on him by the tribal Council of Three Generations, when Diviciacus was became king of the Aedui in his turn."

"So, why can't this ... uh ... generation council just elect another *pendefig*-thing and have done with it?" Labienus interjected.

"It's not that simple ..." Troucillus began.

"Never is with these damned wogs," Labienus said into his wine cup.

Troucillus ignored him. "The tribal king and the *pendefig* are designated at the same time ... it's somewhat like you Romans when your senate designates a *dictator* and a *magister equitium,* a master of the horse. There's always a reason why the two are designated together. In times of crisis, the tribe may need two strong warriors; in times of internal conflict, it may be a political compromise ... one balances out the other. Be that as it may, the high judge of the Aedui has ruled that the position cannot remain vacant ... it must be filled ..."

"So why don't they just fill it," Labienus challenged.

Troucillus nodded, "That they will. But the absence of the designated *pendefig* jeopardizes the legitimacy of the ruling king ..."

"You mean they might dump Diviciacus?" Labienus concluded. "Good riddance to bad rubbish, I say!"

Troucillus actually sighed. "Labienus! Your people have a saying, *daemon apparentus melior quam occultus,* 'the devil you know is better than the one you don't'. Our primary mission from Caesar is to keep the Aedui friendly to Rome and, for that, Diviciacus is the 'devil we know'. If the Aedui should decide to 'dump Diviciacus', as you put it ..."

Troucillus had Labienus' attention now. "What's our bottom line on this?" he interrupted.

Troucillus shrugged, "That I can't say, but let me project some worst-case scenarios. You may not know this, but the Aedui are divided into five major clans. There's the Wolf Clan. That's Diviciacus clan. They've been ruling since Diviciacus' father pulled off a little *coup d'état* during the German wars. They usurped the throne from the Boar Clan, who claim that the gods designated them as the tribal rulers at the time of the great descent. Gai, this is the clan of your acquaintance, Cuhnetha mab Cluhweluhno. His son, Morcant, rode with us part of the way on that boondoggle Caesar sent us on to Ariovistus ..."

I nodded in agreement, then flushed as I realized these were also the people of Rhonwen, the niece of Cuhnetha, the redheaded girl whom I couldn't get out of my mind.

Troucillus continued, "Cuhnetha is sure to use this opportunity to try to take back the throne from the Wolf Clan or at least to weaken Diviciacus. Over the years, Diviciacus has weakened the Boar clan, stripping them of lands and the support of the unaffiliated septs of the tribe. So, Cuhnetha cannot overpower Diviciacus. But that's not where the real danger lies; that lies with Malouuhnos mab Dermuhtos."

Troucillus waited a few heartbeats for Labienus' expected interruption. "Who in the name of Venus' rosy rump is this Malunus Mab What's 'is Name?"

Troucillus smiled, "Malouuhnos mab Dermuhtos is the chief of the Bear Clan. They hold the lands to the west and north of Bibracte, and they may be the most powerful clan militarily of the Aedui."

"What do we know about this Malouuhnos?" I asked Troucillus.

Troucillus nodded. "First and foremost, he is no friend of Rome. He could live with all Romans being pushed back across the Rhodanus, but he wants them all drowned in the Middle Sea. He despises Diviciacus as a collaborator ... a traitor to his tribe. In fact, one of Diviciacus' reasons for encouraging the Helvetii to enter Aeduan lands was to settle them at the expense of Malouuhnos and greatly weaken his clan. Since that has failed, he's using you Romans in the same manner."

"So, what's this Malunus' game, ya think," Labienus asked.

"Trying to put himself on the throne may be a bit beyond his reach," Troucillus explained, "But not completely impossible. A more plausible 'play', as you put it, may be to support Cuhnetha's candidacy and place the new king in his debt. Malouuhnos may even forward himself as *pendefig*. If that were to happen, I wouldn't give a brass *as* for Cuhnetha's longevity ... or Morcant's, for that matter. Be that as it may, if that scenario were to play out, we would be faced with a hostile force ruling the Aedui ... not Caesar's plan at all, I think."

"Can't we do something to prevent this ... this Malunus from participating in this electing council?" Labienus asked.

Troucillus shook his head. "All five clans of the Aedui must participate in the Council of Three Generations or any decision they make will not be accepted as legitimate and binding by the *barnuchela*, the high judges of the tribe. If we were somehow to exclude Malouuhnos' Bear Clan, in order to keep Diviciacus on the throne, there would be civil war, and the tribal high judges would oppose us. Then, the best we could hope for would be a weakened Diviciacus after months of civil war; the worst, a hostile Malouuhnos ruling the Aedui. No, we have to keep Cuhnetha from allying himself with Malouuhnos, and that's where you come in, Gai."

When I heard my name mentioned, I almost choked on some olive pits. "What! What can I do?" I asked after spitting the pits into my hand.

"I don't exactly have a detailed plan," Troucillus admitted, "But you already have an in with Cuhnetha. And, his son, Morcant, seems to like you ... and then there's that business with his niece ... what's her name ... Rhonwen, I believe?"

I'm sure the glow of my face was outshining the lamps in the *cubiculum*, "I ... uh ... what ..."

Troucillus laughed, "Don't choke on those olive pits, Gai! I need you in this. The order for the summoning the clans will be going out in the next couple of days. Our first task is to make sure Diviciacus doesn't do anything stupid. He's probably figured out what the possible political plays against him might be and realizes that Cuhnetha is his most immediate threat. So, you first job is to make sure Cuhnetha gets to Bibracte safe and sound."

"How am I going to do that?" I asked.

"That's where I need your assistance, Labienus," Troucillus said.

Labienus, "How's that?"

"First, I'd like Insubrecus here seconded to me," Troucillus asked.

"Done!" Labienus agreed.

Troucillus nodded his thanks. "I'll also need some troops ... say a *turma* of cavalry ... two would be better ... preferably Gallic speakers from the Eleventh or Twelfth Legions."

Labienus' eyes rolled up while he did some mental calculation. Then he nodded, "I have a *turma* in camp from the Eleventh," he said ignoring the "two would be better" part of Troucillus' request. "They mount twenty-three riders, commanded by a *decurio* called Hirsutus ... one of yours, I think, Gai ... from Insubria ... speaks good Latin and good wog."

"*Bene*," Troucillus concluded. "As soon as the heralds go out summoning the council, we'll have Insubrecus here take the cavalry up to Cuhnetha's settlement and escort him down to Bibracte. Think you can handle that, Gai?"

As I nodded, Troucillus added, "And, while you're up there, you can say hello to this Rhonwen merc Gwen of yours."

II

Caput II. De Itinere Umido ac Frigido
Chapter 2. A Wet and Cold Journey

Troucillus' thinking that we had "a couple of days" before the summons to the Council of Three Generations was dispatched, was a bit optimistic. Two days after our meeting, I was part of Hirsutus' cavalry *turma* riding toward Cuhnetha's settlement hard in the tracks of the royal heralds.

"As part of the *turma*" was the best way I could characterize my participation.

During our first meeting, Hirsutus, *decurio*, a ten-year man, let me know in no uncertain terms who was in command of the troop. Him! Although he didn't say it explicitly, there was no way he was going to let some seventeen-year-old, jumped-up favorite of the current purple-stripe-in-charge usurp his authority and screw up his leadership team simply because that jumped-up favorite of the current purple-stripe-in-charge was sporting a yellow sash.

Although at the time my "seventeen-year-old, jumped-up favorite of the current purple-stripe-in-charge" self had his nose totally out of joint, after many years under the eagles, I fully understand Hirsutus' point.

In combat, there can be no division of authority. When a unit suddenly finds itself *immerda* – totally in it up to their necks – one officer and one officer alone must be recognized as the guy in charge. Even if he goes down – or he isn't about – the chain of command and the succession of authority must be clear. Without this, unit coherence disintegrates, the unit collapses in the chaos of combat, and it's destroyed.

Hirsutus got his command in the Eleventh during the Helvetian campaign through one of the cross-levelings of the new Eleventh and Twelfth Legions with Caesar's veteran legions in Gaul.

Of course, Hirsutus, "Scruffy," was his camp name. After we got to know each other a little better, he shared with me that, when he showed up for his first training formation, he hadn't yet gotten a military haircut and his long, thick Gallic hair was sticking out from under his training helmet like a large stack of hay stuffed under a brass bucket. His training officer took one look at him and dubbed him "Hirsutus." And the name stuck.

Hirsutus was of the Orobii tribe and grew up on a farm near the town of Bergomum in what was then Italian Gaul. After ten years under the eagles, he spoke camp Latin without an accent, but he still spoke and understood the language of his people - a necessity for commanding a *turma* in the Eleventh Legion. Most of his boys knew enough Latin to get through training and to understand basic military commands. Beyond that, they didn't know enough Latin to order a plate of cheese in a *caupona*.

Hirsutus' two sub-officers had the same pedigree as him. His number one was a Gaul from up near *Novum Comum* called Piscis, "The Fish," because his family fished the lake near that town. Piscis was another ten-year man, while Hirsutus junior officer, Murmurus, "Mumbles," was a Gallic-speaker from the hills north of Aquileia with more than five years under the eagles.

They made a good leadership team, so there was no room for a fuzz-face, seventeen-year-old, yellow-sash with one campaign season under his belt.

We departed the camp of the Tenth Legion at the end of the fourth watch of the night, despite *Iove*, in his manifestation of the god of storms, trying his godly best to convince us otherwise. Eurus, the southeast wind, was driving a cold rain hard across the sodden landscape. Hirsutus lifted his face into the rain and declared it good soldiering weather and led us out through the *Porta Praetoria*. The rest of us just wrapped our waterproofs tightly around us as best we could and developed our own theories about soldiering, being wet, and being cold.

We by-passed Bibracte to the east and soon reached what the Aedui call the "great north road." We cut the road a few hundred paces east of a road junction. One branch led south to the town's north gate; another branch led northwest through the highlands toward the territory of the Senones and the Carnutes; a third branch went east toward the Arar and the lands of the Sequani.

In the false dawn beginning to purple the eastern sky, I could see the dark hulk of a Roman camp, a cohort-sized outpost Labienus had established to overlook the road junction and the north gate of Bibracte. The only movement visible on the ramparts was the flapping of the *vexillum*, the standard of the cohort occupying the post. I knew the camp was held by one of the second-line cohorts, the sixth I thought. I could vaguely see the shape of the gate sentry over the camp portal; he was huddled deeply in a rain cloak. Hirsutus signaled to him to let him know we were friendlies, but the figure didn't stir.

"Probably asleep on his feet under that warm cloak," Hirsutus sniffed. "If his *tesserarius*, the officer of the guard, catches his sleeping ass, he'll get one a hell of a beating. *Fungule*! Damned snuffy! Get everybody killed sleeping on guard!"

Hirsutus led us down the east branch of the road. Like most Gallic roads in bad weather, the surface of this one was a quagmire of mud, downed tree branches, and loose stones; so, the going was slow. We were following this road for only a few thousand paces, then we'd pick up a trail leading north toward Cuhnetha's settlement.

I was riding Beorn, my German horse. Clamriu, my favorite mount, seemed to have recovered from her wounding during our retreat from the Hill of Flocks at the start of the Ariovistus campaign, but I didn't want to test her recently healed shoulder on a road like this. Beorn, being a German horse, didn't seem to give a damn about the weather or the road conditions. I just hoped he remembered whose side he was on.

Rain, cold, and darkness conspire to diminish greatly a soldier's visual horizons. That, and our unwillingness to stick our noses too far out of our hoods. Despite this, Hirsutus didn't see fit to send scouts down the road ahead of us, even when the trees crowded the margins of our route. But, either *Domina Fortuna* was with us, or the foul weather had also kept our enemies close to their hearth fires. We encountered no one out on the road that cold, rainy October morning.

By the time the sun was fully up – and we could only guess at that because of a gray, luminescent sky above us – the rain had abated into a wet mist, though the wind had picked up a bit. I, like most of the other riders, had thrown back the hood of my rain cloak. I wore only my woolen pilleus cap on my head. My helmet was tied to my saddle horn next to my *spatha*, my cavalry saber, and my shield was strapped to my back beneath my cloak. So, I was in no way prepared to react should we ride into an ambush. In fact, my infantry sword, my *gladius*, and my dagger, my soldier's *pugio*, were buried deeply somewhere underneath my cloak.

An eccentric thought suddenly popped into my head that I would need to dump the rainwater out of my helmet should I have to plunk the damn thing down on my head. Like any soldier out in the cold rain, preventing a flood of cold water from pouring down my back seemed oddly more important than preventing a sword from splitting my skull.

The rest of the troop was no more prepared for a fight than was I. I knew they all wore the standard, long, chainmail *loricae* of the Roman cavalry; the skirts of their armored coats were visible from underneath their cloaks. None of them wore their helmets and I could see the rounded arch of their cavalry shields, the small *parmae equestris*, poking up behind their necks through their cloaks. None carried the standard, one-handed stabbing spears. Hirsutus had decided to leave them back in cantonment. Being Gauls, they disdained the short Roman *gladius* but, buried deeply under their raingear, they had *spathae*, Gallic long-swords, hanging from baldrics along their left sides.

I was so buried in my own wet misery that, at first, I didn't hear Hirsutus summoning me. "*Insubrece, Decurio! Ad me!* Insubrecus! Get up here!"

I trotted Beorn up along the column to Hirsutus. "*Ti'a'sum, decurio!* Yes, sir!"

"Sorry for disturbing your nap, Insubrece!" Hirsutus snapped. "We should be close to the turnoff north. You've been up here before. Think you'd recognize it?"

Good question, I thought. *That was on a warm, dry day almost eight weeks ago, coming from a different direction.*

"Should be able to," I answered. There was no way I was giving Hirsutus any more reason to doubt my competence. "I'll ride up ahead and find it."

"You do that," Hirsutus agreed.

Then, Hirsutus turned toward his troop and called out in Gah'el, "*Anoule! Dod uhma!* Anoulos! Get up here!"

One of the troopers from Hirsutus' section came forward, "What is it, *a pen?*"

"Go with the ... uh ... the praetorian here ... don't let him get lost," Hirsutus instructed.

I noticed Hirsutus' refusal to name my rank.

Anoulos grinned and nodded, "I'll keep an eye on him for ya, boss!"

I spurred Beorn forward. "Let's go, Anoule," I said in Gah'el to let the Hirsutus' man know I wasn't just a *Roman* popinjay with a purple sash. I was a *Roman* popinjay with a purple sash who spoke Gah'el. "Faster we find this place, the faster we get out of this bloody rain."

We were closer to the intersection with the trail than I thought; it was less than two thousand paces up the road. And it was easy to recognize; it was marked by a stack of three largish rocks.

But there was a problem.

I slipped off Beorn and examined the crossing. Then, "Anoule! Ride back to the troop! Bring Hirsutus, *penaf*, up here to me."

Anoulos delayed a few heartbeats wondering how seriously he needed to take some little Roman tag-along. Then, like every good Roman soldier, he decided there was nothing to be gained arguing with a purple sash. "I go ... uh ... *a pen!*"

The main body was only a few hundred paces down the road, so Hirsutus was up with me in a short time.

"What's the problem, Insubrece?" he demanded in Latin.

I pointed toward the crossing. "*Vestigia equorum*! Horse tracks!" I answered, then switched to Gah'el so Anoulos could follow. "Someone's ridden across this intersection recently ... within the last hour, I'd say."

Hirsutus shrugged. "The heralds from Bibracte?" he offered.

I shook my head. "They went through yesterday, before the rain, and they would have come down the main road from the west like we did. These tracks are up from the south and they were made after the rain started."

My experience with my Sequani trackers was paying off.

I continued, "I'd say about a dozen riders ... shod horses carrying a load ... so I'd guess the riders wore armor. They're heading north, toward Cuhnetha's *dun* ... the horses walked through here, so they're in no hurry ... or the weather slowed them down like it did us."

Hirsutus stared at me for a heartbeat, then said, "Anoule! You're a hunter. What do you say?"

Anoulos slipped off his mount and examined the crossing. Then he shrugged, "*Uh penafboucha* is right, *a pen*. About a dozen riders, armed, riding north ahead of us, going slow."

Uh penafboucha, I thought. *"The little boss." I had a moniker, a nickname among the boys. That's good! A sign of acceptance.*

Hirsutus nodded. "We have to assume they're armed hostiles ... Anoule! Bring up three more boys out of my section ... raingear off, helmets on, shields off the shoulder!

You'll be my scouts up this trail. Insubrece! You've been up this way before, so you're with the point section. You're in charge. Got it."

I nodded and stripped off my rain cloak exposing my yellow officer's sash. I saw Anoulos stare at the sash for a heartbeat, then he spotted the five-strand, golden torc of a Sequani chief around my neck.

"I'll go gather up the boys, *a Pen*," he said to Hirsutus, but his eyes remained fixed on my torc. Then, he turned his horse down the road.

The trail north was in no better shape than the main road, just narrower. As it winded through the low country, it was a sea of mud, branches, and hidden rocks to bruise our horses' hooves.

The forest surrounding the road had changed dramatically since the last time I was through. The good news was that many of the trees had shed their leaves, so visibility was good to both flanks. The other news was many of the leaves had fallen onto our path obscuring it and making it that much more treacherous for our mounts.

Despite the muddy, leaf-covered ground, the tracks of the party in front of us were clear. They were still moving slowly, but they seemed to be proceeding steadily north.

Then, I had a thought. I remembered the Kraut ambush of the Sequani cavalry south of Bibracte when I was up here with Agrippa.

"Anoule!" I summoned my companion.

"Yes, Little Boss?"

"I don't want these bastards doubling back on their trail and ambushing us," I instructed. "I'm going to ride out about twenty paces on point. Have the men watch our flanks!"

Anoulos gave me an affirmative grunt and I road forward.

Fortunately, there was no ambush waiting for us ahead. Soon, we reached the beginnings of some high ground. We would have to cross a series of ridges before we arrived at Cuhnetha's *dun*.

The path became rockier as it climbed the first ridge. There was less mud, but the combination of the slope, loose wet stones, and the sodden leaves made the path hazardous for the horses.

I dismounted and waited for Anoulos and the main body to come up to my position.

"We have to walk them from here," I instructed. "Path's too slippery for the horses."

Anoulos nodded and slipped off his mount. "*Disguhnen!*" he hissed down the line, "Dismount!"

We led our horses to the top of the first ridge. As we climbed, I could easily see the disturbed ground and the stones scored by the iron horseshoes of the band we were following. From what I could tell, they had also dismounted to climb the ridge.

The top of the ridge gave us a bit of a perspective. To the west, I could see the high ground from which, a few weeks ago, the *fintai* of Deluuhnu mab Clethguuhno shadowed my Sequani troop. This was the same bunch who had attacked Cuhnetha's *dun* and had burned his hall. They had had good cover up there in the summer month of *Quintilis*. But now, in October, I could see straight through bare trees across the ridge.

Suddenly, I shivered as the cold wind cut through my sodden clothes. I led Beorn down the trail into the next valley where there'd be some protection for Eurus' cold breath.

If anything, the descent along that muddy path was more difficult than the climb. Our horses, who seemed to have no problem climbing the ridge, wanted nothing to do with descending from it. Twice, Beorn planted his front hooves, stiffened his legs, and dared me to move him farther. I finally had to rest his head on my shoulder and to walk him down the path with his chest pushing against my back, while I cooed to him in German, "*Goot hors ... goot hors.*" Even then, I had to keep a firm handle on his bridle to keep him from rearing his head up and digging in on the path.

At the bottom of the slope, we crossed a small stream swollen with rainwater. After not a few slips, horse snorts, and Gallic curses, we were ascending the next ridge. I focused my attention forward, up the ridge. I had already learned the soldier's lesson, "Going up, ambush front; going down, ambush rear." I didn't want to walk into an unexpected reception along the path above me.

I had climbed about halfway, when I realized the trail we had been following was no longer in front of me. I stopped and hissed for Anoulos to join me.

Before he could ask, I said, "It's gone! The trail we were following, it's gone."

Anoulos too had been occupied with coaxing his mount up the path and had not been concentrating on the trail we were following. "*Cachu!*" he hissed, examining the path before us, "Crap!"

His eyes rolled up as he thought. Then, he said, "The last time I remember seeing it was coming down the ridge."

Then, handing me his reins, "Wait here, Little Boss. I'll be right back."

Anoulos slipped and slid back down our route of march. As he descended, I heard him whisper to the others, "*Arhosen uhma i mi!* Wait here for me!"

He wasn't gone long. "They left the trail at that stream down there," he panted. "They went up stream ... my guess is they're above us to the west ... or they doubled back east and are waiting for us up ahead."

Classic, I thought. *Going up, ambush front.*

I could wait here for Hirsutus to catch up or I could press on and see what was up there.

Or I could just sit here like some pasty-faced, dithering tiro who's never seen a sword out of its sheath.

Then, I remembered my indecision at the Hill of Flocks.

Not again, I decided.

I instructed Anoulos. "Send one man back up the ridge. He's to halt Hirsutus and the main body there. Tell him we're clearing a danger area up ahead. I'm climbing the rest of the way up on foot ... see what's up there. You stay here with the horses. Give me one trooper to go up with me. If something happens to me, he can get back down here and warn you guys."

Anoulos seemed about to say something, then he just nodded. Then he turned to the first trooper in our column. "Calene! Leave your mount with me. You're climbing this hill with the Little Boss."

Calenos nodded and handed his reins to Anoulos. As we started to climb the path, Anoulos hissed, "And, Calene! Bring the Little Boss back with you in one piece. I don't want to have to explain to the Caisar we lost him."

Calenos and I climbed. As our path ascended, the trees receded and opened into a clear area at the top of the ridge. We stayed among the trees trying to keep as much cover as possible. On the ridge, our path turned west and followed the ridge line up to where it again entered a stand of trees above us.

I remembered this place. We were less than three thousand paces from where the trail made its final descent to Cuhnetha's *dun*. From here, after ascending the high ground to the west, the trail again turned north following the upper ridge line until it reached a point directly above Cuhnetha's settlement.

It was just about here last summer that we had first spotted the black smoke rising from Cuhnetha's burned hall. Today, the sky ahead was a filthy gray of scudding, wind-driven rain clouds, but clear of smoke.

My immediate problem was that our trail led uphill directly to where we suspected the hostiles might be hiding. I looked up the trail as far as I could. I saw nothing; no movement except the swaying of bare tree branches and swirls of dead leaves drive by the wet winds.

Going up, ambush front!

I listened. Again, nothing; just the whistling sigh of the cold autumn winds through bare branches.

What was I going to do?

Decide!

I reached out and took hold of Calenos' shoulder armor drawing him close. "We're staying in the tree line and moving up the trail. If these bastards are waiting for us, they'll be straight ahead on the high ground."

Calenos nodded.

"Stay a couple of paces behind me … if anything happens, your job is to get back down to Anoulos and warn the troop."

Again, a nod.

I removed my helmet and secured it to my belt by the chin bindings. I left my pilleus cap on. I removed my sashes and stuffed them down under my *lorica* as best I could. I drew my *gladius*, my short sword, and moved out.

Hunters claim, when stalking prey, they can move through the forest silently. Good luck doing that in Roman combat boots. I tried as best I could to move silently; keep the weight back on the rear foot; place the lead foot down heal to toe, shift the weight forward. I moved about as silently as a bonfire burning wet wood. Pop! Snap! Pop, again! At least the sounds of the wind, the groaning trees, and the blowing leaves covered the racket of my stumbling through the woods.

Finally, I decided to sacrifice stealth for speed. I dashed forward and was soon at top of the ridge where the trail turns north.

No one was there.

There was no sign of anyone having been there.

Dodged another arrow, I thought.

I plopped down on a small boulder. I didn't realize I was panting. I signaled Calenos to get down. Then, I pointed to my eyes and swept my hand in an arch in front of us. Look!

Then I pointed to my ears. Listen!

Men will remain silent in a tactical situation. Horses won't.

Then to my nose. Smell!

The smell of sweaty horses is hard to conceal.

Nothing!

Rolling leaves.

Shaking branches.

Moaning gusts of wind!

Nothing!

Finally, I pulled Calenos into me. "Go back down and bring the rest of the boys up here," I hissed into his ear.

He nodded and made to go, but I held him. "Stay in the trees on the way down ... can't be too careful."

He stared at me for a heartbeat, then nodded.

After Calenos had gone and left me alone on top of the ridge, I realized that I had to find a private spot quickly to relieve myself.

We were soon on the ridgeline above Cuhnetha's settlement. The rain had stopped and the trail along the high ground of the ridge was reasonably dry. I could see that the storage barn that doubled as Cuhnetha's hall had been rebuilt. The brambles that served as the wall of the *dun* had been reinforced. No one had bothered digging out the ditch.

We waited on the top of the ridge for Hirsutus and the main body to catch up to us. Although I could see no movement in the settlement below, I was sure we had been spotted.

When Hirsutus came up to my position, I pointed toward the settlement with my chin. "Cuhnetha's *dun*," I stated in Gah'el.

Hirsutus nodded and made to descend the ridge.

"*A pen*!" I cautioned him. "We can't just ride in there! We should respect custom of our people."

Hirsutus pulled up and looked at me without comprehension. I realized ten years in the Roman army had obliterated in him any sense of the customs of the Gah'el.

"Let me ride ahead to announce our presence and to request admittance as guests," I told him. "Once Cuhnetha greets us as his guests, our safety and lodging are his obligation."

"*Da!*" He nodded, "Okay!"

"Anoule! Calene! You're with me," I ordered.

Before Hirsutus could say anything, I told him, "It's undignified to approach unescorted and threatening to approach with too large a party ... for a *penaf* of your status, three riders are appropriate."

Hirsutus just nodded.

Then, untying the chin straps of my helmet, I said to Anoulos and Calenos, "Helmets off! Shields behind! Look friendly!"

Two affirmative grunts and we turned our horses down the ridge toward the settlement.

As we descended the ridge, three riders appeared from behind the hall in the settlement below. Each was bareheaded and carried no shield.

A good sign.

Each wore a long, Gallic battle-sword on his left side.

We rode to within twenty paces of the opening in the bramble hedge surrounding the dun, a safe and respectful distance. We stopped and waited. The three riders from the settlement approached us at a walk. I recognized the leader from Morcant's *fintai* last summer when he guided our embassy to Ariovistus as far as the fords of the Arar. I did not know the man's name.

When they halted, I lifted my chin so they could see my five-strand golden torc and raised my empty right hand. "May the gods smile down on you and on all in this place! I am Arth mab Secundos of the Insubres, *penaf* of the *Rhufeinai, cuhmaros*, a companion of the Caisar! I speak for Hirsutus, also *penaf* of the *Rhufeinai, decurio*, a leader of thirty, who requests from Cuhnetha mab Cluhweluhno, *Pobl'rix*, clan leader of the *Wuhr Tuurch*, lodging and protection, for himself and for his band."

The leader responded, "I know you, Arth mab Secundos. I am Trahernos mab Nelos, a warrior of five seasons. I rode with the *fintai* of Morcant mab Cuhnetha on our journey to the river of the goddess, Soucanna. Morcant considers you *uh cuhmaros*, a companion. I will relay your request to Cuhnetha."

As he turned his horse, Trahernos nodded to his companions, who remained in place, and cantered back to Cuhnetha's hall. He was behind the hall for less than a few heartbeats when he reappeared with another rider. As they cantered toward us, I recognized the other rider, Morcant mab Cuhnetha.

Having the *pendefig*, the prince of the clan, ride out to welcome us was a very good sign, indeed.

As Morcant neared, he broke into a broad smile. "Arth mab Secundos! Companion of the Caisar, is it? I wondered how long it would be before you showed up ... though I suspect it's not me or my father *you* desire to see."

For a heartbeat, I didn't know what Morcant was saying. Then, it hit me. Rhonwen! Rhonwen merc Gwen, his cousin. My face lit up like a coal in a brazier.

"Ha!" Morcant laughed. "I see I've hit it! I imagine you brought all these *Rhufeinai* along with you to impress my dear cousin! Welcome, Arth mab Secundos. Cuhnetha mab Cluhweluhno, *Pobl'rix* of the *Wuhr Tuurch*, welcomes you and your companions as guests into his *dun*."

III

Caput III. Cave Rufam
Chapter 3. Beware the Redhead

Later, we were all treated to a hot bath, part of the welcoming tradition of the Gah'el. Large tubs were brought down from the rafters of Cuhnetha's hall and set up in the rear, near the portals to the kitchens where the water was heated.

Upon entering the settlement, we had been formally greeted by Cuhnetha on the *lawnt*, the open area fronting the main portal of his hall. Next to him on his left stood a rather stout gray-haired woman, his wife and Morcant's mother, Brida merc Ronos.

It was her brother, Gwen, who was Rhonwen's father.

Cuhnetha intoned the formula of welcome to which I responded. Then, breaking with proper protocol, Cuhnetha greeted me before Hirsutus.

"So, Little Roman, you have come back! I'm glad to see you've escaped that pack of Soucanai brigands you brought with you last time. Now, you've brought me a pack of Rhufeinig mouths to feed!"

I was so busy scanning the area for a red-haired girl, that I almost didn't hear him. Morcant had slid off his horse and taken a position to the right of his parents. He brought me back from my reverie, "What's the matter, Arth? Swallow your tongue?"

"I ... uh ... Cuhnetha mab Cluhweluhno ... uh ... sir ... let me introduce to you Hirsutus, *decurio, penaf*, leader of thirty and warriors of ten seasons ..."

"Welcome, Hirsutus!" Cuhnetha interrupted, smiling at my confusion, "Welcome to my hearth! Please, enter my hall, you and your *aroueinoi*, your officers. My people will lodge your warriors and take care of your horses. Come! I'm sure you want to get out of this weather."

As we entered, I pulled Morcant aside and told him of the trail we had been following in the hills. He looked thoughtful and said, "It's not any of our people ... up from the south, you say ... that's Wolf Clan territory. I'll send out a scouting party to pick up the trail. We'll see what we shall see ... Ah! Arth mab Secundos ... let me introduce you to my wife, Ula merc Tigos."

A heavily pregnant, dark-haired woman with brilliant blue eyes approached us from within the hall. Her eyes seemed for a moment to pierce my *anima*, my life-spirit. I was reminded briefly of Evra, the enchantress from the island of the dead. Then, the blue fires ebbed. Ula halted before us and inclined her head.

"Welcome!" she said. Then, to her husband, "Is this the Arth of whom Rhonwen has told me so much."

My cheeks caught fire. Ula laughed, "No need to answer, *fuh'goure*, my husband. He has answered my question."

She then put her arm through mine and ushered me toward the hall. "Come to the fire, Arth. I'm sure you're chilled after your long ride."

As we walked, Ula said, "You are the one, you know, the one for our Rhonwen. I could see it in you; it's written in your *enaida*, in your spirit-self." Then, she laughed again.

"She has the sight, you know," Morcant laughed. "She tells me that I am destined to become *uucharix*, High King of the Aineduai and live in a great palace of square white stones that shine like silver in the sun!"

"Don't mock the gifts of the gods, *fuh'goure*," Ula chided. "The gods decreed this and all other things before our people descended from the high places. To me, they give but brief glimpses into their plans."

"I surrender, *fuh'gooraige*, my wife," Morcant chuckled. "Arth and Rhonwen shall marry and raise a brood of warriors."

"'Tis!" Ula agreed. "'Tis! But they will journey together through fire and blood before they can sit at peace before their own hearth."

The warm waters of my bath were leeching the chill out of my bones. I shared a tub with Hirsutus. He sat across from me; his head cushioned by a rolled towel on the lip of the tub. His eyes were closed, his breathing steady. He seemed asleep, but the hilt of his *pugio* was within easy reach of his right hand.

I sensed more than saw movement behind my head. I certainly felt a stack of towels thrown down on the table behind me. Suddenly, I was staring up at a tall, red-haired girl, fists on her hips, eyes blazing with green fire.

"So! This is my hero! The great Arth mab Secundos! *Penaf* of five golden strands! Companion of the Caisar! Come all the way up here with his band of Roman brigands to sweep me off my feet, is it!"

Rhonwen!

I lay in the tub staring up at her like the *paganus*, the country bumpkin, for whom my Roman buddies named me. Then, I realized I was naked! My face caught fire. I pulled my knees up to my chest. A wave of bath water broke onto my face. I was choking.

"It's modest now we are!" Rhonwen mocked. "Don't worry yourself, *farour*, my hero! You've nothing down there I haven't seen before ... just a boy's set!"

While I was trying to cough the water out of my lungs, Rhonwen turned to Hirsutus and said, "Cuhnetha is preparing a feast to welcome you, *a pen*! Please come to the hall when you've dried yourself and dressed."

Then she jerked her head in my direction, "And you can bring this one with you, if you want!"

Rhonwen marched off into the adjoining hall with a departing snort in my direction.

Even Hirsutus was impressed. "What in the name of Venus' rosy rump was that all about?"

"Rhonwen," I choked. "Rhonwen merc ... gasp ... merc Gwen ... sputter ... niece of ... choke ... Cuhnetha, our host."

"That might be her pedigree, but why does she have a fly up her nose with you?" he laughed.

"I ... uh ... I don't know ... choke ... I only met her ... sputter ... once," I choked out.

"Well, you seem to have made one hell of an impression ... one hell of an impression, indeed!" Hirsutus chuckled.

Cuhnetha's feast in the main hall was modest, more of an extended-family dinner. We were seated around the central fire at trestle tables set up to face toward each other across the hearth, our backs to the cold outer walls.

Hirsutus, being a Gaul, and understanding the obligations of hospitality, had no qualms about leaving his sword outside the hall. Being disarmed didn't seem to affect either Piscis or Murmurus either.

Cuhnetha and his wife, Brida, sat across the fire, opposite us. To their left sat a stout man in the gray robe of a *derwuhd*, a speaker of the gods; next to him, a gray-haired man in the brown robes of a *barnuchel*, a teller of the laws; finally, in green, Cuhnetha's *pruhduhd*, his bard, the keeper of the past.

To Cuhnetha's right, sat Morcant, as his *pendefig*, his heir and son. Ula sat next to her husband and, next to Ula, Rhonwen, dressed in a long woolen gown of the deepest, forest green which offset her dark, red hair in the shimmering light of the hearth fire.

To Hirsutus right, sat a warrior I did not recognize. He was a dark-haired man with a scowl that seemed to parallel the long, black mustachios that reached down to his chin. He was wearing a tartan of the Aineduai, but it was in the colors of a clan I did not recognize. Around his neck was a five-strand, golden torc whose knobs were shaped into long-taloned bear claws. I caught him staring at me and the other Romans. When our eyes met, his scowl deepened, and he looked away.

On the tables, as an *antepastum*, an appetizer, there were bowls of radishes, leek heads, apples, boiled eggs, scallions, and various nuts. Once everyone was settled, I saw Rhonwen signal toward the back of the hall. Women entered carrying pitchers of beer and red mead. Once all our cups were filled, the women left the pitchers on the tables and retreated toward the kitchens.

Cuhnetha raised his cup and intoned, "May the gods be thanked for this plenty and for these honored guests that grace my table."

We all raised our cups to the king and drank deeply. I noticed Cuhnetha barely wetted his lips then replaced his cup on the table.

"*Cairentoi*! Friends and kin!" Cuhnetha announced. "I welcome you at my table! We all know each other except perhaps for the warrior seated next to the Rhufeinig chief, Hirsutos. This is Malgounos mab Owenos, warrior of five seasons, leader of a hundred, nephew, brother's son of Malouuhnos mab Dermuhtos, *Pobl'rix*, clan leader of the Bear Clan."

Malgounos scowled a greeting in our direction.

Cuhnetha continued, "Malouuhnos dispatched his nephew here to make sure I get to Bibracte safely and on time to attend the Council of Three Generations ... and to make sure that I understood his desired outcome for the selection ..."

Malgounos stared into the fire, refusing to make eye contact with anyone.

Cuhnetha, "Malouuhnos, as I'm sure you are aware, is no friend of *uh Rhufeinai*, the Romans ..."

"Malouuhnos champions the free and independent peoples of the Gah'el ..." Malgounos interrupted the king.

Cuhnetha took a deep breath, then said, "Malgounos! You *are* my guest but pleases remember at whose table to sit!"

Malgounos snapped his jaws shut like a snapping turtle on a snake.

"If I may continue," Cuhnetha then said. "The king of the Bear Clan is no friend of *Rhufain*, Rome, and for this reason he believes Duuhruhda mab Clethguuhno is no longer fit to lead the tribe. He has asked my support in removing Duuhruhda from the high throne and replacing him with myself, as the rightful king of the Aineduai, a proposition to which I am most receptive."

Receptive, I thought, *deposing Duuhruhda and retaking the throne for your clan has been your life's ambition.*

Cuhnetha, "Of course, with the threat of the River People destroyed and *uhr Almaenwuhra*, the Germans, pushed back across the great eastern river, we no longer have any need of the legions. So, as king, I am expected to deliver this message to the Caisar and encourage him, let's say, to withdraw his armies back into his own lands in the south."

I'd like to be a fly on the wall when that message is delivered, I thought.

Cuhnetha continued, "To ensure my cooperation and to strengthen the ties between our clans, Malouuhnos has proposed a marriage ..."

A marriage! Suddenly, I no longer cared about Caesar, armies, and politics. *A marriage! To whom?*

Cuhnetha, "... a marriage between Malgounos here, the brother's son to Malouuhnos, and Rhonwen, wife's sister's daughter to me ..."

Rhonwen! My stomach seemed to contract within me. *What did this mean?*

"Rhonwen has not given her answer to this proposal," Cuhnetha said nodding toward his niece. "Until she does, we will have no more to say about that matter."

Suddenly, I realized Cuhnetha was looking directly at me. As was my newly acquired custom, my cheeks caught flame.

Cuhnetha actually nodded to me.

Then he continued, "I say this, so we all know who is sitting at this table and to remind you that, despite your own interests, tonight you are under my roof and are bound by the conventions of hospitality to me and to each other."

Morcant knuckled the table to demonstrate his understanding. Within a few heartbeats, so were we all.

"*Da!*" Cuhnetha announced. "Good! Rhonwen shall act as *creisawuhda*, our hostess."

Among the Gah'el, at a feast the *creisawuhda* emulates the three-person goddess in her manifestation of Rosmerta, the goddess of plenty. It is she who makes crops grow, cattle thrive, and game to fill the forests.

Rhonwen stood, lifted her cup toward the hearth and asked, "Who is worthy of being served by this cup?"

She then offered the cup to Cuhnetha, the king and host.

He refused it.

She then offered the cup to Morcant, the king's son and champion of the clan.

He refused it!

I thought I detected a slight smirk on his face.

Rhonwen then held the cup toward the hearth. She then said, "I offer this cup to Arth mab Secundos, known among the nations as Arth Uthr."

Again, my face blazed.

I rose, took the cup from Rhonwen's hands, offered it to the assembly and drank deeply.

I handed the cup back to Rhonwen. Her fingers covered mine as she received it. I felt a warm rush travel up my arms.

Rhonwen then signaled to the rear of the hall. Two women appeared, carrying a large, deep serving dish between them, the *duhgsul*. They placed it on the table before Rhonwen. It was a roasted boar.

Rhonwen cut a thick slice away from the haunch and placed the steaming meat on a dish. This was the "hero's portion," the first and choicest cut of the meat served to the best warrior at the table.

In the legends of the Gah'el, wars have been started by warriors contesting the hero's portion.

Rhonwen lifted the hero's portion in both her hands. "I offer this platter to Cuhnetha mab Cluhweluhno!"

"This night, I am not the worthiest of the assembled heroes," Cuhnetha refused the platter.

Rhonwen nodded, then said, "I offer this platter to Morcant mab Cuhnetha!"

"This night, I am not the worthiest of the assembled heroes," Morcant also refused the platter.

Rhonwen nodded, then said, "I offer this platter to Arth Uthr!"

I heard a hiss escape from Malgounos, Rhonwen's putative suitor.

I stood and started to say, "I am not ..."

I caught a look from Morcant at the same time as an elbow in the ribs from Hirsutus.

I started again, "I accept this platter. Let he who can take it from me speak now!"

Every eye around the table looked at Malgounos. He kept his silence.

I accepted the hero's portion from Rhonwen. Again, our fingers touched.

I returned to my place. Hirsutus slapped me across the shoulders. Cuhnetha and Morcant held their cups up to me. My red-cheeked face nodded to them. Morcant drank deeply; Cuhnetha put his cup down untasted.

Rhonwen carved the boar, filling and distributing platters with the steaming meat. Women entered from the rear of the hall, serving bowls of boiled carrots, beets, squash and onions, and loaves of warm bread. They also refilled our pitchers with beer and mead.

We attacked the meat with our *pugiones*, our knives, eating the steaming slices with our fingers. I glanced over toward Malgounos. His head was down seemingly concentrating on his food. I noticed Cuhnetha wasn't touching his food. Brida occasionally leaned over and whispered in his ear. Cuhnetha listened and nodded, his face somewhat pale and unsmiling.

Once the noise of knives scraping plates subsided, Cuhnetha's *pruhduhd*, his bard, rose and intoned, "'*Rando*! '*Rando*! '*Rando*! ... Listen! Listen! Listen!" The *pruhduhd* rehearsed Cuhnetha's royal pedigree beginning with the god, Lugos, ruling in the high places, to Morcant, who would someday rule the clan and the tribe.

Our servers remained at the back of the hall during this recitation. As soon as the bard finished, they rushed out to fill our pitchers, distribute more loaves of warm bread, and platters of a soft goat cheese.

After the servers retreated, the *pruhduhd* again stood, waited for the noise and conversation to subside, and began,

> I sing of the people-king,
> Lord of the land,
> Who extends his power to the shores of the seas.
> In Cair Sidi, strong was the prison of Goualce,
> Through the spite of Gigfrana.
> No one before him had escaped it.
> Heavy blue chains hold the warrior,
> Of the treasures of Annoufn, he laments,
> Until the end of days
> Shall end his woes.
> Thrice enough to fill the ships, we went;
> Except the seven, none returned from Cair Sidi
> Am I not a warrior of renown
> If this song of my deeds is heard?
> In Cair Pedriban, the golden cauldron,
> With the breath of the nine maidens
> It is brought to a boil.
> Is it not the cauldron of the chief of Annoufn?

The edge of its golden rim covered with pearls.
What is its meaning?
It will not boil the meat of a coward,
A warrior who has betrayed his oath,
A man who has not been sworn.
We went with Arth on a glorious quest;
> Except the seven, none returned from Cair Pedriban.
Am I not a warrior of renown,
If this song of my deeds is heard?
In Cair Fedouhd, a bright sword,
Gleaming, white-hilted blade.
It is offered to the warrior,
And in the hand of the hero, it is held.
Iron will not resist its cut;
Time will not heal its wound;
Its blade will not fail the worthy warrior.
When we went with Arth, a splendid battle,
> Except the seven, none returned from Cair Fe-douhd.
Am I not a warrior of renown
If this song of my deeds is heard?
In Cair Pedruhfan, the isle of the strong gate,
In pitchy darkness, water boils,
Heated by the head of the black spear.
Pruhdouen's spear thirsts for blood,
Blood of the people-enemy.
Only the hero can hold it;
Only the hero can cast it.
It is the bringer of death.
We went over the sea, sailed with Arth
> Except the seven, none returned from Cair Pedruh-fan
Am I not a warrior of renown
If this song of my deeds is heard?
The singing stone rests in Cair Rigor.
The stone that knows the king,
The warrior the gods have chosen,
He who is worthy to rule the people,
To make green again the earth,
To vanquish the people-enemy.
For this warrior, the stone shall sing,

> So all shall know the king.
> We filled the ship, sailed across the seas,
> Except the seven, none returned from Cair Rigor
> Am I not a warrior of renown
> If this song of my deeds is heard?
> In Cair Wuhduhr, the black-walled fortress,
> The sentinels will not speak,
> They know not the king;
> The gates will not open.
> From within, we can hear sounds of feasting,
> But we remain on the wind-swept shore,
> Buffeted by the sounding seas.
> In Cair Wuhduhr they saw not the prowess of Arth.
> Except the seven, none returned from Cair Wuhduhr
> Am I not a warrior of renown
> If this song of my deeds is heard?
> In Cair Annoufn, the king sleeps,
> Sleeps until his wounds have healed,
> Sleeps until the people call him forth.
> The king shall not fail the people.
> He shall bring forth grain from the earth;
> He shall put fruit on the trees;
> He shall bring game back into the forests;
> The white-handed goddess shall be his queen;
> And our enemies shall be cast into the sea.
> For him, the stone shall sing;
> For him, the white sword shall cut;
> For him, the black spear shall fly;
> For him, the cauldron shall boil the meat;
> For him, the blue-chained prisoner sings.
> In Cair Annoufn, we awake the king.
>
> > Except the seven, none returned from Cair An-
> > noufn.
>
> Am I not a warrior of renown
> If this song of my deeds is heard?

When the bard finished, we slammed the table tops with our hands and fists to show our appreciation. Even Hirsutus and his mates joined in.

I'm not sure how much of this Hirsutus and the other "Romans" understood. This was the saga of Arth Mawr's raid into the underworld, the realm of Annoufn, and his overthrow of the five great fortresses of that place.

Arth sailed across the western ocean in order to capture the treasures of Annoufn, the wonder weapons he would wield against the Romans when he destroyed their city: *Carreg o Duhnged*, the stone that proclaimed the rightful king; the sword, *Duhrnouuh*, from whose cut no armor could protect an enemy; *Gae o Melcht*, the black spear of the god, Lugos, that thirsted after the blood of its enemies; *Pairu Duhrnouchos Gaour*, the Giant's Cauldron that fed an army as long as its courage did not fail; and the blue-chained prisoner, Muhrdinos mab Wuhlcht, who could read the hearts of men.

According to legend, Arth Mawr never died, but sleeps in the fortress of Annoufn until the people again call him forth to defeat their enemies. Considering the political situation in Bibracte, this tale could easily be seen as an anti-Roman statement by Cuhnetha, who hoped to wrest the crown from Caesar's ally, Duuhruhda mab Clethguuhno.

As the noise resided, the servers again rushed out to re-fill our pitchers. Then, I saw Cuhnetha rise; his face was pasty-white; his right hand rubbed his chest. Brida rose with him. She put an arm around him. He seemed to lean heavily on her. Quickly, Ula also rose and helped Brida support Cuhnetha. The women guided him away from the table.

Rhonwen also rose. She leaned over and whispered something in her cousin's ear. Morcant nodded. Then she rushed away, following the women as they guided Cuhnetha to the side of the hall where I assumed his apartments lay.

Morcant rose. "The king, my father, retires! He invites you to stay! Enjoy his hospitality as his guests."

As Morcant spoke, I saw Malgounos watching Cuhnetha retreating from the hall. When he caught me looking, he quickly focused back on his cup.

We continued to drink. Cuhnetha's *barnuchel* betrayed a ribald sense of humor, telling a series of jokes that began with a Greek, a Roman and a Gaul walking into a *taberna*.

"... so the Greek lifts his cup of ale and sees a dead fly in it, so he slams down the cup and tells the landlord to take it away and pour him another; the Gaul lifts his cup, sees a dead fly, picks it out and flicks it away and drains his beer; the Roman sees the dead fly, picks it out, and starts squeezing the little body shouting 'spit it out you lousy barbarian ... it's mine!'"

Even the gray-robed *derwuhd*, smiled at that one.

Suddenly I felt a hand on my shoulder. It was Morcant. "Can I have a bit of a word with you, Arth?" he asked.

I got up and followed him out of the hall.

All that was left of the day was a band of glowing red gold outlining the hills to the west. Morcant began, "My father's health has not been good. He has stomach pains and nausea ... sometimes he can't catch his breath. My mother tells me it started when those bastards from Bibracte came up here and burned our hall, and he couldn't do a thing to stop them. His *meduhg* originally thought it was his stomach, so he put him on a bland diet ... water, porridge, milk ... essentially baby food. But his condition hasn't improved. In fact, its gotten worse."

I remained silent; what could I have said?

Morcant continued, "This council to replace the tribal *pendefig* and Malouuhnos' plot to replace Duuhruhda as tribal king has gotten my father's hopes up to reclaim his father's legacy as king of the Aineduai ..." Morcant shook his head, "I'm afraid if the journey and the strain of attending the council doesn't kill him, the disappointment of having the throne slip through his fingers will."

I continued to remain silent.

Morcant sighed. "Tell me, Arth. You're close to the Caisar. Will he support my father's taking the throne?"

Now I was on the spot. I remained silent trying to compose a response that would satisfy Morcant, not reveal too much of Caesar's plans, and still not be an outright lie.

"The Caisar desires a strong and stable Aineduai friendly to Rome," I began. "He's no friend of Duuhruhda; he doesn't trust him. But an enemy you know is sometimes better than one you do not. The key to this may be Malouuhnos. The Caisar will not tolerate an enemy of Rome ruling the Aineduai."

It was Morcant's turn to be silent. Then he asked, "So, it is the Caisar's intention to keep his army north of the Rodonos?"

This was dangerous ground!

"The Caisar has not been clear," I prevaricated. "I believe his interests lie not in Gaul, but in Rome. A stable Aineduai protecting the border and a peaceful Gaul would make it easier for the Caisar to focus his attentions away from these lands."

I certainly didn't share with Morcant Caesar's new interest in the Belgae. But, at the time, I didn't believe I was telling him an outright lie. Caesar did seem focused on Rome and the on the east as his comments about Alexandria and his desire for me to learn the *koine* seemed to indicate.

History reveals a clear horizon while the present tries to peer through obscurity, as the philosophers say. As Morcant and I stood there outside his father's hall, I had no idea that we would spend the next six years waging a war of conquest in the north. I told Morcant what I believed to be the truth, or at least hoped for.

Morcant sucked through his teeth, "I worry about my father," he said to no one in particular, "These are difficult times for our people."

Then, "Oh! Before I forget! The scouts I sent out to investigate that trail you discovered have returned. Whoever it was, they failed to make contact. It was as you suspected, a war party, not a hunting party. From the direction they came, I suspect they were from a sept of the Wolf Clan, Duuhruhda's people. I imagine a *fintai* of Rhufeinai and Malouuhnos' band congregating here before the Council of Three Generations has peeked Duuhruhda's curiosity. The trail swung west and south in the direction of Bibracte. I'm sure whoever it was, they're now drinking Duuhruhda's beer and telling him what they saw."

I responded with an affirmative grunt.

Morcant slapped a hand on my shoulder. "Let's get back inside before the mead runs out ... I image Rhonwen's little performance with the cup and platter was her answer to Malgounos' wedding proposal ... so the road remains wide open for you there, Arth!" he chuckled.

The road remains wide open for me, I thought. *First, she tells me I'm a little boy in a man's armor, then she offers me the hero's portion at a feast!*

Bloody redheads!

IV

Caput IV. Ad Aquilam Revenio
Chapter 4. I Return to the Army

The ride back to Bibracte was uneventful. As if to demonstrate how fickle the weather gods can be, the morning of our departure dawned clear, dry and warm. The day felt more like early September than it did mid-October.

Whoever's trail we were following on the way north did not make an appearance. If it were indeed a scouting party sent out by Duuhruhda, they would have returned to the king with a confusing report. His perceived rival for the throne, Cuhnetha, was being shepherded to his capital by both the Roman army and by the anti-Roman faction of the tribe headed by Malouuhnos mab Dermuhtos.

We departed the morning after the feast, despite our heavy heads from Cuhnetha's beer and mead the night before. Morcant told me that his father had to get us out of his *dun*. He couldn't afford to feed that many mouths and still make it through the winter without starving his people.

Cuhnetha seemed to have recovered from his illness of the night before. His wife, Brida, bid him farewell on the *lawnt*. She was staying back in the *dun* to be on hand for the expected arrival of their first grandchild. Ula, Morcant's wife, stood next to her, her right hand resting on her distended abdomen that looked like it was straining to hold back the warrior within. As Ula turned away, I saw a tear falling down her cheek. She said something to her husband, who shook his head. He placed his hands on Ula's shoulders and said something to her. He then caressed her cheek with his hand, kissed her, and mounted his horse.

We were ready to depart when Rhonwen, her red hair tied back in a tail, hurriedly exited the hall. She was wearing riding boots, dark green woolen *bracae*, and a cream-colored, long-sleeved woolen tunic. She quickly kissed Ula on the cheek, said a few words to Brida, then vaulted onto a dappled, gray mare.

I caught Morcant's eye and raised my eyebrows. He smiled and sidled next to me, "Since my mother is not making the trip, Rhonwen is coming along to run Cuhnetha's household while we're in Bibracte ... she readily volunteered to do it ... almost demanded it as if she had some other motive for wanting to go to Bibracte with us."

When Morcant's "some other motive" crack sunk in, my face lit up like a coal in a winter brazier. Seeing this, Morcant laughed and gave me a punch in the shoulder.

Desperate to change the subject, I asked, "Is Ula alright? Were her tears for you?"

Morcant dropped his smile, "It's that cursed 'second sight' of hers. She's convinced Cuhnetha will not return from Bibracte ... he's going to die there."

I shrugged, not knowing what to say about dire prophesies and the "second sight."

"I'll do my best to see that doesn't happen, *fuh'cuhfail*, my friend," I stammered.

Morcant smiled again, "Thank you ... I'm sure there's nothing to worry about. Ula's vision is probably just a bit of indigestion from last night's feast."

We took our time riding south and arrived at the road junction to Bibracte during the fifth hour. The Roman *castrum* overlooking the site was clearly visible from the road as it was intended to be. Hirsutus had sent a detachment ahead under Piscis to inform the garrison that an armed party was coming down the road. Despite that, there was a reception committee waiting for us at the junction. Piscis' riders were dismounted and standing at ease around the road junction with their mounts; that is, standing as much at ease as a Roman soldier dared in the presence of a senior centurion.

The centurion was kitted out, his helmet straps tied tightly under his jutting, shaved chin, his left hand firmly grasping the hilt of his *gladius*, and his *vitis*, his cudgel, clamped tightly under his right arm. To his left and slightly behind him stood his *optio* by the red feathers protruding from his helmet and the long staff clasped in his left hand. Behind them, a *contubernium*, a squad of *muli*, standing at ease, their shields and pila grounded the points slanted forward.

My initial impression of the group was the inane and unmilitary grin on the face of the *optio*.

I was waiting for Hirsutus to greet the centurion when he stepped forward and greeted me. "So, it's true! In less than a year, a rank-breaking *fungulus* went from a pile of fish cac' on the bottom of *Oceanus* to an officer with a purple sash! Miracles can still happen in the Roman army!"

It was Strabo, my training officer in basic!

He was referring to an ambush we encountered while coming over the Alps last spring. Minutus, my *geminus*, and I broke ranks from a *testudo* to protect Strabo when a sling bullet slammed into his helmet and knocked him senseless. My jaw still ached from the *castigatio*, the "correction," Bantus, my *optio* at the time, delivered for my breaking ranks.

Strabo was still talking, "I believe you remember this reprobate here who's disguised himself as an *optio*."

As I slid off my horse, I recognized the grinning *optio* as Tulli, a *veteranus* who served as our assistant squad leader in basic. He threw out a right hand in my direction, "*Pagane*! Bumpkin! It's good to see you again!"

As I grasped Tulli's right arm, I heard Strabo saying, "I'm a *centurio prior pilus* of the second line, commander of the Sixth Cohort of the Tenth ... we're holding down the fort up on the hill there until we're relieved by the Seventh Cohort on the calends. 'Fish' here told me you were part of this mounted circus ... good to see you again and still in one piece." Strabo squeezed my shoulder.

Then he turned to Hirsutus, our commander. "You must be Hirsutus, *decurio* ... heard good things about you ... Strabo ... commander Sixth Cohort, Tenth Legion ... your junior *decurio* here tells me you're escorting some wog VIP to Bibracte then heading back down to base camp."

"Correct, *centurio*!" Hirsutus responded. "I'm escorting one Cuhnetha mab Cluhweluhno, clan leader of the Aedui, to the gates of Bibracte under orders of the legate, Labienus."

Strabo nodded. "*Bene*. I have a change of orders for you. Your *turma* has been assigned to this post under my command. I need cavalry scouts up here, so you'll be bunking in with my cohort at least until the calends. Have your *tesserarius*, or whatever you call it in the cavalry, get with mine to go over the passwords."

While Strabo was talking, Morcant approached us on foot, leading his horse. "Arth," he asked me in Gah'el, "Is there a problem."

"*Na!*" I started to answer in Gah'el, then I realized there was a protocol to be observed. "This is Strabo, the commander of the *Rhufeinai* on the hill ..."

Then I noticed Strabo looking at us. "Centurion!" I announced in Latin, "This is Morcant, Cuhnetha's son ... he rode with us against the Helvetii ..."

"Does he speak any Latin?" Strabo interjected.

"To speak little," Morcant answered in halting Latin.

"*Bene*! Then, welcome, Morcant, son of Cuhnetha ..." Strabo started.

Then a voice from behind me speaking in Gah'el. "So, this is what we've come to now! *Uh Rhufeinos*, a Roman welcoming *us* to our *own* lands!"

It was Malgounos.

"Who's the wog with the sour puss?" Strabo asked me.

"Malgounos mab Owenos," I responded. "He's from the north, ... not of Morcant's clan ... and since he understood enough Latin to know you were welcoming us, I believe he can speak it well enough, if he chooses."

In response, Malgounos snorted and returned to his men at the end of the column.

"Don't think he's any more pleased to have us here than we are to be here," Strabo muttered as Malgounos retreated.

Then to Morcant, "We were told you'd be through and to pass you right on ... I just came down to greet an old comrade and to see if the Bumpkin here has started shaving yet."

Morcant might have understood half of that. But he did understand the gist of it. He smiled, nodded and said, "*Gratias ti'ago, centurio*! I thank you!"

Then to me, Strabo said, "Bantus, that lucky bastard, is basking in the sunshine on the docks down in Massalia with the *frumentarii* while the rest of us freeze our *coleones* off up here."

I noticed Strabo was still bare-legged. "You may want to invest in a nice pair of woolen bracae before it really gets cold, sir."

"Pah!" he snorted. "And the next thing you'll be telling me is grow mustachios, drink beer, and chew on raw meat! *Quam inromanitas*! Not 'Roman' at all"

I wondered briefly how well Strabo's sense of *romanitas* would keep his *coleones* warm when the snows of *Ianuarius* blew up his tunic.

We split from our party at the crossroad. Cuhnetha's group along with Malgounos' *fintai* continued south down the road to the north gate of Bibracte. We pulled off along the side of the road to let them pass us. I noticed that the lead riders of Cuhnetha's group had the white, wooden wands of a peaceful negotiation conspicuously displayed as they approached Duuhruhda's town.

As Rhonwen rode past me, she looked straight ahead, seeming to make an effort not to look in my direction. I felt a wave of disappointment wash over me. I assumed she was purposely cutting me. Then, at the last instant, she looked back over her shoulder. She must have detected something in my face because I saw a smirk break out across hers. Then, she quickly turned her head, her red ponytail leaping off her shoulder and plunging down her back.

Hirsutus was next to me watching her little act, "I have to tell you, Insubrece," he chuckled, "You let that one get her claws into you, you'll never get them out."

He glanced over at me, was silent for a heartbeat, then chuckled, "But it's much too late for that advice, I think."

I was seventeen; I hadn't yet learned to keep my feelings off my face. In fact, I was too young to have an inkling what my feelings were before they overwhelmed me.

I completed the journey to basecamp with Murmurus' section. Hirsutus sent him south as an escort and to pick up their remounts and "trinkets and trash" from camp. We arrived at the *castrum* of the Tenth Legion early in the seventh hour. We were quickly passed through the gate and were walking our mounts down the *Via Praetoria*. This was "officers' country," and the purple stripers hate having the dust stirred up and getting all over their nice shiny gewgaws.

When we arrived at the assembly area in the *praetorium*, I decided to report to Labienus at the *principia*. We halted at the *groma*, the survey stake marking the center of the *castrum*. "Murmure!" I started. "Mumbles! This is where I get off. I have to report to the boss."

Mumbles nodded and stuck out his hand, "*Va'bene, Pagane! A' prope vicem!* Be safe, Bumkin! Until the next time."

I took Mumbles arm, "*E'tu!* And you, Murmure! Be safe!"

Then to the rest of the troop in Gah'el, "*Huhd nes uh buht'oun uhn court' eto, cuhmroduhr!* Until we meet again, boys!"

A few nods, a few hands raised, some mumbled, "*Uh tro nesav, cuhd!* Next time, buddy!" And we parted. The troop continued south toward the stables. I walked my horse over to the *principia*.

When I entered the headquarters tent, I got a big surprise; Dion was sitting behind Ebrius' desk. Ebrius himself was nowhere to be seen.

"Dion! Where's Ebrius?" I started "What are you doing here?"

Dion got to his feet. "This is where Tutor sends me every morning, *decurio*, just like you instructed ... as far as Ebrius ... he's probably sharing a jug with some mates down in the *quaestorium* ... he should be along in a bit."

"Does the legate know?" I asked.

Dion shrugged. "Does he know, or does he care? Yes, to the first, no, it seems, to the second. As long as the paper flows smoothly, and he can find the report he needs, the legate doesn't seem a bit concerned about the situation."

I had been in the army long enough to understand the principle, "if it's not broken, don't fix it." So, I didn't pursue the issue. I asked, "Is the legate available?"

"Let me see," Dion offered.

He walked over to portal of Labienus' *cubiculum* and stuck his head in. I heard a short, mumbled conversation, then Dion stepped back, holding open the tent flap. "Go right in, *decurio*," he invited.

Labienus was planted in his accustomed position, sitting behind his field desk, surrounded by tablets. "To what do I owe the honor of the visit, Gai?" he said.

He called me Gai, so the meeting was informal. So, I just announced, "I'm back from that mission to fetch Cuhnetha, so I'm reporting in ..."

Labienus raised a hand to stop me, "I appreciate that but, for the time being, you don't work for me."

Before I could respond, Labienus continued, "You've been seconded to the legate, Troucillus. You're to report to him in Bibracte ... Ebri! Ebri! Where are you, lad?"

It was Dion who stick his head through the tent flap, "*Ti'a'sum, Legate*! I'm here, sir!"

"Oh ... Dion ... where's uh ... never mind ... can you put your hands on the decurion's orders?"

"*A'mperi'tu, legate*! Immediately, sir"

I was marveling about how quickly Dion had adapted himself to the army, when Labienus started, "Good lad you got there, Gai ... a real help around here ... don't imagine you'd be willing to leave him here while you're in Bibracte?"

Before I could respond, Ebrius rushed in carrying a small *tabula*. As he handed it to Labienus, the legate quipped, "Hope I didn't disturb your siesta, soldier."

"Uh ... no, sir ... I mean ... yes..."

Labienus took the tablet and held up his hand, "*Abi, Ebri*! Get outta here, Ebrius!"

"*A'mperi'tu, legate*!" Ebrius sputtered and beat a hasty retreat out of the office leaving a swirl of wine fumes in his wake.

"Admin's running smoother and Ebrius is getting his afternoon beauty rest," Labienus muttered, while examining the tablet. "Everybody wins!"

Review over, Labienus snapped the tablet shut and handed it to me, "These are your orders attaching you to Troucillus. It's also your authorization to sleep outside the camp and dress in civilian clothes. Keep it in a safe place; it's also your ID as a Roman officer."

I took the *tabula*. I didn't read it; I had a lot to process. "Civilian clothes?" I asked.

"Yes," Labienus nodded. "Troucillus didn't think dressing as a Roman officer in the middle of Bibracte would serve you well, especially considering the hostility of the northern clans. So, you're to dress up as one of the wogs. Troucillus' man delivered a parcel to your quarters. I imagine that's your getup while you're away on this little boondoggle."

I nodded my head dumbly. Labienus continued, "So, you might as well get to it. Take your horse, equipment, and iron with you; you may need it ... any questions?"

"*N'abeo, legate*," I muttered. "No sir!"

"*Bene*," Labienus nodded. "And Dion? Will you be leaving him here? I could use the help?"

When I got back to my quarters, Calo, our orderly, greeted me. "Ah! *Decurio*! It's good to see you back. There's a parcel for you. Shall I fetch it?"

"In a bit, Calo," I responded. "Would you help me out of this iron first? My shoulders are aching."

I dropped my helmet and *spatha*, my cavalry saber, on my bunk, unbuckled my belt, and ducked out of my baldric. Calo unfastened my *chlamydes*, my shoulder armor, and began unlacing my *lorica*. Finally, I was able to slip out of my chainmail.

Calo examined my rig. "Perhaps I should give these a good brushing," he suggested. "And a light coat of oil?"

I was still luxuriating in those first moments of being out of my iron, when my shoulders are finally freed and want to stretch up into the clouds.

"You do that, Calo," I sighed.

As Calo carried my rig over to his work area, I untied my *sudarium*, my sweat scarf, and began to unlace my *subarmalis*, the padded jacket I wore under my *lorica*. As soon as I opened the jacket, I was engulfed with the unmistakable miasma of "under-armor odor." There's nothing like it! It's one of the unmistakable signs of the Roman army. Purple striper or *mulus*, under the iron, we all smell alike.

I sat down on my cot with a sigh and wondered if I had enough time for a trip to the bathing point.

Calo returned carrying a large cloth bag. "Here is your parcel, *decurio* ... ah ... perhaps a fresh tunic? And ... yes ... a clean *subligar* ... I think your tighty-whities have outlived their usefulness."

I pulled off my tunic and tossed it to Calo. Then I sat down on my bunk to unlace my boots. Calo beat a hasty retreat with my stinking tunic; he didn't want to spend any more time with it than he had to.

While I was unfastening my boot laces, I noticed the parcel Calo had left on my bunk. Curiosity got the better of me. I opened it and looked inside. I saw a folded piece of cloth. I removed it. As, it unfolded itself in the light of the tent, I could see it was a knee-length, long-sleeved tunic in dark green wool. It was well dyed and woven in a good tight weave with tight stitching along the seams – the garment of a wealthy man.

The next piece was a pair of *bracae*, trousers, of the same color and quality. Underneath that, I retrieved a shoulder cape, a tartan displaying an intricate plaid of red, blue, and yellow over a dark green background.

"The colors of the Helvi," Calo's voice announced from behind me. I turned and he stood there with a clean military tunic draped over his arm.

"You recognize these colors?" I asked.

"Indeed, sir," Calo nodded. "My people traded with the Helvi when I was a child. I know their colors well. Seeing them meant we didn't have to run and hide for our lives."

I'm sure there was a story there.

"I suppose you won't be needing this tunic then, sir," Calo was saying. "Let me find some fresh linens for you."

As Calo retreated, I reached back into the bag and withdrew a white, wooden wand capped in silver on both ends. Finally, I found a tabula. I opened it and read,

> *Gaius Valerius Troucillus, Legatus ad Manum to Gaius Iulius Caesar, Proconsul, to Gaius Marius Insubrecus, Decurio, Sends Greetings*
>
> *I have sent you the clothing of a noble of my tribe. I think it best that you assume this "disguise" while you are working with me in Bibracte of the Aedui. Not that the Aedui will not know you for a Roman with that short haircut and shaved face. But it's best I think not to flaunt it in front of them.*
>
> *You may wear your own armor and bring one of the Roman mounts. Roman armor is essentially the same as ours and I have a member of my staff who can easily obscure the army brand on your horse, a skill at which he has had much practice. But that will remain our secret.*
>
> *Also, I have sent you a wand of negotiation which will identify you as a protected emissary and as part of my familia. Keep this with you at all times. Even if one of the northerners recognizes you as a Roman, he will not violate the decorum of diplomacy. Such an act would forfeit his head-price and send him into exile as an outlaw.*
>
> *Finally, you need to find my house.*
>
> *Enter Bibracte through the southern gate. After you enter, the main road will bear somewhat to the left and begin to climb a small ridge. After a few hundred paces, you will come to a junction. On your left is the spring of Anouba; on your right, a trail climbs up to the citadel and the hall of the tribal king, Duuhruhda. Bear to the left at this crossing. You will continue to climb until you come to the top of a saddle. On your left, a*

trail leads up to the western tower, on your right, the walls of the citadel. Go straight here and follow the trail down from the ridge. After about two hundred paces, you will find a flat, open area on the right where there are a number of large houses. Mine is in the middle of the grouping about a hundred paces east of the trail you came in one. It's marked by a pennant displaying my tribal colors, the same as the tartan I gave you. My doorman is expecting you.

If all else fails, ask directions. Everyone in town knows where the "Romans" are.

And, while I'm thinking of it, lose that short Roman sword of yours. Wear your long sword on your left hip like the Gallic warrior you're supposed to be.

Until I see you, Vale!

As I finished reading, I sensed a presence standing behind me.

I turned.

It was Calo holding clean linens. "Perhaps you'd like to change into these *before* you get into your new clothes, *decurio*."

BIBRACTE
AEDUORUM

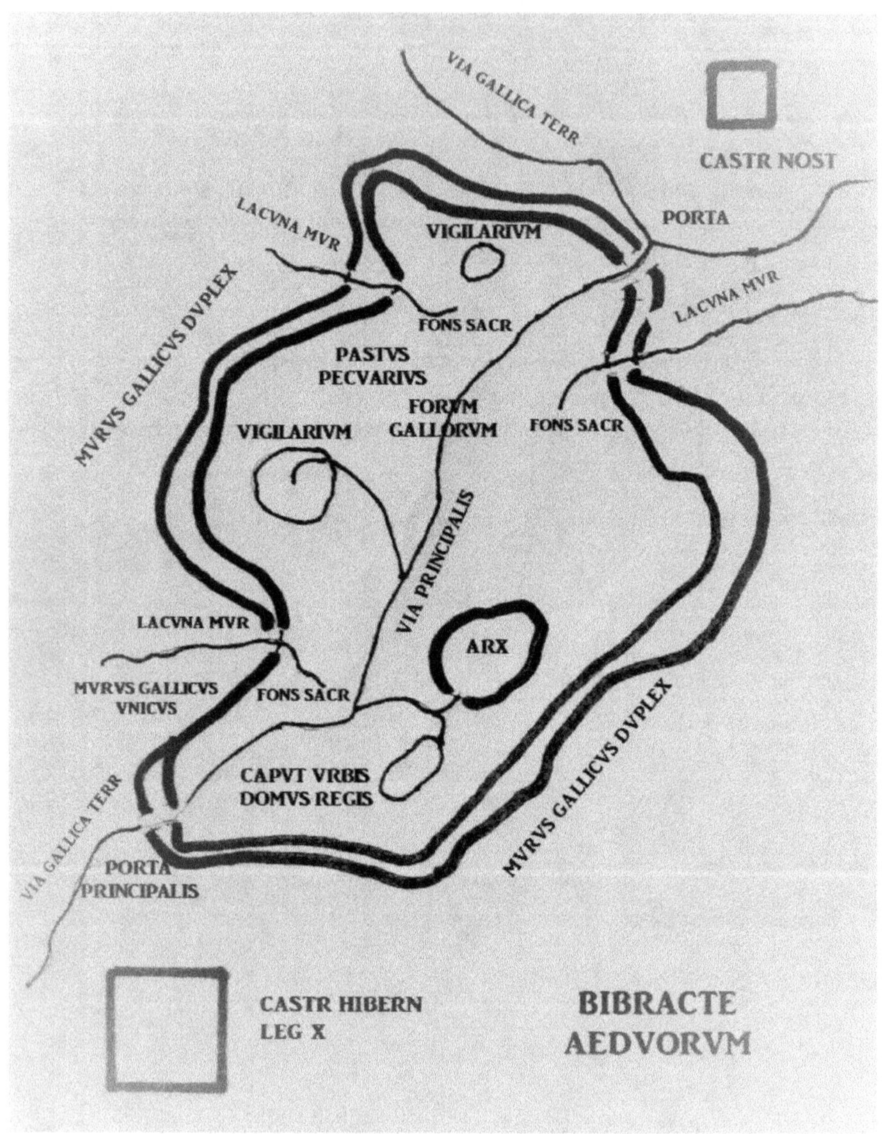

BIBRACTE OF THE AEDUI

V

Caput V. De Ludo Regium
Chapter 5. The Game of Kings

By sundown, I was seated by the fire in Troucillus' house, bathed, fed, and a cup of red mead in my hand.

I didn't have too much trouble finding the place. I rode Clamriu into Bibracte; she needed the exercise, and I didn't think the short ride would strain her injured shoulder.

By Roman military standards, security on the city gate was informal, at best. A loose detail of warriors was posted there, but the officer in charge saw I was mounted, carried the iron of a warrior, held a white wand in in my right hand, and wore a five-strand golden torc around my neck. I'm sure my lack of luxuriant, Gallic facial hair confused him a bit – he couldn't see my short hair underneath my helmet – but there were nobles and warriors arriving from all over Duuhruhda's territories. Perhaps one of the septs that lived too close to the Roman *provincia* had taken to scraping their faces and looking like women in armor. Besides, there was nothing to be gained in challenging a well-mounted warrior wearing a five-strand torc. The guard commander passed me through with a nod.

Troucillus' directions were fairly straightforward. I stayed on the main road keeping the citadel to my right. On my left, I passed the *fuhnon Abnoba*, the spring of the goddess, Abnoba, and the city's western tower located on a small hill called *Gropar Craig*, "Hill of the Rock," where the bone-fires of the *Samon'win* would soon be lit. As I descended from the low ridge, an open area, *Tir Pori Gouart'eg*, the Cattle Pasture, opened to my left. This, I learned, was where the Council of Three Generations was to be held. To my right, a collection of large, prosperous-looking round houses, most surrounded by wooden stockades.

I learned later that beyond the houses to the northeast was the *Fuhnon Ancamna*, the spring of the water goddess, Ancamna, one of the three sacred springs of Bibracte. The first was the *fuhnon Abnoba* in the southwest; the second, the *Fuhnon Ancamna* in the northeast; and the third, *Fuhnon Maru Rignai*, the Spring of the Phantom Queen, was below the *Craig uh Ouraig*, the Rock of the Wife, where the city's northern tower stood.

Explaining the *Maru Rignai*, the three-personed phantom queen, is difficult; there is no equivalent concept in the Roman or Greek pantheons. The nearest the Romans can come to understanding the phantom queen of the Gah'el is their own three-faced Hecate, goddess of crossroads and of dark places.

The closest word in Latin to the Gallic *maru*, is *simulacrum* which indicates an indistinct image, a shadowy manifestation. The Gallic word *maru* can mean all this, but it is a dark, fleeting image seen only through a dream or in a trance. In fact, the word *maru* is often used to describe a nightmare.

The *Maru Rignai* manifests herself – or themselves – in three forms: the white, the red and the black.

The white goddess is Andraste, the eagle, the goddess who brings victory in battle. It is she who lures men into battle to gain riches, destroy their enemies, and conquer other lands.

The red is Andarta, the hawk, the blood goddess who brings the battle madness. It is she that emboldens warriors to slaughter their enemies without fear. But it is also she who brings the madness that enables a man to slaughter friend and foe alike.

The black is Catubodua, the direst manifestation of the *Maru Rignai*. Catubodua is the hooded crow, the harbinger of death. She feasts on the blood and the flesh of those slain in battle.

At any time, the *Maru Rignai* is any one of these and yet all of them together. These are goddesses to be appeased and to be avoided. Their desire is death, blood, and destruction.

As I approached Troucillus' house, little did I realize that I was but a few hundred paces from the sacred spring of the *Maru Rignai*. The *Samon'win* was fast approaching, a time when men believe the boundaries between their middle world and the world of the gods is most porous. With the Aedui in crisis, it was the opportune time for unscrupulous men to take advantage of the people's fear of the Nightmare Queen.

As I sampled Troucillus' red mead by the fire, he sat on my right. We had been joined by his *barnuchel*, Aderuhn mab Enit, who had presided over the inquest into the murder of Rhuhderc mab Touhim, a warrior in Morcant's troop, during our journey to the Arar in pursuit of Ariovistus. His handling of the trial of Arion mab Cadarn, one of Athauhnu's men accused of the murder, had prevented a war from breaking out between the Aedui and the Sequani on the eve of Caesar's campaign against the Swabii.

Across the central hearth sat a man in the brown robes of a *derwuhd*, a speaker of the gods. He was another of Troucillus' Romanized clan, Spurius Fulvius, but as we were speaking in Gah'el, we addressed him by his Gallic name, Trahernos mab Adair.

Trahernos was saying, "The Aineduai are by tradition divided into five clans, each claiming descent from one of the five sons of Ci, the "Hound," the eldest son of the god, Lugos. Ci was Lugos' champion in the wars against *Uh Thloo uth uh Doo T'wil*, the People of Dana. These lands from the mountains to the sea were given to the Hound by the god and the Hound divided them up between his five sons – Gouuhn, Du, Coch, Glasach and Melwuhn ..."

"Wait," I interrupted. "Those aren't names. They're colors."

"Yes," Trahernos nodded. "Each has significance ... white is all colors, therefore the strongest ... black defies all color, therefore it cannot be understood ..."

"Traherne!" Troucillus said, "You can explain that to Arth later. For now, we need to understand what we're dealing with in the council tomorrow."

"Of course, *a pen*," Trahernos agreed. "As I said, each of the five clans of the Aineduai claim descent from one of the sons of Ci. The clan of the Hound's oldest son, Gouuhn, is the *Wuhr Tuurch*, the Boar Clan, the clan of Cuhnetha mab Cluhweluhno. As the eldest clan, the tribal kingship traditionally resided with the *Wuhr Tuurch*; that is, until recently. During the *Cad Almaeneg*, the German wars, Duuhruhda's father, Clethguuhno, who is of the *Wuhr Blath*, the Wolf clan, descended from the Hound's middle son, Coch, pulled off a neat *coup d'état*. He convinced the council that the tribe was facing such a crisis with the Cimbri and the Teutones rampaging through their territory that Cuhnetha's father, Cluhweluhno, was far too weak and Cuhnetha too young. So, the council elected Clethguuhno to replace Cluhweluhno as the tribal king and war chief ..."

"I don't understand something, Traherne," I interjected. "You said Cluhweluhno's clan descends from Ci's *middle* son, Coch. Why didn't the clan of Du, Ci's second son, claim the kingship?"

"Ah," Trahernos answered. "Good question ... one that points directly to the heart of the issue we will be facing tomorrow ... the clan of Du mab Ci is the *Wuhr Arth*, the Bear Clan, the clan of our friend, Malouuhnos mab Dermuhtos. That clan was devastated during the German wars ... Dermuhtos, Malouuhnos' father, was killed in a battle with the Cimbri, a battle that Malouuhnos believes should never have been fought. The *Rhufeinig* consul, Gnaeus Mallius Maximus, promised to support Dermuhtos, but did not. Instead, Maximus used Dermuhtos to slow down the Cimbri long enough for him to withdraw his legions across the Rotonos, while Dermuhtos' army was destroyed. So complete was the destruction of Dermuhtos' clan that it could not participate in the council that designated Cluhweluhno king."

Aderuhn, Troucillus' *barnuchel* nodded, "This is permitted by the laws of Lugos in times of crisis. It is somewhat like the Roman tradition of appointing a dictator in an emergency."

"But the *Rhufeinig* appointment of a *dictator* is temporary," I protested. "It rarely lasts more than a year."

Aderuhn agreed, "And, so it is with our people. But the law does not specify a time limit for the appointment, and this is what Malouuhnos may try to use to unseat Duuhruhda before the council. One, his father's elevation was temporary, only meant to face the *Almaeneg* crisis; and two, Duuhruhda's father was not elected by the full tribal council of three generations."

Troucillus spoke, "Our interests lie in a strong *Aineduai* nation friendly towards the *Rhufeinai*. A dynastic struggle will weaken the tribe and any increase of Malouuhnos' influence will turn the *Aineduai* away from their alliance with Rome. What can we do to keep the alliance with the *Aineduai* ... uh ... shall we say, reliable?"

"Directly, nothing," Aderuhn stated. "The law prohibits our direct participation in the election. We are free to observe as are any of the people, but we cannot participate or be seen influencing the election. That would play into the hands of Malouuhnos and the anti-*Rhufeinig* factions of the tribe."

Troucillus nodded, then asked, "Traherne! How do you expect Malouuhnos to use the gods to support his putative coup?"

Trahernos shrugged. "The tradition is that the king requires the favor of the gods to rule. If Malouuhnos can convince the council that the gods have withdrawn their favor from Duuhruhda, the tribe is obliged to unseat him and elect another."

"How could Malouuhnos convince the council that the gods have turned against the king?" I asked.

Again, Trahernos shrugged, "In times of famine and war, hunger and defeat are looked on as evidence that the gods are punishing the people because of an unworthy king. As far as I can see, the *Aineduai* are prosperous. That leaves war. So, I imagine Malouuhnos will attribute the invasion of the River People and the presence of the legions in *Aineduai* lands to the displeasure of the gods with Duuhruhda's rule."

Aderuhn nodded counting off on his fingers, "That! And the alleged conspiracy of Duuhruhda's brother, Deluuhnu, with the River People. And the irregularity of the election of Duuhruhda's father, Clethguuhno, to the throne. And the stop-gap nature of that appointment ..."

"In order to put Cuhnetha on the throne?" I interjected.

"That would be my guess," Troucillus agreed. "And I imagine Malouuhnos will propose himself as *pendefig*, since Cuhnetha's clan is so weak."

"And there goes Caesar's alliance with the *Aineduai* ..." I mused.

Troucillus agreed, "I imagine that was part of Malouuhnos' proposition to Cuhnetha, 'I support you taking the throne; you throw the *Rhufeinai* out'."

I remembered Caesar's growing concern with the *Belgae*. If Caesar were to march north, the lands of the *Aineduai* would lie right across his lines of communication. Caesar needed the *Aineduai* peaceful, united, and supportive.

"Caesar will not agree..." I started.

"Not agree!" Troucillus snorted. "It will mean war. It will start here at Bibracte. And, with the legions dispersed, only the Tenth Legion stands between Malouuhnos and the river, Rotonos."

We were all silent for a few heartbeats, then I asked, "There are two other clans in the tribe. Will they support Malouuhnos in this?"

Troucillus answered, "My best guess is that the *Wuhr Gadno*, the Fox Clan will not. They live along the Rotonos and have been trading with the *Rhufeinai* for decades. They will not support anything that will interrupt their access to Roman goods, especially wine and *garum*, of which they have become overly fond. The Badger Clan, the *Wuhr Broch*, live in the west. They have little contact with the *Rhufeinai* and depend on Malouuhnos' support in their contstant wars with the Senones and the Bituriges. They'll do anything Malouuhnos wants of them."

"So, going into this, the legal and religious reasons for deposing Duuhruhda are questionable and the tribe is split on the issue," I summed up. "So, how do you expect Malouuhnos to go about it?"

Aderuhn answered, "The council is held out in the open. All the people are encouraged to witness how their king is selected. Although they have no legal right to participate in the debate or in the acclamation of the king, they can always make their desires known and influence the selection. If I were Malouuhnos, I would enlist the people's aid by appealing not to the law, but to the will of the gods. He will convince them that the gods have abandoned Duuhruhda and, if he is retained as king, the gods will abandon the tribe. Unless they restore Cuhnetha to the throne with him as *pendefig*, the gods will offer the *Aineduai* as slaves to the *Rhufeinai*. He will place his own people among the crowds to stir them up. They must put Cuhnetha on the throne and rise up to destroy the *Rhufeinig* invaders. Unless they do, the gods will abandon them."

We all sat in silence after Aderuhn's summary. The council was to be held the next day, starting at the sixth hour when fire-chariot of Lugus was at its zenith.

We would soon discover that we had had badly underestimated Malouuhnos.

VI

Caput VI. De Maledicto Catuboduae
Chapter 6. The Curse of Catubodua

The *cuhmooliat*, the council of three generations, began at midday so Lugos, the god himself, could witness the justice of the proceedings. How the Aedui decided it was midday or how the god could actually see the proceedings was anyone's guess. The sky was obscured with thick, threatening, gray clouds, and chilly breezes from the western mountains whipped across the field where the council was held.

Tir Pori Gouart'eg, the Cattle Pasture, was located just west of the main road running through Bibracte. Based on the piles of *merd'* scattered throughout, the place was aptly named. In fact, a few head of placidly-munching cattle were on hand to witness the event. They didn't seem at all impressed.

The pasture sat behind a row of workshops, shops and taverns that lined the west side of the road. To the south, the Rock of Ambisagros and its tower rose; to the north, the Rock of the Wife and the northern tower. The inner wall of Bibracte's double wall bordered the pasture to the the west.

The five clans of the Aedui were situated facing each other in a rough circle. Reflecting the confusion of the dynastic situation, Cuhnetha, as head of the Boar clan descended from the eldest son of the Hound, occupied the place of honor on the east of the circle where the sun rises. The delegation from the Badger Clan, descended from the Hound's youngest son, faced Cuhnetha from the west where the sun descends into the underworld. To Cuhnetha's immediate right, Malouuhnos' Bear Clan. Duuhruhda's Wolf Clan, despite his being the ruling *Uucharix*, tribal king, was situated to the right of Malouuhnos. The remaining Fox Clan had most of the southern circumference to themselves.

Our entourage, as observers and guests, sat outside the circle. Troucillus picked a spot between Malouuhnos and Cuhnetha – distant enough from Duuhruhda not to suggest Caesar's influence on the king but still where Troucillus expected most of the action. Troucillus had arrived early setting up field chairs for himself, me, Aderuhn, his *barnuchel*, and Trahernos, the *derwuhd*.

We were all dressed in the colors of Troucillus' people, the Helvi. I was wearing the dark green attire that Troucillus had given me. When I awoke that morning, I found a pair of soft, brown leather boots in place of my hobnailed Roman *caligae* – Troucillus felt that he wanted to downplay any apparent Roman military connections. Also, Troucillus had left me a long, gray, hooded cloak of tightly woven wool, for which I gave thanks while sitting in the chilly breezes blowing in off the already white-capped mountains.

Despite all this, I couldn't help noticing around our group a perimeter of seven guards dressed as Gah'el but with Roman, military haircuts. All carried Roman *pugiones* on their belts and one even had the collar of a chainmail *lorica* peeking out from under his tunic.

Troucillus caught me looking. "Labienus loaned me a squad of *muli* from the Eleventh Legion ... they're all Gallic speakers and I told them not to shave ... couldn't do much about the short hair, though."

The rest of us wore our longswords. This was permitted as long as we remained outside the circle of the council.

Members of each clan's delegation were slowly wandering in and gathering at their assigned positions, which were marked by a pennant hung on a pole and crossbar displaying the clan colors. The pennants snapped sharply in the cool western breezes. At first glance, they all seemed to be the tartan colors of the Aineduai. But, upon closer examination, subtle differences in the pattern and colors could be detected.

Cuhnetha was the first of the "major players" to arrive. Although he seemed healthy, I did notice Morcant, his son, walking closely on Cuhnetha's right side and occasionally supported him by subtly placing his hand under his father's elbow. He was accompanied by his *barnuchel* and his joke-cracking *derwuhd*, whom I remembered from the feast. Trailing behind, I recognized Tegid mab Davuhd, Morcant's shield-bearer and, on Cuhnetha's left side, Rhonwen.

Aderuhn was explaining, "Each of the clan chiefs will have his *barnuchel* and *derwuhd* to advise him on the legalities and the will of the gods in these proceedings. Also, selected members of three generations – father, son, and grandson, if you wish – and yes, Arth ... I know you've lived among the Rhufeinai all your life ... women of the warrior class participate in the council."

Before I could respond, Malouuhnos' entourage began to arrive. I recognized the sour faced Malgounos from Cuhnetha's feast. I assumed the warrior walking to his right was Malouuhnos. He was not a physically imposing man. He stood little more than five Roman *pedes* in height. His long hair fell to his shoulders in a cascade of black and gray. But it was the way he walked that signaled his strength and dexterity. His hips were slightly thrust forward; his shoulders and arms moved along with an easy, confident fluidity. This was a man who could move quickly, with strength and dexterity, and betray no warning of an attack.

Along with Malouuhnos came a browned-robe man, whom I assumed was the *barnuchel*, and behind him, a tall, gaunt man in black robes.

I heard Trahernos hiss, "Malouuhnos' *derwuhd*! He's a member of the *froduhr du*!"

"The Black Brethren?" I asked.

"I have only heard of this order," Trahernos explained. "They practice ... uh ... 'fundamentalism' is the best way of describing their doctrine ... they want to re-assert the will of the gods as it was at the time of the great descent from the high places. They believe that the gods favor only the Gah'el; all other people are *tramorwuhrai*, outsiders, a contamination, and an abomination to the purity of the nations. They preach 'holy war'; the nations must rise up and expel all foreigners, especially the *Rhufeinai*, from the lands granted the Gah'el by the gods. It's said they still practice human sacrifice to appease the gods."

"The Black Brethren," Troucillus commented. "This may be more interesting than I anticipated."

As we watched, a tall, blond-haired warrior separated himself from the Badger Clan and began to walk toward Malouuhnos. He got no more than two or three paces into the circle when a gray-robed *barnuchel* called over to him. The warrior stopped and waited while the *barnuchel* approached him. They had a quick conversation during which the *barnuchel* pointed to the warrior's sword and gestured into the council circle. The warrior raised his hands seemingly in protest, but the gray-clad barnuchel pointed to his sword with increasing emphasis. Finally, the warrior shrugged his shoulders in exasperation. He grabbed the handle of his longsword with his left hand drawing it from its scabbard. He handed the sword over to the *barnuchel*, spun on his heals, and continued his journey across the circle to the area of Malouuhnos' Bear Clan.

"Bruhchamos mab Euhdulf," I heard Troucillus say, "Or, Bruhchamos Gwen, the "White," for his white-blond hair, *pobl'rix* of the Badger Clan ... he almost screwed the dog violating the circle."

"He did 'screw the dog'," Aderuhn answered. "But I doubt Duuhruhda will allow the tribal *barnuchel* make an issue of it. He wants to force the issue of the new *pendefig* through as quickly as possible, if he can."

As we watched, Bruhchamos greeted Malouuhnos. The blond warrior stood a full head over the leader of the Bear Clan, but there seemed no doubt who was in charge. It was Bruhchamos who had taken the walk across the circle and, as Malouuhnos spoke, it was the tall blond warrior who bent forward to hear his instructions.

"I'd say the fix is in," I heard Troucillus mutter.

We then noticed some movement approaching from the road. I recognized Duuhruhda mab Clethguuhno, the current tribal king of the Aedui, leading a group of men and a few women towards the council circle.

"The games begin," Troucillus muttered.

As Duuhruhda and the representatives of his Wolf Clan approached the circle, a man detached himself from the Fox Clan's grouping and walked over to greet the king. The man had short hair and a cleanly shaven face; in other words, he looked like a Roman in Gallic clothing.

"Ah! The plot thickens!" Troucillus narrated. "Karadogos mab Toutoualos, or Primus Caratagus Aeduanus as he prefers to be called, the leader of the Fox Clan. It's as we expected. The Fox Clan has allied itself with Duuhruhda as the pro-Roman faction, while Malouuhnos has Brychamos in his *marsupium* to put Cuhnetha on the throne with an anti-Roman platform. Aderuhn! I don't think Malouuhnos has the horses to pull off a regime change. Do you agree?"

Aderuhn nodded. "Cuhnetha's clan has no teeth. Duuhruhda has stripped it of any real power and isolated it from its putative allies in the west. Karadogos' clan is not strong militarily, but because of its extensive trade with the *Rhufeinai* across the Rotonos, it's quite prosperous. I agree with you. Malouuhnos can make some noise, but I doubt he can win adequate support to put Cuhnetha on the throne."

We watched as Duuhruhda and his Wolf Clan assembled themselves in their assigned spot. As reigning tribal king, Duuhruhda would have the privilege of the "first baton"; he would be given the speaking staff first allowing him to address the assembly. We expected him to propose his choice of *pendefig* immediately and hope the motion would carry.

"Arth?" I heard Troucillus call my name. "What would you do if you were Duuhruhda?"

"I don't know," I shrugged. "As you say, he's sure to win in the long run."

Troucillus nodded. "Yes! You're correct as far as his short-term goal of staying on the throne. But, in the long run, he will still have to deal with the hostility of Malouuhnos and the western clans to his alliance with Caesar. And now that Caesar has liberated the Soucanai from Ariovistus, the frontiers of the Aineduai lands along Arar will be become unstable, and Cuhnetha is too weak to hold them. So, what's Duuhruhda's best play here."

I thought about it for a few heartbeats, then said, "Nominate Morcant as his *pendefig?*"

"Exactly!" Troucillus agreed. "He'd change the whole balance of power in the tribe. And how could Cuhnetha's Boar Clan not acclaim one of their own as the tribal *pendefig*. It would be a master stroke!"

"So, you think that's what Duuhruhda will proclaim?" I asked.

"Not a chance!" Troucillus snorted. "He's not that smart!"

As we spoke, a tall man dressed in a white robe entered the circle. As everyone around the circle rose, he raised an oaken staff in his right hand, a tree sacred to the gods. On the top of the staff was a silver hand, fingers extended, palm open, the sign of peaceful deliberation. The man waited as all conversation around the council circle ceased and the assembly stopped fidgeting.

"Anionos mab Kamehros," Aderuhn whispered. "Duuhruhda's *barnuchel* ... the senior justice of the Aineduai.

Anionos intoned, *"Mai cuhmooliat uh popl bellac uhn decrau* ... The assembly of the peoples now begins!"

Anionos intoned his qualifications as *barnuchel*, *"Uhr wuhf uhn Anionos, mab Kamehros, mab Gwehnios ..."* He listed all his ancestors, mentors, teachers, schools. I was brought back momentarily to a field near the banks of the Arar, where Aderuhn officiated over the murder trial of Arion mab Cadarn on our way to face the German warlord, Ariovistus.

When Anionos chant ended, I quipped, "Not a student of the "blue people" of Pridain or of the Irioudinai of the western isles ... how disappointing."

"Not everyone is schooled in the ancient ways," Aderuhn chuckled.

Troucillus hissed us back into silence

Anionos' assistant intoned, "*A oes unrhuhw un uhmginnull uhn i che hoon uhn herio awdurdod i barnuchel i benderfuhnu materion hin?* ... Does anyone assembled here challenge the authority of the *barnuchel* to decide these matters?" No one in the assembly answered. Anionos took his seat in a chair placed within the circle for him. The assembly then took their seats.

Duuhruhda entered the circle and faced Anionos. Anionos nodded to his assistant, who handed Duuhruhda an oaken wand, the "speaking staff." Duuhruhda inclined his head in Anionos' direction and turned to face the clans assembled around the council circle. Duuhruhda raised the speaking staff in his right hand so all could see.

"Let's see just how big an idiot our friend, Duuhruhda, is," Troucillus' chuckled.

The king began, "I am Duuhruhda, son of Clethguuhno, *Pobl'rix*, clan leader of the *Wuhr Blath*, the Wolf clan, and *Uucharix*, tribal king of the Aineduai ..."

When Duuhruhda made *that* claim, Cuhnetha snorted loudly, earning him a dirty look from Anionos, the presiding justice.

"Not an auspicious start!" Troucillus muttered.

Duuhruhda continued, "I come before this assembly of three generations to nominate a successor to ..."

"Don't say that name!" Troucillus urged in a whisper.

Almost as if he heard, Duuhruhda corrected himself, "Uh ... a successor ... a successor to the station and rank of tribal *pendefig* ... a warrior of proven worth over five seasons. I nominate ..."

"Wait for it," Troucillus hissed.

"... I nominate my sister's son ... Eogahnos mab Gwitheri!"

As Troucillus groaned, the members of Duuhruhda's allied clans rose in acclaim. Cuhnetha's clan and the two western clans remained silent and seated.

"Eogahnos mab Gwitheri!" Troucillus spat. "A complete nonentity ... a nobody ... he might just as well have nominated his wife's pet lap dog!"

Duuhruhda handed back the speaking staff, inclined his head in Anionos' direction and rejoined his clan.

"Who will speak to this proposal?" Anionos asked.

Malouuhnos immediately stepped into the circle. But, before he could be recognized, Morcant helped his father, Cuhnetha, rise from his chair and supported him into the circle. As the descendant of the eldest son of the Hound, Cuhnetha had precedence in council.

Anionos inclined his head in Cuhnetha's direction. His assistant walked across the circle and presented the staff to Cuhnetha. Cuhnetha took the staff and raised it for all in the assembly to see. Morcant steadied his father, then retreated to his assembled clan.

"I am Cuhnetha mab Cluhweluhno, *pobl'rix* of the *Wuhr Tuurch*, the Boar Clan, descended from Gouuhn mab Ci, the eldest son of the Hound, the eldest grandson of the god, Lugos, and by the will of the god, the rightful *uucharix* of the Aineduai ..."

Cuhnetha stopped, seemingly struggling to catch his breath. Morcant took a step into the circle toward his father, but stopped as Cuhnetha continued, "This ... this man ... this Duuhruhda ... this son of the murdering usurper, Clethguuhno ... this brother of a traitor and outlaw, Deluuhnu ... this man has no right to sit on the throne of the Aineduai ... such a claim is in itself an offense to the god! To tolerate such a claim will invite the wrath of Lugos to be visited on the nation! The signs are clear! First, the River People burn and murder across our lands. Now, the *Rhufeinai* camp before the very gates of this city ..."

"And there it is," Troucillus hissed.

"... Soon, our traditional enemies, the Soucanai, freed from their bondage, will again run rampant in our lands along the Arar! Murder and treason run through this man's very veins, this man who calls himself our king! I say this! This impiety should not be allowed to stand for another day. I propose ... no ... in the name of the god, Lugos, I demand that the rule of the nation be restored to the proper clan, the clan of Gouuhn mab Ci, as Lugos himself decreed when the nation descended from the high places! I propose that the throne be restored to me, as the eldest son of Cluhweluhno, the last legitimate king of the Aineduai!"

Cuhnetha paused, whether to catch his breath or to let his message sink in being anybody's guess. Then, "I propose further that in this time of crisis to the nation the place of *pendefig* be granted to Malouuhnos mab Dermuhtos, who will lead the clans of the north to defend our lands from our enemies!"

With this, the members of the three clans supporting Cuhnetha and Malouuhnos rose in acclaim. I looked to see how Cuhnetha's son, Morcant, reacted to his father having passed him over for *pendefig*. But I could get no reading except Morcant's concern for his father, who was near collapse after delivering this harangue. Morcant quickly strode into the circle to keep his father from collapsing. He removed the staff from his father's right hand and gave it back to Anionos' assistant. Then he half carried the old man back to his seat.

"We're still in good shape here," Troucillus was saying. "I'm sure the council has heard this rant before ... even with Malouuhnos in play, there's not enough momentum to overthrow Duuhruhda.

Anionos assistant walked across the circle to Malouuhnos. He took the speaking staff and lifted it in his right hand until those assembled around the council circle quieted.

"Here we go," Troucillus predicted. "The speech about how the gods have cursed the land because of Duuhruhda ... crops will not grow ... mares with not foal ... lambs are born deformed ... soon a dark mist will cover the land obscuring Lugos' fiery eye."

"You mean winter's here," Trahernos chuckled.

"I am Malouuhnos mab Dermuhtos, *pobl'rix* of the Bear Clan," the speaker began. "With the consent of the presiding justice, I wish to bring forward one of my people to report to the council what the *Maru Rignai*, the Phantom Queen, has revealed to her!"

With the mention of the Phantom Queen, Malouuhnos had everyone's attention. I saw men and women around the circle make hand gestures to ward off the malignance of those goddesses. These movements also caused me to notice for the first time that a large crowd had gathered in the field around us to witness the proceedings. Hundreds of idle warriors and town-folk touched their foreheads, kissed their fingertips and raised them north to keep the menace of the *Maru Rignai* away from their hearths.

Without waiting for Anionos' response, Malouuhnos' black-clad *derwuhd* led a woman into the council circle. Her hair was a wild tangle of black and gray. She was thin as a spear shaft, her face ashen. Her cheek bones seemed to be pushing up through the almost translucent flesh of her face. The fabric of her dirty, undyed gown hung from her shoulders like a tattered curtain from a rod. She shuffled forward to assume a position next to Malouuhnos.

"*Wraig uh Tomen!*" Trahernos gasped.

"The Woman of the Mound?" Troucillus answered him. "That's a story to frighten children into their beds. This is theater ... pure theater!"

Wraig uh Tomen! That was a story my Nana used to frighten *me* into *my* bed when I was a child. *Wraig uh Tomen* is a fey who appeared as an ugly, frightful hag. She haunted the burial mounds of the old ones. Her keening death chant was both a lament for those who had died as well as a warning of imminent death to the living. Nana told me anyone who looks into the eyes of the Woman of the Mound sees his own death there. But this woman could not be the *Wraig uh Tomen*; she never appears in the sight of Lugos' eye.

Anionos was speaking, "Your request will be honored, Malouuhne, if the speaker is a free member of the nation."

"Examine her, Anione!" Malouuhnos invited.

"Woman!" the high justice said. "Tell this council your name and station!"

The old woman hesitated a few heartbeats. The she raised her head looking directly at Anionos. I noticed her eyes were of a blue so pale, so washed out, that she could easily be mistaken as blind.

"Me name, is't, yer'onor," she answered in a high-pitched croak. "What would me name tell yer that's worth an acorn? I'm called Gourach ... Gourach merc Fetroda ...

"'Witch, daughter of the Tomb'!" Troucillus spat. "This is too much ..."

"... daughter of a mother to whose womb we all must return ..."

"Please, sir," Aderuhn was cautioning Troucillus. "We are guests here ... we have no legal standing in council ..."

"... when I walked with mortals, me name was Morna ... me husband was a miller ... we had a home on a river west a here ... the River People came ... they burned our mill

... killed me husband ... our two sons ... carried away our daughter ... me they used and left for dead and I would have died had not the goddess come for me in the night ... then I was reborn as Gourach mec Fetroda, speaker of the *Maru Rignai*!"

"'When I walked with mortals'! Mad as a drunken Sybil," Troucillus dismissed her.

I was not as sure. I felt the chill that runs up a mortal's spine and makes the hairs on the neck tingle when in the presence of a creature from the earthen mounds.

Anionos was speaking, "Malouuhnos mab Dermuhtos! As clan chief, do you affirm that this woman is a free member of your clan and that her recounting of her history is true and accurate?"

"I do!" Malouuhnos answered.

Anionos continued, "Morna! As wife of a miller, you are of the rank of free clansmen who own property. Since you owned neither land nor cattle, you are of the station and rank of *keilos bach*, and as such, you have the right to speak in the tribal council."

"Anionos is completely ignoring the fact that this woman is crazy as a rabid squirrel," Troucillos spat.

"Or, truly touched by the goddesses," Trahernos suggested.

"Pah," Troucillus dismissed him.

"Tell the council of your vision," Malouuhnos encouraged the woman.

The woman was silent for a few heartbeats, then she began relating her tale in a voice other than the one I had just heard, a high-pitched chant-like narrative.

"I were at the sacred spring of the *Maru Rignai* to make me offerin' ... I wanted the Phantom Queen to rain blood and terror on them what murdered me family. I was layin' some sweet cakes and honey there where the waters emerge from the underworld, when I sees this old woman washin' somethin' in the stream. I says to 'er, I goes, 'What're ya doin' here? These waters're sacred to the goddess', but she answers me not. So, I says again, 'Woman! Ya canna be washing ya rags in these here waters! You offend the goddess!' With that she looks up at me and I freeze at the sight of 'er! She were the most ugly thing I've ever laid me eyes on ...'"

"Uglier than herself," Troucillus scoffed. "That would be a stretch."

"... 'er skin were the color of a cured hide ... 'er nose were all twisted ... there were running sores on 'er face ... but it were the eyes that froze me ... they were black, black as the midnight sky an' they were deep as the grave ... there were no white in 'em ... I felt meself being drawn into 'em an' tumblin' down a black pit into the dark places ... she held up the rag she were washin' an' I saw it were a tunic, a tunic covered in blood ... the fabric were pierced and ripped apart ...'"

"*Wraig golchour*!" Trahernos said. "The Washer Woman!"

I knew the "Washer Woman" from the tales of my nana. She was the harbinger of death, the messenger of the Phantom Queen. She washes the grave clothes of those who are about to die.

'... then I says to 'er, I goes, 'Whose tunic are ye washin' there, mother?' An' I hears her voice not in me ears, but in me head. She says, 'This is the tunic of the king! This is the shroud of Duuhruhda mab Clethguuhno!'

When the old woman said that name, I heard a collective gasp from those gathered about to watch the council. *Wraig golchour* was a powerful portent. I looked over to where the still-quite-alive king sat. His face was gray as the sky, his lips tight, colorless.

"... so I says to 'er, I goes, 'The king! Is 'e dead?' but she doesn't answer a word. Then she says to me, she goes, 'We have a message for 'im who is not king ... 'im whose father's treason blackens 'is 'eart ... 'im whose brother's betrayal rests on his shoulders ... 'im whose own treachery curses 'im' ..."

"Laying on a bit thick," Troucillus muttered.

Trahernos actually shushed his *pendefig*.

"... 'tell 'im who is not king that he is an offense to the gods ... tell 'im the throne must be returned to its rightful heir ... tell 'im unless it be done the wrath of Catubodua will be visited upon the nation ... the dark foreigners from the south will bare their swords against the throats of the people ... the Black Queen will feast upon the flesh and upon the blood of the Aineduai ..."

With the mention of the black goddess, Catubodua, a moaning arose from those standing around us. I looked and saw a woman swaying back and forth, her arms locked across her chest; the face of the man standing next to her, white as winter snow.

"... then she began keening a chant,

I see a world not dear to me
People without a king
Land without people
Spring without rain
Summer without warmth
Fall without harvest
Winter without food
I see a world not dear to me
People without a king.
Land without people
Kine without calf
Ewe without kid
Sow without piglet
Bitch without pup
I see a world not dear to me
People without a king.
Land without people
Earth without grain
Streams without fish
Sky without sun
Night without stars
I see a world not dear to me
People without a king.

> Land without people
> Young men without valor
> Warriors without loyalty
> Old men without wisdom
> Women without wombs
> Children without reverence
> I see a world not dear to me
> People without a king.
> Land without people
> Priests without gods
> Justices without laws
> Bards without words
> I see a world not dear to me
> People without a king.
> Land without people
> Son will deceive father
> Daughter will deceive mother
> The Son will enter the father's bed
> Father will enter the daughter's bed
> I see a world not dear to me
> People without a king.
> Land without people

"*Can Catubodua!*" Trahernos hissed. "The Song of Catubodua. The Prophecy of the Last Battle, *Mai Darogan Brouuhdr Diouedaf*, when Lugos will close his eye on the middle lands and the world will be reduced to perpetual darkness and cold!"

"Malouuhnos wants the council to believe that the gods have allowed the *Rhufeinai* to invade the nation as a punishment for tolerating the cursed reign of Duuhruhda," Troucillus commented. "And, unless the nation rejects him as king, Catubodua will blight the land."

The old woman seemed in a state of collapse with Malouuhnos' black-clad *derwuhd* supporting her, trying to walk her out of the council circle. Malouuhnos continued to hold the speaking-staff while his ally, Bruhchamos Gwen, sat complacently in his seat his legs stretched out before him and a satisfied smirk on his face.

Duuhruhda seemed to have collapsed into his seat, his face ashen white. Anionos, the presiding justice, was leaning over the king urgently whispering into his ear. Karadogos, Duuhruhda's ally, stood up and gestured urgently for the speaking staff. Anionos' assistant stood in the center of the council circle seemingly dumbfounded.

Voices surrounding the council circle moaned in fear while others yelled for Duuhruhda's removal. The chant "Cuhnetha! Cuhnetha! Cuhnetha!" was rising up from various places in the crowd.

Troucillus was watching the conversation between Duuhruhda and Anionos. "Even a dolt like Duuhruhda has to understand there's no coming back from that," he commented.

"Do you mean Malouuhnos has won?" I asked.

"This battle," Troucillus agreed. "Duuhruhda needs to come up with an excuse to suspend the council until this hubbub dies down … Aderuhn! Are there precedents?"

"For suspending a council of three generations?" Aderuhn answered. "Yes! It has been done. But the cause must be extraordinary …"

"Like a malediction being delivered from the Queen of the Hooded Crows?" Troucillus interrupted.

The chant for Cuhnetha was growing around us.

"I see Malouuhnos has planted people among the crowd to good effect," Troucillus commented.

Finally, Anionos reentered the council circle. His assistant seemed to break free of his trance and retrieved the speaking staff from Malouuhnos. Anionos raised his staff of office and held it high until the chatter, moaning, and chants for Cuhnetha finally died down.

Anionos spoke, "Until the priests have had a chance to examine this witness, the council of the three generations is suspended!"

VII

The eighth hour saw Troucillus and I sitting before Labienus in the *principia* of the Tenth Legion. As usual, Labienus was sitting behind a barricade of wooden tablets recording every jot and tittle of the army's condition.

"Tell me again why I should give a *cacula*, a turd, for what this ... this senate of the Aedui is doing?" Labienus challenged.

Troucillus sighed. "First, Labiene, if Malouuhnos is successful in ousting Duuhruhda, he will weaken, if not destroy, Caesar's alliance with the Aedui ..."

"Duuhruhda?" Labienus interrupted. "You're talking about Diviciacus, the king, right? And who is this ... uh ... this Malounus fellow again?"

"Malounus, as you call him, is the leader of the anti-Roman faction in the Aeduan ... uh ... the Aeduan senate," Troucillus said, expressing the issue in terms that Labienus, a Roman, could reasonably understand. "He wants to depose Diviciacus and put Cuhnetha on the throne with himself as ... uh ..." Troucillus struggled to come up with a Latin term for *pendefig*, saying finally, his "*Magister Equitum.*"

"His Master of the Horses?" Labienus repeated. "Why doesn't Diviciacus just arrest this Malounus, and that Cunneta fellow for good measure, and have done with it. Certainly, the king has more troops at hand than they do! Cunneta? Isn't that your friend, Insubrece?"

Before I could answer, Troucillus said, "That's not how the Gauls do these things, Labiene. It would be illegal ..."

"Illegal! Pah!" Labienus spat. "And treason isn't illegal? Just throw those *mentulae* into a hole somewhere and have done with it!"

Labienus' shoulders seemed to sink. "Labiene! That would mean a civil war between the clans," he tried to explain. "Whoever prevailed, the tribe would be greatly weakened and that would destroy the keystone of Caesar's alliances north of the Rhodanus."

Labienus did the math. Caesar's ambitions in the north against the Belgae would be frustrated if a war broke out along the Rhodanus. "Can't you talk to this Cunneta? Gai! You're in good with the son, right? What's his name ... Morcantus? Can't you talk some sense into him?"

Labienus shook his head. "We cannot be seen getting involved in tribal matters. Malouuhnos ... Malounus as you call him, has already denounced Diviciacus as ... uh

... *deliciae Caesaris* ... Caesar's little bitch ... if the tribe detect Roman interference, it will undermine the king's position. No! Let me work in the background as a prince of the Helvi. We had a setback today, but the game is still in play."

Labienus seemed relieved by Troucillus releasing him of any responsibility in this "Gallic" mess. Then another thought occurred to him. "Then, what do you want of me, Troucille?"

"In order to succeed, Malounus must not only get the Aeduan senate to elect Cuhnetha king, but he also has to pull off a military coup against Rome. Specifically, he has to push this legion back across the Rhodanus or destroy it."

Labienus again did the math. He nodded and said, "I see your point. But they're barbarians! They'd never be able to marshal an adequate force and get them down here in time after the election."

"*Exacte*!" Troucillus agreed, ignoring the "barbarian" jibe. "Exactly! So, Malounus wouldn't wait for the election! We must assume he's already marshalling the Aeduan warbands from the north and west and moving them in this direction! The timing's perfect! The *Samon'win* is almost here, so the crops are in. The men do not have to work the fields and there's plenty of surplus food for a campaign. Besides, if the election doesn't go his way, Malounus could use his troops to push Diviciacus off the throne. Then, he can attend to the Tenth Legion."

Labienus got it. "*Verpa Martis*! None of my recons are going out in that direction! I assumed the Aedui friendly! They could be up my arse before I had a chance to scratch!"

Then, "Ebri! Get those troop disposition reports in here. QC!"

It was Dion who responded carrying in a stack of *tabulae*. "Here they are, Legate!"

Thanks, Dion!" Labienus said getting up from his seat. "Where's Ebri... never mind ... bring 'em here."

"Ebrius is Caesar's man, so he's Caesar's problem," Labienus muttered as he walked over to the operations maps, Dion in his wake.

Labienus stared at the map for a few heartbeats then said, "Give me the tablet for the Eleventh!"

Without fumbling, Dion handed Labienus one of the *tabulae*. Labienus opened it, then looked back at the map. "The Eleventh's the closest to our position ... but they're spread out on road building details and they're still a new formation ... the Eighth is in camp at the confluence of the Arar and Dubis ... that's a two-day march ... the tablet for the Eighth!" Labienus snapped his fingers and Dion immediately handed him another *tabula*.

Labienus referred to the *tablula*, then snapped it shut. "Troucille! Is there any chance the Sequani are caught up in this plot??"

Troucillus shrugged. "Doubtful, Labiene! The Sequani have their hands full sweeping up the remnants of Ariovistus' lot. Besides, they hate the Aedui. If the Aedui were beer, the Sequani would only drink water!"

Labienus nodded, "*Bene*! So ... a threat in the east is doubtful ... the crossings of the Arar are secure ... that frees up the Eighth ... I'm getting ahead of myself here ... Dion ... go outside and send in two runners ... leave the rest of those *tabulae* on my desk!"

"*A'mperi'tu, legate*!" Dion snapped. "Yes, sir!" It took Dion a few heartbeats to find a spot on Labienus' cluttered desktop to drop the remaining tablets, but he was soon out the door.

Labienus was still staring at his operations map. "The terrain in the west is a blank. We have no information about rivers ... roads ..."

Two *muli* entered the cubiculum. Both were dressed in red military tunics, wide leather belts with their *pugiones*, military knives; both wore narrow purple headquarter sashes. Labienus heard them enter and without turning away from his map, he ordered, "One of you get Malleus, the *Primus Pilus*; the other the *Praefectus Castrorum*, Gemellus. Inform them that I need to see them here, QC ... ASAP! *Inrite* ... Informal ... just come as they are ... time's of the essence ... *Abite*! Go!"

Both men gave an "*A'mperi'tu, legate*!" as they turned on their heels. Labienus showed his complete confidence in his acceptance with the rank and file by QC'ing both top soldiers in camp. Over my years of service, I've seen seasoned legates who wouldn't dare attempt that!

Labienus returned to us from his maps. "I've got do get some recon out west beyond Bibracte," he started. "I imagine you'd recommend Gallic speakers, Troucillus?"

Troucillus nodded, "Yes! The political balance in Bibracte is delicate. We don't want this to look like a Roman invasion. That would just play into the hands of the anti-Roman faction."

As Labienus' perused the tablets on his desk, he also nodded. "I've got that *turma* of cavalry from the Eleventh north of town with the Sixth Cohort. We can send them out to the northwest. I should have most of the Twelfth's cavalry here in camp with me ... hopefully I have a rested *turma* that's ready to go ..."

Labienus' head jerked up from his *tabula*. "Troucille! What am I looking for out there? All wogs look alike to my boys."

Troucillus ignored the "wog" remark and answered, "I can give you swatches of the tartans for the rebel clans ..."

Labienus gave Troucillus a blank look.

"Clan tartans..." Troucillus began to explain. "... they're plaids ... the colors that identify the clans ... Never mind, Labiene! If you're sending out Gallic troopers, they'll know what to do with them."

"Have to be good enough," Labienus mumbled diving back into his reports.

Suddenly, two figures burst into the cubiculum. Malleus and Gemellus. Both men were turned out in full combat gear-*lorica*, belt, baldric; *gladius* strapped on the left hip, *pugio* on the right; helmet clamped under the left forearm; vine cudgel grasped in the left hand. For two senior centurions, who had served under the eagles for their entire adult lives, "informal," *inrite*, when reporting to a senior officer meant only helmet crests, leg greaves, and their multiple military awards for bravery in combat – *phalerae*, *hastae*, torcs and arm bands – were left back in their quarters. I would have sworn both men managed a shave between the time they were notified and the time they reported.

Malleus was limping noticeably. From under the skirt of his chainmail *lorica*, the jagged end of a red, half-healed wound extended down his left thigh.

Both men nodded toward Troucillus as they entered, their eyes passing over me seemingly without recognition. Then, Malleus' head jerked back to me. "Insubrece? That *is* you! Why are you out of uniform?"

"The *decurio* has been seconded to me, centurion," Troucillus answered. "He is in mufti at my instruction"

Malleus nodded slightly in Troucillus' direction, his lips a bloodless straight line cut across his face. Regardless of the reason, a Roman soldier out of uniform while on duty was still an offense in Malleus' mind. Especially, when the authorization came from a "civilian."

"Gentlemen!" Labienus announced. "I asked you here to discuss a possible threat to this command brought to my attention by Gaius Valerius Troucillus, the *imperator*'s legate to Diviciacus, King of the Aedui."

Labienus briefed the centurions on the situation. When he was done, he asked, "Any questions, gentlemen?"

Gemellus, "So, sir ... this threat ... if it materializes ... will be coming at us from the west and northwest?"

Labienus nodded, "That's what we believe, Gemelle!"

When there were no more questions, Labienus asked, "Malle! What's the status of the Tenth?"

Malleus, "As of this morning's manning report, I can put 3,296 *muli* into the battle line with nine of ten present in the first line cohorts ... all critical leadership positions are filled ... no critical equipment shortages to speak of ... we're still a bit low on *pila* and scorpion bolts, but not critically ..."

Labienus held up his hand and asked, "Tell me about the security of the camp."

"Camp's in good shape, Legate," Malleus started. "Ditch and ramparts are complete ... the four gates are secure ... towers and platforms constructed ... *scorpiones* and *ballistae* mounted ... wells dug ... ten-day's ready rations available, about half the winter reserve in storage ... men are still under leather, but the log walls are going up ..."

"What would be our most immediate problems if we were under siege?" Labienus asked.

"Sanitation," Malleus answered immediately. "We haven't diverted any water through the camp to wash away waste ... the men are still squatting in trenches dug in the *intervallos* ... that and feed for the horses ... we have four extra *turmae* of cavalry on post from other legions."

Labienus nodded. "We can send the cavalry away if the threat becomes immediate ... what's our current alert status?"

"Two in ten in accordance with standard operating procedures for a winter camp," Malleus answered indicating two of the ten legionary cohorts were always under arms and ready for battle. "And, we have one cohort away at the northern camp."

"That position may become quickly untenable if we're attacked," Labienus stated. "We'll need adequate warning to withdraw that cohort, which leads me to my next point ... the cavalry *turmae* we have in camp ... are any from the Twelfth?"

Malleus nodded, "Two of the seven."

"*Bene*!" Labienus said. "I want to send both west on a scout and screen, them and the *turma* from the Eleventh that's up in the northern camp ... we have no idea of the avenues of approach from the north and west, so the cavalry will have to figure that one out, too ... but I don't want a mouse to be able to approach from that direction unless we know about it."

Malleus nodded.

"Effective immediately, the camp is going to three in ten alert status ... same as a marching camp," Labienus directed. "Frequent infantry patrols, no smaller than century in size, as far as the wood line to the west ... continue to have the *frumentarii* collect and bring in winter rations ... do we need a second ditch, Malle?"

Malleus shrugged, "Couldn't hurt ... digging'll keep the men occupied and we could use the spoil to reinforce and heighten the walls."

Labienus nodded, "*Bene*! What about the *Porta Decumena*, the supply gate? Last time I looked it was straight through and wide open ... nothing but a barricade to block it."

"Has to be that way," Malleus agreed. "Can't get the supply carts in otherwise ... the oxcarts can't be turned through a folded gate. We have that gate covered with two platforms mounting two *scorpiones* each."

"That may not be good enough if we get hit hard." Labienus said. "Get with the engineers ... there's plenty of lumber ... have them fabricate a swinging gate, same as in a permanent camp ... also extend the two rear corner platforms forward to provide flanking fire to support that gate ... that should be a priority task!"

Labienus continued, "As far as diverting water through the camp for a sewer, save that one for after the second ditch and fortifying the *Porta Decumena*. I agree, we would need that in case of an extended siege, but the enemy would probably cut the water supply anyway ... instruct the century-level officers to enforce waste discipline strictly ... if worse comes to worse, we can use oil to burn the solid waste ... but I don't think it'll come to that ... if the wogs can't overrun us in the first couple of weeks, they'll lose interest and go home."

Malleus was taking notes in a small tablet he pulled out from under his belt.

"That's all I can think of, Malle," Labienus said. "You got anything?"

"*N'abeo, legate*," Malleus shook his head, "No, sir!"

"How's the leg, Malle?" Labienus asked.

Malleus was silent for a heartbeat, then said, "Not a problem, legate. I've cut myself worse shaving."

Only if Malleus shaves with a leaf-bladed, German, stabbing spear, I thought.

Labienus nodded, accepting Malleus' excuse. Then he said, "Go ahead a take a seat while I talk to Gemellus about a few things."

Malleus was about to protest, then shrugged and sat down with an audible grunt on one of the camp stools. For a *centurio primus pilus* to agree to sit in the presence of the legate commanding the army, he had to be in significant pain.

Labienus and Gemellus walked over to the operations map; Troucillus trailed a pace behind them. I watched as the color returned to Malleus' cheeks. Then, he said to me, "Still riding ponies, Pagane?"

His addressing me by my camp name, Paganus, "Bumpkin," indicated that our conversation was *inrite*, informal. But there's nothing to be gained by a junior officer acting too familiar with the top soldier of a legion.

"*Veho, centurio*," I answered. "Yes, sir."

Malleus nodded. "Over the winter, I want you to train with one of my cohorts. There's no future in the cavalry. If you ever want to make centurion-grade, you have to be in the infantry."

The good news was that Malleus saw potential in me; the other news was that I was going back to basic training.

Malleus continued, "Strabo *Centurio* was your training officer down in Aquileia ... he's got the sixth cohort now up in the northern camp ... I'm thinking of moving him up to a *centuria prior* position the third cohort ... nice little promotion for him. I'll assign you to his century for training. I'm sure the legate will not object as long as you have enough time for that Greekling of yours to teach you how to talk like some prancing, perfumed, eastern *irrumtor*."

Malleus must have detected the look on my face when he referred to Dion and his teaching me the *koine*. "Surprised I know, Pagane? I noticed the *Graeculus* on Tutor's manning chart the day he arrived. A good leader knows every detail about the unit he commands and the men he leads. Doesn't mean he always makes good decisions, but without knowing his men, he can never make good decisions. Remember that! Someday you may find yourself carrying the *vitis* and leading men into combat. Know your people!"

Labienus and Gemellus were approaching. Malleus was making to get off the stool when Gemellus extended his hand. Malleus hesitated for a heartbeat, then accepted the prefect's help. Gemellus pulled Malleus up on his feet.

Labienus was speaking, "You gentlemen are dismissed. You know what needs to be done. I'll let you get to it."

Both centurions assumed the position of attention, nodded toward Labienus, and barked "*A'mperi'tu, legate*! Yes, sir!" And, marched out of the *cubiculum*.

Labienus watched them depart. "Good thing we're in winter camp," he said. "Malleus wouldn't be able to keep up with the daily marches with that leg ..."

Then he remembered Troucillus and me, "He got cut off with the First Cohort when the krauts rushed our right flank at the River of Lilies. By the time the second line broke through, he was standing with what was left of his men, surrounded by dead *Grunni*, and a spear head embedded into the bone of his right leg ... he had had one of the *muli* hack the spear handle off so he could still fight. Can't imagine the pain. Spina didn't think he could save the leg. Malleus told the doc if he cuts off the leg, he'd cut off the doc's head. Spina made the right decision on that one."

Labienus just shook his head. Then he said, "Troucille! I'm going to need to take Insubrecus here back. I need him out on this recce."

When Troucillus didn't object, Labienus continued. "I understand there was a bit of ... uh ... shall we call it awkwardness when you went out with that troop from the Eleventh ... their senior *decurio* was keen to protect his turf ..."

When I didn't respond, Labienus went on, "I need you to go back out with them, but I'm going to smooth over the rough patches. I'm promoting you to a *decurio duplicarius*, a "double-pay" *decurio*; that will make you equal in rank to Hirsutus' number one ... what's his name ... yes ... the Fish. Also, I'm assigning one of the squads from the praetorian cavalry to you for this mission. They'll remain independent from the boys from the Eleventh and Twelfth, so there's no reason for Hirsutus to get his hackles up ..."

Labienus had just promoted me to the equivalent of an infantry *optio*, the number two man in an infantry century, just below the centurion. Granted, a cavalry rank did not have the same *auctoritas*, prestige, as an infantry position, but with the double-pay for the rank and the bonus for being in the *praetoria*, I was making over three-times what a third-line *mulus* earned.

Labienus was talking, "... I'm sending Hirsutus' boys north and west of Bibracte ... the two cavalry *turmae* from the Twelfth Legion will by-pass Bibracte to the south, one will go west and the other will swing to the northwest ..."

Suddenly there was a commotion outside the entry to the cubiculum. Ebrius burst into the room immediately followed by another man dressed in Gallic costume but with a Roman military haircut.

"I told this man you were busy, legate ..." Ebrius was saying.

Troucillus interrupted, "*Decane*! Sergeant! What is it?"

I then recognized the other man as a member of Troucillus' security detail from Bibracte.

"Legate!" he was saying, "You're needed in Bibracte! Immediately! Cuhnetha ..."

"What about Cuhnetha?" Troucillus interrupted him. "What has happened! Has he moved on Diviciacus?"

The decanus shook his head, "No, legate! Cuhnetha can't move on nobody no more. He's dead!"

Troucillus and I rushed back to Bibracte.

Labienus decided that, due to my relationship with Morcant, Cuhnetha's son and heir, I was more valuable helping Troucillus' investigation in Bibracte than I was riding out on some boondoggle into the "wilds of long-haired Gaul," as he put it.

We rode directly to the roundhouse in Bibracte where Cuhnetha had established himself and his entourage. Troucillus dispatched the *decanus* in charge of his security detail to his quarters to gather his bodyguards and meet us at Cuhnetha's place. Not surprisingly, we were met there by Malgounos, Malouuhnos' nephew, and a group of warriors from the Bear Clan.

"It doesn't take long for vultures to gather! What do you want here, *Rhufeinai*?" Malgounos challenged us.

Troucillus ignored the barb, slid off his horse, and passed Malgounos without a word. As Troucillus passed, Malgounos' hand dropped toward the handle of his sword. I was off Clamriu in a heartbeat reaching for my *pugio* when I heard Troucillus' voice say, "We carry the white wand! Unless you're as mad as *uh moucuhn treisgar*, a rabid swine, you'll take your hand away from that weapon ... you're with me, Arth!"

Attacking a diplomat protected by the white wand was a grievous felony under the law of the Gah'el. If blood were drawn, Malgounos would be liable to three times Troucillus' honor price which, as *pendefig* of the Helvi, was substantial. If Troucillus died of his wounds, Malgounos could be *roi mioun couc*, "placed in the boat," meaning branded as an outlaw and cast into exile. No one in the nations would offer him bread or fire.

Malgounos hand immediately dropped away from his sword. As I walked past him, he hissed, "This isn't over. I'm not done with you, you stinking Roman bum-boy!"

The white wand works both ways; so, I had to ignore his insult. I followed Troucillus into the house.

We walked into the central room of the house; it seemed empty. Regardless, Troucillus announced our arrival with the formula of entry, "May the gods smile on all in this place!"

Rhonwen appeared from a dark corner. Her eyes were red from crying, her face pale. "You are welcome here, friends!" she answered. "But the gods have chosen not to smile this day."

"We come to pay our respects ..." Troucillus started.

"Respect from the tame, lapdog bitch of the *Rhufeinai*," Malouuhnos said emerging suddenly from a side room. "How can one who has no respect, give respect!"

Morcant appeared behind Malouuhnos, "Please! You are under my roof. Respect my hospitality!"

Malouuhnos grunted, then said, "I will take my leave of you, Morcant. My deepest sympathies for your loss!"

Malouuhnos walked past us without a word.

"*Cefndere*!" Morcant said to Rhonwen. "Cousin! Have you offered our callers the *duhgsul*?"

Among the Gah'el, it is customary to offer callers to the house of the recent dead the *duhgsul*, a flat platter of bread, and a cup of water, so the spirit of the departed understands they are welcome guests and will not afflict them.

Rhonwen brought a platter of bread cut into small squares. We each took piece and ate it. Then Rhonwen offered the cup of water. We both drank.

Morcant then said, "We are observing the *dichuno*. Please enter the chamber of Cuhnetha and see."

The *dichuno*, the waking, is a period of one day during which the body of the dead is displayed. It is thought that, if the person is not dead but in a state of deep unconsciousness, what my friend Spina would call *sopor profundus*, a coma, the period of waking would give the person the opportunity to recover before being buried.

My grandpa used to scare the daylights out of me with tales of people being buried prematurely and waking up sealed in a tomb. There, they would die a horrible death, and their *bougana*, their wrathful night phantom, would wreak a terrible vengeance on those who buried them prematurely. First, the specter would feast on the blood of the livestock and cattle; then the *bougana* would attack the children.

In the old days, a blood sacrifice had to be offered to the dark god, Dana, to appease the *bougana*, typically a young woman, if the specter had been a man, or a child, if the specter had been a woman. Today, after a recent death, a bowl of animal blood is often left on the doorstep for the *bougana*.

Gran'pa told me that the *bougana*'s strength waxed and waned with the moon. When the specter approached the abode of the living, a mist would rise to hide the phantom's approach. If it found no blood offering on the doorstep, it would scratch at the door with its long talons seeking entry and access to the still warm blood of the living.

When gran'pa said this, he would scratch the side of his wooden chair with his fingernails. That sound was enough to send me scurrying up into the sleeping loft and burying myself as deeply into my blankets as I could. For some reason, as a child, I believed that the blankets would protect me from any monsters who might lurk in the dark of night.

As soon as I saw Cuhnetha, I knew he would not be emerging from his grave. His face was gray-green, bloodless; his eyes sunken into his skull; his face had the waxy sheen of the recently dead.

As is our custom during the *dichuno*, both Troucillus and I placed a finger below the corpse's nose to test for breathing. There was none, of course. I noticed that Cuhnetha's flesh had cooled.

"May he feast in the Land of Youth with the red-haired goddess until the end of days," we both intoned.

Troucillus placed a hand on Morcant's shoulder and said, "I grieve for your loss, Son of Cuhnetha."

Morcant nodded in response. I muttered my condolences also. We all left the room.

Troucillus was saying, "I know this is a bad time, but to you have some time to talk?"

Morcant nodded, then said to Rhonwen, "Cousin, would you keep watch over Cuhnetha?"

During the *dichuno*, the body should not be left unattended in case in shows some sign of life.

Rhonwen nodded and entered Cuhnetha's chamber.

"Please sit," Morcant was saying. "I have some red mead."

We sat near the central hearth. Morcant filled our cups and joined us.

"What happened?" Troucillus asked.

Morcant shrugged. "My father has not been well for some weeks. We thought it was stomach problems, so he was on a bland diet. The journey here to Bibracte and the council seemed to make his condition worse. He almost collapsed after his testimony. We came back here. He had some porridge and water. Then he went into his room … 'for a nap,' he said. When Rhonwen went in to check on him a while later, he wasn't breathing. We couldn't wake him …" Morcant's narrative trailed off.

"Any idea why…" Troucillus asked.

Morcant shrugged, "People … people just die … the gods rarely give an explanation … he hasn't been well … the council exhausted him …" Again, he just trailed off.

Then from behind us, Rhonwen's voice, "Malouuhnos wants us to believe that Duuhruhda had him poisoned! He did it for you *Rhufeinai*. The Caisar wants to keep Duuhruhda on the throne and Cuhnetha threatened him."

"Cousin!" Morcant protested, "Cuhnetha …"

"Tegid is sitting *dichuno*," Rhonwen dismissed Morcant's objection. "You didn't think I'd stay away while you talked to this bunch, did you?"

She poured herself a beaker of mead and took a seat.

"Malouuhnos claims you *Rhufeinai* had Cuhnetha poisoned," Rhonwen accused. "That makes sense! You certainly had motive. But, in my opinion, as good as you *Rhufeinai* think you are, the timing doesn't make sense. How could you have moved so quickly. And, you certainly didn't have access to our quarters! No! If Cuhnetha were poisoned, you lot didn't do it."

Troucillus was nodding, a slight smile across his lips, "Very good … *cui bono* … yes."

"Koo we boh noh?" Rhonwen repeated, her eyebrows knotted.

"It's Latin, my lady," Troucillus explained. "It means 'to whom the benefit'; in other words, who would profit from Cuhnetha's death. Certainly, as long as Cuhnetha had a strong claim to the throne, and as long as he seemed to be in league with Malouuhnos, and as long as Malouuhnos seemed to be an enemy of the *Rhufeinai*, the Caisar would benefit from Cuhnetha's removal. So, as you stated, the principle of *cui bono* would point to the Caisar. But, such a chain of events could only be considered likely, if the Caisar believed that Cuhnetha had a reasonable chance of taking the throne from Duuhruhda. And that, my lady, is where the chain of causes breaks down. And, even if I were to grant that the little performance of the 'hag of the tomb' changed things, then, as you yourself pointed out, we would have the problem of 'opportunity'."

Rhonwen nodded, but Morcant injected, "What if Duuhruhda poisoned Cuhnetha on his own? There is a long history of animosity between our clans and Duuhruhda would like nothing more than to remove a perceived threat to his power, regardless of how unlikely."

Again, Troucillus nodded, "Right you are, but that still leaves the problem of opportunity. How did Duuhruhda get to Cuhnetha? You trust everyone in your household, do you not?"

Morcant nodded, "Of course. They are family or have been sworn to us for years."

"Based solely on *cui bono*," Troucillus said, giving Rhonwen a slight wink, "There is another suspect. Malouuhnos himself."

"Why would Malouuhnos poison my uncle?" Rhonwen challenged. "He was using Cuhnetha's claim to the throne to leverage his own election to *pendefig*!"

"If Malouuhnos believed that Cuhnetha had a reasonable chance to overthrow Duuhruhda, then you are correct, my lady." Troucillus agreed. "In that case, he needed Cuhnetha alive to further his own ambitions. But Malouuhnos' long game was removing the *Rhufeinai* from the lands of the Aineduai. If murdering Cuhnetha and blaming it on the Caisar is a better way of achieving that than hoping the council will actually believe that the Phantom Queens oppose Duuhruhda's reign, then I have no doubt he'd act on it."

"But how?" Rhonwen disputed.

"Indeed, my lady ... How?" Troucillus nodded. "It keeps coming back to that."

We were all silent for a few heartbeats. Then, Troucillus, "I have a suggestion. It may sound a bit ... uh ... extreme, let's say ... but I ask that you consider it before saying no."

"What is it, Troucille?" Morcant asked.

Troucillus nodded, "We do not actually *know* that Cuhnetha was poisoned. It is most likely that the gods simply called him out of this life. However, one thing the army of the *Rhufeinai* is quite proficient in is medical knowledge. Again, please hear me out on this. I suggest that we have one of their *meduhgai*, their doctors, examine Cuhnetha for signs of poisoning or violence. Then we'll know, or at least we'll have reasonable evidence, of what might have caused Cuhnetha's death. Perhaps, all this suspicion of poisoning is just the howling of the winds through the trees and the only ones culpable in Cuhnetha's death are the gods themselves."

There was silence for a few heartbeats, then Rhonwen, "A Roman doctor! Are you completely daft, man?"

Then, Morcant, "No! Wait, cousin ... if only for my own peace of mind, I would like to know my father was not murdered ... Troucille! If I were to allow this examination, I would insist on a couple of conditions."

Troucillus nodded.

"First," Morcant said, "There must be complete secrecy ... no one outside this household must know."

Troucillus answered, "Of course."

"Further," Morcant continued, "My father's *meduhg* must observe the examination."

"Yes ... of course." Troucillus nodded.

"And, finally," Morcant said, "I have heard that the doctors of the *Rhufeinai* sometimes ... uh ... sometimes *interfere* with the bodies of dead ..."

"Interfere?" I asked.

"*Incidere corpus post mortem*," Troucillus explained to me in Latin. "Perform an autopsy."

Then, to Morcant, "Please continue, *a pen*."

"I will have none of that with my father!" Morcant insisted. "Such a ... such an act would offend the gods."

Then to Rhonwen, "Please understand, cousin ... I must know ... for my own peace of mind ... besides ... I will not have that *moch*, that pig, Malouuhnos, use my father's death to further his own ambitions!"

Rhonwen nodded, her lips a tight, bloodless slash across her face.

"Go ahead and make whatever arrangements you need to, Troucille," Morcant said. "I will inform my father's *meduhg*.

Troucillus nodded, then said, "One more thing, *a pen*. You said that your father had a meal right before he went in to lie down. Have those dishes been cleaned."

Morcant stared at Troucillus for a couple of heartbeats, then answered, "Uh ... no ... I don't think so ... things here have been quite ... uh ... quite confused ... why do you ask?"

"I would need to examine them," Troucillus replied. "Will you secure them until the *meduhg* gets here?"

Morcant just nodded, then, "Please excuse me, *a pen* ... and you too, friend Arth ... I wish to sit *dichuno* with my father."

When Morcant left the room, Rhonwen also rose. As she stood before me, her shoulders seemed to sag, her eyes took on a watery gleam. "Thank ... thank you for attending ... *dichuno* ..."

I stood there before her stiff as a *tiro* on inspection parade. I caught sight of Troucillus standing behind her. He was making a circling motion with his arms and mouthing something to me.

I finally caught, "*Quam complectare!*"

I stepped forward and put my arms around Rhonwen's shoulders. At first, she stiffened. Then, she seemed to melt into me. Her shoulders heaved as she began to cry.

I had no idea what to do. So, I stood there and, after a bit, began to pat her shoulders.

I again caught sight of Troucillus. He just rolled his eyes.

Spina arrived just before sunset.

He was accompanied by one of his "crows," a medical corpsman carrying a satchel. Both were wrapped in Gallic cloaks; neither Troucillus nor Morcant wanted to advertise the fact that Cuhnetha's corpse was being examined by a Roman doctor.

Spina was none too happy about being outside camp at night in the middle of a "native town". Despite his Aventine street savvy, being in the middle of a "barbarian" settlement at night was a bit beyond his ability to abide gracefully.

I spotted me as soon as he entered the round house, "I shudda known you'd be at da bottom a dis! Whadda you doin' draggin' me out heah at dis time a day. I'll nevah get back to camp befaw dawk!"

I realized then we had a communication problem. Not only did Spina not speak or understand Gah'el, but also most Latin speakers could hardly understand him.

Morcant who had a little Latin just stared at the doctor, then said, "This is the Roman *meduhg*? What language is he speaking?"

"This is Spina," I explained. "He's the Caisar's personal physician. He says the blessings of the gods be on all in this place."

Troucillus barely suppressed a smirk at my "liberal" translation.

Morcant shrugged, "Tell him he's welcome. Ask him if he would like some refreshment before he examines my father."

I translated for Spina.

He responded, "Refreshment? Whadda's dat mean ... fermented mare's piss served up in a human skull ... let's get dis ovah wit'! Whayah's da patient?"

To Morcant, "The doctor thanks you but would like to start his examination."

Then to Spina, "Come with me, *medice*! He's in here."

As soon as we walked into Cuhnetha's chamber, Spina stopped in his tracks. "Whad'is dis? Some kind a joke? Dis guy's dead!"

Rhonwen rose from her vigil beside Cuhnetha's bedside as we entered. "Who is this, Arth? Is this the Roman doctor?"

As I nodded to Rhonwen, I heard Troucillus behind me, "I apologize doctor ... Spina, isn't it? Perhaps my men didn't explain ... this is Cuhnetha, an important man among these people ... a king. He passed away earlier today. We invited you here to examine him. We want to know whether he was poisoned."

"Poisoned?" Spina exclaimed. "Whadduh I know about poison? I'm an army doctah, not some Aventine witch. I know about stabbings, hackings, bashings ... I don't know nothin' about poison! If its bleedin' I sow it up; if it's broken, I splint it; if its swellin', I put a salve on it. I'm no good at poison!"

Troucillus shrugged. "You're the best we got, Spina. The Aedui, who are against us, are going to claim Caesar had this man poisoned. We need you to prove that false ... that he died of ... well, shall we say, 'natural causes.'"

Morcant whispered in my ear, "What's going on, Arth?"

"Negotiating," I said.

Morcant stared at me for a heartbeat, shook his head and muttered, "Rhufeinai."

Spina in turn shook his head, muttered, "Natural causes," then walked over to where Cuhnetha was lying. He placed his hand on the corpse's forehead. Then, he attempted to move Cuhnetha's jaw. He then lifted Cuhnetha's right arm, which was quite stiff.

"Rigor's set ... body temperature has cooled," Spina muttered. His assistant had entered the chamber and was taking notes on a small tablet. Spina lifted up Cuhnetha's coverlet and examined the body. "Blood is settlin' in da lowah extremities ... dead for what ... six hours ... eight?"

Spina didn't wait for an answer. "Dis guy's definitely dead! Why? I got no idear! I'm gonna examine da body for wounds."

I translated this for Morcant, who just nodded.

After a bit, another man entered the room, a tall, thin, gray-haired individual in dark robes. "This is Arwuhnos mab Iforos, our household *meduhg*," Morcant said without taking his eyes of what Spina was doing. "He's here to observe."

I nodded. Spina was rolling Cuhnetha's corpse over on its side. That was the cue for Rhonwen to leave the room. Which was a good thing because after Spina examined Cuhnetha's trunk, arms and legs, he began to examine the corpse's anus.

"What is he doing?" Morcant complained.

Spina didn't need that translated. "Dere was dis murduh I heard about down in Rome yeahs back ... a wife had her husband bumped off ... a loan shark, gambler and drunk ... real sonofabitch, he was ... used to get drunk every afternoon, come home, and kick the *merd'* outta huh and dere son ... finally she had enough ... she hired dis hitter from the local fountain gang ... she wanted it to look like ... whaddid you call it ... yeah ... 'natural causes' ... so dis hitter stabbed da husband up de arse wit' a red-hot iron ... killed him and cauterized da wound ... no blood at all.

"Did she get away with it?" I asked.

"You could say dat," Spina said, continuing his examination. "She got dragged into cawt by some tight-arsed broad-striper in da senate who took it upon himself to defend *Romanitas* ... Romans don't like it when a wife offs 'er husband regardless a da reason ... gives noble women too many ideas, I guess ... he hired another broad-striped prig to prosecute huh before the urban praetor ... problem was dat, everytime dis prosecutor mentioned how dey thought the husband was killed, da jury, mostly plebs, cracked up ... by da time da purple-stripuh delivered his summary, da jury had to go out and change dere underwear dey were laughin' so hard."

Spina continued his story while he examined Cuhnetha, "Da wife woulda still got convicted except no one on the jury liked huh husband either ... dat an' a lot a people on da jury owed him money ... a lot of it at twelve points on da *denarius* ... da wife put it out dat, if she got off, she'd forgive all da debts ... dat, an' she spread some silvah out on the jury ... in Rome, de only honest jury's a rich one, dey say ... besides, da way she done it made for an entertainin' story ... an entertained jury always acquits."

The only honest jury's a rich jury, I thought. That's what got me into the army. I'd never would have survived a trial ... justice stacked against Gabinius' silver ... that is, if I lived long enough to get to trial. Hard to believe that was less than a year ago.

Spina finished his examination of Cuhnetha's body. "Can't find any wounds on 'im. Now, what makes ya think he was poisoned?"

"Nothing specific," Troucillus answered, while I translated for Morcant and the Gallic doctor. "He's been feeling poorly for a while. Earlier, he had a meal, came in here to lie down and rest, and just died."

Spina shook his head. "Died after eatin'? I don't suppose ya still got dat food he ate?"

"Actually, we do," Troucillus answered.

"*Bene*," Spina said. "Can you find me a couple a rats?"

"Rats?" Troucillus asked.

"Yeah, rats are da best, but a small dog'll do in a pinch," Spina said. "We'll feed 'em dis guy's last meal an' see what happens. Most dings that poison humans kills rats too. If dere's poison in his food, we'll know."

Troucillus translated this for Morcant, who then sent his doctor out of the room in search of subjects for Spina's experiment.

Spina was saying, "One a my teachers back in Rome had a little side business. He read up on Theophastus' *Plants* and ... uh ... consulted on pharmaceuticals, is probably da best way to put it ... most poisons are also drugs ... depends on the dosage. He had a nice little side business goin' for himself. He taught me a little. Most poisons come from plants an' work fast. Best way to slip dem to da victim is in food or wine. Dat way da victim don't taste 'em. Let's see if I remember dis ... most common poisons are opium, mandragora, henbane, belladonna, thorn apple, hemlock, aconite, dagga, an' poisonous mushrooms ... each has different symptoms, So, aftuh his last meal, did dis guy display anything like dry mouth, tingling in his hands and feet, paralysis, shortness a breath, dimming of his vision, nausea, vomiting ... anything like dat?"

After Troucillus translated this for Morcant, he said, "No! He was just tired. He has been suffering from stomach problems for the last few weeks. He tired quickly; he was weak at times and ... oh, yes ... he sometimes complained about pain in his jaw and arm."

After Troucillus' translation, Spina was quiet for a few heart beats, then asked, "Pain in one arm? Which one?"

"The left," Morcant answered.

Spina nodded, "Did he have shortness of breath ... pain in his chest ... sweatin' ... cold. clammy skin?"

Morcant's eyes widened, "Yes ... now that he mentions it ... my father sometimes became very pale and rubbed his chest as if he were in pain."

When he was told what Morcant said, Spina again nodded, "These are signs sent by da gods. They always presage death. Why dey do it, no one knows ... to tease ... to torment ... to warn ... no one knows. But it sounds like dis guy's fahdduh died of dem 'natural causes,' as you called 'em. But, if you t'ink dis guy coulda been poisoned, dere's one udder possibility heah?"

"And that would be?" Troucillus asked.

"I got no experience wit' dis," Spina started, "But I heard in dee east dey use a poison dey call da 'yellow' ... da Greeks call it *arsenikon* ... if ya give da victim small doses, it takes a while to kill ... weeks, even months ... da victim thinks he's just sick ... feels increasingly weak ... stomach problems are one of the symptoms of dis poison."

The east, I thought. Grennadios the Trader passed through Bibracte often, and Grennadios is an agent of the Egyptian king, Ptolemy. The Egyptians are infamous for poisoning, almost as bad as the Parthians. What's the old saying? "It's better to be an Egyptian's pig than his child because an Egyptian won't poison his food." Grennadios also did work for Pompeius who, despite all appearances, was no friend of Caesar.

Spina was asking, "Did dis guy experience any muscle cramps, loss a hair, vomiting, fatigue, headaches, confusion ... any'ding like dat?"

Morcant shook his head, "No ... just the stomach problems and occasional chest pain."

Spina was examining Cuhnetha's hair and fingers. "I don't see any sign of da poison. I think the gods just decided it was dis guy's time. Let's see what happens to da rats when dey eat 'is last meal."

While we were waiting for the results of Spina's experiment, Morcant offered the doctor the hospitality of his hearth. The late October evening was cool, so there was a fire burning in the central fireplace. We were treated to fresh bread, olive oil, sliced apples, carrots, a soft, creamy cheese and red mead.

Spina was relieved that the mead wasn't served in the skull of some long-vanquished enemy, but in ceramic cups. However, he still sniffed the mead suspiciously.

"Don't worry, doctor," I reassured him. "That didn't come out from under the tail of a horse. It's made from honey."

Despite my assurances, Spina was still suspicious of the dark amber liquid in his cup. It was only after we all drank and didn't wretch, that he sampled it. That was all it took. Before we left, Spina downed at least four cups of the mead.

Rhonwen had returned to her vigil at Cuhnetha's bedside. I tried to explain the custom of sitting *dichuno* to the doctor. He just shook his head saying, "She can sit dere all she wants. Dat guy ain't comin' back."

VIII

Caput VIII. De Machina Intra Machinam
Chapter 8. Wheels Within Wheels

While we waited for the rat verdict, Troucillus asked Morcant, "How does your father's death affect your clan's participation in the council?"

Morcant shrugged, "Participation? Not at all. I'm my father's *pendefig* and, as you know, my duty is to stand in for the *pobl'rix*, the clan Chieftain, when he's ... uh ... incapacitated."

As Troucillus nodded, Morcant continued, "I am going to send to Duuhruhda and ask for a five-day suspension of the council, while I bury my father and mourn his passing. It's traditional, so I do not anticipate my request being denied."

Again, Troucillus nodded, but I could see some concern in his face.

Morcant continued, "Five days is more than enough time for our clan council to confirm me as my father's successor. So, when the council here resumes, I will be the *Pobl'rix*, clan leader of the Boar Clan."

Troucillus asked, "Is it your intention to take your father's place as Malouuhnos' candidate for the tribal king to replace Duuhruhda?"

Morcant considered the question for a while, then answered, "No! I don't think so. Restoring our clan to the throne of the Aineduai is ... uh ... was my father's dream. I think he wanted revenge for his father's death more than regain the throne he lost. No ... I will support Duuhruhda as king in return for Duuhruhda restoring the lands he has taken from my clan. I will tell him that he has strong enemies in the west and now needs a strong ally in the east, especially now that the Soucanai are free of the *anwariaid Almaeneg*, the German savages, and will soon be pushing again against our borders. I think he'll agree to my proposal. Especially since, without my assuming my father's candidacy for king, Malouuhnos' proposal hasn't a leg to stand on."

Troucillus nodded, but again I detected some concern in his face.

It was well after sundown when the rats were declared healthy and unpoisoned. Cuhnetha's food had little effect on the rodents, except perhaps fattening them up a bit.

It was too late to return Spina and his assistant to camp, so Troucillus offered to put them up for the night at his place. Spina was a solid four cups of mead into the evening, so the thought of having to spend the night in a "barbarian shantytown" didn't seem to alarm him anymore. The fact that Troucillus had a full squad of Roman *muli* guarding his quarters certainly helped to allay any fears the doctor may have had about closing his eyes in the midst of "wild, long-haired savages." I certainly didn't mention to Spina that Troucillus' security detail were all Gah'el from Caesar's Eleventh Legion, now sprouting beards and in native mufti. Besides, Troucillus' larder was well supplied with wine, which won the day with our dear doctor.

We were not long returned to Troucillus' quarters, when Spina, after his long day of hunting for poison in the porridge, succumbed to a pitcher of Troucillus' finest *rhaeticum*, a gift Caesar had sent up from Massalia to his personal emissary to the king of the Aedui. The doctor's chin dropped down to his chest and his wine cup clattered to the floor. Soon, his mouth was open, and he was serenading us with a chorus of baritone snuffles. I noticed that the doctor snored without any trace of an Aventine accent.

I also noticed that my friend, Troucillus was silent and pensive. "A brass *as* for your thoughts, Troucille," I said to draw him out.

"A brass *as*? That's about all they're worth, Gai," he answered.

"Certainly, being able to demonstrate reasonably that Cuhnetha had not been poisoned is good news," I pressed.

"Oh that? Yes ... I agree," Troucillus said. "I never thought he was. The challenge was never in proving it; it was in being able to convince the council of it. Now, if Malouuhnos were to make such an accusation, Morcant could demand a hearing before the high judge of the tribe. I'm confident that Morcant's testimony and that of Cuhnetha's household physician will demonstrate that the old king died of natural causes."

There was that expression again. "'Natural causes'," I asked. "You keep saying this, *mi amice*. Don't you believe the gods decide these things?"

Troucillus stared into his cup for a few heartbeats, then said, "The gods? I'm not sure of them at all ... or of their participation in the day to day lives of mortals. At best, if the gods exist, they allow human history to take its own course ... a complex myriad of cause and effect impossible for us to predict or even to understand."

"*Deos negas tu?*" I asked. "Do you deny the gods exist?"

"No!" Troucillus shook his head. "Not at all! I just do not rely on their participation or their favor. As far as their existence, I believe establishing that is beyond the power of human reason. Plato may teach that we can reach some sort of union with the divine, but Aristotle's logic cannot build the staircase on which humans can ascend to that Olympus. Me? I'm caught in the middle. I'm *willing* to believe in the existence of gods, or of a god, or of some sort of intelligent, creative entity ... that's the only safe course for a mortal. But I rely on facts, evidence, logic, reason to understand the acts of men."

"Why do you characterize this as the 'only safe course'", I asked.

Troucillus chuckled, "The most pedestrian reason is that of the state cults. The Romans, like most peoples, believe their welfare is dependent on the benevolence of their state gods ... Iove, Mars, Venus, Mercury ... that lot. I've even heard of a bunch who live out in eastern reaches of Syria, who believe their god will inflict horrific plagues on them if they as much as eat pork or shellfish! In order to ensure their gods' blessings, the Romans, like most peoples, act out rituals, make sacrifices, and they expect everyone in the state to participate. To refuse to do so would invite the wrath of these deities and so is considered *sacrilegium*, treason against the state. I certainly would not want to be strangled in a pit or crucified simply because I refused to toss a pinch of incense onto a holy flame kept in some ancient and moldy pile of brick, mortar, and marble on the Capitoline. It's just smoke!"

Troucillus took a drink, then continued, "Look at it this way, Gai. Human reason can neither *prove nor disprove* the existence of gods. A mortal must *choose* either to believe or not to believe. If a man chooses to believe in the gods, and they do not exist, is that man any worse off? No! When he dies, he'll descend into the same nothingness as the man who chooses not to believe. The rub comes if gods *do* exist. Then, the believer may be rewarded after death for his belief, while the *atheos*, the atheist, will be punished. So, the only reasonable course for a mortal is to choose to believe. That of course ignores the possibility that the gods don't give a *cacula*, a turd, for our credulity and sycophancy and, after our death, don't simply ignore our descent into some dark, cold, subterranean prison in the bowels of the earth."

As Troucillus rambled on about his philosophy of gods and the afterlife, I found myself rubbing the *Bona Fortuna* medallion hanging under my tunic. Despite anything Troucillus might say, or believe, a soldier's god is his luck. I didn't want to become a part in some blasphemous discussion that would cause *Bona Fortuna* to turn against me. I needed to change the subject.

"The five-day delay for reconvening the Council of Three Generations ... this is good news for us, is it not," I asked.

Troucillus seemed to return from his musings on dark, subterranean prisons and unreachable gods. "Good news ... Yes and no," he answered.

"*Explanes tu ista, mi amice*," I said. "Please explain, my friend."

"It's a complicated situation," Troucillus continued. "It could be good for us, or bad, or neither, but most likely both."

I felt like I was tumbling back into our discussion of gods and the causes of human events.

Troucillus continued, "The death of Cuhnetha destroys Malouuhnos plan to elevate himself to tribal *pendefig* under Cuhnetha's cloak. But, as our Greek friends say, 'The daemon you know is safer than the daemon you don't know.' Will Malouuhnos give up trying to turn the tribe against Caesar. *Dubitissime*! Very doubtful. So, what will be his next play?"

Troucillus took another sip of his wine.

"The way I read his dice cup he could still attempt to convince the council that Caesar had Cuhnetha murdered ... we already discussed that ... at best that would be a difficult toss for him. Then, there's the possibility of armed intervention ... a *coup* ... he has the forces of both his own clan and that of Bruhchamos behind him ... that of course would put him at odds with the council and tribal tradition ... but sharpened swords can overcome law and tradition until he has established his regime and come up with some facile rationalization why his seizure of power was necessary. Finally, he has this melodrama playing of that crazed hag who claims the dark goddess is denouncing Duuhruhda's kingship ... I think he might believe that fable supported by some military move may give him the Venus throw."

I thought about that, then said, "But certainly, Labienus would not permit an armed *coup d'état* overthrowing Caesar's key ally up here."

Labienus shrugged, "Direct Roman intervention into the internal affairs of the Aedui could easily backfire on Caesar and play right into Malouuhnos' hands. In fact, that may be a critical element of his endgame."

I resisted the temptation of pointing out to Troucillus that he had just mixed his dicing metaphor with the game of *latrunculi*. And, as Spina's snores reminded me, it was late and quite a bit of wine had flowed through our cups.

"*Quomodo*?" I asked, "In what way?"

"Malouuhnos may be provoking Caesar into taking an ... uh ... let's say an inciting action against him. And, in my opinion, Labienus is just the man to do that; he tends to be a bit '*parare, oppugnare, cogitare* – prepare, attack, think' at times."

I nodded in agreement.

"Up until this point," Troucillus continued, "Our theory was that Malouuhnos, using this 'dark goddess' ploy, would try to force the council to accept Cuhnetha as the tribal king and himself as *pendefig*. Then, he would bring his and Bruhchamos' tribal bands down from the north and west to seal the deal and intimidate the Romans into inaction. Now, with Cuhnetha dead and a five-day delay in the council, that plan is no longer viable ... not completely anyway ..."

Troucillus broke off to gather his thoughts, then continued. "Here's what I'd do in Malouuhnos' place. I would continue to play up his dark-goddess ploy to undermine the council's power to confirm Duuhruhda as king. Meanwhile, I would assemble my warriors and infiltrate them into Bibracte, while undermining the loyalty of Duuhruhda's troops ... that dark-goddess fable and a bit of silver would go a long way to accomplishing that ... then, when the council reconvenes, I would force through a proposal naming myself as the tribal king. When the council finds itself surrounded by my men, and Duuhruhda's bands are standing down, they would have little choice but to confirm me."

I nodded, but ask, "Do you think Labienus would accept that?"

"Labienus would have to send down to Massalia for Caesar's instructions," Troucillus answered. "That would give Malouuhnos time to reinforce his position in Bibracte. I imagine he would hold both Morcant and Karadogos hostage to ensure the cooperation of their clans. He doesn't even have to attack. He could hunker down in Bibracte and dare Caesar to attack him. Then, instead of having an alliance of tribes friendly to Rome anchored on the Aedui, Caesar would be faced with a potential war all along the borders of the *provincia*. In fact, I have little doubt that Malouuhnos has sent feelers out to the bordering tribes – Bituriges, Carnutes, Senones, even the Parisi – he may have reached as far afield as the Belgae. Seven battered and understrength Roman legions would be stretched thin just holding the border against such a threat."

"What about the Sequani," I asked.

Again, Troucillus shrugged. "The Sequani would never join an alliance headed by the Aedui. And they're much too weak to oppose it; they haven't begun to recover from the ravages of Ariovistus and the Suebii. Their only possible course would be to lie low and hope Malouuhnos stays focused on the Romans and doesn't turn his attention on them."

Everything Troucillus was saying seemed to make sense. Cuhnetha's death, far from weakening Malouuhnos' position, seemed to strengthen it. With Cuhnetha out of the picture, Malouuhnos had one less complication to worry about.

"What can we do?" I asked Troucillus.

"We need to act quickly," he answered without hesitation. "And one of the critical pieces to this puzzle is whether Malouuhnos is marshalling his forces, where are they gathering, and in what strength. That's where Labienus' immediate efforts should be directed. Tomorrow we must dispatch those cavalry recces into the west and north that we discussed. I believe once I've had a chance to brief Duuhruhda on what we believe Malouuhnos is up to, he will authorize a small and discrete Roman incursion into his lands and perhaps even lend us guides to direct the effort."

As I nodded, Troucillus continued, "That's where I need you to be, Gai. You'll be my eyes and ears on that reconnaissance. We're not only looking for assembly areas for Malouuhnos' troops, but small bands of his warriors attempting to infiltrate into Bibracte. Tradition would forbid them to carry a white wand of peaceful assembly, but I wouldn't put it past Malouuhnos to violate even that."

Troucillus was silent for a few heartbeats, then continued. "If I am successful in convincing Duuhruhda of his danger and focus him on ensuring the integrity of his household troops, I will try to sell him on a counterstroke to defeat any legitimate proposal Malouuhnos may present to the Council of Three Generations."

"And that would be?" I prompted him.

"I will certainly support Morcant's demand that his clan be strengthened by the return of their traditional lands. But, in order to checkmate Malouuhnos before the council, Duuhruhda must propose Morcant as his *pendefig*."

"Do you think Duuhruhda will cooperate?" I challenged.

"Oh, I'm sure I can scare Duuhruhda badly enough to agree to that. Courage and insightfulness are not two of his gifts. It's Morcant I'm not so sure of. I get the feeling that his father's death has caused him to want to withdraw from tribal politics. He just wants to restore the wealth and power of his clan and live quietly on his lands. I think I can convince him that, as long as his clan has a traditional claim on the high kingship of the tribe, Malouuhnos will never allow him or his people to live in peace."

"What then?" I asked.

"What then, indeed," Troucillus repeated. "The answer to that is still obscured in the mists. Certainly, we'll know more when you get back from the west with information about Malouuhnos' troop movements and dispositions. But, if we detect them early enough and prepare ourselves, I'm confident that they can be kept out of play. But it's not the enemy outside the walls I'm so concerned about; it's the enemy within the walls."

"The enemy within the walls?" I questioned.

"Yes!" Troucillus nodded. "The acts of men I can understand and counter; it's the acts of human fear and superstation that are capricious and unpredictably powerful. How will Malouuhnos deploy this so-called Curse of the Catubodua against Du-uhruhda."

I had no answer for that. Our mutual silence, however, was interrupted by the snorts and snores of our comatose doctor. It was late. We helped Spina stumble onto a cot set up for him near the hearth and we called it a night.

Troucillus was right about one thing. The battle we were about to fight would not be one fought against mortals with shining steel and bright banners under a midday sun. It would be fought in the murky recesses of human credulity against the dark powers of the Queen of the Hooded Crows.

IX

Caput IX. De Tempestate Imminente
Chapter 9. The Gathering Storm

Troucillus coordinated things with Labienus and Duuhruhda in less than a day
The king was most willing take Troucillus' counsel. Despite Caesar' treatment of Duuhruhda's younger brother, Deluuhnu, at the height of the Helvetian war, the king now had no doubt to whose toga he was tied. If he did have any doubt, he merely had to gaze southward from his own battlements to see an entire Roman legion snugging in for the winter right outside his gate.

Besides, Duuhruhda, never a man of great fortitude or initiative, was frightened to the marrow by Malouuhnos' aggressive ploys against him and his throne. And, the thought of his rival martialing the aid of the dark goddess, Catubodua, to overthrow him, put the king into a mild state of panic.

Duuhruhda readily accepted that Cuhnetha's death was not due to any devious Roman plot, readily agreed to authorize a limited and somewhat discrete Roman reconnaissance into the western marches of his territories and designated trusted officers from his household cavalry to "lead" these intrusions.

Troucillus, the king, and Anionos mab Kamehros, the senior justice of the Aineduai, then met in private. After listening to Troucillus' report concerning the death of Cuhnetha and the investigation of our competent, albeit reluctant, medical examiner, Spina, Anionus readily agreed to grant a five-day suspension of the council as soon as Morcant requested it.

The traditional and seemly period to suspend tribal business to observe the rites and mourning period appropriate to the death of a pobl'rix, a clan king of the tribe, as Anionos termed it.

After the period of Cuhnetha's *dichuno* had passed, Morcant, as the provisional chief of his clan, presented himself to the king requesting a delay in the council proceedings and leave to return to his *dun* to bury his father. These requests were readily granted, condolences given, and funereal gifts to accompany Cuhnetha into his tomb distributed.

Duuhruhda appeared so distraught by his sorrow over Cuhnetha passing, actually shedding a tear or two, that a casual observer would never suspect that the two men had spent their entire lives detesting each other. But, as Caesar often said, the only difference between a politician and an actor, is that the actor earns his money honestly.

Labienus, of course, was ready to launch his part of the mission *statim*, immediately. He had already identified the resources available for the reconnaissance - the *turma* of cavalry from the Eleventh Legion under Hirsutus, which he had posted to the northern camp, and two *turmae* from the Twelfth Legion which were in the main camp – all Gallic speakers.

There was some discussion between Labienus and Troucillus about uniforms and equipment; Troucillus wanted the men in *mufti*, while Labienus insisted Roman soldiers should look like Roman soldiers, even if they were merely cavalrymen. The compromise was that the troops would be armed with Roman equipment, but they would neither wear standard mud-red military tunics nor Gallic tartans. The troops themselves came up with a motley collection of tunics acquired from the *vicus*, military stores, and their own private clothing stashes.

Labienus and Troucillus quickly coordinated the linkup between the Roman cavalry commanders and the Aeduan guides and briefed them on their mission. By the eighth hour of that very day, the last horse tale disappeared into the west. The units were expected to return and debrief Labienus in a market cycle, giving us plenty of time to collect, analyze, and theorize on any intelligence they discovered. Troucillus wanted to be ready for anything Malouuhnos might pull when the Council of Three Generations recommenced.

Then, Troucillus pulled off a complete surprise. "Gai! We have to return to the king's hall, you and I. I managed to get an audience with *Mair Duhn Mawr*."

"*Mair Duhn Mawr*?" I questioned. "The Big Guy? Who is that? Why would we want to see him?"

"*Mair Duhn Mawr* ... Druce mab Cadmanos," Troucillus answered. "A cousin of our dear friend and ally, Duuhruhda ... an older and wiser cousin on his mother's side. He serves as the king's chief of intelligence, his head spy. If anything's going on in the lands of the Aedui ... or in the nations for that matter ... *Mair Duhn Mawr* will know about it."

We rode south to Duuhruhda's hall. The king's *dun* sat below and facing the *arx*, the citadel, which was located on the highest peak in the town. To get there, Troucillus and I, escorted by two of his ersatz Gauls from the Twelfth legion and a scribe, rode down the main street through the center of Bibracte.

Bibracte is not a town in the Roman sense. It is more of a collection of villages, clustered around the *dun* of the king, all enclosed within a common wall. Be that as it may, Romans would be amazed to witness the degree of commercial and social activity carried on in the place. Romans believe that, north of the Rhodanus, in "long-haired" Gaul, as they call it, people live with their cattle in small, smoke-filled, round wooden huts.

Bibracte would have demonstrated the error of that belief.

Wooden buildings, some three stories in height, bordered the main street along which Troucillus and I rode. The quarter, through which we passed, was dominated by weavers and dyers. The finely woven garments being manufactured and sold were displayed on racks along the street and strung on lines between the buildings. I was fascinated by the dominance of colors – bright reds, greens, and blues - and the movement of the fabric on the racks and lines as it swayed in a gentle breeze. Although, it was late in the day, there seemed no shortage of stock or of interested shoppers.

Scattered between the fabric shops were *tafarndai*, taverns selling beer, wine, mead – and even wine – to thirsty customers, workers, and passers-by. Unlike a Roman city, women mixed easily with men at the tables outside the *tafarndai*, some even sitting at tables by themselves. Packs of running, screaming children, seemed to flow through all the cracks of this arrangement of urbanity, joining the rendering together into a portrayal of an industrious, prosperous, and peaceful community.

As we rode south and began to climb the shallow saddle between the two southern hills of the town, the buildings fell away, and groves of hardwood trees crowded the road. To my right, the western watchtower rose over *Gropar Craig*, the Hill of the Rock, the second highest point within the town walls. Then, to my left I saw the gray walls of the town citadel crowning the heights of *Uh Graig*, the Rock.

According to the legends of the Aineduai, when the nations descended from the Lands in the Sky, the people did not know where to settle themselves in the new lands gifted to them by the gods. Ambisagros, the god of sky, thunder, and lightening, much like the Roman, Iove, picked up a huge border and flung it out over the western horizon. "Where *uh graig*, the rock, settles is your new home," he told the Aineduai, whether to bless their migration or just get rid of them is anyone's guess. *Uh Graig* is Ambisagros' boulder and *Gropar Craig*, is a shard that broke off when it landed. These two hills mark the center of the Aineduai; as long as the people live around them, the nation will thrive.

As soon as we cleared the western sloping of *Uh Graig*, Duuhruhda's *dun*, his residence and administrative center, appeared to our front. We followed a road which branched off the main street to the left up onto a saddle connecting the *dun* to the citadel. We climbed the saddle bearing right to the gate which led us through a twelve-foot wall of what Roman engineers call *murus Gallicus*, the Gallic fortification.

Although initially Roman sappers and siege specialists dismissed these constructions as primitive and weak, they soon discovered, at times to their own loss, that the *muri Gallici* were deceptively sturdy and able to resist direct assault, even by some of the largest Roman rams and bombardment techniques.

The Gallic wall is characterized externally by an outer stone facing with the butt ends of transverse hardwood, cross beams, one *pes* by one *pes* square, positioned in parallel stacks at intervals of approximately two *pedes*. These cross beams are the only external evidence of the wooden structure around which the external stone facing is constructed.

Internally, longitudinal timbers are laid across these cross beams and attached to them with mortice joints and iron spikes through augured holes. Depending on the planned height and thickness of the wall, before the fill is poured and the outer stone facing set, *murus Gallicus* resembles a honeycomb of small, square rooms constructed from an interlocking network of sturdy, hardwood beams.

Once the wooden frame has been built, the space between the beams is filled with earth and rubble. The Gauls prefer a mix of loose soil and river gravel which, along with the honeycomb construction of the wooden frame, gives the structure flexibility and the ability to absorb the blows of battering rams and projectiles.

Finally, the wall is covered by a thick outer facing of well-cut and tightly fit stone. These stones are firmly mortared and positioned in such a manner that they support the ends of the traverse beams of the wall's wooden frame, giving the structure additional strength and flexibility.

I have seen the projectiles from the most powerful pieces of Roman siege artillery bounce off these walls without any effect. Battering rams, when they can be positioned and operated against the fortification, seem to have no more effect than to keep the defenders awake at night with their incessant and ineffectual pounding.

Roman engineers explain that the interlock construction of the *murus Gallicus* enables it to "absorb" the blows of the rams and projectiles. In fact, they point out, the protruding ends of the traverse, wooden beams, which give these walls a rustic and primitive appearance in the eyes of Roman siege experts, serve to buffer the stone facings of the wall walls from projectiles.

As we approached the portal of Duuhruhda's *dun*, I noticed a carving on each of the facing gate pillars. Initially, the sculpture looked like a white triangle, an upside-down cluster of grapes. On closer inspection, I realized each of the "grapes" was a human head, the head of a dead warrior, eyes closed, mouths agape, agony etched across the faces. The head which served as the apex of the cluster, was grasped by its hair by a huge, human fist.

This was a warning to those who were enemies of the Aedui.

When I was a child, my gran'pa, usually after a few tankards of beer, told me lurid tales about our ancestors, the Gallic Insubres. The Gah'el believe that the essence of a warrior, his *virtus* as the Romans would call it, resides in his head. Any warrior worth his salt ration can kill his opponent. But, to dominate him, to possess him in servitude for all eternity, his head had to be taken, preserved, and displayed as a trophy so all could see and admire the prowess of the taker.

So, these grotesque stone heads festooned down the gate posts of Duuhruhda's fortress served as a warning to those who would dare to oppose the power of the king. "Oppose me and you will serve at my feet forever!"

How ironic! After his performance during our campaign against the Helvetii, I have trouble seeing Duuhruhda as an effective administrator, much less a fearsome warrior-king of the Gah'el!

But, as Caesar later taught me, belief is stronger than reality ... perceptions stronger than truth. Show people what you want them to believe, and most of them will. Hence, my work re-writing Caesar's "field journals."

We rode through the gate unchallenged; the officer of the guard nodding in Troucillus' direction as we passed through. The interior of the *dun* was dominated by Duuhruhda's hall, a typical, round pile of wooden posts, wattle-and-daub panels, and a conical thatched roof. Side buildings protruded out of the central structure in a somewhat haphazard fashion. Surprisingly, we did not ride up to the *lawnt*, the grassy area in front of the main entrance, the traditional place of greeting guests, but Troucillus turned to the right. There, to my surprise, tucked into the west wall of the *dun*, was a stone building, a small Roman house with a red-tile roof.

As we approached the entrance of the house, its double doors swung open and, from between them, stepped a man. My immediate impression was "diminutive, thin and gray." He stood no more than five Roman *pedes* in height. His hair, cut short in the Roman fashion, was gray as was the closely cropped beard that covered his face. He wore an unadorned, finely woven, knee-length, Gallic tunic of silver-gray. A broad, leather belt of reddish cordovan circled his waist from which hung a Gallic *dagr* in a richly decorated sheath of red leather wrapped in silver wire.

The man halted a pace in front of the doors and awaited our approach. We pulled up our horses a polite five paces before him. As we dismounted, I expected Troucillus to announce our visit to whom I assumed was the *maior domus* of the house.

Then, the man spoke, "*Salve*, Gai Valeri Troucille! Welcome to my home. I have looked forward to finally meeting the legate of the Roman *proconsul* and *imperator*, Caesar."

Latin! In the accent of Rome!

The man continued. "And this young man must be Gaius Marius Insubrecus, *decurio* of Caesar's praetorian cavalry and *comes*, companion of the great man himself. Congratulations on your recent promotion to *duplicarius*, young man! For one so young, you have made great progress in the legions."

I was speechless. How could this man, an Aeduan living in the midst of Bibracte, know what had happened in the *principia* of a Roman military castrum less than a day ago!

Troucillus however seemed unaffected. "*Salve*, Druce mab Cadmanos! Thank you for agreeing to meet with us on such short notice."

The man's face cracked into a humorless grin. "Notice is only as short as its urgency, my dear Troucille. And, I agree with you, the issue for which you come here is pressing ... please ... come into my home ... I have laid out some refreshments for you and young Insubrecus here ... my staff will attend to your escorts and your mounts... please, come in."

Druce led us into his home. We passed through a small *vestibulum* and crossed the *atrium*. The air in the room felt warm and dry; Druce had somehow managed to transport a Roman hypocaust system, central heating, into the "wilds" of long-haired Gaul. The walls of the room were plastered and decorated with three-dimensional square patterns executed in earthen tones giving the room a perception of depth. The floors were of tightly fitted, polished slabs of black slate. I could feel the warmth of the furnace rising from them.

We followed Druce into his *triclinium*, the formal reception room. There, a table was laid out with platters of bread, olive oil, various cheeses, bowls of fruit, olives ... even *garum*. Druce gestured us toward chairs arranged around the table. "I have some *baeterrae* just up from your *provincia* ... I just unsealed an *amphora* ... will that be satisfactory, gentlemen?"

"Most kind of you, Druce," Troucillus responded.

Druce nodded and a servant filled our cups from a ceramic pitcher.

"Leave the pitcher and please leave us," Druce instructed the man. Then, raising his cup to us, Druce toasted, "Fortune and long life!"

"Fortune and long life," we responded. The wine had a somewhat sweet taste, but its after-taste, whose fumes seemed to rise up into my brain, left no doubt of its strength. I spotted a pitcher of water on the table. I poured a few drops into my cup.

"So, tell me, Troucille," Druce was saying. "You spent some time as the 'guest' of the German, Ariovistus. How was it among those savages?"

Troucillus shook his head. "As long as he believed I was more valuable to him alive than dead, he was somewhat ... shall we say ... accommodating. I imagine if Caesar had been taken out of the picture, my value would have diminished along with the quality of his hospitality. Fortunately, I did not have to press that theory to its limits ... this is quite a home you've build for yourself, Druce ... nostalgia for your time living in Rome?"

Druce smiled and shook his head, "Nostalgia? No! Comfort is the key here ... ah ... young Insubrecus here does not know *that* story. He's wondering what a square Roman stone house containing a man who speaks forum-Latin is doing in middle of Bibracte of the Aedui, I imagine."

Druce paused to sip his wine. Troucillus took up the narrative. "After the defeat of the Cimbri, the Romans were ... shall we say ... not comfortable with the role of the Aedui in that war. So, they demanded hostages from the leading families be handed over."

Druce nodded, "I was barely seven years old ... wild as a colt and just as filthy. I was shipped down to Massalia, put on a ship, dropped off in Ostia, and taken by barge up the Tiber to Rome. I was in shock. I hadn't recovered from the *sight* of the great Middle Sea to say nothing of being trapped for weeks out on the water in a great pile of creaking lumber with no sight of land anywhere, when I was plunked down in a massive pile of masonry teaming with rank-smelling strangers babbling in a language I could not even begin to understand ... seven years old!

"Your family's patron, Gaius Marius, was still in charge of things back then, Insubrece. I was lodged with the household of Quintus Hortensius Hortalus, the father of the orator. I was treated well ... almost like a son. I even attended tutoring with the younger Quintus. By the time I reached my majority, I was a Roman's Roman ... lisped my Latin like a Palatine fop, wore my hair short, my face shaved, my body bathed and scented. I even assumed a *toga virilis* on my sixteenth birthday.

"I returned to Gaul, part of the staff of the proconsul, Gaius Cassius Longinus Varus. After Varus disgraced himself against the slave army near Mutina, I returned to my people. My uncle, Clethguuhno, still ruled here in Bibracte. He welcomed me and asked me to mentor his sons, Duuhruhda and Deluuhnu. The old man knew they would eventually have to deal with Rome.

"Now that day has arrived. Here sitting in my *triclinium* are the companions of the Roman proconsul wanting to discuss Roman interests in the royal succession of the Aedui, while an entire Roman legion is encamped less than five hundred paces beyond the south gate of the city."

As Druce took a sip of his wine, Troucillus asked, "Deluuhnu? What have you heard of him?"

Druce gave Troucillus a long stare then broke into a humorless grin, "Please, Troucille, you know better than to ask me that. Deluuhnu is *proscriptus ... aqua et igni interdictus ...* outlawed at the demand of Caesar. Neither I nor the king have had any contact with him. You did not come here to ask me about him. You want to discover what I know about the plans of Malouuhnos mab Dermuhtos and the death of the unfortunate Cuhnetha mab Cluhweluhno."

Troucillus put down his cup and nodded, "Fair enough, Druce. What do your sources tell you about Malouuhnos?"

"Cuhnetha's unexpected death has tossed a spanner into his little plot to depose my cousin," Druce answered. "Never a deep thinker, our friend Malouuhnos ... that's not to say he can't be dangerous ... he's simply not clever."

"So, what do you think is his next move?" Troucillus pressed.

"His next move?" Druce repeated. "Let's back up just a bit, here. I wish you had consulted me earlier; I could have saved you a bit of effort."

"*In quo modo,*" Troucillus asked. "How?"

"Those patrols you had my cousin authorize," Druce grinned. "I'm afraid they're going to find exactly what you feared they would."

"What?" Troucillus exclaimed. "Malouuhnos is gathering troops ..."

Druce chuckled. "Of course, he is ... but it's not what you think. Malouuhnos is a 'marcher lord'; his clan buffers our lands from the western tribes. The crops are in, but it's still seasonable enough for raiding parties of bored young warriors to take the field. It's especially tempting since the winter food supplies are piled in barns and storage sheds, ripe for the taking.

"Every fall, both Malouuhnos and his toady, Bruhchamos mab Euhdulf, assemble war parties in key locations along the borders to counter any raids from our neighbors to the west ... mostly the young bachelors and newly married ... five-season warriors ... they'll stay in place until the danger is past or it gets too damned cold to be sleeping rough. They're usually back to their hearths by the Ides of November at the latest.

"Even a pack of Roman cavalry should have no problem finding that bunch ... just look for the smoke from their fires or follow the sounds of their drinking parties ... great fun actually ... that is, as long as there's no real fighting to do."

Druce was enjoying setting Troucillus right, so he continued. "As far as your fears that Malouuhnos may have forged alliances with the western tribes to oust you Romans, that would never happen. Gauls don't think like you Romans do, my dear Troucillus. What is it that you say? 'The enemy of my enemy is my friend'? In the west, it's simply 'my enemy is my enemy' ... has been for generations and so it will remain. They've been killing each other over cows, crops, women, and land since they descended from the high places.

"If Malouuhnos were to move his war bands against Bibracte, his neighbors would invade his lands, steal everything they could carry, and burn everything they couldn't. They have no strategic sense, as you Romans would characterize it ... no, 'long-term' vision ... they'd rather steal a few head of cattle today than worry about the inevitability of a Roman invasion tomorrow. No, Malouuhnos wouldn't dare move his war bands east to pull off a coup ... there'd be nothing left for him to go home to."

"So, you believe a Roman invasion inevitable, Druce?" Troucillus pressed.

"Inevitable?" Druce snorted. "You're already here on our doorstep! And, from what my sources report about your road building south of the Rhodanus and up through the Sequani lands, Caesar is establishing logistical lines for a push north in the spring. The Belgae, this time, Troucille?

"That weasel of his, Marcus Metius, is up in Durocortorum gathering intelligence from the Remi. If Caesar tries to take on Galba and then the Nervii confederation, he may be biting off more than he can swallow. But I am willing to leave that as Caesar's problem. My concern is that Bibracte lies between Caesar and his ambitions with the Belgae.

"So, my dear Troucille, what does Caesar intend for us? I am willing to work with you as long as I can be reasonably certain that the interests of my people, and certainly those of my dear cousin, the king, are best served."

Troucillus took a long sip from his wine cup, then began, "Caesar considers the Aedui friends and allies of the Roman people ..."

Druce interrupted, "Please! Troucille! We are far beyond euphemisms and political formulae here. Bottom-line this for me!"

"Very well," Troucillus nodded. "My instructions from the proconsul are to support Duuhruhda. Caesar desires a strong confederation of tribes friendly to Rome north of the Rhodanus centered on the Aedui. He sees Duuhruhda as the best option to achieve that. Caesar does not wish to be distracted by the nations to the north; he understands clearly that his interests lie in Rome and his enemies are in the senate.

"His 'ambitions with the Belgae', as you put it, are to ensure that they do not act in a manner that would disturb the peace along the *limes*, the frontier of the *imperium Romanum*, and threaten the *provincia*. Metius' instructions are to attempt to come to some sort of agreement with Galba and the Nervii. Caesar does not care a whit if those barbarians shag squirrels and drink mare piss out of human skulls as long as they stay in their forests and do not stir up trouble in the south."

Druce grinned into his wine cup. "Negotiate with the Nervii," he chuckled, "*That* I'd like to see. They still don't allow Roman merchants to cross the Mosa into their lands for fear that Roman wine and *garum* will turn their warriors into little girls ... I wish Caesar's weasel luck *negotiating* with that lot."

Druce put down his cup, straightened in his chair and said, "Very well, Troucille! You've been as open and forthright with me as your patron, Caesar, will allow. Let me share with you what I believe is our greatest vulnerability in this issue."

Druce remained silent for a few heartbeats. I found myself leaning toward him in anticipation. He began, "What do you know about the *derwuhdai du*, the Black Druids?"

Troucillus shrugged, "We've heard very little about them south of the Rhodanus. They preach that the traditional gods of the Gah'el are the only gods. Those worshipped by other peoples, especially the Romans and the Greeks, are *daimonoi*, demons who seduce the nations from their true beliefs. Unless the 'true belief', as they put it, is restored among the nations, the gods of the Gah'el will allow *tramenouur*, foreigners, to punish the nations with fire, steel and servitude."

"Essentially correct, Troucille," Druce nodded. "Until recently, these black druids have been active only in the north, on the coast facing the islands of the Pretani, among the Morini, and the Manapii. Recently, my sources tell me that they are stirring up the Veneti and the other tribes along the coasts of Amorica.

"The movement seems to have originated in the islands of the Pretani. I am told the black druids have a sacred island there in the far west, facing the Island of the Dead, a place they call *Inis Afalon*, the Island of Afalanos. Be that as it may, they preach that this god, Afalanos, is preparing to return to the middle lands.

"In preparation for this, the nations must revert to the old ways, the customs of the peoples uncontaminated by foreign influence. We're talking human sacrifice, the burning of prisoners, a complete purging of all foreigners from the scared lands granted us by the gods. If Afalanos is pleased by the people's efforts, he will beget a son on a mortal woman, a great hero who will become the *Vercingetorix*, the great Warrior King of the Gah'el, a new Arth Mawr. He will lead the nations to restoring their greatness. Rome will burn, along with Athens and the cities of the Great Middle Sea, until the Gah'el are again masters of the middle lands."

Troucillus shook his head, "Certainly, you don't believe this nonsense."

Druce shrugged, "It doesn't matter what *I* believe, Troucille. The nations feel threatened by Rome ... they look for ... for some glimmer of hope ... some succor ... any dream they can rely on ... but we have a more pressing problem facing us."

"And that would be," Troucillus asked.

"These Black Druids do not rely only on their preaching," Druce explained. "They recruit ... shall we call them 'acolytes' ... disaffected young men whom they train, arm, and brainwash ... fanatics who do the bidding of these bent priests. These men are convinced that they are fulfilling the will of the gods by murdering foreigners and any among the nations who oppose the Black Druids. Murder for them is their entry into a paradise reserved for them in the lands beyond the skies."

"And your sources tell you these bands of ... of religious terrorists are operating in Aeduan territory?" Troucillus asked.

Druce nodded and continued, "This talk of the Maru Rignai, the Phantom Queen, is consistent with the ... shall we call it, the *theologia* of these Black Druids. The rise of the Phantom Queen is a sign of the imminent advent of Afalanos, a sign for the nations to rise up against foreigners. I'm afraid that a legion of Romans camped on our doorstep as if they belonged here will only serve to encourage the worst fears of our people ... and that is what threatens the stability of my cousin's throne, and any hope Caesar has of building a stable alliance around the Aedui."

"So, you are with us against these fanatics?" Troucillus asked.

"'With us'?" Druce repeated. "What a curiously deceptive way of asking, Troucille. Let us just say that we have a common goal, the elimination of these Black Druids and the prevention of Malouuhnos mab Dermuhtos from deposing my cousin."

"Fair enough," Troucillus nodded. "What do you propose."

Druce took a long drink from his wine cup. "We must act with dispatch. Whatever Malouuhnos and that druid of his have planned will probably be timed to coincide with the *Samon'win*. That gives us just a bit longer than a market cycle to act. You were concerned about Malouuhnos infiltrating his warriors into Bibracte. I too am concerned about infiltration; not by Malouuhnos' men but by *sicarii*, assassins of the *brawdoliait du*, "The Black Brotherhood," as these fanatics call themselves. I have agents watching for these *scelesti*, these thugs. I'm about to dispatch one of my most trusted men north. I will have information for you by the time the council reconvenes."

Troucillus nodded, "May I ask that one of my people accompany him?"

Druce chuckled, "Not one of your ersatz Gauls from the legions, I hope."

"No!" Troucillus shook his head. "I was thinking of Insubrecus here."

X

Caput X. De Collegio Nigro
Chapter 10. The Black Brotherhood

"I was thinking of Insubrecus here."

Somehow in my short army career, I had accumulated a veritable triumvirate of bosses who were all too ready to volunteer me for dangerous and dirty details. Caesar, Labienus and now Troucillus.

The next day, before the trumpets in the Roman camp had signaled the end of the fourth watch, I was riding out through the northern gate of Bibracte with Druce's man, Catouallaunos mab Dubnogenos. Catouallaunos, or Clou as he preferred to be called, was a warrior in his mid-twenties, with eight campaign seasons to his credit. He was technically a member of the king's *fintai*, his household troop, but he had served Druce directly for the last four years.

We rode out without helmets or armor. Our "cover," as Druce termed it, was we were two warriors traveling north to hunt a boar that was terrorizing a farming village. We wore our long swords and *dagrai*, short knives; mine was actually my Roman blade, my *pugio*, despite Troucillus' advice I carry nothing that could identify me as a Roman soldier.

I rationalized carrying the *pugio* - to myself at least - by imagining that, since I was supposedly a warrior of the Helvi, who had lived under Roman influence for decades, my carrying a Roman weapon would reinforce my cover story.

My real reason was that I believed my *pugio* brought me luck. It got me through the attack of the two thugs sent up from Mediolanum to kill me last *Samon'win*, and the murderous encounter with Aulus Gabinius, *Iunior*, and his *gladiatores* at the senator's estate a few weeks after that. So, I carried a Roman soldier's knife on my belt, and my *Bona Fortuna* medallion hung from around my neck under my tunic.

It was a cold morning. I wore my Gallic tunic, a pair of woolen bracae, the heavy woolen cloak, and the high leather boots given to me by Troucillus. I had a warm woolen pilleus cap pulled down over my ears. Instead of Clamriu, I rode a dark bay gelding from Troucillus' stable. Troucillus drew the line at my riding a horse with "SPQR" branded on its rump while pretending to be a member of his tribe. For a bit of prestige, should I need it, he gave me a silver torc of three strands capped with the heads of bears, the totem animal of his clan, designating me as a "leader of ten."

We were accompanied by one of Clou's "servants," Pruhderos, whom I was sure from his scars and the way he moved was a veteran warrior. He led a packhorse to

113

which were tied our boar spears, a stack of *gaea* javelins, a tent, a couple of camp stools, cooking gear, a couple of skins of beer and mead, and some rations.

For all appearances, we were just two young warriors out for a bit of hunting and drinking.

The first test of our "cover" came sooner than I expected. No sooner had we left Bibracte and reached the road leading north, when we discovered that Strabo's cohort, which was stationed in the northern *castrum*, had set up a roadblock. We spotted torches burning on both sides of the road and a log barricade blocking the right of way. As soon as we were within twenty *passus* from the barricade, a voice challenged us out of the dark in Latin.

"*Insistit'! Qu'estis*? Halt! Who goes there?"

Our cover was that we did not understand Latin. But a roadblock and a voice yelling out of the dark was enough to stop us dead in our tracks.

Then, I heard the voice say in Latin, "Where's the wog? Wake that lazy *mentula* up! There are riders on the rode!"

We held our ground and soon a figure approached us out of the gloom. A tall man, yawning broadly while trying to adjust his belts and armor.

"*Uh mochuhn Rhufeinig*, the Roman pig wants to know why Gah'el travel in their own land and who they are," he announced to us once he identified us as Gauls.

"Tell that short-haired, girly-faced sow we're going to visit his mother for some sport," Clou shot back. I had no doubt working for Druce, Clou understood Latin and caught the "wog" remark.

The man smiled and said, "I'd love to, but unless you want to spend the next few hours of your life having your mounts, packs, and every cavity in your body searched, I'll need a better story."

Clou snorted, "Tell the pig we're members of the king's *fintai*. We're going north to hunt a boar."

The man nodded, "That's a better story."

The man walked back to the checkpoint and reported to a Roman officer in his halting Latin. I heard a Roman voice say, "All that jabbering just to say, 'We're going hunting"? No wonder you wogs can't get anything done!"

The Roman then came forward with two legionaries in tow. He was a *decanus*, a squad leader. I had no doubt the rest of his *contubernium*, his tent-squad, were hidden in the shadows with their javelins at the ready.

The Roman gave us the once over. "Only three ... what harm could three wogs going north do?" he shrugged

Then he called over his shoulder, "Remove the barricade! Three wogs to pass through!"

Then to the interpreter, "Tell them they can go!"

Before the man could translate, Clou said, "What was that all about?"

The man shrugged, "The Romans have their loincloths all up in a knot about something. They started all this yesterday, right around the time their cavalry rode north.

They seem more concerned about traffic moving south. Going north, just a quick sniff and off you go."

Clou started his horse down the road. "I'll be a happy man when 'off they go'!"

The man shrugged again, "Hopefully in the spring. Word is they're heading north up into Belgica."

I wondered briefly if everyone this side of the Rhodanus knew of Caesar's intention of confronting the Belgae!

Clou just snorted in response as we headed north.

As we rode through the Roman roadblock, the *decanus* stood at the side of the road at rigid attention. He was grasping the hilt of his gladius so tightly that his knuckles were white. His eyes glared at us from below the brim of his *galea* helmet, and he thrust his chin forward like the ram of a trireme rushing toward the side of a Carthaginian ship.

For the first time, I saw Rome the way the Gah'el must see it, an arrogant, unstoppable power, now in their midst, and daring them to do something about it.

As we rode past, the *decanus'* chin seemed to jut out farther against the rawhide straps of his cheek guards. I was tempted to turn my head and say to him in camp Latin, "Ey! *Mentula*! Go tell your *capu'*, your boss, Strabo, Paganus says hey!" But, had I done that, I'd be "blowing my cover," as Troucillus would put it. So, I averted my eyes like "a good, little wog" and rode north.

We rode north and west for the rest of the morning. We passed though clusters of round houses which served as market towns, passed small farmsteads carved out of the forests, and rode up into the hill country. We saw nothing suspicious. The crops were in. The men were out repairing equipment and harnesses. Women were mending and washing. Children were feeding the livestock.

We passed other groups of travelers heading south. Most were headed to Bibracte for the *Samon'win* celebrations. Others were bringing in their excess harvest to sell in the markets. Some were hoping to witness the Council of Three Generations before it ended. The news from the north was there was no news. The borders were quiet; the countryside seemed to be settling down into its long winter slumber.

The Gah'el believe the king is the land; a good king meant a fertile, peaceful land. Duuhruhda's land was peaceful, prosperous, and tranquil despite the presence of Roman legions in the south.

Lugos' fiery chariot was traveling low in the southern sky signaling the People of Danu that it was almost time for them to emerge into the middle world from the *crugiau*, the barrows. The shadows of the trees pointed north. I estimated that it was *naouniau, meridies* as the Romans call it, midday. We came to a cluster of buildings in a clearing seemingly tucked between the sides of two heavily wooded hills. Smoke emerged from the smoke hole of the largest building. Around the entryway, men sat drinking from ceramic cups. They eyed us suspiciously as we approached from the road.

Clou raised an empty right hand in their direction. "Good fortune to all in this place," he announced.

The men relaxed. I heard mutterings of 'welcome'. Then, they went back to their drinking and talk.

"This is Ludnert's place," Clou said to me. "The last inn before we pass into the lands of the *Wuhr Math*, the Bear Clan. A good place to fill our bellies and collect any rumors from the north."

No sooner did Clou mention "fill our bellies," than mine rumbled reminding me I hadn't eaten since leaving Bibracte before dawn.

No sooner had we jumped down from our horses, then a stout, grey-haired man in a leather apron emerged from the inn. Wiping his hands on a cloth, he greeted us, "Clou! You lazy excuse for a soldier! What's so important that it brings ya so far from your incessant feasting and fornicating down in Bibracte. And, who's this with ya? He looks like he hasn't had his first shave yet."

"The aroma of your cooking, of course. Ludnert," Clou shot back. "What's in the stew today? Old plow horse? Or were you lucky enough to trap a few squirrels to fill your pot?"

"Had I known yer smelly arse was going to walk through me door, I would've put more effort into catching those busy-tailed rats," Ludnert chuckled. I assumed this was a time honored ritual of insults between the two.

"This here's Arth mab ... uh ... mab Cunorud ... he's one of the Elvai in the south."

Ludnert's eyebrows rose, "The Elvai! That explains his bare face and short hair. I thought the Elvai had been swallowed up by the *Rhufeinai* long before the krauts came.

Ludnert was referring to in Cimbrian wars some fifty years past.

Clou shrugged. "There's a *pendefig* of the Elvai who's a guest of the king. This one's part of his *fintai*. I'm taking him up north to hunt a boar. Seems the *Rhufeinai* have stolen all the pigs in the south."

Ludnert's eyes became guarded. "Going north, are ya?" We'd better talk. But, where's me manners. Get your dusty arse in 'ere and wet ya whistle. Is that Pruhde I see back there with the pack 'orse. Prude! Leave the beasts with the boy in the stable and get in 'ere and fill ya belly!"

We entered the inn. Ludnert sat us down at a table near the open door. A tow-headed boy delivered some rough ceramic mugs and a large pitcher of beer. Ludnert rubbed the boys head and told him to fetch some stew and bread, then he joined us. While Clou was filling the cups, Pruhderos arrived and sat down.

"I was hoping this was the day I'd at least get the cups filled before you arrived, Pruhde!" Clou quipped.

"In yer dreams, boss," Pruhderos answered and drained half his cup.

I loosened my belt and pulled me baldric up over my head. I leaned my *spatha*, my long sword, against the wall in easy arm's reach. I tasted the beer; it was good, strong, still fresh with a deep nutty flavor. I took a longer drink, put my cup down, and belched to show my appreciation.

Ludnert was talking to me, "Arth mab Cunorud, is it … a 'leader of ten' by that torc. So, do you Elvai keep to the old ways, despite the *Rhufeinai*?"

"Not all," I shook my head. "We are forbidden to form war bands like in the old days. Young men who want to be warriors have two choices. If they're citizens, they can join the legions. If not, there's an auxiliary cohort."

"Bah!" Ludnert dismissed my answer. "What glory is there in that! What's yer story? You scrape yer face like a *Rhufeinos*, but yer riding with a member of the king's *fintai*. Be you *Rhufeinos* or *Gah'el*?"

"Both," I shrugged. "And, neither."

"Both and neither!" Ludnert challenged. "What kind a answer's that?"

I had to be careful here. My cover was being pressed. I remember Troucillus counselling me. The best lies sail close to the truth.

"My grandfather, Cunomaro mab Arth, joined the war bands when the krauts came down from the north, not to help the *Rhufeinai*, but to protect our lands and people. His band was with the *Rhufeinai* when the krauts destroyed their armies and killed their chiefs. So, he and the warriors who survived took to the hills and did their best to protect the women and children."

"No shame in that," Ludnert belched through his beer. "No shame in that at'all. Protecting the people is the second mandate of the warrior, right after obeying the king. Right, Clou."

Clou nodded over his beaker, then said, "You got that right, Ludnert!"

The boy brought us three steaming bowls of stew and a couple of loaves of bread, still warm from the oven. I ripped off a piece of the bread and dipped it into the brown gravy. Pork, with a good portion of red carrots, leeks, turnips, celery, and some sort of bean. Delicious!

I ate a few bites, washed it down with a long draught of beer, and continued, "When the *Rhufeinai* returned north over the great mountains, my grandfather's *fintai* came down from the hills and joined them. When their *brennos*, Marios the Dictator, destroyed the krauts at *Dun Mawr*, a place the *Rhufeinai* call *Aquae Sextiae*, my grandfather was with the horsemen that attacked the krauts from the rear and panicked their army.

"My grandfather took six heads that day, three golden torcs, seven gold armbands, three horses, and a dozen prisoners. Marios himself gave him the handshake and made him a *Rhufeinos*. Gaius Marius Helvianus, he called himself."

"So, yes, my family are *Rhufeinai* over three generations. But some of our young men, like me, long for the old days, when a warrior met his enemies, face to face, alone, between the armies, not hiding behind a shield wall with a short sword. The days when the champions of our people fought each other warrior to warrior and the *chruhduh- dai*, the bards, sang their exploits for all the nations to hear."

"So, when our king's younger son, Gaius Valerius Troucillus, went north with the Caisar into the lands of the free nations, I went with him to see how the gods intended our people to live."

Ludnert put down his beer, belching loudly, "That's quite a tale, Arth *glas*, Young Art. Ya mean to tell me you Elvai still have a king despite the *Rhufeinai*?"

I put down my cup. The beer was starting to make my head spin a bit. "First, Ludnert, I am not *glas*! Yes! This was my first campaign! But I have fought the River People and beat them! I have fought the krauts along the great eastern river and beat them! I killed one of their *brennoi*, one of their battle-lords, and took his horse, his sword, and his gold! When the kraut *brennos*, Ariovistos, captured my king's son, Troucillus, it was I who led the *fintai* that took him back. I pursued Ariovistos to the banks of the great eastern river! There I shouted challenges and insults at him, and no one dared cross over to answer my challenge!"

My heard my voice getting louder as I delivered my *brolio chruhfeluhr*, my warriors boast. Even Clou's jaw dropped a bit and Pruhderos stopped chewing his food. I thought I'd better quit while I was ahead. I was repeating phrases from sagas I had heard as a boy. So, I drained my cup and slammed it down in the middle of the table. Ludnert immediately refilled it.

I grabbed my cup, let out a long belch for effect, and continued, "You asked about our king, Ludnert. Only my people recognize him as such. The *Rhufeinai* will have no kings! They are strange in this way. But they are not true warriors. The *Rhufeinai* made our king a ... a ..." There was no good word in Gah'el for this. "... a *marchog* ... a 'rider'... a 'knight'... he wears a narrow purple stripe on his tunic indicating that he is a leader even among the *Rhufeinai*. When the Caisar holds court, our king advises him as a noble of the *Rhufeinai*."

Ludnert let out a great sigh, then took a drink from his cup. "You're a braver man than I thought, Clou," he started. "Travellin' north with such a warrior who at any moment might glow red, when the battle frenzy takes him, and slaughter all around him, friend and foe, alike."

Ludnert was alluding to the saga of Ci Mawr, the Great Hound, whose battle rage, *Gouachlgofrouuhd Coch*, the Red Frenzy, made him unbeatable in battle. Ci Mawr had offended the Maru Rignai, the Phantom Queen, by refusing to sleep with them in their manifestation as the *Forouuhn Coch*, the Red Maiden. As revenge, the Maru Rignai caused the *Gouachlgofrouuhd Coch* to descend on him during a feast in the king's hall. Before he came to himself, Ci had slaughtered dozens, including his shield bearer and his own son.

As a self-inflicted punishment, Ci wandered the lands fighting impossible battles. Finally, he was mortally wounded when his own spear, *Gae Bolga*, turned on him and gave him a poisoned wound in his thigh. As he lay dying, the Maru Rignai appeared to him in their manifestation as the *Gourach Louuhd*, the Gray Hag, and taunted him. Despite his weakness, Ci Mawr cut the Gray Hag across the face with his great sword, *Duhrnwuhn* White-Hilt, a scar that the goddesses manifest to this day.

I remember years ago, after Gran'pa told me this story, he took a long drink from his cup and asked me what I thought the moral was. When I said I didn't know, he looked at me and winked, "When a goddess tells you to hump her, you do it!"

All that accomplished was Gran'pa receiving the sharp end of Nana's elbow in his ribs and getting a sour look from my dear, Roman mother, Valeria.

I was all of ten years old; I had no idea what "humping" meant.

When Ludnert said this, Pruhderos reached over and squeezed my shoulder indicating that Ludnert's remark was just a "guy thing," no malice intended, and I was talking too much. I decided to concentrate on my lunch.

Clou asked, "So, Ludnert! Do you have news from the north?"

"Aye," he nodded, refilling his cup. "Some bloody strange happ'nin's up there ... bloody strange ..."

Ludnert shook his head and took a drink, "That *moch*, Malouuhnos mab Dermuhtos, came through here a couple a weeks back on 'is way down to Bibracte ... 'e had a strange little man with him ... a priest ... a *derwuhd* ... but 'e was like no druid I've ever seen ... you know how that bunch are ... free drinks, free food, kiss that tree an' the gods'll love ya ... no, this gobshite looked like he never had a decent meal in 'is life ... pale, sunkin' cheeks, lank 'air ... wouldn't touch the beer ... drank only well water, ate only bread ... said 'e was fastin' in preparation of 'The Comin'', he called it ... dressed all in black. Well, Malouuhnos headed on down the road and I didn't give 'im or 'is bloody druid much thought after that."

Ludnert paused long enough to wet his whistle, then continued. "Then, travelers down from the north started telling these strange stories ... people up there disappearin' ... no trace of 'em ... who leaves 'is 'ome this time a year? There's this mound ... supposed to be one of the *crugiau*, the barrows that connect the middle lands and the underworld ... built by the old ones in the time before time ... strange lights at night ... screams in the darkness ... all this so close to the *Samon'win*. People up there think the old ones are going to break the *adawid*, the ancient agreement. When they emerge into the middle lands it's to take them back from the nations ... they're gonna make slaves of us ... they say we broke our word and we're surrendering the middle lands to the southerners, the *Rhufeinai* ... the gods're angry ... they want to punish the nations ... it's daft ... but so close to the *Samon'win*, it has some of the countryfolk worked up."

"Worked up how?" Clou asked.

Ludnert shrugged, "Prayin' mostly!"

"Praying mostly," Clou challenged. "What the hell does that mean?"

"Accordin' to me sources," Ludnert started, "Bunches of 'em gather at the *Crugmawr* at night and beg the old ones not to attack 'em when they return at the *Samon'win*. They swear they'll destroy the southerners, drive 'em from the middle lands ... swear if their king canna do it ... or won't do it ... they'll offer his blood to appease the gods and find a true warrior king, a *brennos*, to lead 'em against the *Rhufeinai*."

"Bloody *gouladourai*," Pruhderos snorted. "Ignorant rednecks!"

Ludnert shrugged, "Maybe, Pruhde. But remember, the world is different up here. The nights're darker; the forests deeper. The old ways still survive up here. But that's not the worst of it."

"Not the worst of it?" Clou repeated.

"Aye!" Ludnert responded. He took a long drink from his cup. "A merchant came through here a few days back, a guy I know from Bibracte. Anyway, 'e says 'e heard that a boy was sacrificed on the *Crugmawr* to some god called Afalanos. I've never heard of that one."

"He's a god of the Pretani," Clou told him. "The male equivalent of our Danu."

"Danu!" Ludnert's eyes widened. "The Dark One! The queen a the underworld!"

He spat toward the north and made the "horns" with his right hand to ward off evil. I felt myself rubbing my *Bona Fortuna*. Danu! Even her name should not be spoken out loud lest she appear as if summoned. She comes from the north and casts no shadow on the ground. I rubbed *Bona Fortuna*, again,

"Tell me more about this ... this sacrifice," Clou urged.

Ludnert shook his head and drank more beer. "Seems one a the farmers up there has this son ... a boy the gods cursed ... almost twelve years old ... can hardly speak 'cept in gibberish ... can't work round the farm ... goes into rages at the slightest thing ... they took the boy up to the *Crugmawr* ... on the top of the mound's a hole, like a bowl carved outta the earth ... it's *uh port* ... a passageway to the otherworld where the old ones emerge at the Samon'win ... they took the boy there, then they cut 'is throat ... let the blood sink down through the portal into the ground to appease this Afalanos ... let 'im know that the old ways are remembered by the nations ..."

"*Hurtuhnai*!" spat Pruhderos. "Idiots!"

"Aye!" nodded Ludnert. "The boy was ... was defective ... not a worthy sacrifice ... the gods canna be happy with it."

"That's not what Pruhde meant, Ludnert," said Clou. "We do not offer the blood of our children to the gods. It's ... it's unnatural ... perverted. The true gods cannot be pleased with it. You said, 'they took the boy there'? Who took him? The *gouladourai*? The farmers themselves did this?"

"The farmers?" Ludnert repeated. "No! Not them. There's a band a ... a priests, I guess they'd be ... they're preaching this 'comin' nonsense ... this Afalanos is coming at the *Samon'win* to judge the nations ... if he doesn't like what 'e sees, 'e's gonna unleash the old ones against us ... it'll be like in the old tales ... a war with no mercy to clean the middle lands a ... a *anghredadunai* ... infidels, unbelievers, heretics, they calls us ... no mercy ... we're all to die ... our blood drunk by the old ones to give 'em strength ... the middle lands are to be purged."

I was rubbing *Bona Fortuna*, again. The Romans have a myth about a monster, the *Stryx* they call her because after she kills, she keens out a sound like that of the owl.

According to the old stories, the *Stryx* was a mortal woman named Polyphonte, who resisted Aphrodite's commands because she wished to remain a virgin. Aphrodite cursed her with an unnatural desire for a bear, with whom she mated and bore two sons, Agrios and Oreios. Her two, darling bear-boys went about killing travelers and eating their flesh.

This cannibalism enraged Zeus, so he transformed Agrios and Oreios into vultures, the eaters of the dead. Polyphonte, he changed into an owl, the *stryx*, in Latin. Polyphonte cried by night, without food or drink, until Hecate, the Roman's equivalent of Danu, took mercy on her and taught her how to get her nourishment from the veins of mortals who were foolish enough to go about at night.

The *Stryx*, or as the Greeks call her, the *Lamia*, hunts in the darkness. She tears open the throats of her victims and gorges herself with their living blood. She celebrates her kills with the high-pitched screech of her owl persona. Her devotees, all women, are called *strigae*.

Caesar later told me that the Roman Senate had passed a law years ago declaring the worship of the *Stryx exsecratio*, cursed, anathema, repugnant to the gods. Being a *striga* was punishable by death, being buried alive outside the *pomerium*, the sacred boundary of the city.

Then, Caesar, after a few cups of wine, shared that his own niece, Atia Balba Caesonia, was a *striga*, as well as many of the rich, high-born women of the Roman society, such as Clodia, the sister of his client, Publius Clodius Pulcher, and even his own lover, Servilia.

Ironically, Servilia was also the half-sister of Marcus Porcius Cato, Caesar's most strident political enemy. Cato had the tightest arse of all the tight-arsed *Optimates* in the senate. There was no doubt in Caesar's mind that Cato would push for the internment of half the female population of Rome, if he got a so much of a whiff of the *strigae*, and his darling, half-sister, Servilia, would be the first one dropped into the pit to demonstrate Cato's unshakable and uncompromising *dignitas*.

Caesar said the *strigae* often met in the homes of one of the goddess' devotees under the guise of worshipping *Magna Mater*, the "Great Mother," from whose rites all men are banned. Unlike *Magna Mater*, who's an ascetic and temperate goddess - in many ways a Cato in skirts - the worship of the *Stryx* entails drinking red wine as a reenactment of drinking the blood of her victims, who, according to the *strigae*, are all men.

Caesar believes that during their rites, the *strigae* drink the "blood" of all their husbands – divorced and current; their lovers, who forgot their birthdays; their sons, who control their property and monthly stipends; the chariot drivers, on whom they lost money; the gladiators, who failed to return their attentions; and any other male, who had crossed them in any way. After that, the *strigae* can hardly walk far enough to get into any real mischief.

Caesar quipped that if the senate started burying all the *strigae* in Rome, they'd quickly run out of grave diggers and the places to dig the holes. Besides, most men winked at these rites because they'd rather have their women take out their frustrations ritually with red wine than bringing them home and doctoring their husbands' wine supply or mushroom larder.

I have no idea what the source of Caesar's information was, but we were half an amphora of wine into the evening when Caesar shared this with me.

When Clou heard these tales from Ludnert, he insisted on pressing on to this *Crugmawr*. So, by the seventh hour, while the shadows of the trees were pointing northeast, we were remounted and heading north. By the time we passed into Malouuhnos' lands, my nice little beer-buzz had turned into a dull ache in my forehead.

We passed through what Clou called the "water gap." We climbed a wooded valley, following a small stream uphill, then rode over a narrow saddle between two hills. On the other side of the water gap, we arrived in a land seemingly under an enchantment, as if cursed by some god.

In contrast to the clan holdings of Duuhruhda, where people were visible, working to get ready for the winter, and anticipating the festival of Samon'win, the lands of Malouuhnos seemed deserted. Silent! No one was visible. However, as we passed farmsteads, we could feel the eyes of the crofters following us from within their darkened huts. On more than one occasion, we saw or heard a door or shutter slam shut as we came into view.

I was reminded of my ride through the valley of the Dubis, approaching Vesantio, where the crofters were hiding from the murdering raiding parties of Ariovistus.

Or, of a story my gran'pa told me years ago of Pruhderos and Rhiannon, the goddess of the birds, and the enchantment of the Mouse Lord which covered the middle lands in a white mist and made all living things disappear.

In fact, here in Malouuhnos' lands, even the birds seemed reluctant to sing.

"Don't much like strangers up here," Pruhderos' voice cut through the unease.

"Don't like *us* is more like it!" Clou shot back. "I've had warmer receptions from people I was raiding! You'd think we were a band of murderous Soucanai on a cattle raid!"

We rode for a couple of hours in silence, until the sun was settling behind the hills in the southwest. Clou estimated we were about half the distance to the *Crugmawr* and we should stop for the night. We passed a farm with a fair-sized roundhouse. There was smoke rising through the roof, so we knew someone was home.

As we rode into the yard, Clou quipped, "Let's see if the law of hospitality still applies in this blighted place."

We sat on our horses before the door and waited for the farmer to offer greetings and hospitality.

Nothing happened.

Clou called out a ritual blessing on the dwelling and its inhabitants.

Still, nothing happened.

Finally, Clou said, "Enough of this!" He jumped down from his horse and pounded on the barred door of the dwelling.

Still, nothing happened.

Clou continued to pound and called out, "We are travelers up from Bibracte! We ask hospitality for the night!"

Nothing.

"You give offense to the king and to the gods by turning us away!" Clou persisted.

Then a voice from behind the door. "Go 'way! You're strangers! You're not welcomed!"

"Of course, we're bloody strangers!" Clou yelled at the closed door. "The gods demand you offer hospitality to travelers! You insult the king by turning us away! Open this bloody door, before I kick it down!"

Again, the voice. "It's not that we turn our backs on the gods! You're in danger 'ere and you endanger us! Go 'way afore they find you 'ere!"

"Danger!" Clou yelled back. "I'll show you danger! Open this bloody door and look! We're warriors! Who is going to *find* us?"

There was silence for a few heartbeats. I could swear I heard voices in a whispered conversation from behind the door. Then, "Please! There's a shed behind the house! You can use that for the night! The well is there, too. Please! Stop shouting or they'll 'ear you! Go back to the shed before you're seen!"

Clou walked away from the door. This was the best deal he could hope for unless he kicked down the door and forced whoever was inside to accommodate us.

"It's the shed or the woods, boys," he shrugged. "Who's he worried about? Who's going to hear us way out here? Why should we give a turd?"

We led our horses around the house. The shed was a storage barn. It was full of forage for the winter, so we could at least spend the night on a bed of hay. The animals, a plough horse and a couple of head of cattle. were in stalls at the rear of the building. The pigs were in pens outside and the chicken coop was down wind, praise the gods!

Pruhderos unloaded the pack horse, and we tied our mounts behind the building out of sight from the road. We had no idea from whom we were hiding, but the atmosphere of this place had spooked us enough not to take any unnecessary chances. We fed and watered our horses, then settled down to a meal of jerky and beer.

We could smell the cooking of the family's dinner. Chicken stew, I thought. My mouth watered, so I ripped a shard of jerky off my strip with my teeth.

So could Clou, "Bastards!" he spat through a mouthful of dried jerky. "Having a nice hot meal while we sit out here chewing on this shoe leather."

Pruhderos seemed more affected by our situation than we did. "You think we should post a watch tonight, *a pen*?" he asked Clou through a mouthful of jerky.

"A watch?" Clou challenged. "Why? We're in our own lands!"

Pruhderos shrugged. "Our lands are on the other side of the water gap," he stated. "This place is ... uh ... this place is ... uh ... *diert*!"

Diert! Pruhderos used a word meaning alien, mysterious, dangerous.

Clou didn't contradict him. Then, we heard a knock on the door of the hut. I reached for my sword which I had leaned against the wall.

Clou opened the door, *dagr* in his right hand, the blade down along his upper leg. It was a girl about twelve years. She was holding a tray with three steaming bowls and a loaf of bread.

"Me ma sent this over, lor'" she said. "I'll go back fer some beer."

Pruhderos brushed past Clou and took the food. "Tell your ma we thank her," he said.

The girl nodded and retreated back into the darkness of the farmyard. Pruhderos brought the food into the hut as Clou closed the door. "Praise the gods," he said over the stew. "Now I can hold on to this bloody jerky in case my boots need mending."

We didn't wait for the beer but dug into the stew. My bowl was about halfway down when I again heard a knock on the door of the hut. Pruhderos went over and let the girl in. She was holding a pitcher.

"Ma says we got no cups. You'll 'ave to share and drink right out a the pi'cher," the girl announced.

"That'll be no problem at all," Pruhderos said taking the pitcher.

"What's your name, girl," Clou called out of the shadows.

The girl's eyes widened, "I canna be givin' me name to no strangers!"

"Strangers!" Clou challenged her. "We're no strangers! We're of your own people."

"You're southerners!" the girl argued. "You're ... you're contaminated."

The girl used the word *halogai*, a strange word to come out of the mouth of a farm girl.

Clou challenged it. "'Contaminated' Who told you such claptrap?"

"The priest, lor'" she answered. "The black priest said all southerners are contaminated by false gods?"

"False gods?" Clou repeated rising and walking toward the girl. "Is Lugos, who gave us these lands, a false god ... Lugos, who demands we respect strangers ... offer them hospitality?"

The girl recoiled toward the open door as Clou advanced. "Lugos 'as abandoned us, lor'! His great fiery cart is fleeing south. 'E has joined the gods of our enemies!"

"That happens every year," I chimed in. "It's almost Samon'win. Lugos always returns with the spring."

"Not this time, lor'!" the girl argued. "A new god is comin' out of the north! Lugos is fleeing from 'im! If we don't keep faith with the new god, 'e will lead the dark ones against us. 'E will give them our blood to drink!"

"That's nonsense ..." Clou began.

"No, lor'!" the girl almost screamed, her hand on the door. "It's already started! The priests are takin' children ... the children of disbelievers! They take 'em to the great mound north a 'ere! If they find out I've been talkin' to yas, they'll come 'n' take me! No one comes back from that place!"

"Do you have your *dagr*, girl?" Clou challenged her.

The girl's hand dropped down to her belt.

"You're a woman of the Gah'el!" Clou continued. "No man, priest or otherwise, can attack a woman of the Gah'el with impunity!"

The girl shook her head. "It's not the priests who come, lor'! They send the *groudruhn*! The *cerdournos*! Steel is no good against the *groudruhn*!"

The "Wanderer"! The "Night Walker"! This was the bogyman! My gran'pa threatened me with when I was a child and refused to go to bed. A flesh-eating, blood drinking monster who lurks in the darkness and preys on unsuspecting travelers and naughty children who stay up too late!

"He'll come fer me if the black priests know I been talkin' to disbelievers!" the girl screamed and bolted out of the shed. She disappeared into the darkness of the farmyard.

We were all silent for a few heartbeats. Then Pruhderos said, "What rubbish ..."

"It may be, Pruhde," I agreed, "But these people believe it and it seems these priests enforce it with fear ..."

"Or worse!" Clou added. "We need to see this mound ... find out what these priests are doing up there. Taking children ... I hope that's just a rumor they spread to frighten these people. Let's finish our food and get some sleep. I want to be on the road before the sun's up. And Pruhde ... your idea about keeping a watch is a good one ... we don't seem to be in our own lands anymore."

We were on the road north before sunrise, before the morning birdsong. Although none of us believed in the girl's nightwalker tale, we did not want to expose these people to punishment by these fanatical druids. By the time the eye of Lugos rose above the hills in the southeast, we were miles away from the farmstead. Although none of us said it, I got the feeling that we were all relieved when the warmth of Lugos' bright eye banished the cold shadows where this new god was said to lurk.

It was Pruhderos who finally broke our silence. "What kind of bloody people are these Pretanai that they worship a god who demands human blood and will have no other god but himself? That's *anfrouthau*."

Pruhde used the term "unbelieving." Many of the Gah'el – Romans, too - were devoted to a particular god, but this devotion did not cause them to deny the other gods. Such an attitude would invite enmity and vengeance from the neglected deities. The Roman term for such a person is *atheos*, an atheist. *Negare deos*, to deny the gods, was a crime among the Romans, who believed the benevolence of the gods made their nation great, protected it from their enemies.

As a soldier, I take pains to appease *Bona Fortuna*, the goddess of luck. Mars, the god of war, keeps me strong in battle, and Iove, the king of the gods, makes my legion victorious. As a client of Caesar, I offer sacrifice and prayer to Venus, the mother of Aeneas, the founder of the *gens Iulia*. As a member of the *gens Maria*, I keep the mask of Gaius Marius in my *vestibulum* to appease the *lar* of the man who granted my family the franchise and our name.

But I do not ignore the other gods; I certainly do not voice my distain for them. Such for a mortal would be *demens*, madness!

Little did I know at the time that, in a couple of years, I would follow Caesar over *Oceanus* and into the lands of these Pretani, the "Blue-Paints," the *Picti*. And even more, I would live among the people of the Isle of the Dead, Evra's people, the *Galighe*, whom the Romans call the *Scoti*. There, I would discover many new gods. But none of these gods demanded that I reject the other gods; none of these demanded human blood be spilled on their altars.

This blood-god of the black druids was not merely *inromanitas*, uncivilized; it was *maledictus*, cursed; *turpis*, disgusting.

"We need to get up to this *Crugmawr*, the Great Barrow," Clou was saying. "That seems to be the center of it. Then, we'll have an idea what's going on up here."

Pruhderos and I both answered with affirmative grunts.

We rode northwest the rest of the morning. We were now in the heart of Malouuhnos' holdings. The lands were quiet. We saw no human activity; people kept themselves behind closed doors as we rode by. Even the birds, the servants of bright Rhiannon, singer of the dawn and evening song, were silent.

It was past midday by the shadows cast by the trees. Clou halted and pointed to a piece of cloth tied to the branch of a tree on the east side of the road. "That's a sign ... I'd say the *Crugmawr* is nearby. Pruhde! See if there's a trail leading east.

Although it was late in October, the oaks still held most of their leaves, though they had turned golden brown. The other trees - maple, birch, chestnut, ash, elm, and dogwood - had passed the time of their bright colors and had dropped most of their leaves. The next heavy rain or strong wind would strip them bare down to their skeletal remains. The pines and spruce had assumed their winter colors, a green so dark as to appear as black patches in the forest.

Pruhderos jumped down from his horse and examined the ground around the marked tree. He kicked aside some of the fallen leaves, then he crouched down and stared out across the forest floor.

"There's a trail here, *a pen*," he said finally. "It leads off to the east. I'd say it's been used recently but someone's tried to cover the tracks by sweeping the dead leaves over them. I can still see the indentation of the travel over them."

"Can you follow it, Pruhde?" Clou asked.

Pruhde nodded, "Yes ... it's like most forest trails ... it wraps around the terrain features but essentially leads directly to a destination. If this is the trail to the barrow, we should find it out in that direction." Pruhderos pointed almost due east with his arm and hand.

Clou nodded and jumped down from his horse. "We'll lead the horses," he said. "I don't think they'll be too happy in among the trees."

I dismounted and followed Clou and Pruhde into the forest. Pruhde followed the trail while Clou over watched him. I led the horses.

As soon as the trees closed in around us, we seemed to have entered a different world, a world of shadowy silence cut off from the sun. I felt the horses shy back from the forest; they wanted to remain on the road, out from under the murky wood. I didn't blame them. This place turned my gut into water, made my legs feel weak.

We tried to move silently, but the dead leaves on the ground rustled and cracked under our boots. Pruhde stopped suddenly. Then he turned toward us and pointed to the trunk of a maple. Clou and I moved forward and joined him.

"The trail is marked," he breathed in our direction. "Look!"

It took me a few heartbeats to see what he was indicating. Finally, I made out some lines carved into the tree.

"What is it?" I asked.

Pruhde shrugged, "A trail marker? Maybe the old writing ..."

"The old writing?" I interrupted.

Pruhde nodded. "It's what the nations used before they adopted the symbols of the Greeks and Romans. The top one's '*alm*', the fir tree. It's the equivalent of the Roman 'A'. The bottom one's '*fern*'," the alder, a Roman 'F'.

"'A' 'F'?" I questioned.

"Afalanos?" Clou asked.

"Aye! That would make sense," Pruhderos agreed. "They're using the old symbols because they reject any influence of southerners. They're marking the way to the Mound of Afalanos."

Once we saw the trail markers, following the path was easy. We had gone about five hundred paces when I detected movement to our right out of the corner of my eye. I got the impression of a black, flowing haze moving along in the same direction as us. When I looked directly, there was nothing, just the gray-brown trunks of half-shorn trees, a forest floor carpeted in dead, brown leaves, and the naked stalks of the underbrush.

I hissed to my companions, "Movement! Right!"

They immediately halted. We all squatted down on our haunches and examined the terrain. Even our horses looked right, their eyes wide.

"What did you see," Clou hissed back to me.

"Not sure ... looked black ... moved quickly ... made no noise," I whispered back.

We waited and watched for a few more heartbeats.

"You get spooked by a squirrel?" Clou chuckled.

"Seemed too big," I answered, ignoring the jibe. "Squirrels up here are reddish, aren't they? Besides, squirrels would have rattled the leaves when they ran. A wolf, maybe?"

"Too early for them to be down this low," Pruhderos said. "Besides, they don't like hunting during the day and, unless they're starving, they avoid humans."

"A bear?" I asked.

Pruhderos shrugged. "Maybe. But I haven't seen any droppings and the horses are too calm. Bears aren't usually shy when something they don't like comes into their territory."

We waited for a few more heartbeats. Finally, Clou rose to his feet. "Let's keep going," he ordered.

We rose and continued along the trail. As we walked, I searched my memory. Did the *cerdournos*, the night walker, roam in the daylight? What about the *groudruhn*, the wanderer ... didn't gran'pa once tell me a tale of the Arth Mawr tracking the *groudruhn* in the daylight?

We halted. Pruhderos indicated what seemed to be a dark patch in the forest about fifty paces to our front. "A hill of some sort," he hissed.

We both nodded. We continued along the trail. Soon, the "hill" was apparent. The fact that someone had festooned its trees with strips of cloth didn't serve to obscure it. The strips of whitish cloth swayed in a gentle breeze giving the hill the appearance of a place covered by a magic mist, a place of enchantment.

"The *Crugmawr*?" Pruhderos asked.

Clou nodded. We could see the imprint of a well-worn trail leading up to its summit. By the looks of it, it was both heavily and recently traveled.

"Up we go," Clou instructed. Then, "The horses are a problem. The slope may be too steep and the trail's narrow ... we'll have trouble getting them back down ..."

Clou looked around. "Let's hide them in that stand of spruce over there!"

"And leave them alone?" I protested. "What if someone steals them? Or bears?"

"Still haven't seen any bear signs," Clou said. "I think the human activity here keeps them away. They'll be hidden from view. You have a better idea, Arth?"

I examined the trail leading up the mound. Clou was right. We could coax the horses up but getting them back down would be a chore. Too steep; too narrow. If we had to leave in a hurry, we'd have to abandon them on the summit.

Finally, I nodded in agreement.

I led the horses into the stand of spruce. I could tell they were not happy about our plan. They grunted, snorted, and stamped in protest. They did however accept their feedbags as an acceptable bribe for their cooperation.

I was wondering whether I should blindfold them, when Pruhderos came in behind me and removed a couple of the *gaea*, hunting javelins, from the pack horse.

"Better safe than sorry," he winked at me.

Pruhderos saw the blindfold in my hand, "Don't! Let them see. They'll be our early warning system if something ... I mean if someone comes up behind us."

I nodded, hoping our horses didn't understand Gah'el. *Something*!

We left our horses in the thicket and climbed the mound. It was easier than I had expected. The trail was clear, and the slope was not that steep. We quickly reached the top, where we saw *Uh Port*, The Portal, a cavity seeming scooped out of the top of the mound. We halted just below the lip and examined the hollow.

We waited but nothing was moving below us except the stripped branches of trees moving in the gentle late afternoon breeze. The movement of the branches cast lengthening shadows from the sun low in the south making detection of movement in the hollow almost impossible. All we could hear was the whistling of the airs and the clicking and groaning of the trees.

Then we heard a low, buzzing sound.

"Can you hear that, boss?" I heard Pruhderos hiss to Clou.

Clou nodded and shrugged. Then he pointed to where the trail seemed to lead down in the hollow. "The Portal should be in that direction. I'll go down and take Arth with me. You stay and over watch our movement. Keep an ear out for the horses if something comes up behind us."

Pruhderos nodded; he spread the four *gaea* he had taken from the pack horse along the ground. Clou started down into the cavity. I followed. I noticed Clou had unsheathed his *dagr*.

We soon reached the bottom and, as soon as we did, *Uh Port* was visible before us. The portal to the underworld was marked by a large, granite stone carved in the shape of a table with no legs, just a solid, gray mass of ancient stone covered with lichen and moss except where someone had scratched into the surface the symbol

I heard Clou suck in his breath. "Afalanos' sign!"

As we approached the altar, we realized that the buzzing had grown louder. Afalanos' table was surrounded by a dark moving cloud.

I recognized the sound from the battlefield.

Flies! Clusters of fat, black flies!

Whatever was attracting the flies was on and around this stone altar.

Then, the smell hit us.

The stench of rotten meat and curdled blood - a battlefield where the dead had been left to rot. What seemed to be broken ground and small black stones at the foot of this altar, were clots of thickened, putrid blood.

Whatever was left in my stomach from breakfast rose up into my gullet; my throat muscles began to spasm. I managed to control my impulse until a cloud of the black, fattened flies flew up into my face. Then, my head was down behind a tree vacating whatever was left in my stomach.

I steadied myself by holding on to the small tree. I spat and wiped the watery bile off my chin. Then, I saw Clou waving the flies away from his face while poking at the blackened clots with a stick.

I quickly realized my stomach wasn't as empty as I had thought.

"No shame in it, Arth," he said without turning his attention from the carnage on the ground. "Even a warrior of ten seasons would have trouble stomaching this."

I was again wiping my chin.

Clou continued. "This blood is no more than two ... three days old. And there's a lot of it ... looks like it spilled down from the top of this stone here. And there's blood on top too ... what bled out here is anybody's guess."

Clou seemed to be struggling not to suggest that it was human blood, that these priests of Afalanos were offering human victims at The Portal to feed their god and the dark ones, who were readying themselves to emerge into our world at the *Samon'win.*

Then, we heard a scream. "*Guhsegerladra*! Sacrilege! You unbelievers desecrate the altar of Afalanos!"

I looked and saw a tall, thin man in a black robe appear from out of the trees on the far side of the altar. His unbound hair was long, thin, and stringy; strands of it fell across his pale, closely shaven face. He was grasping a rope in his right hand; he was dragging something behind him ... a captive.

Clou quickly rose to his feet. He circled the altar widely avoiding the pool of rotted blood at its feet. I rounded the altar on the opposite side. The tall man's captive was a child! A young girl, no more than nine or ten winters! Her hands were bound before her; there was a red, angry bruise on her left cheek. She was crying.

Clou had his knife out, held low below his waist. "Whatta you got there, priest? Another victim to add to the sickening rites you're performing in this place."

The tall man seemed to raise up. He sneered at Clou, "You have no idea what's about to happen here, unbeliever. Afalanos grows strong on the blood of our offerings. When he arises, he will scour the middle lands clean of the unworthy."

While the tall man was spouting his nonsense to Clou, I sliced the rope with which he was holding the girl. I was starting to unbind her hands, when the man turned on me and shrieked, "That one belongs to the god! You will suffer ..."

He never finished. Clou drove his blade into the man's abdomen, low, so he would be a long time dying. The man looked down where Clou had stabbed him. Then, he fell to his knees. With his failing strength, he unleashed an unearthly keening. Then, he fell forward into the clouds of flies and the congealed blood.

I had the girl's hands free. From the other side of the hollow, I heard answering cries.

"I think that's our signal to get out of here," Clou said.

We turned back toward our trail. The girl seemed to be in shock, unable to run. So, I threw her over my shoulder. I could see movement through the trees, the pursuit behind us and moving around us on both sides to cut us off.

The priest Clou had stabbed managed to lift himself up, his face covered in black, crusted gore. "Kill them! Kill them, my brothers! They have stolen Afalanos' offering! Kill them!"

We ran. By the time we reached to bottom of the trail leading to the rim, our pursuers were almost on us. I was just about to put the girl down and make my stand against them, when I sensed something whizz past my head. I heard a wet, meaty thump behind me. Then, a scream.

Pruhderos was covering our retreat with his javelins.

I struggled up the slope, the girl limp over my shoulder. I sensed Pruhderos' last three javelins flying past my head into the rout below. Clou thrust his arm up under mine and drove me up the hill. Almost at the top, Pruhderos grabbed the front of my tunic and pulled me up to the rim. I fell to my knees, panting. Clou took the girl from me and descended toward our horses.

Pruhderos dragged me to my feet. "Plenty a time to rest when you're dead, mate. Not now!"

Pruhderos thrust his arm through mine and drove me down the hill. We reached the thicket where we had left our horses. Clou had cut the feed bags off and we mounted. Horses are smart. They never wanted to enter these woods, but as soon as they realized we were escaping them, they ran like the wind down the narrow trail.

When we reached the road, Clou led us southeast. He had placed the girl in the saddle in front of himself. We ran south for about three thousand Roman paces before Clou pulled up.

"We dismount and walk the horses," he ordered jumping down from his saddle. He left the girl to ride. "Let the horses catch their breath. Those bastards might come after us."

I didn't know how a bunch of mad priests could pursue a group of mounted warriors. But we had to get out of these lands where human blood was being spilt and an apocalyptic struggle between light and darkness was being preached.

The girl we rescued still seemed to be in a state of shock barely clinging to Clou's saddle. Finally, Clou asked, "What's your name, girl?"

When she didn't respond, he again asked. "Girl! I asked you what's your name?"

She seemed to re-enter our world. "They sent the *cerdournos* to take me ... took me right out a me bed, 'e did ..."

"Who sent the nightwalker," Pruhderos asked.

"Them! The black'ins! The priests of the dark'ins!" the girl almost shrieked.

"I asked your name," Clou said again, almost in a whisper.

"Me name?" the girl repeated.

"Yes! Your name," Clou insisted. "You do have a name, don't you?"

The girl had to think about it. "Me name? I'm called ... uh ... Modrona ... Modrona, daughter of Cardros, the smith."

"Well, Modrona merc Cardros, I'm called Clou. The ugly one back there is Pruhde and this handsome young hero is Arth," Clou explained.

The girl examined our faces but didn't respond.

"So, Modrona merc Cardros, tell me what happened with this *cerdournos* and those black-clad bastards," Clou asked her.

"Me da would have no part of the black'ins and their mad sayin'," the girl started, "So's they cursed 'im ... told 'im 'e'd be dragged under by the dark 'ins at the turnin'.

But me da just laughed at 'em ... told 'em to peddle their cheap wares som'wheres else ... so they come fer me in the night ... they sent the nightwalker ...”

"They nightwalker's just a tale ...” I started.

"No!” the girl shrieked. "'e's real, 'e is! 'E come fer me 'e did ... 'e come at night ... took me from me bed ... 'e took me to the black'ins in the mound!”

Clou gave me a look and shook his head. Then, he asked the girl, "What did you see there at the mound.”

The girl seemed to calm a bit, then continued, "There was another 'un there ... this boy ... said 'e come from a farm up in the hills ... said 'is da wouldn't give the black'ins 'is sheep when they wanted 'em ... the nightwalker took 'im too ... brought 'im to the mound like me ... the black'ins come at sundown 'n' took 'im away ... I 'eard him screamin' then 'e stopped real sudden like ... then the black'ins started chantin' ... 'e never come back ... just the black'ins chantin' ...”

The tale seemed to exhaust the girl. Clou reached out and pressed her shoulder, "You're alright ... you're safe now. The black'ins can't get to you while you're with us.”

The druids didn't seem to be chasing us, so our first problem was the girl. Should we take her with us or return her to her people? Bringing her back to Bibracte would slow us down. But, if we brought her back to her father, what would prevent the priests from snatching her again?

The sun was low in the sky – late into the eleventh hour, I guessed – and we were still far from the water gap separating Malouuhnos' holdings from those of Du-uhruhda, the king. According to the Modrona, the trail that led south to her father's village was still a couple thousand paces down the road. We could detect no pursuit. So, thinking we were reasonably safe, we decided to halt for the night. The horses needed rest and so did we. And we gave no credence to the girl's story of the *cerdournos*, the nightwalker, stalking the dark forests.

There's a saying among my people, "*O enau plantai uhn dohd dim ond uh gwir*” – "From the lips of children comes only the truth.”

Had only we remembered it that evening when we decided to stop.

We found a small, wooded hillock a few hundred paces back from the road for our night laager. There was a small spring below the hill for fresh water and we believed that the trees, brush, and dead leaves would prevent anyone – or anything – from ap-proaching us undetected. We secured the horses and boiled a few pieces of the leather-like jerky for our dinner.

At first, Modrona didn't seem interested in eating but, after the boiling water had rendered the jerky into something edible, she recovered her appetite and ate more than the three of us combined. I guessed Afalanos likes his sacrificial victims hungry when they arrive in the underworld, so the druids hadn't fed her.

There was no question about posting a guard. We put the fire out for security and Pruhderos took the first watch. I had the second and Clou would relieve me.

I wrapped myself up in my blanket against the autumn chill and was soon asleep. When Pruhderos woke me, the darkness was complete. I could not see my hand in front of my face.

"Moon set a while ago," he whispered in my ear. "Can't see a bloody thing out there. Doubt anything'll be movin' about tonight ... at least nothin'll be movin' quiet."

We were sleeping in a tight circle. Pruhderos slipped into my already warm blanket. I leaned my back against a tree. I felt around for a water skin and, when I found one, began drinking. I had learned in the legions the best way to keep from falling asleep on night watch was to fill your bladder almost to the point of pain.

We couldn't burn a watch candle, so I had to measure time by the stars. Luckily, most of the leaves were down and the night sky was clear, so I could clearly see the star in Cynosura, the "Dog's Tail." Then, I found the "Plough" in Calisto, the "Great Bear." In my mind, I drew a line from the always visible star in the Dog's Tail through the two leading stars of the Plough which became the radius of an imaginary circle. Using that radius, I imagined a circle in the heavens and marked where the "blade" of the Plough was on the circumference. Assuming my watch lasted four "night hours," I picked the spot where the edge of the Plough should be when it was time to awaken Clou.

Out in the darkness, Pruhderos was starting to snort. I kicked out my leg in the direction of the sounds and made contact with something that felt like his arm.

"Wha ..." I heard his voice.

"You're snoring," In hissed into the darkness.

There was no response, so I kicked his arm again.

"Sta ... why you kickin' me ... need to sleep ..." Pruheros' voice.

"Turn over! You're snoring," I whispered.

"Ya ... ya ... no problem ..." I heard a body and blankets shuffling in the dark.

Despite the cold air and the pressure building on my bladder, I must have dozed. I don't remember falling asleep. In fact, I would have sworn I never closed my eyes. But suddenly, I was jolted into a more alert state of consciousness.

Something had changed.

I looked up at my sky clock. The edge of the Plough had moved about halfway through my allotted arc, two hours. It was past midnight.

I moderated my breathing and remained very still. I listened. I could hear nothing except the soft breathing of my companions around me in the darkness.

I continued to remain still and to listen. It was all I could do in that complete darkness. Nothing. I heard no movement.

Still, I sensed something had changed; something was different, not right. The darkness felt "heavier," more oppressive, more threatening.

The horses were stamping and making deep snorts and nickers. They were nervous. They sensed something too, something threatening out in the darkness.

Then, I caught a whiff of something. A gamey smell, like the wet fur of a wild animal wafting across the night airs. I no sooner became aware of the smell and focused on it, then it was gone.

I lay very still. I tried to sense the direction of the breeze. I could not. Very carefully, I raised my hand, placing a finger in my mouth to wet it. I held my finger up in the darkness. The colder side told me there was a slight movement of air across our campsite.

We were being stalked by something. Something large enough that I could sense its odor; something stealthy enough that I could not hear its approach.

Using the tree as a support, I slowly raised myself up. Despite my efforts to remain absolutely silent, I could hear every scrape my body made against the tree and a rustle on the twigs and dead leaves as my weight bore down on them. Slowly, in a deep crouch almost on all fours, I inched my way toward where I thought the creature lurked, moving closer to my sleeping companions.

My thought was that whatever was out there, once it sensed my movement, once it understood that its human prey was awake and alert, it would retreat into the forest. My gran'pa used to tell me when we hunted together that the animals in the forest were more afraid of us than we were of them. As long as we didn't startle them, threaten their young, or give them no avenue of escape, they preferred to avoid us.

Gran'pa never encountered the creature that was stalking us that night.

I crossed our campsite. I stopped. I didn't want to stumble on my sleeping friends.

Then, the stench hit me. It seemed to surround me suddenly, embracing me out or the darkness, cutting off all the wholesome air. I was smothered by a thick, unbreathable miasma of a rotten, wet, strangely "meaty" stench which seemed to make the darkness of the moonless night darker, closer, suffocating.

I heard groaning to my left. I reached out. I felt a small body rocking back and forth. Modrona. She had wrapped herself in a tight knot, arms wrapped around her knees, head tucked tightly down against her knees and thighs. She was moaning, "*Uh cerdournos ... uh cerdournos* ... the nightwalker ... the nightwalker ...*"

Suddenly, I was pulled upwards into the night. I thought for a heartbeat I was flying ... tossed off into the darkness by an irresistible force. But my flight ended abruptly. I stopped, trapped a steal-like grasp, pressed against a wall of stinking, bristly fur. A hot, rotten, meaty stench of stinking animal-like breath washed over me. I was being crushed. My arms were trapped against my body. I could not reach my *pugio*; I could hardly feel my fingers. I expected razor teeth to rip open my throat.

Then, I fell to the ground. I heard the creature bellow in pain as it loomed over me. I felt the movement of its paw, heard a meaty impact, then a human grunt. I pulled my *pugio* from my belt. I wanted to run, but I knew my only chance of survival was to attack. I rose and lunged at the monster thrusting my knife where I thought its chest would be. I felt the blade bite thought flesh and muscle.

My knife seemed to have had no effect. The creature grabbed me again. Its embrace again forced the breath from my body. I saw lights dancing in the darkness, tiny fireflies in the night, as I began to die.

Then I was on the ground again. The creature was still looming over me, bellowing. I detected pain and even fear in its cries. I heard something from behind the deeper shadow of the monster, a wet, constant pounding, and the gasps of strained human panting.

Something massive fell next to where I lay. A smaller figure jumped on top of the massive pile, seemingly pounding it with both hands.

Then, I heard Clou's voice, "Die! Die, you rotten son of a bitch! Die!"

I rolled to my right and tried to get up. I felt a sharp, stabbing pain low across my ribs. My head spun. I almost collapsed back down on my knees. I reached out and steadied myself against a tree.

"Clou! Clou!" I gasped. "Stop! I think it's dead."

Clou reached out to my voice. Using me to steady himself, he pulled himself up off the creature. I realized he had been stabbing down on it with his longsword.

"Bear ... I think ..." he panted. "Never saw one ... attack like that ... in the night ... no reason ... pure malice ..."

Modrona's voice was still moaning in the darkness off to my left, "*Uh cerdournos ... uh cerdournos ...*"

"Where's Pruhde ..." Clou panted. "He ... he stabbed it first ... made it drop you ... thing flung him off ... over there somewhere."

The darkness was still complete. Clou and I had to get the fire going so we could see. We found Pruhde lying against a tree. His eyes were glazed; he was semi-conscious. "Wha ... wha the hell was tha' bleedin' thing," he managed to pant out.

We examined him and found, in addition to the shock of being hurled into a tree, his left shoulder was out. Clou managed to manipulate the arm back into the shoulder socket. He immobilized Pruhderos' arm by securing his forearm across his chest with his belt.

"I'll rig a sling for you when there's light to see," Clou told him. "But that shoulder's going to hurt."

Pruhderos was back with us and panted, "I've had worse. What was that thing? I had my knife in it and it tossed me away like I was a sack of feathers!"

I was trying to calm the girl. "It wasn't a monster. It was just a bear."

"It was the nightwalker," she insisted. "That smell! I remember it! It was 'im! The nightwalker!"

Clou rigged a torch with some burning faggots and examined the mountain of fur lying across our sleeping blankets. Something wasn't right. Then, Clou pulled on the fur, and it came away.

"By the balls of the Great Bear," Clou gasped.

Under the fur was a man

"The bastard's still breathing!" Pruhderos warned.

"Hold this," Clou said, handing me the torch. Then he reached down, pulled the man's head back by his hair and cut his throat with his *dagr*. Blood spilled out from the wound soaking the fur cloak the man had worn.

"Even the nightwalker couldn't survive that," Pruhderos nodded.

Clou pulled the cloak back. The man underneath was a giant, one of the Titans of Greek myth. He must have been almost seven Roman *pedes* in length, at least four hundred Roman *librae* in heft. His head was the size of an *onager* stone but covered in black matted hair and a beard. Underneath the cape, he was naked but for the thick black hair covering his entire body. Just looking at him made my crushed ribs ache.

"There's your nightwalker," Clou said, kicking the corpse.

"What now?" Pruhderos asked.

"It's still too dark to move," Clou judged. "We don't know whether whoever sent this ... this thing ... is still out there waiting to ambush us."

"You mean we're going to sit here in the dark with ... with that?" I protested.

"It's dead. It can't hurt us now," Clou said. "But I get your point.

We moved off a few paces away from the dead monster. We sat together in a close circle for the rest of the night. None of us slept.

When there was enough light to see, we were quite a sight. Clou rigged a sling for Pruhderos injured arm; he also had a long, purpling bruise between his shoulder and the middle of his back where he was slammed into the tree.

I was in agony every time I breathed. I gingerly lifted my tunic and found a deep, purple bruise under my left ribcage. Clou examined me and said he didn't think any of my ribs were broken. He guessed that one or two of my ribs might be fractured, or my pain was caused by the compression of my lower ribs and the strain on the muscles. He managed to bind me up so I could at least ride without screaming with every hoof-beat.

Clou had a black eye. He couldn't remember how it happened. Modrona's only "injury" were her red eyes and tear-stained face. She still wasn't convinced that the man we killed wasn't the nightwalker.

We walked over to our campsite to examine our "monster."

In the morning light, our "nightwalker" was still there, still in the shape of a man, and still apparently quite dead. For the first time, we noticed his tattoos, swirling patterns of half circles and arcs in blue ink on his face, down his arms, and across his chest. Neither Clou nor Pruhderos had ever seen anything quite like it.

We brought Modrona over to convince her that there was no *cerdournos* lurking in the night. Clou even had her kick the body a couple of times.

"You see, darlin'," Clou told her. "Not a monster, just a man."

I'm not sure Clou's lesson did her much good. In a way, it's better to be able to attribute evil to mythical monsters than to be forced the accept it in humans.

I estimated it was near the end of the third hour before we reached Modrona's settlement. We were riding slowly because of the beating we had just taken. I winced and hissed every time my horse planted a hoof.

Modrona's people were overjoyed to have her back. Clou explained to her father, Cardros the smith, that his daughter had been kidnapped by a madman whom we had killed. He also warned him against the black druids. He didn't share with him what we suspected was happening in the portal of the *Crugmawr*.

Cardros, like most men who make their living pounding lumps of glowing iron into useful shapes, was not a man one would choose the confront willingly. His forearms were the size of most men's thighs. Also, he was a veteran of the muster, a trained and experienced spear man. He assured Clou that, should "any of those black bastards" dare show his face at the smithy, he'd make him sorry he'd ever heard of Afalanos.

Before we left, Clou took something out of his saddlebags and presented it to Modrona. It was a small *dagr* in a leather sheath.

"Modrona," he said to here as he attached the knife to her belt. "You are soon to be a woman of the Gah'el and expected to stand in the battle line against our enemies. You are never again to allow yourself to become the helpless victim of any enemy, man or monster! This *dagr* was given to me by my father when I was about your age. Use it well; use it bravely."

I measured the rest of our journey that day by the pain that shot through my side every time my horse took a step. Pruhderos wasn't in much better shape. So, our going was slow. It was the well into the tenth hour before we approached the water gap leading back into Duuhruhda's lands. Our plan was to pass through the gap before stopping for the night.

At least, that was the plan before we heard the pounding of horses driving up the trail behind us. Travelers and merchants did not normally move with such urgency; it was soldiers. And we were the object of their urgency.

We turned our horses around to face the approaching troop. We were in no condition to flee or to fight.

It was a troop of five armed riders. As they approached, we raised our empty right hands to indicate we had no hostile intent. They pulled up some three paces before us.

The lead rider raised an empty right hand in our direction. "I am looking for a group of three warriors who were at the *Crugmawr* yesterday around midday. Are you they?"

We dropped our hands. Clou responded. "I am Catouallaunos mab Dubnogenos, called Clou by my comrades. I am a leader of a hundred, a warrior of eight seasons, and an officer in the *fintai* of Duuhruhda mab Clethguuhno, *Uucharix*, tribal king of the Aineduai, and *Pobl'rix*, clan leader of the Wuhr Blath, the Wolf clan. Whom do I have the honor of addressing."

I saw color rise in the leader's cheeks. "Forgive me, Catouallaunos mab Dubnogenos ... I forget my manners. I am Tahernos mab Malagronos, leader of ten, warrior of five seasons, an officer in the *fintai* of Malouuhnos mab Dermuhtos, clan leader of the Bear Clan and ruler of these lands. Again, I ask you, are you the men who were at the great mound yesterday afternoon?"

Then, I heard a voice from the rear of Tahernos' troop, "They're the ones! Let's get on with this, Taherne!"

Tahernos looked back toward where the voice was coming. Again, color rose on his cheeks. I saw a figure in black skulking at the rear of the column.

Tahernos turned back to Clou, "Catouallaunos mab Dubnogenos! I must ask you and your companions to accompany me back to the *dun* of Malouuhnos."

"For what reason?" Clou asked.

"To stand before the chief *barnuchel* of the province to answer charges lodged against you," Tahernos stated.

"What charges?" Clou asked.

Before Trahernos could respond, the black priest rode forward. "You desecrated the shrine of Afalanos! You stole offerings meant for the god."

I noticed the druid did not accuse us of murder; I doubted his compatriot survived the knife thrust to his abdomen.

Clou ignored the priest, "Traherne! I know of no law of the nations termed 'desecration'. Such things are for the gods to judge, not men. Also, is not your head *barnuchel* in Bibracte with your chief for the Council of Three Generations? Who has given the order for our arrest?"

Trahernos shrugged his shoulders, "I have been ordered to bring you back ..."

"By whom?" Clou again challenged. "By this black-clad, gobshite of a bent druid? Do you have any idea what these demon-worshipping frauds are doing at The Portal ..."?

"Enough of this talk!" the druid interrupted before Clou could finish. "You have your instructions, Traherne! Take them now! Gag them before they utter more blasphemies and incur the wrath of the god on you and all your men!"

Trahernos face glowed red being addressed by a druid in that manner. "I ... I have no choice in this, Clou ... either you must come with us now, bound and disarmed, or I will be forced to take you."

Bound and disarmed, I heard. We'd never make it to stand before any *barnuchel* on these trumped-up charges. We were marked for death in The Portal.

Clou understood what was in store for us, too. Better to die fighting than having your throat slit in the woods.

Before we could act, we heard more hoof beats approaching on the road. Trahernos' men turned as two riders appeared on the road behind them.

They were Gah'el. Scouts.

The lead rider raised an empty right hand. "We are part of the *fintai* of the king, Du-uhruhda mab Clethguuhno. We ride under his authority. I am Sheridos, head scout. Whom do I have the honor of addressing?"

Trahernos identified himself as did Clou. Sheridos nodded and spoke to his companion. "Go tell the chief we've encountered friendlies on the road."

As the other scout rode back down the trail, Trahernos told Sheridos, "I am arresting these men by the authority of Malouuhnos mab Dermuhtos. I ask you not interfere."

Sheridos shrugged. "That's not my call."

Then to Clou, "What the hell are you doin' this far north, Clou? I thought you'd be tucked up nice and cozy down in Bibracte with your woman."

Clou grinned, "It's a long story, Sheride! But not one for these ears."

Sheridos nodded, then said, "I hate to piss on your cooking fire, Traherne! But this here's the king's man. I doubt he'll be going anywhere with you."

Three more riders approached from the rear. I recognized two of them as Roman cavalry in mufti. It was one of Labienus' recon parties. The leader spoke, "What the hell's the hold up, Sheride? If they're friendlies, just nod and wave as we pass. We have to get back to Bibracte!"

"As do we, *decurio*," I addressed the leader in Gah'el. "We have vital information for the *legad uh Rhufeinai*, Troucillos."

I saw the man's eyes widen. "You are Troucillus' man?" he asked me in Latin.

"*Comes Caesaris sum*," I answered. "I'm a companion of Caesar and a *decurio* in his praetorian cavalry. But my information is for Troucillus *Legatus*. And it is vital!"

The man nodded, then said in Gah'el. "These men are coming with us to Bibracte. Any problem with that?"

No one spoke. Trahernos looked relieved and shrugged. The black druid scowled.

"One other thing, *decurio*," I said to the Roman commander in Latin. "Bind and gag that priest. The legate will want to talk to him."

XI

Caput XI. De Adventu Strigis
Chapter 11. The Vampire Appears

Two days later, I was laid up in Troucillus' house nursing my bruised ribs. I was set up on a couch near the central fire while Troucillus attended the reconvening of the Council of Three Generations.

We had arrived back at Bibracte late in the afternoon of the day before. We travelled too slowly for the Roman cavalry but much too quickly for my aching ribs. By the time I finally reached Troucillus' house, my face was white as a candidate's toga.

As we approached Bibracte, I noticed that Strabo had torn down his roadblock and withdrawn his troops back into their camp. I wondered briefly if Troucillus had anything to do with explaining to a veteran Roman centurion the importance of not ruffling the feathers of "friendly wogs," forcibly enough to get said centurion to countermand his own orders.

This new spirit of Roman-Gallic detente almost broke down over an argument about what to do with our prisoner. The Roman commander, a *decurio* who went by the moniker, "Capillus" – "Shaggy" – obviously because of his thick, bushy main, insisted on delivering the druid to Labienus down in the main Roman camp south of the town. Clou wanted the man delivered to Druce mab Cadmanos, the king's spymaster. Since we were significantly outnumbered by Capillus' boys, there was no way we were going to win the argument. We settled it by agreeing that the priest be delivered to Labienus, but Troucillus could participate in the interrogation, if he chose, and share the information with Druce.

Personally, I doubted we'd get any useful information out of that gobshite priest other than rantings about Afalanos' coming at the *Samon'win* to lead the Dark Ones to reconquer the middle lands. All foreigners and heretics would be destroyed! Gibberish we had already heard.

Labienus might see this as evidence of a military threat in the north.

Troucillus needed to understand how this perverted cult affected the stability of Duuhruhda's regime and Caesar's alliance with the Aedui.

The Romans bypassed the town riding south with their prisoner. Clou, Pruhderos, and I entered Bibracte through the northern gate. We soon parted company; they continued south to the king's stronghold, and I rode east to Troucillus' residence. As soon as Troucillus laid eyes on me, he put me to bed with a cup of *mulsus*, warm honeyed wine, and sent a runner down to the *castrum* to fetch Spina.

While we waited for the doctor, Troucillus debriefed me on my mission.

"You're telling me these madmen are sacrificing children to this god of theirs?" Troucillus pressed me.

I wasn't sure whether his question was rhetorical, so I answered, "We didn't actually witness it, but the evidence of the altar in The Portal and the tales we heard indicate it as a reasonable conclusion."

Troucillus shook his head, "And the people up there allow this?"

Again, not sure of Troucillus' intent. "Not all ... I wouldn't envy the next druid who shows up at Cardros' smithy. My guess is they were using the people's fear of the night-walker to cover what they were doing ..."

"Are the troops reliable?" Troucillus interrupted.

I shrugged and immediately regretted it. "Depends what you mean by 'reliable' ... the bunch that tried to arrest us were acting on orders from the priests, but their officer didn't seem too happy about it. How much control Malouuhnos has or will have once he goes back north is anyone's guess ..."

"That's the critical question," Troucillus again interposed. "Malouuhnos is like the boy who thinks he's captured a lion because he has hold of its tail. He may think that he is using this Afalanos nonsense to control political events in Bibracte ... perhaps seize the throne for himself now that Cuhnetha is out of the picture. The black druids may have an altogether different plan. If the people in the north are more afraid of the priests than they are loyal to their chief, Malouuhnos may have quite a surprise in store for himself once he returns to his holdings."

An attendant entered the room and announced the arrival of the Roman doctor. Troucillus dismissed the man. He patted my shoulder, "Get some rest, Gai. I must see Druce and the king. We'll talk when I get back."

A few heartbeats after Troucillus left, Spina entered followed by one of his medics carrying a large *capsa*, a box containing medical supplies. Spina already had a winecup in his hand.

"*Bene*, Insubrece, you got yer own," he said noticing my winecup on the table next to my coach. "Now I don't have ta shayah."

I assumed "shayah" was Spina's Aventine Latin for "share."

Spina put his cup next to mine and continued," "Let's see what we got heah ... wheah's da pain?"

"My ribs," I told him. "Mostly on my lower right side ..."

"*Bene*," Spina nodded, "Let's take a look ... can ya stand up?"

I nodded but I needed the medic's assistance to get to my feet. I unfastened my trousers and pulled the tail of my tunic up to expose my side.

Spina bent forward to look. Then, he ordered his medic to bring a lamp over. He whistled and said, "You got mowah colah down heah than a wall painting in a brothel... dat hoit?"

I groaned as Spina pressed my ribs, "*Cac't*! Yeah! That *hoits*! What'd you think!"

"*Bene!*" Spina chuckled. "You can put ya shirt down ... help dee officah back onto da couch," to his assistant.

Once I got settled as best I could, Spina took a swig of his wine. "Don't t'ink anyt'ing's broke ... ya may have cracked a rib aw two, aw ya might have just a bad bruise ... looks like somethin' displaced ya lowah ribs ... dey aint' attached to ya breast bone so dey'll move if ya press 'em hard enough ... ain't pleasant ... see a lot a dis 'specially when guys take a fall offa hawse or take a blow in da side from somet'in' blunt like a centurion's cudgel... good news is you'll be fine ... bad news is it'll hurt woise den a crucifixion for a few days ... can't do anyt'in' for ya, it'll heal itself ... just try to take it easy for a few days."

I nodded as the pain of having to move around and Spina's examination began to subside.

Spina rummaged through the *capsa* finally extracting a small bottle. "Dis is to help ya sleep," he said uncapping the bottle. The cap had a glass stem which was submerged in the bottle. Spina let a drop of brownish-liquid drop from the stem into my wine then mixed the concoction with the stem.

"*Papaver somniferum*," he said. "*Opion* da Greeks call it ... juice a de'eastan poppy ... one a drop ... you'll sleep like a baby ... t'ree drops, you'll nevah wake up." He recapped the bottle. "I wouldn't drink dat stuff till yer ready to go ta sleep ... I'll be back aftah sick parade in dah mawnin' to check on yas."

I lifted my wine cup and sniffed.

"One utter t'ing, ..." Spina started.

"What's that?" I said putting down the cup.

"You don't wanna sneeze ... dat'll kill ya!"

I decided to put off my date with Somnium, the god of dreams, until Troucillus returned from his meeting.

I was pretty sure that Spina's remark about a sneeze killing me was just part of his caustic bedside manner, but I wish he hadn't said it. Now, that I was focused on not sneezing, not sneezing was a problem. Twice, I felt a sneeze coming on but was able to suppress it by holding my nose and breathing through my mouth. The second one caused a slight convulsion in my upper abdomen which made me see stars.

Troucillus got back just before dark. I must have dozed a bit, because one instant I was alone trying not to sneeze and the next Troucillus was standing over me.

"Back in the world of the living, I see," Troucillus chuckled.

His sudden appearance startled me a bit, but a sudden stabbing pain in my side made me settle down. "Uh ... yeah ... Spina was here ... how'd your meeting go?"

Troucillus shrugged, "Morcant has returned from burying his father and is ready to take his place as the head of his clan ..."

"Have he and Duuhruhda found common ground against Malouuhnos?" I interrupted.

Troucillus shook his head, "No ... if anything they're further apart. Duuhruhda despite the urging of both Druce and myself refuses to reach out to him ... it's not at all clear what Malouuhnos's play will be now that Cuhnetha is dead. Perhaps he'll nominate Morcant for the throne in place of his father. That may be what Morcant is waiting to see ... I don't know."

"Could that sway the council in Malouuhnos' favor?" I asked.

"Malouuhnos still seems to have Bruhchamos' clan behind him and Karadogos still supports the king and the Roman alliance," Troucillus mused. "So, theoretically Morcant can sway the balance in either the King's or Malouuhnos' favor. We think if Morcant comes in on Duuhruhda's side, that will decide the issue ... Morcant's clan may be too weak to overthrow the king, unless Malouuhnos were to propose restoring the throne to Morcant ... we just have to wait and see ... I'd intervene with Morcant myself but Druce thinks that would smack of Roman interference in the selection and could actually play out in Malouuhnos' favor ... so ... we wait. But that's not the worst of it."

"The worst of it?" I repeated.

Troucillus nodded. "Yes ... Malouuhnos' creature, this so-called Gourach merc Fetroda, 'Witch, daughter of the Tomb', has taken up residence at the fount of the *Maru Rignai*, the Phantom Queen. She's babbling her nonsense about the Washer Woman and the wrath of Catubodua if the king is not overthrown. Now, Malouuhnos' black druid is saying that this Catubodua is a precursor of Afalanos, the vengeful god of the north who will purge the land of foreigners and heretics. If the people do not heed the words of Catubodua, overthrow Duuhruhda, and cast out the invaders, Afalanos will destroy them as he will destroy all unbelievers."

"Do the people believe this gibberish?" I asked.

Again, Troucillus shrugged, "Some ... not many ... Duuhruhda has brought prosperity to Bibracte ... the people feel safe ... they're well-fed ... content. There are some who do not like the sight of Romans camped outside their town. This Catubodua noise is feeding their discontent and becomes another dynamic affecting the deliberations of the council. By itself, it's merely a nuisance. I doubt it can materially change the balance of the forces vying for the throne. As long as it stays under control ... as long as nothing else happens to convince the people that the gods have turned against Duuhruhda and his alliance with Caesar."

Troucillus sat silently for a few heartbeats, then took a deep breath. "Well, my friend, there is nothing we can do about any of this tonight. Why don't you get some rest. I think I'm going to need your help the next few days."

Troucillus' addressing me as *"mi amice,"* "my friend," was a significant indication how he viewed our relationship. To this point, I considered myself somehow subordinate to him by age, experience and by our relationship to Caesar. However, in Roman culture, *amicitia*, friendship, could only exist between equals.

The Roman concept of *clientela*, patronage, best described my relationship with Caesar. This relationship was strictly hierarchical, with Caesar, the *patronus*, in the superior position to me, the *cliens*. The patron always held greater power and prestige than his clients, whose interests he was expected to protect and advance. In turn, the clients owed their patron complete loyalty and service.

Certainly, one of the issues that Troucillus had to skirt around was the fact that, in many ways, as the Aedui became allies of Rome, their king, Duuhruhda, also assumed the role of client to Caesar.

Amicitia, friendship, on the other hand, was a relationship between equals. Like *clientela*, it could exist only between free men. However, the *pietas* between friends, the sense of loyalty and service, was given out of *caritas*, affection, not *officium*, obligation.

It could be said that, whereas *clientela* describes a "parent-child" relationship between patron and client, *amicitia* is an ideal brotherhood between equals.

As I write this, I realize that I am most fortunate having Rhonwen as my wife and having our children with us, healthy, content, and safe. But my life has also been enriched by my friends - Macro, Spina, and even Dion when he is not playing the Greek philosopher. I have not seen Troucillus in many years. After the wars, Octavius sent him out to Aegyptus to manage Roman - that is Octavius' - interests there. I imagine the Macedonian would spin in her tomb at the thought of a Romanized Gaul ruling her empire.

Troucillus bade me good night and one of his retainers came in to stoke the fire so I would be warm through the late fall evening. Although I had little pain when I lay still, I was worried that I would not be able to fall asleep after having awoken from my late afternoon nap.

Then I remembered Spina's concoction.

I picked up my wine cup and sniffed. It smelled like *mulsus*, honeyed wine, but there was a furtive odor of something bitter. I stilled the wine around with my finger and sniffed again.

Then, I took a sip. Yes, there was something lurking under the taste of the *mulsus*. I waited a few heartbeats, but nothing happened. I literally shrugged and took a deeper drink.

That's the last thing I remember.

A black wave washed over me, and I tumbled down into complete darkness.

I seem to have struggled back to consciousness sometime during the night. I remember listening, but hearing nothing out of the ordinary, just the normal sounds of the autumn winds rustling through the thatch and whistling across the smoke hole in the roof. I'm not sure I even opened my eyes. I felt warm and safe, and curiously free of pain. I plunged back down into the stygian depths of blissful unconsciousness.

I became vaguely aware of the sounds of human activity around me; then, a reddish glow of light through my closed eyelids. I blinked my eyes a few times then opened them. It was morning. Troucillus' retainers were tiptoeing around me, trying to perform their morning duties without disturbing me. I stretched a bit but stopped when I felt a pang in my side. I tested my ability to move again. The pain was still there in my side but seemed less than it had been.

I looked over and saw that my wine cup was gone. I hope no one had sampled it. Spina's brew had been more powerful than I had anticipated. But it seemed to have done the trick.

"*Quot'orarum?*" I croaked. "What hour?"

Someone answered, "Still the first."

I nodded and pulled myself up into a sitting position. Carefully! My side still ached, and I didn't feel like testing it.

Someone dropped a basket of rolls on the table next to my couch, then a cup of wine, *bene mixtum*, mostly water. I took a long drink to wash away the dryness in my mouth and throat.

"*Ub'est Troucillus?*" I asked. "Where's Troucillus?"

"The boss is already out and about," one of Troucillus' minders from the legion told me, a Cisalpine Gaul called Pugnus, "Knuckles."

"He didn't go out alone, did he?" I asked.

"Nah! Not a chance!" Pugnus said. "A couple a the boys and our *decanus* went out with him. Anything happens to the boss and our arses are tall weeds in the defensive ditch and our centurion will chop them fine."

I nodded and took another drink of the wine. I was just starting on the rolls when Pugnus came back into the room.

"*Decurio*, there's a lady here to see you," he announced.

The "lady" burst into the room behind Pugnus and was by him before he could re-act.

Rhonwen.

Pugnus made to grab for her, but I said, "*Es' bene, Pugne*! It's OK, Pugnus!"

Then I remembered that all three of us spoke Gah'el, so I switched to that language. "The lady Rhonwen is a ... is a friend."

Pugnus nodded and retreated. But, Rhonwen shot back, "A *friend* is it! Is that all I am to you, Arth mab Secundos?"

I felt my face begin to glow. Then, I realized Rhonwen was teasing me. My face glowed redder.

I noticed that Rhonwen was carrying two sealed clay pitchers. Rhonwen followed my eyes and explained, "I heard you were injured, so a brought you some healing foods."

She placed the first pitcher on my table. "Red mead," she announced. Then the second pitcher, "Chicken soup!"

I nodded. "Pugne! Can I have a couple of cups! And a ... uh ..."

"Drinking bowl," Rhonwen coached.

"... and a drinking bowl!" I finished.

One of Troucillus attendants brought in the cups and bowl and placed them on my table while Rhonwen unplugged the pitchers. She poured each of us a healthy dollop of the mead.

She picked up one of the cups and sniffed. "This'll put some fire in your belly," she said and drank.

I imitated her. She was right. The mead warmed me all the way down to my October-chilled toes.

"Nothing like some red mead on a chilly morning," she said opening her second pitcher. She poured the contents into the drinking bowl, a steaming, golden-yellow liquid with a strong aroma of cooked chicken.

She handed me the bowl. "Drink this down, Arth … good for what ails you."

I sniffed the liquid, then barely wet my lips. I tasted delicious.

"Drink it down," Rhonwen urged. "You don't think I'd waste a good broth just to poison *you*, do you?"

Our eyes met, and I could see the gleam of playful teasing in hers. I drank my soup as ordered. Strangely, it did make me feel stronger.

"So, I hear you were hurt defeating a monster in the northern forests," Rhonwen teased. "The nightwalker itself, I've been told."

I put my bowl down, shaking my head. "No … it was a man … a very large man in a bear skin … and I didn't kill him … someone else did."

Rhonwen's eyebrows went up. "A man, eh? He must have been a giant to crush your ribs like that! So, you killed a giant, then!"

I suspected she was still teasing me. "No … someone else killed him … an Aineduai in the king's service named Catouallaunos mab Dubnogenos …"

"Ah!" Rhonwen interrupted. "One of Druce mab Cadmanos' people."

Rhonwen detected the surprise on my face.

She laughed. "You don't think for a moment that my cousin would walk into Bibracte without knowing who all the players are, do you? Have some more broth." She refilled my bowl.

As I drank, Rhonwen continued, "My visit to you is not simply to bring you soup. My cousin knows you are a friend of Troucillos and Troucillos is an agent of the Caisar. So, I am here in what the *Rhufeinai* call a 'back-road approach'. Did I get that right?"

"Close enough," I agreed putting down my soup bowl.

Rhonwen nodded. "My cousin is willing to cooperate with Troucillos' plan and accept the role of Duuhruhda's *pendefig*, but he has two conditions."

"And they are?" I asked.

"First, Duuhruhda is to restore to us all our traditional clan holdings as they were when my grandfather, Cluhweluhno, was *uucharix* of the Aineduai," Rhonwen stated.

I nodded. This was essentially Troucillus' plan.

Rhonwen continued. "The second is he wants the Caisar's word that he will respect and preserve the nation. Morcant will support the nation's alliance with the *Rhufeinai* as a friend and ally, I think it's called. The Caisar will allow the Aineduai to rule themselves without taxation, tribute, or occupation by the legions. Can Troucillos make such a promise?"

Again, I nodded but said, "Only Troucillos can speak to that. But it sounds consistent with the Caisar's wishes."

Rhonwen seemed to accept my somewhat weaselly answer. She continued, "Morcant offers something as a token of his goodwill."

I nodded then thought I realized why Morcant had sent Rhonwen to approach *me* with this proposal. Again, my face caught fire.

Rhonwen immediately understood my reaction. "Don't be daft, Arth. I'm a free woman of the Gah'el, not a piece of *Rhufeinig* marriage chattel! I cannot be offered as a peace-weaver without my own consent. What my cousin offers is Deluuhnu mab Clethguuhno."

"Deluuhnu mab Clethguuhno!" I repeated. "The king's brother? The outlaw? He fled north to the Bolgai, the Belgians"

"The same!" Rhonwen agreed. "My cousin has had word of him, and that word is he is no longer among the Bolgai."

"How did Morcant receive intelligence about Deluuhnu" I challenged.

"From an unexpected source," Rhonwen stated, "But one that is reliable. Your mate, Athauhnu mab Hergest."

"Athauhnu!" I repeated. "Since when are the Soucanai trading information with the Aineduai?"

Rhonwen rolled her eyes. "This is going to take all day if you keep challenging everything I tell you! Now listen! Athauhnu's lands are in the north. He is more concerned with the Bolgai than he is with the Aineduai."

I nodded, accepting her explanation.

"Have you ever heard of Belimawros Golba? She asked.

Belimor the Fat, I thought.

"No," I answered.

"No reason why you should," Rhonwen continued. "Golba is what the Bolgai call an *oberkunig*; he rules a coalition of tribes both in *goulag Bolg*, the lands of the Belgians, and in *goulag Pruhdain*, Britain. Golba is well aware of the Caisar's ambition to move north against him in the spring. His plan is to disrupt the Caisar's supply lines by destroying the Caisar's alliance with the Aineduai *before* he can move against his confederation among the Bolgai."

"How can Morcant possibly know this," I challenged.

"Not only has the Caisar's campaign against the Almaenwuhr brought my cousin close to your friend, Athauhnu, but he has contacts among the Parisai, who have never been friends of the Bolgai," Rhonwen stated. "Now, may I continue?"

I nodded.

"Good!" Rhonwen said. "My cousin believes that Golba is behind this Afalanos scheme ... that he has brought these black druids down here from his holdings in *Pruhdain* to undermine Duuhruhda's rule and his alliance with the *Rhufeinai*. But, when my uncle, Cuhnetha, died suddenly, Golba realized that he needed another credible candidate for the throne of the Aineduai ... Malouuhnos wouldn't do except as *pendefig*. So, he dispatched the king's brother, Deluuhnu ..."

"But, Deluuhnu has been outlawed!" I objected.

"Outlawed! By whom?" Rhonwen countered. "The Caisar? The Caisar's mandate has no standing in the nation. Deluuhnu has never been charged with a crime! He has never stood before a barnuchel in council! Many of the people are sympathetic to what they consider his unjust exile at the behest of the Caisar. There are even those among the Duuhruhda's own *fintai* who would gladly support Deluuhnu against the king! They see Deluuhnu's exile as unjustified Rhufeinig interference in the affairs of the nation and Duuhruhda has allowed himself to become the Caisar's puppet!"

I nodded seeing her point.

"The Parisai report a large armed party moving south from the lands of the Bolgai," Rhonwen continued, "Much too late in the season for a sustained campaign or even a major raid. My cousin believes it is Deluuhnu moving south the join Malouuhnos. If Malouuhnos cannot get the council to declare Deluuhnu king, he will stage a coup and seize the throne or at least set up a rival king in the north."

"Either way, Labienus would feel forced to intervene with the legions," I mused.

"Exactly!" Rhonwen agreed. "If the Rhufeinai are fighting the Aineduai in the south, they cannot move against the Bolgai ... that is the essence of Golba's plan ... but there's more."

"What more can there be?" I asked, my head spinning.

"My cousin's contacts among the Parisai say that their nation has been approached with silver by agents of the Rhufeinai to ally themselves with Deluuhnu against the Caisar. They have no doubt that these agents are also active among the tribes bordering our lands to the north and west."

I had no doubt that, if large amounts of silver were changing hands, Metius was right in the middle of it.

Rhonwen was talking, "My cousin doesn't believe that Golba's plot and Deluuhnu's bid for the throne are in the best interest of the nation. So, he is willing to cooperate with the Caisar as long as his two conditions are met."

I nodded. "And you want me to deliver this message to Troucillos."

Rhonwen nodded. "Yes. Morcant feels it's better that way. He does not wish to appear too complicit with the Rhufeinai."

Again, I nodded.

"And one more thing," Rhonwen offered rising from her chair.

I looked up at her.

"If ever I offer myself to you, it will be of my own choosing and not part of some political deal."

She leaned down and kissed me on the side of my mouth. My face caught fire.

"Finish your soup!" she ordered on her way out.

Troucillus returned from the council during the ninth hour in a black mood.

"*Stulti*!" he almost shouted, "Idiots! They'd rather oppose each other and let Mal-ouuhnos take the throne."

"Morcant and Duuhruhda"" I offered.

"*Exacte*!" Troucillus spat. "Right! Both offered themselves as *uucharix* with some complete non-entity as *pendefig*! Duuhruhda's candidate hasn't changed, and Morcant nominated some maternal uncle of his who must be close the forty! But the real surprise was Malouuhnos ..."

"He nominated the king's brother, Deluuhnu mab Clethguuhno, with himself as *pendefig*?" I offered.

That stopped Troucillus in his tracks. "Yes ... but, how did you know?"

"Rhonwen came by earlier with a message from her cousin," I told him.

"That explains why she wasn't with Morcant at the council," he nodded.

"How did the council react to Deluuhnu's nomination?" I asked.

Troucillus was silent for a heartbeat, then said, "I thought Duuhruhda, the king, was going to have a seizure ... he went gray in the face and seemed to have trouble breathing. Of course, I couldn't say anything, but Anionos, the king's barnuchel, questioned Deluuhnu's eligibility. Malouuhnos answered Anionos' objection by ask-ing for what crime against the nation had Deluuhnu been exiled and what barnuchel had decided his guilt. Of course, there was no answer for that ... then that black druid of Malouuhnos started yammering about Afalanos favoring Deluuhnu and how he would expel the foreigners from the lands of the free nations ... made him up to be a *vercingetorix* ... a national champion. After that, all order broke down. Anionos called an end to the session supposedly to consider Deluuhnu's status ... but I see no alterna-tive there. Deluuhnu's only crime is opposing Caesar and *that* is an endorsement for his ascending the throne according to Malouuhnos and his crazed priest."

Troucillus was again silent for a heartbeat, then asked, "What else did Rhonwen have to say?"

I told him ... Morcant's willingness to make a deal with Duuhruhda ... his two con-ditions ... Rhonwen's report of Belgian involvement in the scheme to place the king's brother on the throne, the possibility of Deluuhnu's incursion in the north, and Ro-man agents stirring up the northern tribes.

Troucillus' face turned red. "How stupid of me! Druce! I trusted that snake! He must have known about Deluuhnu's plot! In fact, he knew this when we met with him before we sent our patrols north! He played the oldest trick in the book on us. We told him we were hunting for a rabid boar. But he told us all we'd find were tran-quil, harmless sows So, that's what we saw ... exactly what we were told we'd see. When Deluuhnu sweeps down from the north, he'll pick up those seemingly harmless border assemblies of Malouuhnos and Bruhchamos. By the time he approaches Bibracte, he'll have a small army at his back. Those troops were exactly what we suspected all along, but I let Druce convince me otherwise."

"Druce betrayed us?" I asked.

Troucillus shook his head. "Druce's loyalties are to himself, his family, his clan, and his tribe, not to Caesar. He may have decided that his nephew Duuhruhda is too weak to hold the throne ... that he has become a pawn of Caesar and the Aedui will be swallowed up by Rome ... or ..."

"Or what?" I prompted.

"... he's playing a very clever game of *latrunculi*," Troucillus mused. "He wants each side to see him as an ally. That way, whichever brother wins, Druce wins."

"What can we do?" I asked.

"Act quickly and decidedly!" Troucillus answered. "I will send word to Labienus. We need eyes and ears back in the north, and the legions need to be put on alert. Druce's trick has cost us almost a market cycle in preparing our forces. Then, we inform Morcant that we will support his two demands. Once I tell Duuhruhda of his brother's plot, I believe he'll cooperate with us. As far as Caesar goes ... well ... this is consistent with his instructions to keep his alliance with the Aedui intact ... what is it that Caesar is fond of saying ... *Fortuna audaces iuvat* ... "Fortune favors the bold"? I'll send him a message telling him *what we have done*. At worst, it supports his belief that the Belgae are actively working against us."

Pugnus burst into the room, "Legate! There's a messenger here from Labienus *Legatus*! The man says it's urgent"

"Send him in," Troucillus granted.

A member of the praetorian guard in full kit and purple sashes marched into the room. He assumed the position of attention in front of us. "I have a message for Troucillus *Legatus* from Labienus *Legatus*," he announced in a parade-ground voice.

"*Troucillus Legatus egome*'," Troucillus nodded. "I am Legate Troucillus. But lower your voice, praetorian. In Bibracte, even the statues listen."

The man nodded. "Labienus *Legatus* requests your immediate presence at the northern camp. legate!"

"*Pro qua*?" Troucillus asked. "Why?"

The praetorian was not used to the demands of his legate being questioned. He hesitated for a heartbeat, then he remembered that it was a legate asking the question. He said almost in a whisper. "A body has been found in the woods outside the northern camp, legate."

"A body," Troucillus repeated. "Why would that be of any interest to me?"

"It's one of us ... a Roman soldier!" the praetorian insisted. "He's been killed by the *stryx*!"

When we arrived at the northern camp, we immediately saw a gaggle of Roman soldiers standing along the road below the main gate. Roman soldiers typically do not "gaggle" during the duty day; so, whatever had happened here was significant enough to cause discipline to slip.

We saw a line of horses being shepherded by a group of praetorians. Labienus was already here. They directed us into the woods west of the camp. There was a well beaten trail to follow, and we quickly found our second Roman gaggle of the afternoon. This one had more prestige, however, since it was being overseen by Labienus himself.

"Ah! Troucille! Insubrece! You got here quickly ... *bene,*" he greeted us. "Bad situation ... terrible ... one of our soldiers murdered ..."

"Murdered?" Troucillus responded. "You think one of the Aedui did it?"

"Who else?" Labienus shrugged. "Some isolated act, I imagine ... sneaking around outside the camp ... looking for something to steal or weaknesses in the defenses."

Troucillus drew close to Labienus. "The man you sent to fetch us said the *stryx* did it."

"The *stryx!*" Labienus shook his head. "The stryx is a myth ... a fairy tale to scare children ... no! This man was murdered by another human being ... a Gaul."

"Why a Gaul and not a Roman?" I interrupted.

Instead of being reprimanded for interrupting my superior, Labienus answered the question. "The way he was killed ... not clean like a Roman would do it. His throat was ripped open as if an animal attacked him. No ... no Roman would kill like this ... it's *inromanitas* ... barbaric!"

"Why did you ask us here"? asked Troucillus.

"Why?" Labienus responded. "Oh ... two reasons. First, you are Caesar's liaison with the wogs here ... I need you to deliver a message from me to their king. I want the murderer found and, when he is, I'm going to crucify him on the road junction below this camp. None of this Gallic 'pay a fine' business. I'm going to string his arse up on a pole for everyone to see what happens when a Roman soldier is attacked. And second, I understand you're a good ... uh ... good tracker. I'd like you to look at the scene and see if you can find any indication how this happened."

"But no *stryx,*" I asked.

"*Landica Veneris*! No!" Labienus almost shuttered. "You know how superstitious these *muli* can be! If they thought the *stryx* was roaming about in these woods, they'd be too frightened to stick their noses out of their squad tents all winter!"

I didn't think it my job to inform Labienus that that particular weasel was already out of the bag.

Troucillus nodded to me, and I followed him farther along the trail. After a few paces, we found another gaggle of *muli,* this one clustered around Strabo, the commanding centurion of the cohort stationed in the camp.

When Strabo saw me, he shouted, "No bloody wogs up here! Who allowed this damned ..."

Then he recognized me. "Pagane? That *is* you! I damn near didn't recognize you! What's going on? You lose your shaving razor?"

"I'm on detached duty, *centurio,*" I began to explain, "Assigned to the legate, here..."

Then Strabo spotted Troucillus and his purple strip. He stiffened to attention. "*Legate*! Forgive me ... I didn't see you ... I thought I was dealing with a new Gallic invasion with Pagane ... I mean, Insubrecus here! *Cossus Lollius Strabo, Centurio Prior, centuria una, cohors octo, legio decem ...*"

Troucillus held up his hand, "Centurion! Don't worry about a mouse when a bear is loose ... show me the body, please."

"Follow me, legate," Strabo said and led us farther along the trail.

We soon came to the putative crime scene.

My first impression was a man in a military tunic lying on the ground like a fallen statue. But, unlike a statue, there was little color to him except for his mud-red tunic and black hair. His face was the whitish green of the recently dead without the rouged cheeks and lips of a marble god. His eyes, almost black in the dapple shade of the woods, stared sightlessly toward the heavens from under their half-closed lids. His arms, covered by long, winter sleeves, stretched out along his side as if he were on parade. His *bracae*, brown leather trousers, ended mid-calf. His *caligae*, military boots, were missing. His feet, white as if carved from ivory, pointed toes up toward the treetops.

There was a man, a *medicus*, bent over the body. He was examining a large, ragged wound, a black and red jagged chasm that seemed to stretch ear to ear from the man's chin to his collar bone.

I realized it was Spina.

Strabo's voice brought me out of my contemplation, "*Optio*! *Nuntia*! Report!"

Tullius, Strabo's number one, separated himself from Spina and, tipped off by the tone of Strabo's command, assumed the position of attention in front of us. Despite that, I could swear he gave me the wink.

He correctly spotted Troucillus' stripe and started his report, "*Tribune*! Tullius Norbanus, *optio* ..."

"'*Legate*'," Strabo coached.

Tullius eyes widened a bit, his cheeks reddened, "*Legate*! Tullius Norbanus, *optio, centuria una* ..."

Troucillus held up his hand, "Forget the pedigree, *optio*. Just tell me what's happening."

Tullius nodded. "Legate! The IBO is ..."

"Ee Bay Oh?" Troucillus interrupted.

"*In Bello Occisus*," Strabo explained. "Killed in Action. Continue, Tulli!"

Tullius nodded. "The IBO is Titus Rutilius, soldier, tent-squad three, century four, cohort ..."

Again, Troucillus interrupted. "Just tell me how he got out here into these woods, please, *optio*."

Tullius glanced over to Strabo, who nodded. "Rutilius, or Rufus, "Red," as he's called by his mates, was assigned to the SA last night ..."

"Es Ah?" Troucillus asked.

"'*Statio ad Auscultandum* ... a Listening Post'," Strabo explained. Every night just after dark, we put a screening force out beyond the camp parapet to detect enemy approach and give the camp early warning. It's called a 'listening post' because the men will hear the enemy approaching in the dark, not see them. Continue, Tulli."

Tullius nodded. "Rufus was standing watch with his *geminus*, his battle-mate, a trooper called Lupus. Sometime during the night, he went off to take a leak and never came back. Lupus thought he got lost and would make it back to camp when the SA ... I mean the Listening Post ... came back in at dawn. But no Rufus. So, as soon as it was light enough, we sent out a search party ... Rufus wasn't the kind to desert ... he's a second enlistment man ... a *vet'ranus* ... we found him here, as you can see."

Troucillus glanced over at the body, "You strip his lorica?" he asked.

Tullius shook his head, "The SA go out as *velites* ... no armor, so they can get back here fast ... it's not their job to tangle with the enemy ... just get back here and warn the camp ... his belt, sword, and boots are missing, though."

"See!" Strabo stated. "The *stryx* doesn't need a Roman sword, but it's a great prize for some thieving wog ..."

I bent into Tullius, "Tulli, when you get a chance, tell Strabo that the legate's a "wog" ... he's a member of the Helvi tribe south of here, but he's a favored client of Caesar."

Again, Tullius' eyes widened a bit.

Strabo was saved further embarrassment when Spina joined us. He looked at me and asked, "So? How da ribs doin'? Much pain?"

"Only when I breathe, doc!" I said.

"*Bene*! Don't breathe, then!"

Then, Spina noticed Troucillus. "Ah! Troucille ..." he started. Then, he noticed Strabo and Tullius standing straight as two wooden training stakes and realized the meeting was "formal."

"*Legate*!" Spina corrected himself. "I assume you've come up heah to see da body?"

"Yes, I have! Please show me what we have, *medice*!" Troucillus answered, then nodded to Tullius, "*Multas gratias*! Thank you, optio."

"Follow me," Spina invited walking back toward the body.

As we walked away, I saw Tullius deliver my message to Strabo. The centurion's face turned bright red.

I rejoined Troucillus and Spina over the dead man. "What do you think, Spina?" Troucillus was asking.

"Whadda I t'ink," Spina quipped. "I t'ink da guy's dead."

Troucillus ignored Spina's sarcasm. "What did this? An animal."

"Not unless da critters up heah smack deah victims ovah da head, gag 'em, and tie 'em up before dey kill 'em." Spina said.

Spina squatted down next to the body and lifted one of it's arms. I noticed the arm was stiff, so stiff that the body shifted when the doctor lifted it.

"See heah on da wrist," Spina was saying. "Dat's a ligature mahk ... deah's one on dee udder wrist and on both ankles ... dis guy was tied up while he was still alive."

"Mahk?" repeated Troucillus. "Oh ... 'mark' ... yes, please go on, Spina."

Spina nodded. "You can see how stiff da guy is ... in dis wedder I'd say he's been dead at least twelve hours, give a take. He's got a bump on his head da size of a goose egg. Dat means he got clobbered before he got killed. I found fibahs in da guy's mout' meaning he was gagged ... whoevah it was probably used dis guy's *sudarium*, his scahf, on 'im ..."

Spina paused while Troucillus and I made sense of "fibahs," "mout'," and "scahf" - fibers, mouth and scarf. Then, he continued, "... but heah's da t'ing ... deah ain't a drop a blood left in dis guy, but deah ain't no blood heah ..."

"So, he was killed someplace else," Troucillus finished the thought.

"Yeah, unless the *stryx* drank it all," Spina snickered.

Then, Spina continued. "Look at dis wound in 'is neck. It looks like a mangled mess, like some frenzied animal tore 'is t'roat apaht. But if ya look real close at dee edges, dere smooth ..."

"Which means?" Troucillus prompted.

"Which means dis guys t'roat was cut wit' a knife ... a shawp one wit' a smooth edge by da look o' it," Spina explained. "Den, da wound was mangled to make it look like somethin' else."

"So, murdered by men, not monsters," Troucillus concluded.

"Yeah," Spina agreed. "At least twelve hours ago ... somewheah else ... not heah."

Troucillus nodded his thanks to Spina. He pulled my sleeve and we moved off to the side.

"So ... two immediate questions," Troucillus mused, "The first ... how'd the body get to its present position? And second, how'd it get there without being detected by a picket line of Roman soldiers?"

I shrugged. "The second is easy ... they were asleep."

Troucillus nodded. "That would be the most likely solution ... makes more sense than his being transported there by a supernatural, blood-sucking, she-owl ... we need to speak to this ... uh ... this ..."

"*Geminus*" I suggested. "His 'battle-mate'?"

"Yes ... yes ... his 'battle-mate', Troucillus agreed. "But where did the body come from ... we figure that out and we find where he was murdered."

Troucillus led me back to where the body lay. He positioned himself near the feet and squat down. He motioned me down next to him.

"Gai?" he asked. "Do you remember what I said to you when we found the body of that Aeduan trooper on our way to confront Ariovistus?"

I thought for a few heartbeats. So much had happened since then that I had almost forgotten about the murder of Teguhd, Rhonwen's erstwhile "fiancé," by Metius' enforcer, Bulla.

Then, I remember, "To a hunter, no animal can pass through a place without leaving some trace ... something left behind ... no man either ..."

"*Exacte*!" Troucillus agreed. "Now look around us. Whoever dumped this body here had to have left some evidence."

I scanned the area concentrating on the downhill slope of the land. The main road was down there somewhere. And, beyond that, Bibracte. The road would have been the best approach; it was free of brush, clear of the fallen leaves and the Romans didn't patrol it at night. In the woods themselves, most of the leaves were down – the oaks were still stubbornly holding on to their now golden-brown coiffures – the underbrush was mostly bare – a tangled maze of thin brown branches ... some described graceful arcs ... others, straight lines intersecting at varied angles.

Then I saw it! A branch, black against the afternoon sunlight ... broken ... first arching from the trees then sharply angled down toward the ground. Someone or something had broken it as they passed.

"There!" I pointed it out to Troucillus, "A broken branch."

Troucillus grunted and squeezed my shoulder. He moved carefully to the broken branch. He examined the edges of the break.

"This was done recently," he said to no one in particular. "The dead leaves on the ground mask tracks ..."

He picked up a dead twig from the ground. "... hard to say for sure, but this looks like it's been stepped on ..."

He worked his way down the slope then stopped. "Brambles never fail ..." He picked something off some brush and held it up over his shoulder for me to see. "Fibers ... hard to tell the color ... may be red like his tunic ..."

A bit farther down, Troucillus stooped. He placed the fingers of his right hand to the ground, held his fingertips up to his eyes, then rubbed them together. "Blood ..." he whispered over his shoulder to me. "The body was still leaking when they hauled the poor sod up this way ..."

"'They'?" I challenged.

Troucillus nodded, "Yes ... 'they' ... carrying a dead body's no easy task ... carrying it up a slope, through the brush and trying to stay quiet enough not to wake up the Roman pickets even more difficult ... six at least ... maybe more ..."

Then, Troucillus laughed.

"What's so funny?" I asked.

Troucillus shook his head. "I was just visualizing six or seven men struggling up this slope dragging a limp, leaking body while being serenaded by the snores of the sleeping Roman pickets ... I wish I was around for that one ..."

We soon broke out onto the northern road. Troucillus examined it for some tracks, but the daily traffic had wiped out most traces. In fact, there was a comet of fresh horse droppings right across our putative trail. Despite this, Troucillus still found a trace.

"*Vide!*" he said pointing to a spot at the edge of the road. "Look!"

I looked where he was indicating. A clear footprint at a right angle to the direction of the road pointed straight at the trail we had followed down the slope.

"Not a Roman boot ..." Troucillus was saying. "Looks like whoever wore it was carrying something heavy ... and awkward. Look at this scraping here as he stepped off the roadway ... he stumbled a bit ..."

Troucillus straightened himself up and looked beyond the road toward the southwest. "Bibracte is down there," he said. "Between here and the walls, woods, and fields

... about a thousand paces to the walls, more than that to the northern gate ... I seriously doubt anyone would carry a body that far ... they killed our man somewhere near here ... down in these woods I imagine ... but why drag him down here to kill him then drag the body back up the slope ...”

Troucillus took his *pugio* off his belt and carved a sign about head-height on a tree bordering the road. Then, he arranged some stones pointing in the supposed direction of travel.

“I’ll get that centurion ... Strabo? I’ll get Strabo to sweep through these woods before dark ... I think he’ll find the place where his man was killed ... that might tell us why they dragged him away to kill him. The question why they dragged his body back is easy to answer.”

“Easy to answer?” I asked. “How so?”

Troucillus gave me a humorless grin. “An act of terrorism, pure and simple. Whoever did this wanted the Romans to discover the blood-drained corpse of their comrade; they wanted the Romans to think the *stryx* killed him. If Strabo tries to send out another tent-squad beyond the walls of the camp tonight, he may be faced with a mutiny. If Labienus actually does crucify a tribe member for the murder of a Roman soldier, he’ll face a revolt ... a revolt that will probably put Malouuhnos on the throne and chase the Roman army down the valley of the Rhodanus.”

I nodded. It made sense to me.

“And now that I’ve said that out loud, I have an idea who did this,” Troucillus continued. “Gai! I’ll bet you a *denarius* against a brass *as* that crazed witch, Gourach merc Fetroda, is preaching that the Catubodua has developed a taste for the blood of Duuhruhda’s Roman allies, and Malouuhnos’ black druids are saying this is a sign of the imminent arrival of Afalanos.”

XII

Caput XII. Pactum Est Factum
Chapter 12. A Deal Is Made

Based on a conversation I had with Caesar in Alexandria many years ago, I can now understand why Caesar placed so much faith in Troucillus.

One night as Caesar and I drank a sweet Greek wine on a terrace of the Macedonian's palace in Alexandria, he fell into one of his "philosophical" moods often brought on by inactivity and the grape. He told me all history lies. All of it is written for some political or moral theme or to make a people feel good about themselves – or bad, depending on the historian's prejudices.

Considering that I had written Caesar's "history" of his Gallic campaigns and was at that time finishing up his history of the civil wars, I thought Caesar's comment somewhat ironic. But irony and wine rarely mix in the same cup.

Caesar continued explaining that the actual facts of history – if they are even reliably known - are distorted in their telling to support some nationalistic or moral theme. For Romans, the usual prattle is the nation is the darling of the gods and they manifest their favor by delivering the peoples of other lands, and their gods, and their gold, to us.

"Look at the Aegypti," Caesar gestured toward the city of Alexandria with his winecup. "They were building magnificent stone temples and pyramids capped with pure gold when Romulus was huddling in a waddle hut clinging to the muddy sides of the Palatine warming himself with a dung fire. The Aegypti believed *their* gods, as grotesque as they seem to us ..." Caesar gestured with his wine cup to a statue of a hawk-headed man with a large red disk on his head. "... favored them above all nations as long as the Aegypti sang their praises, burned incense in their temples, and gave silver to their priests. And for this, the gods delivered to them the wealth of all the lands – the 'red' lands and the 'black' lands, as they call them - from the cataracts to the delta."

Caesar took a long drink and shook his head. "Then, along came Alexander and his ragtag crew of Macedonian hill-farmers still scraping sheep dung off their boots. According to *their* histories, Ares had a bigger pair than old bird-face over there and delivered Aegyptus along with the empires of the east to *his* darling, Alexander."

Caesar shook his head again and chuckled. "Now it's our turn. I'm sure we Romans will convince ourselves that Aegyptus is ours because Iove wants it that way. Why? Because he loves us above all others. Why? Because we pile gold up in his temple on the

Capitoline ... we build temples to him in the lands we conquer ... we banish the foreign gods, or just rename them so we can pronounce their bloody names ...”

Caesar chuckled again. “There's an old story I heard many years ago ... the King of the Persians, Cyrus the Great, summoned all the *magi*, the wisest men in his empire, to come before his throne. He commanded them to develop a universal principle ... a maxim that would be true in all situations. He gave them one year to do it or he'd crucify the lot of them ...”

Caesar stopped speaking, took another drink of wine, and chuckled.

“What is it, *patrone*?” I asked. “What's so amusing?”

Caesar shook his head, still smiling. “I've often wondered whether the world would be a better place if we executed all academics ... those people'll argue about anything ... the direction of the wind ... why fire's hot ... anything ... viciously, too ... no quarter given ... most of it's useless ... just noise ... empty prattling about issues that aren't important at all ... why should I care whether the gods are *spiritus*, made of air, or of particles so fine that humans cannot see them ...”

Caesar looked out over the balustrade toward the great Museum from which I imagined I heard the humming of thousands of endless and meaningless arguments - a veritable beehive of intellectual vacuity that yielded no honey.

Caesar gestured toward the great marble buildings saying, “Catula got that right ... as long as she supplies those freeloaders with free food and wine, those philosophers of airs and doctors of the vapors will never wander far from its walls ...”

“Catula?” I asked, “Kitten?”

Caesar looked over, “Oh ... yes ... the queen, Cleopatra, wants me to call her Catula ... at times I think the child is flirting with me ... ridiculous really ... where was I?”

Caesar surreptitiously checked his hairline and discovered it still started back on the top of his head despite the comb-over.

“Killing academics,” I told him. “Before that, Cyrus the Great's universal principle.”

“Ah... yes ...” Caesar pulled a few longer strands of his hair across the top of his forehead and continued. “So, Cyrus commanded the *magi* to develop a universal principle, true in all situations ... gave the eggheads a year to do it or he'd kill the lot of them.

“Finally, the day arrived. The head scholar prostrated himself before the throne of the great king, the rest of the academics were on their bellies behind him. Cyrus spoke, ‘Have you obeyed my command and developed a principle that applies in all situations?’ ‘We have, oh, king of kings!’ the man said not daring to look up. ‘Tell it to me!’ the great king demanded. Speaking into the marble floor of Cyrus’ great palace the man said, ‘The universal principle of all human history is this, my king, that this too shall pass away!’”

It took me a few heartbeats to digest what I had just heard. Then I said, “I don't imagine old Cyrus was too pleased with that.”

Caesar shrugged. “The story ends there. But Cyrus was not known for his sense of humor, so I imagine the lions in the royal menagerie ate well that day.”

Caesar chuckled again, refilling his winecup. "I'll tell you another problem with historians," he started.

Caesar had entered the cosmic introspective stage of his drinking. I had discovered long before this that it's best just to let Caesar talk himself out. Usually, these sessions ended with him snoring in his chair.

"What's that, *patrone*?" I prompted.

"They represent human history as if it were a logical chain of events ... because this happened then that happened ... it's almost as if history were the plot line of some cheap, Greek romance."

"And you don't believe that?" I asked.

Caesar shook his head. "Come now, Gai ... you didn't just fall off the farm cart ... we've been comrades now for how long? At least ten years! *Merda cadit* ... crap happens ... and when it does, there's no rhyme or reason to it ... no grand, divine plan manifested through the acts of men ... when turds fall on you, you just have to deal with it the best you can."

Caesar was warming to his subject, a sure sign that he would soon be slipping off into the dark realm of Somnium.

"Think about Gallia," he was saying. "Most of the time we didn't have a clue what was going on. Why did the Vercingetorix lock himself up in Alesia when he had us outnumbered and running in circles? Why did Pompeius and the Optimates in the senate flee Rome when they could have crushed us with two legions? Pure chaos!"

Caesar yawned and hiccupped almost simultaneously. He examined the contents of his cup, shrugged, and emptied it. He went on, "Most of the time we weren't faced with one big crucial event ... we were unusually dealing with dozens of seemingly minor things ... we didn't know what was true and what was false ... what was important and what was insignificant ... I had you write it up as if I understood it all, but even after it was over, I wasn't sure at times what had happened ..."

Caesar filled his cup from the pitcher and took another draft of inspiration, "The one thing I did ... or we did right ... was we didn't let the confusion paralyze us ... that's what bad commanders do ... wait until the situation has completely clarified itself before they act. By that time, the opportunity is lost and so is the war ... we just laid down our money and made our bet, as the bookies around the great Circus say ... we made a decision. If things seemed to be working, we pressed on; if not, we tried something else."

Caesar leaned his head back in his chair and closed his eyes. The end of this evening's lecture was near.

"That's what poor commanders do, Gai," Caesar said to me from the road to unconsciousness. "When they're faced with too many choices ... things they can't understand because critical information is not available ... they just freeze ... do nothing ... it's better to move ahead ... even run away ... at least you're doing something ... not just stand there with a confused look on your puss ..."

Caesar stopped talking. His eyes were closed. I waited a bit, but he didn't speak. Soon I noticed his breathing became regular, deeper. His head nodded, and his mouth opened slightly.

I removed the wine cup from his hand and summoned the two praetorians standing outside the door of his chamber. We eased him up out of the chair and walked him inside and over to his bed. We got his boots off, and I threw the comforter over him. He began to snore.

I noticed the sash of a *decanus* on one of the guards.

"*Decane*! I want two men on this door all night," I told him. "No one in, no one out, unless I say so ... and that includes that little Macedonian *vacca ... compre'endisne*, got it?"

"*Compre'endo, centurio*," the man snapped. "Yes, sir!"

"And, put two men out on that balcony all night," I continued. "It's too easy a climb from the courtyard."

"*A'mperi'tu', centurio*!" again, "Yes, sir!"

"I'll be in my quarters! Come get me if anything happens!"

"*A'mperi'tu', centurio*!"

I started to walk away, then stopped. "One other thing, *decane*."

"*Centurio*?" the squad leader responded.

"Send one of the boys down to the kitchens for a pitcher of water and a cup ... put them next to the boss' bed ... he's going to need it when he wakes up."

Troucillus and I were faced with a number of events, facts and rumors, none of which we fully understood – the murder of a Roman soldier made to look like an attack by the *stryx*; the intrigue around selecting a ruler for the Aedui; rumors of Deluuhnu, the king's brother, approaching from the north with a band of Aeduan rebels and Belgae; a crazed witch preaching that Catubodua, a manifestation of the Maru Rignai, thirsted for the blood of foreigners; black druids from Britain proclaiming an imminent apocalypse; Romans bribing the northern tribes to attack Caesar's army.

We also knew we were running out of time. The *Samon'win,* the suspected trigger date for the coming of Afalanos and an uprising of the northern clans, was just a couple of days off.

Also, Labienus' patience was wearing thin. At any moment, he might order a *vexillatio*, a detachment from the Tenth Legion, north to sort things out. Or he might string up a few "wogs" as a warning against attacking Roman soldiers. Either action would likely trigger a revolt in Bibracte itself, push Caesar's ally, Duuhruhda, off the throne, and destroy the Roman alliance with the Aedui.

Finally, what game was Morcant playing? Was he content with accepting the role of Duuhruhda's *pendefig*? Or was his end game seizing the throne with Malouuhnos' help? Did he believe that his father, Cuhnetha, died of "natural causes," as Spina would call it, or was he convinced that Duuhruhda had him poisoned to remove him as a threat?

And, most importantly to my seventeen-year-old self at that time, what was Rhonwen up to? She kissed me! Did she really like me? Or was she playing with me to help her cousin, Morcant?

All Gallia could explode in the next couple of days, and I was fixated on the flirtations of that redheaded coquette!

She kissed me!

The spot where her lips torched mine still felt warm!

As Troucillus and I walked along the road back to the northern camp, I could sense his mind sorting through what had to be done.

Finally, Troucillus broke the silence. "I hope Labienus is still at the camp ... we need to get eyes in the north," he said. "Labienus is not going to be happy when I tell him about Deluuhnu and his connection with Galba of the Belgae ... and how the king's uncle, Druce, may have conned us ... but that can't be helped now ... we have to find out whether Deluuhnu is in the north and gathering the clans."

I nodded, then added, "And he not crucify anyone on the crossroad."

"That too," Troucillus agreed. "But first, I need to get a squad of *muli* out in the woods to find where this Rufus was killed. If we find the crime scene, we may find out more about who killed him."

"But we already know that," I pointed out. "It had to be something with Catubodua's witch and those black priests."

"Troucillus nodded. "I don't disagree with you, Gai. But knowing something and being able to prove it are two very different things."

As we approached the camp, we saw that Labienus was still there. He seemed surprised to see us approach along the road. "I thought you two were above," he said. "Never know where you'll pop up, Troucille."

Troucillus nodded. "Yes ... we were following some clues ... Labiene! A word ... *clam* ... in private."

Troucillus and Labienus stepped off to the side. I noticed that Labienus' praetorian detail positioned themselves between me and their boss. I half recognized most of these guys, but they obviously saw me as some shaggy "wog" wearing a long sword. Potentially dangerous. My "cover" disguise was working even with them.

As I watched, Labienus' face went white ... Troucillus was obviously telling him about Deluuhnu, the Belgae and the northern clans ... then red ... Druce conning us. Labienus' head bobs and his thrusting jaw gave violent emphasis to whatever point he was trying to impress on Troucillus. Troucillus nodded, shrugged, and held up his hands toward Labienus. Finally, Labienus nodded, turned away from Troucillus, and called up the hill for Strabo.

Troucillus walked back over to me. "*Infelissime*!" Troucillus shook his head. "He's not a happy man. The nearest *turma* of Gallic-speaking cavalry is that one from the Eleventh, but they're east of here on the Arar near Venta Cavillonum ... a day to fetch them and a day to get them back here with tired horses. As we feared, he wanted to send a couple of cohorts of *muli* from the Tenth directly north, but I talked him out of that. And no reprisals for the killing of his man. He's got Strabo putting together a detail to search for where his man was killed and he's going to send Rufus' buddy, Lupus, down to talk to us. So, let's head back up the road where we marked the trail.

Lupus was no help at all. He insisted that Rufus had wandered away from their post in the middle of the night to take a leak and never returned. He heard nothing, saw nothing. It was obvious that he and most of his mates had fallen asleep. But Lupus denied that; falling asleep on guard was a serious offense. He would at least be beaten with his centurion's cudgel. Since a mate was killed while they slept, Lupus could be beaten to death and his entire tent-squad shut out of the camp on rations of barley and water.

Strabo's search detail didn't take long to find where Rufus had been killed. Despite the cool October weather, the flies drew them to the site.

We were led there by one of the *muli*. We found the rest of the squad grouped near a large holm oak. They seemed to be avoiding an area directly under the bows. A cloud of flies, the stench, and the crusted gore on the ground immediately told us the reason for their reluctance. This was the spot where Rufus was murdered and bled out.

Troucillus and I also avoided disturbing the feasting insects. The branches of the oak were draped with strips of white cloth that drooped in the still airs. I noticed one swatch that seemed larger than the rest.

"*Cac't! Vide, legate!*" I pointed. "Crap! Look at that, sir!"

A tunic hung from one of the branches. It appeared dirty-white in the lengthening shadows of the late afternoon. But there was no mistaking the crude purple strip painted across it. The tunic was pierced by multiple knife thrusts; blood had been smeared around the slashes.

"A warning?" Troucillus mused out loud.

"*Wraig golchour!*" I told him. "The Washer Woman ... the messenger of the Phantom Queen. It's a warning of imminent death."

"And by the look of the purple stripe, mine ... or perhaps Labienus," Troucillus completed my thought.

"Look there, sir!" one of the *muli* said pointing at the trunk of the tree.

Both Troucillus and I leaned forward toward the tree to see what the man was indicating; neither of us wished to enter the feeding frenzy of the flies or step into the blood that was exciting them so. Then, I spotted it.

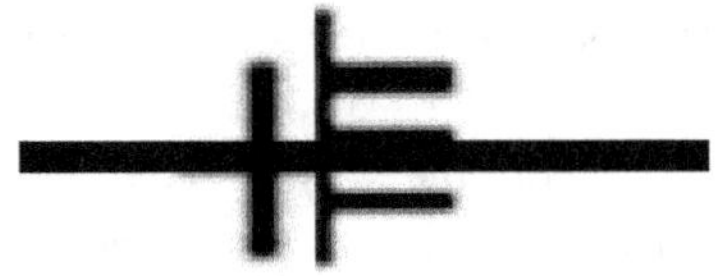

"I've seen that before," I told Troucillus. "Up north ... that's the sign for Afalanos. The black priests carved it into his altar."

Troucillus nodded. "The old writing. So, the dark god of the Britanni and the Maru Rignai, the Phantom Queen of the Gah'el, are mated, and Catubodua has drunk blood to celebrate the marriage ..."

Then, Troucillus remembered where he was and with whom, men who would not understand his metaphor.

He turned to the *muli*. "*Milites*! Soldiers! Look here! This is where your mate was murdered. That is his blood on the ground! He was killed by men, not a monster! His blood lies there, not carried off by the *stryx* ..."

At the very mention of the *stryx*, some of the men spit toward the north; others made the hand sign to ward off evil.

"... you can defeat men with good Roman steel. There is no need to fear that our gods cannot protect us here ... that our gods cannot overcome any powers evoked against us. Tell your mates! The night should hold no fear for Roman soldiers!"

It was a good speech. But I have since learned that, once the fear of some terrifying, malignant force of darkness takes hold of men's hearts, the logic of what is right before them in the daylight has little power. Despite what Troucillus said, despite the physical evidence before them, most of these men believed that this was the place where the *stryx* had dragged their mate to feast on his blood before magically depositing his lifeless corpse back on their doorstep.

The *stryx* had sent them a warning; this place was cursed.

We arrived back in Bibracte just after dark. We stopped just inside the north gate. "I'm riding down to the king's stronghold," Troucillus began. "This has gone on too long ... I need to nail down his agreement with Morcant as we discussed and get him to rein in his uncle, Druce ..."

Troucillus didn't wait for my response. "Gai, I want you to pay a visit to Morcant ... confirm everything that his cousin, Rhonwen, told you this morning ... get him to commit to it if possible ... I'd like to get a proposal appointing Morcant as Duuhruhda's *pendefig* before the council tomorrow. I need to stabilize affairs here in Bibracte; then we'd be free to move north against Deluuhnu and his Belgian friends ..."

I was nodding but realized that Troucillus may not be able to see me in the dark. So, I grunted "*Bene!*"

"Take a couple of the boys with you for security," Troucillus was saying. "Pugnus and two of the other *muli* ..."

I remembered the cut-up and bloody tunic hanging from Afalanos' tree. "No, Troucille! I'll be fine. Morcant's quarters are just a short walk from where we're staying ... it's you that the druids have targeted. My death is of no value to them."

I was wrong.

To promote terror, one man's death could be as useful as the next.

I left my mount with the stable attendant at Troucillus' place. I told the porter where I was headed. The porter recommended I take a torch bearer; the night was as dark as a root cellar in Hades. But I was in too much of a hurry. Besides, my seventeen-year-old hubris told me I was a Roman soldier; I could move in the night, and I wasn't afraid of the dark.

I made my way to see Morcant alone and on foot.

I almost got to Morcant's place. I was navigating a narrow passageway between two buildings when I heard what sounded like moaning. I looked around in the dark and spotted a shape lying on the ground. It seemed to be a man. I went down on one knee and bent over the shape to investigate.

I saw the blow more than felt it, an explosion of frenzied, fireflies schooled before my eyes in the night. I tumbled forward, over the moaning body, which came suddenly alive, and rising, pushed me against a wall.

The darkness saved me. The blow, which was intended for my head and would probably have killed me, landed high on my shoulders. I managed to get my *pugio* out of its sheath and pressed my back against a wall. I sensed dark shapes around me. One came at me. I kicked out with a heavily booted foot. I felt the impact, heard a satisfying grunt of pain, and the shape tumble back into the darkness.

I tried to rise but seemed to be having trouble breathing. Another dark shape closed in from my right. I reversed the knife in my right hand and thrust a back-handed stab in the shadow's direction. I felt a ripping impact, heard a painful curse in Gah'el.

I needed to get to my feet to draw my longsword. I pressed my back into the wall and tried to leverage my body into a standing position by digging my heels into the ground and driving myself up along the wall. I again changed my hold on the *pugio*, bringing the blade forward. I slashed wildly in front of myself trying to keep my shadowy attackers away. I felt an impact on my forearm. No pain, just a blow.

To my left, I saw a light coming down the ally. My attackers brought a torch to take advantage of their numbers. I had to get to my sword.

More shapes filled my narrow battlefield, but the pressure on me seemed to lessen! The reinforcements were attacking my assailants! I could hear the impact of fists, cudgels, and steel on bodies; heard the grunts of dying men; saw bodies fall.

I heard a familiar voice call out in Gah'el, "Arth! Arth! You okay?"

It was Pruhderos, Clou's man.

"Here! I'm over here against the wall," I heard myself say.

Pruhderos approached out of the melee, a *dagr* in his right hand. He stopped when he saw me. I realized I was still holding out my knife in my right hand. I had my sword halfway out of its sheath, the hilt grasped in my left hand.

Pruhderos raised both his hands so I could see them against the torch light. "It's me, Arth! Pruhde! You remember! We went north together."

I lowered the point of my knife, let my sword drop back down into its sheath. I felt my body slumping into a sitting position against the wall. "Give me a chance to clear my head ... those bastards hit me pretty hard."

Pruhde looked down at me. "We better get a cloth around your arm, Arth. You're bleeding all over yerself."

I raised my right arm up in front of my eyes. I realized I was still holding my *pugio*. I saw the ripped, blood-soaked cloth of my sleeve. I watched as a stream of reddish black liquid oozed down my forearm and plopped down into my lap.

That's the last thing I remember.

Pruhde took me to Morcant's quarters. It was the nearest safe haven. I was placed in a chair, my wounded arm on a table next to me.

Pruhderos' voice. "Do you have a *meduhg*? A doctor? This man is hurt."

A woman's voice. "Let me see! Unwrap the arm."

Rhonwen!

I felt someone tug away the cloth wrapping my forearm.

Rhonwen. "That's just a scratch ... we don't need a doctor for this!"

A cup was thrust into my left hand, I sniffed it. *Dur*. Whiskey.

Pruhderos. "I think he took a blow to the head, lady!"

Rhonwen. "Let's take a look, then ... that might explain why he's so woozy."

Fingers probe the back of my head.

Rhonwen. "Drink some of that, Arth. It'll warm you up and get some blood flowing to your head."

Fingers pulled back the collar of my tunic and probed my shoulders and upper back. Pain exploded red in my brain.

Rhonwen. "His head's fine ... the blow landed across his shoulders ... still feels hot to the touch ... can you raise your arms, Arth?"

For a few heartbeats, I wasn't sure to whom Rhonwen was speaking.

Then, she was nose to nose in my face. "Arth! Look at me! Do you know who I am?"

I nodded and croaked, "Rhonwen."

"*Da!*" she nodded squeezing my shoulder. "Good! Do you know where you are?"

Before I could answer, another voice behind me, "*Cefndir*! Cousin! What's all this? Who are these men?"

Morcant.

"It's Arth, cousin. He was attacked. These men brought him here."

Then Pruhderos, "*A pen*! We are members of the king's *fintai*! I'm called Pruhde, a warrior of five seasons. We were sent out by the king's uncle, Druce, to find Arth here. We came across him being attacked in an alley near here. We kept one of them alive to talk to."

"Later," Morcant said. "Let's see to Arth first."

Rhonwen to me, "Arth! Can you lift your arms?"

I nodded and started to raise them. Then I felt a pain on my upper leg. Rhonwen had pinched me.

"*Da!* Good! You felt that," she said. "Put your arms down ... and drink some of that *dur* before you spill the rest of it!"

I did as I was told. I felt the fumes of the liquor flow up through my abdomen into my head.

Rhonwen. "I don't think the blow he took to the back did any real damage ... he's going to be sore for a few days ... we need to see to the cut on his arm."

"Do I need to summon Arwuhnos?" Morcant asked.

"*Nac*!" Rhonwen shook her head. "No need for the doctor! The cut is deep but no major blood tubes have been severed."

Then to me, "Arth! Make a fist with your right hand."

I did what I was told. The pain in my arm jumped from a dull throb to a red, stabbing pain. I gasped

"Don't be such a baby!" Rhonwen scolded. "Now, wiggle your fingers for me!"

I did as I was told.

"*Da*!" Rhonwen judged. "Good! Just needs a good cleaning and a few stitches. A girl of twelve summers could do this job."

She snatched the cup of *dur* from my hand and poured it over my wounded arm. The entire cosmos went red.

Later, we were sitting at table. My arm was stitched, tightly wrapped, and propped on top of small packing box Rhonwen had found in one of the storage spaces. The residual throbbing was being dulled further by my second cup of *dur*. I think Spina would have been jealous of Rhonwen's work. She used a small needle, and her stiches were close and tight. She joked that all I would have to impress the girls was a thin, white line visible only in the summer when my skin darkened.

Pruhde reported he had been sent out by Clou to find me and make sure I was safe. He was told that his boss, Druce, had decided that he didn't want any more dead Romans lying around Bibracte. Bad for business, he said.

At Morcant's request, we dragged in the survivor from the gang that attacked me. At first the man was reluctant to talk. Pruhde whispered something in his ear. The man went deathly pale, then nodded.

To my surprise, we discovered that he was a two-year man from the king's *fintai*. He told us that he and a number of his mates wanted the king's brother, Deluuhnu, back from exile. It was the Caisar's doing that he was outlawed. This faction of the king's guard had allied themselves with the black druids. The only way to right the injustice of Deluuhnu's exile was to rid the nation of the Rhufeinai, the Romans.

I asked him what was Malouuhnos mab Dermuhtos' involvement in his "cause." He said that he had no knowledge of Malouuhnos' part, but his nephew, Malgounos mab Owenos, had been present at a few of their gatherings, so it was reasonable to assume that Malouuhnos knew what they were up to.

After we were sure the man had nothing more to tell us, Pruhde got up and excused himself. He said he needed to get back and report to Druce. He grabbed the prisoner by his collar and dragged him to his feet.

Then I thought occurred to me.

"Pruhde! I need to get word to Troucillos. There must be more gangs of these killers out there hunting Rhufeinai," I advised.

Pruhderos shook his head. "Druce anticipated that. Clou is out looking for him. He'll be fine."

I nodded, then asked, "What did you say to the prisoner that frightened him into speaking.

Pruhderos shrugged, "That I was going to let the Rhufeinig purple-shirt have him ... the one down in the camp with the curly hair ... and he was going to hoist him up on a stake and let the ravens feast."

After Pruhderos left with the prisoner, I addressed Morcant, "Troucillos has asked me to speak to you about your offer."

"To ally myself with Duuhruhda against Malouuhnos and his crazed druids?" Morcant nodded. "It is as my cousin told you. Duuhruhda restores my clan, nominates me as his *pendefig*, and I support him against the northern clans."

I responded, "Rhonwen said you want the king to 'restore to all your traditional clan holdings as they were when your grandfather, Cluhweluhno, was *uucharix* of the Aineduai' ..."

"Ah... he does listen," Rhonwen chortled into her mead cup.

I continued, "... I imagine you have a complete list of holdings that we can put before Duuhruhda to get his agreement."

Morcant nodded, "Duuhruhda's own *pruhduhd*, his bard, could recite that list, as well as my own. That's not a problem. What about the Caisar? Is he willing to respect the sovereignty of the Aineduai?"

I nodded. "Troucillus, the Caisar's *pendefig*, has given his word."

Caesar did honor Troucillus' promise. The Aedui never became *victi*, a subjugated people, even after their northern clans joined the Vercingetorix. After the great revolt, Caesar had Duuhruhda replaced as king by Morcant; the former king of the Aedui spent the rest of his days as Caesar's "guest" in a villa near Baiae. Octavius also respected Caesar's pledge. Morcant still holds Bibracte as a friend and ally of the Roman people, although his spends most of his time living in a villa built for him by our "Exalted One" in the new Roman *colonia*, Augustodunum.

After Pruhderos left, the humors that flow through our bodies to give us strength in times of crisis began to ebb. My arm throbbed; the blow I took across my upper back ached so badly, I could hardly turn my head; and the struggle inflamed my already injured ribs. I would have dedicated ten pounds of silver to the gods Hypnos, Nyx, and even Thanatos, for a few drops of Spina's juice, the Greek *opion*.

I felt I needed to get up and walk away, as if movement would allow me to escape the pain I was in. Before I could attempt this, Troucillus arrived.

Blessedly, Spina was with him.

After Rhonwen had poured him a cup of red mead, Troucillus briefed us on what he had discussed with Duuhruhda. The king's uncle, Druce, was present at the meeting. The excesses of Malouuhnos' black druids, Deluuhnu's alliance with Galba of the Belgae, and the ritualistic murder of a Roman soldier had pushed Druce over the line.

He now favored an alliance with Caesar to protect the nation and Duuhruhda's throne.

It was Druce, Troucillus said, who had proposed to the king an alliance with Morcant's clan and the restoration of his lands in return for his support. Again, this was dependent on Caesar's promise to respect and preserve the independence of the Aedui. Troucillus said that Druce's proposal was consistent to his own thoughts on the matter and with the offer from Morcant brought to me by Rhonwen earlier in the day. Troucillus suspected that the staff serving him in the quarters he had been given by the king were on Druce's payroll.

After Druce's proposal, Duuhruhda just bowed his head and said that this was his desire also. If Morcant was in agreement, he would propose him as *pendefig* to the Council of Three Generations when they convened in the morning.

No sooner had Troucillus agreed to approach Morcant, then Druce announced that he had dispatched detachments of reliable members of the king's *fintai* into the town to arrest the black druids and the so-called "Witch, Daughter of the Tomb." He had reliable information that the murdered Roman soldier was the victim of malcontents within the king's guard, who were working with Malouuhnos and his black priests to place Deluuhnu on the throne and expel the Romans. Even as we spoke, his own household guard was out hunting the dissidents down before they could do anymore violence.

Troucillus took a long sip of his mead and chuckled, "I imagine Druce did a quick calculation and realized he had an army of Rhufeinai right on his doorstep while Deluuhnu and his Bolgai were wandering around somewhere in the northern marches. What is the old saying? 'A single enemy on your shield is more dangerous than a troop of enemies over the mountain'."

Troucillus continued his account. "Druce then announced that his men were at that very moment rolling up an ambush by members of the king's *fintai* meant for me when I left the stronghold. The plan was to make it look to the Caisar as if I were killed as a result of Duuhruhda's treachery. The killing of a Rhufeinig *pendefig*, the personal representative of the Caisar himself, would leave the Rhufeinai no choice but to exact vengeance. If the Aineduai were still split over who should be their king and whether they should go to war with the Rhufeinai, this would force their hand."

While Troucillus spoke, Spina was splitting his attention between examining me and Rhonwen's red mead.

"*Cac't*, Insubrece!" Spina was saying, while balancing a mead cup in one hand and pulling back my collar to examine my injured shoulder with the other, "Keep still, will ya! Dat looks like it hoits like all da torments of Hades! Wad dey hit you wit'? A club?"

My mind was floating somewhere between Troucillus' Gah'el, Spina's fractured Latin, and the excruciating pain of his examination. "*Nesc', med'*! Don't know, doc! I wasn't looking when they did it, now was I!"

"Not a good idear mockin' the guy who's got yer pain killah," Spina retorted taking a long drink. "Any point in my lookin' at da woik *she* did on yer ahm?" Spina asked nodding toward Rhonwen.

"Not unless you want her to do some surgery on you with that knife she's got in her belt," I warned.

Spina shook his head, "Ah all dese Gallic broads dat ferocious?"

"Only the redheads," I retorted.

Then, I remembered the verse of a Gallic drinking song, "... *a'r faun, a'r buhr, a'r tal* 'and the long, and the short, and the tall'."

"Ya got phlegm stuck in ya t'roat? Or ya tryin' to tell me something?" Spina asked.

Rhonwen, who had kept at least one eye on Spina since he started examining me, heard me mutter in Gah'el. "What's he saying to you, Arth? Is that Rhufeinig horse doctor criticizing my work?"

"*Na!*" I told her in Gah'el. "No! He wouldn't dare!"

Rhonwen snorted and went back to her mead.

"Wad she want?" Spina asked.

"*Nil!* Nothing. Wanted to know if you needed more mead," I told him.

"Shuwah!" Spina said, "Nothin' sadder dan an empty cup."

He pushed his cup across the table in Rhonwen's direction. She gave him a dark look, then remembered her manners. She refilled his cup, not too neatly.

Spina sat and took the cup. "She's not too good at dis, is she. Whatta she do heah? She the big guys' squeeze?"

"No! No!" I sputtered a bit. "She's his cousin ..."

"That like a 'Roman cousin'?" Spina winked.

"*Verpa Martis!* No!" I said a bit too strongly. "That's forbidden by tradition and law! It offends the gods! It breeds weak warriors, idiots, and monsters!"

Spina grinned into his cup, "Well, dat'd explain a lot about what's going on down in Rome dese days."

Then, Spina chuckled, "What's a matter? I hit a noive wit' dis one?"

I felt my face go red. Rhonwen sensed she was being talked about. "What's he saying, Arth?"

"*Nil!*" I started, then realized Rhonwen didn't understand Latin. "*Dim!* Nothing! He's saying nothing!"

"Many words to say *nothing*, Arth" Rhonwen countered.

Spina chimed in, "*Art*' ... is that how these people say 'sweetie'?"

My cheeks warmed.

"*Verpa Martis?*" I heard Rhonwen muse. "Is that what a girl has to look forward to with you ... *dulcissime?*"

I realized Rhonwen wasn't completely ignorant of Latin.

My face caught fire.

Both Spina and Rhonwen were laughing at me.

XIII

Caput XIII. Altera Quaestio Resolvita Altera Aperta
Chapter 13. One Problem Solved; Another Revealed

I spent that night in Morcant's quarters. Spina thought it best I didn't move any more than I had to and Troucillus agreed.

I was set up in one of the side rooms. Because of the injury to my shoulders, I wasn't comfortable lying down, so I was propped up in a reclining position on some sort of couch. Spina put a dose of his "juice" into a cup of mead and had me drink it.

As I was beginning to fade away, Rhonwen came into the room and covered me with a thick comforter. In my stupor, I thought I heard her say to Spina, "Is he going to be completely out, Doctor?"

Spina, "A sleep so deep he can almost see da banks a da Styx."

Rhonwen. Sigh, "So much for a maiden's dreams."

Then, she winked at me!

I could have sworn they were both speaking Latin! Or Gah'el? Or maybe it was an hallucination caused by the "juice."

The next morning, I was roused up at dawn. I pulled back my blanket and realized that someone had stripped me down to my skivvies. But Rhonwen's thick comforter ... and the "juice" ... had kept me warm throughout the late October night. As soon as my mind put my semi-naked condition, the comforter, and Rhonwen in the same picture, my cheeks caught fire.

One of Morcant's attendants brought me a breakfast of hot porridge and watered beer. When I tried to swing my legs up off the couch, I realized that parts of my body seemed to have stopped functioning. My head would turn only a few degrees left and right, and my right arm couldn't be raised above my shoulder, at least not without my seeing stars in the daylight.

I checked the bandages with which Rhonwen had wrapped my wounded right arm. They were dry; I felt no throbbing pain and could smell no sign of infection.

I remember Spina telling me last spring, after I was attacked by the *sicarius*, the hitman from Rome, disguised as a legionary slave, "If ya get dis painful lump above da wound, right wheyah da limb meets da body, ... dee ahmpit or da groin usually ... dat ain't good ... means *daemones* got into da wound ... not good at all ..."

I reached over and felt around my armpit. *Grat'is diis*! Thank the gods! There was no painful lump.

I tried to take a deep breath to test my bruised ribs and quickly decided not to repeat the experiment.

I ate my breakfast sitting on the side of my couch in a somewhat hunched position. I'd save trying to stand and walk for when I had to. While I was eating, an attendant came in and delivered my boots. I hadn't noticed they were gone! They gleamed with a deep, brown luster having been brushed, cleaned, and rubbed with a fresh coat of sheep fat.

I had almost finished my meal when Rhonwen entered the room with what appeared to be a bundle of fabric in her arms. As I struggled to cover myself with the tangled comforter, she said, "Ah, the sleeper awakes! And, he has a good appetite!"

Without waiting for a response, Rhonwen continued, "I brought you these to wear. Your tunic's fit for nothing but cleaning rags and your *loudrau*, your trousers, had to be sent out to see if they could be salvaged. So, I brought you these. They're the colors of our clan, but you must be used to dressing up like an Aineduai by now."

I noted she was speaking Gah'el. Then I recalled my "vision" last night of her speaking Latin. So, I answered her in that language, "*Habes tu dormita bene, Ronvena*? Did you sleep well, Rhonwen?"

Rhonwen looked at me for a few heartbeats; I could almost *see* the mischief dancing in her green eyes. Then, she answered in Gah'el, "Are you trying to say something to me, Arth? Or just clearing your throat?"

I felt my face heat up. Rhonwen seemed to ignore my embarrassment. "When you're done eating, get yourself dressed. My cousin has news, and we expect your friend Troucillos to come by soon."

Then she paused, her green eyes dancing. "You *can* get dressed yourself, can't you? Or should I stay and help?"

When I finally did manage to get myself dressed and out into the main room. Troucillus had already arrived. He and Morcant were sitting next to the central fire sipping from ceramic cups. Rhonwen stood behind her cousin's chair.

"Ah!" Morcant announced as I entered the room. "He lives! Come join us! Troucillos here has news."

As I bent myself piece by piece into a chair, with no few grunts, Troucillus began, "It was a busy night in Bibracte ... you alright, Arth? I've seen fifty-year-olds with arthritis move better than you?"

As I finally got myself seated with an explosive sigh, Morcant said, "After-battle pains. Any warrior worth his salt has them after a fight ... bumps, bruises, cuts ... it means he was up close to the enemy."

I thought I heard Rhonwen snort.

"So, my news," Troucillus started. "Druce purged the king's guard last night. A lot of them were swept up with the ambush squads along with most of the henchmen of that black druid of Malouuhnos ..."

"Wouldn't members of the *gorchuhmuhn derwuhdai*, the order of priests, be ... uh ... *imiouned* ..." I asked.

"'Sacrosanct'?" Troucillus answered. "Immunity is a concept Rhufeinai and the Groegai use to protect their elite from prosecution for their crimes. Among the Gah'el, no one is immune from the laws of Lugos, not even the king."

Troucillus continued, "Besides, most of those arrested were thugs and landless men enlisted by Malouuhnos' crazed priest and dressed up in black robes. Be that as it may, you'll never guess who else was caught in Druce's net."

Troucillus leaned in as if he were going to tell a great secret. I did my best to emulate him, but my aching ribs and shoulder stopped me.

In a stage whisper, Troucillus said, "Malgounos! Malouuhnos' own nephew, Malgounos! He was with the bunch who were waiting to ambush me down the hill from Duuhruhda's stronghold!"

Troucillus sat up with a satisfied look on his face.

"So ... this means ..." Morcant started.

"This means we have Malouuhnos by his short and curlies!" Troucillus announced.

Then, he remembered Rhonwen, "My apologies, lady..."

"Don't fret yourself, Troucille," Rhonwen laughed. "I'm not some *gouraic Rhufeinig*, 'Roman her-ladyship', pretending to be an untouched blossom!"

Troucillus nodded and continued, "So, Druce is delivering the bad news to Malouuhnos! Either he cooperates with the king's proposal in council to appoint you his *pendefig* and brings his ally Bruhchamos with him, or he hands Malgounos over to Anionos, Duuhruhda's barnuchel, for judgment on charges of breaking the king's peace, a breach of the king's hospitality, and attempting to kill a king's guest with the rank of *pendefig*. The honor-price alone would be crippling!"

"What about the others ... those black druids and the traitors?" Rhonwen asked.

Troucillus shrugged, "They will be tried, found guilty, stripped, and banished, I imagine. The collaborators among the king's *fintai* will be fined, I'm sure. The officers and veterans among them may be stripped of their honor price and put on the road. The younger soldiers, a fine and some lessor punishment. That's Druce's plan, anyway."

"So, it's over?" Morcant asked.

Troucillus shrugged, "Malouuhnos' druid hasn't been found yet. The king's men are searching Bibracte for him. And, the so-called "Witch of the Tomb" seems to have gone missing as well. They may have fled the town. Duuhruhda is putting out the word that if they surrender themselves, they will only face the judgment of his barnuchel ..."

"And, if they do not?" I interrupted.

Troucillus shrugged, "And, if they do not, they'll be turned over to the Rhufeinai for the murder of their soldier."

"*Erunt cruci suffecti*! I blurted in Latin. Then, I remembered where I was. "They'll be hung!"

Troucillus nodded. "Labienos wants revenge for his man! And the soldiers need to see that *men* killed their mate, not some mythical blood-drinking monster. Labienus will string both up, right where everybody can see it. And he'll have Duuhruhda's blessing."

There was silence for a few heartbeats. Then, Troucillus said, "I don't imagine you've heard yet what Labienos did this morning?"

We shook our heads

"Apparently before dawn, Labienos marched seven cohorts of the Tenth legion north in full battle array to witness the funeral of his murdered soldier, this Rufus fellow. They burned the man right in the crossroad with all seven cohorts plus that of Strabo lined up for him. They sang a funeral paean loud enough to wake the infernal gods. The guards manning the northern gate thought the town was being attacked. They almost lit the beacon on the northern tower."

I had seen how the legions honor their dead after the fight with the Helvetii and again after our fight with the Suabii at the Hill of Flocks. It was the way the Romans appeased the *lemures* of their slain comrades.

"That is nothing remarkable," I said. "The fact that Labienos marched almost an entire legion north for one man, maybe …"

"Ah! But you haven't heard all of it," Troucillus continued. "After the funeral, when the sun was fully up, Labienos marched the Tenth south, right under the walls of the town, drums beating, *cornua* and trumpets blaring. When he got opposite the king's stronghold, he halted, arrayed the troops in battle formation facing the town, *acies simplex*, one long battle line of cohorts. There they stood and serenaded the king for almost an hour. I watched Labienos' little show myself alongside Duuhruhda and Druce. And believe me … they got Labienos' message! Justice for my man, or I'll exact it myself."

"Certainly, the Caisar would not authorize an attack on Bibracte!" Rhonwen protested.

Troucillus shrugged, "And, that is what I have advised Labienos. But should Labienos ignore my warnings, Bibracte could be ashes before the Caisar could stop it. Besides, there are many in Rome who would applaud Labienos' action. In their histories, the Rhufeinai boast of destroying entire civilizations for less an insult than murdering one of their soldiers. Their senate might award Labienos an ovation for destroying a mere town to avenge the murder of *un milour Rhufeinig, a single* Roman soldier."

We were silent again. I thought I detected a slight smile cross Morcant's lips. Despite recent developments, he and his clan were still no friend of Duuhruhda.

Troucillus started again, "That just leaves the small matter of Deluuhnu and his Bolgai …"

"Certainly, they'll turn back once they hear of king's purge in Bibracte and Malouuhnos' submission," Morcant suggested.

Troucillus shrugged, "That would make sense, Morcant, but we can't assume that Deluuhnu will act rationally. He is still furious over his unjust treatment by the Caisar and his brother's seeming collaboration in his banishment … no … we cannot depend on Deluuhnu being rational. Besides, despite Malouuhnos giving in to the king, Druce warns there are no assurances that Malouuhnos' war bands will not still join Delu-uhnu. They have been proselytized by the black druids to believe in this Afalanos apoc-alypse and the destruction of all foreigners contaminating the nation."

"What then," asked Rhonwen.

"What then?" Troucillus echoed. "Duuhruhda is sending word to Labienos that he has the king's authorization to send troops north, even if they are clearly seen as Rhufeinai. And Morcant, I believe your first job as *pendefig uhr Aineduai*, high prince of the nation, will be to lead a war band north against the invaders."

The Council of Three Generations was due to convene at the sixth hour when the eye of Lugos would be high above the proceedings. Troucillus wanted me to attend as part of his entourage. I was feeling a bit better now that I had stretched out my limbs and moved around a bit. But I dreaded the idea of having to climb up on a horse, even for the short trot over to the *Tir Pori Gouart'eg*, the Cattle Pasture.

Little did I know what Fate and Morcant had in mind for me!

Spina appeared halfway through the fourth hour. He announced that he had fin-ished sick parade down in the Roman camp and now wanted to examine his "favorite patient." Since he announced this while filling a cup with Rhonwen's red mead, his sincerity was at best questionable.

But examine me he did. We went back into my sleeping chamber; Rhonwen fol-lowed. She stood back and said nothing while Spina checked my ribs: "Dat hoit? ... How 'bout dat?" Then my shoulders: "Can ya feel me touchin' you heah? ... You got pain heah?" But, when Spina unwrapped the bandages around my wounded forearm, Rhonwen got in as close as a hungry puppy to its mam.

"Ah ... dat's good woik!" Spina exclaimed as he unwrapped the arm.

Rhonwen smiled and nodded.

I looked. There was a reddish black line down the flesh of my arm almost two *pal-mae* in length held together tightly by a series of small black stitches. I noticed it inter-sected the white, jagged scar from the faux slave in Aquileia to form a distorted X.

Spina was saying, "*Bene ... bene ...* no maw red den expected ... little swelling ... nice 'n' dry ... no pus ... blood ..."

Spina bent over the wound and sniffed, "Don't' smell nothin'," he muttered.

Then he reached up and examined my armpit, "Nuttin' swollen... dat hoit?"

"*Bene!*" Spina finally announced. "Insubrece! Would you ask da lady heah to reban-dage dee arm?" He toasted himself with a long sip of the mead.

Rhonwen was nodding as if she understood what the doctor was saying. Did she, I wondered. I was still not sure of what went between those two last night while I was slipping away into the land of poppy dreams. I felt a strange pang in my chest. I didn't then understand this reaction, but I have since come to recognize it as an early symp-tom of jealousy.

Ah! We're only teenagers once! *Laus diis*! Praise the gods for that!

Spina was sitting in a chair working on his mead while Rhonwen wrapped my arm. "I don't see anyt'ing seriously wrong wit' youse, Insubrece. So, I'm declarin' youse fit for light duty ... no fatigue details ... try not to use dee ahm too much ... no weapons practice. Keep da wrappings clean 'n' dry."

Spina took a drink and continued. "If ya get feverish ... dee ahm gets swollen, hot, aw painful ... ya get a painful swellin' in ya ahmpit ... come see me quick ..."

"Tell the *meduhg* we have herbs for that," Rhonwen muttered as she wrapped my arm.

She *did* understand him!

Spina asked, "Wha'd she say?"

"She said you do good work," I told him.

Spina nodded and took another drink. Rhonwen clucked her tongue and shook her head.

"Ya gonna have some pain," Spina was saying. "Especially in ya neck and shouldah ... it should be manageable ..."

I have learned over the years that one thing a soldier gets good at is "managing" pain." One really doesn't "manage" pain; pain has a will of its own. The best a man can do is "endure" pain, and remain functional, as best he can.

Over the years, I've learned to classify my pain into two categories in relation to my ability to function as a soldier. The first is, I'm aware of the pain, but I'm still able to concentrate on my duties mentally and physically. In the second, my entire conscious world is subsumed into the pain; the pain becomes the world in which I live, a world where time seems to creep, a world I fear I'll never escape, but I'll be trapped in it until I pray the gods to end me.

As I write this, I can still see those two scars running down my right forearm in a distorted X. The cut from the *sicarius* in Aquileia that Spina stitched up when I was sixteen; the cut from the black druid in Bibracte that Rhonwen attended to when I was seventeen. Since then, they have been joined by countless others.

A soldier's sword arm has to expose itself to do its work properly.

If I think about it, I can still feel the presence in remembered or actual pain of every injury I ever received during my years under the eagles. These pains I find easy to "manage." It's the memories that lurk in the darkness of my *anima* that are "unmanageable." Those, and my fear for my family in this sinister and unknown future I seemed to help establish – the intrigues of Octavius, Livia's *frumentarii* lurking about, or the actions of soulless madmen, like Thraex.

At times, these fears threaten to render me immobile, unable to function.

Like a good soldier, I have to remind myself that there is nothing I can do about an unknown future. The threads of my life are on the loom of the *Parcae*, the Fates: Nona, who spins the thread of my future from her distaff onto her spindle; Decima, who measures it with her rod; and Morta, who will cut it, choosing the time and manner of my death.

In many ways, it is easier to cope with the willful malevolence of a *stryx* or a Catubodua than with the cruel indifference of the Fates. I rub my *Bona Fortuna* in the hopes that she will somehow influence the Parcae in my favor. Then, I take these fears of the unknown and lock them away deep in my *anima*, so that I can continue to function as a soldier, a husband, and a father.

Whatever happens tomorrow, it will be said, *"Sic dictu Fata ...* it is as the Fates decree."

Compared to this, the physical pains of my body are nothing

The most difficult part of my attending the council was getting on the horse. When I stood at my horse's left side and tried to will my body to mount, nothing happened; my body simply refused to function. Finally, I had to ask one of Morcant's soldiers to give me a hands-up. I grabbed the left, front saddle horn with my left hand as the warrior boosted up my left leg and I threw my right leg across the saddle. Even with that, it took a few heartbeats of deep breathing before the pain in my side and shoulder passed, and I felt somewhat comfortable with my seat.

My mount was a gentle beast, a light bay gelding a bit past its prime and in no hurry to get anywhere. So, we walked gently down to the main street where Pugnus, one of Troucillus' bodyguards, was waiting for us. Pugnus took one look at my pale face and decided not to bother asking me *"quomo vadi*? ... how's it going?" He just nodded and led me - slowly - toward the meeting place in the *Tir Pori Gouart'eg*, the Cattle Pasture.

By the time we arrived, I could see most of the principal players were there. Noticeably missing was Malouuhnos' nephew, Malgounos mab Owenos, and that damnable black priest. At least at this meeting there'd be no blood and brimstone rantings about the coming Afalanos, the chosen, and the damned.

Troucillus waved us over to where he had set himself up outside the council circle. When we arrived, Pugnus quickly dismounted and helped me down from my horse. At first, I though dismounting would be easier than the mounting; then, my feet hit the ground and I saw stars.

I was still panting a bit when I lowered myself into the chair next to Troucillus. *"Ecce*! Here! Drink this," he told me handing me a cup.

It was wine, *merum*, straight up. I took a long draft, felt the heat of the alcohol fill my body. My muscles seemed to relax; the pain faded a bit. I sighed.

As I squirmed in my seat to find a comfortable position, I noticed the crowds of townspeople who had assembled to watch the proceedings. "Quite an audience for this little show," I quipped.

Troucillus nodded, "No use in putting on a show unless there's someone there to watch it."

Then, after a heartbeat, he said, "Druce sent out his men this morning to, let's say, 'encourage' attendance. I think free mead and food were involved ... see ... the Aedui are learning well from Roman politics."

I looked over at the gathering of the "three generations" of the *Wuhr Blath*, the Wolf clan. Duuhruhda, his uncle, Druce, his *barnuchel*, Anionos, and another man, a tall, stocky warrior, were hunched together in conference around the king's seat. For the first time, I noticed a force of warriors, at least a dozen, members of the king's *fintai* by their single-strand golden torcs, gathered around a covered wagon behind where the king's clan was gathered. Druce's men, Clou and Pruhderos, were standing directly behind the wagon.

Suddenly, the conference around the king's seat broke up and the tall warrior strode into the circle.

"Bledigos mab Eurig," Troucillos explained, "A ten-season warrior ... interim commander of Duuhruhda's *fintai* since Deluuhnu's downfall ... I'll bet his ears are ringing since that little palace revolt among his men last night. I believe our little drama is about to begin."

Bledigos threw up his hands until the movement and murmurings of the crowd ceased. Then, in a parade-ground voice, "*Rando! Rando! Rando*! Hear! Hear! Hear! Duuhruhda mab Clethguuhno, *Uucharix*, tribal king of the Aineduai, *Pobl'rix* of the *Wuhr Blath*, will address you!"

Duuhruhda rose from his seat and slowly entered the circle as his man, Bledigos, retreated. Duuhruhda was dressed for battle. His head was bare, but he wore a long jacket of polished chainmail extending down to his knees, split front and back for riding. A thick belt of brown leather festooned with silver disks circled his waist securing the longsword hanging from his shoulder by a reddish-brown baldric. The sword was encased in a red, leather-wrapped scabbard, secured with gold wires.

Duuhruhda entered the circle armed – a signal that his was not council business – and he halted near the middle of the circle. For a few heartbeats he remained motionless, said nothing. Then he raised his right hand to the heavy seven-strand gold torc around his neck, the symbol of the *uucharix*, the high-king of the Aineduai. Again, he remained motionless for a few heartbeats.

He began, "My people! By now I'm sure you have heard reports and rumors of violence in our streets! Groups of armed men attacking strangers, guests, and citizens alike! Revolt in our streets led by members of my own guard and incited by the black priests of this Afalanos!"

Duuhruhda stopped speaking. I could hear a low, rumbling murmur from the gathered crowd. I looked and saw nodding heads, grim faces.

Duuhruhda, "I regret to inform you that what you heard is true!"

A moan went up from the mass of people surrounding us and the council circle.

Duuhruhda raised his hands and held them up until the noise from the throng subsided.

"He's playing it well," I heard Troucillus whisper in Latin.

Duuhruhda began again. "It is over! Your king has restored the peace! Bibracte is safe again!"

A sigh!

"The agitators have been killed or captured by troops loyal to you and to your king!"

Seeds of a cheer planted among the crowd began to bloom. Cries of "Duuhruhda!" "Duuhruhda!"

"Druce placed agents among the crowd," Troucillus in Latin.

Duuhruhda remained silent as the cheering and acclamations spread across the mob like flames across dry grasslands.

Finally, he raised his hands for silence. "There is one piece of unfinished business, which I call upon the nation to witness!"

Duuhruhda remained motionless in the circle.

Bledigos urged two of his troopers forward. Each carried a thick, forked, wooden pole. They marched past the king and stood the sticks upright in the soil about three *pedes*, three Roman feet, before him. Each pole stood about six *pedes* in height, with the bottom of the forks at least five *pedes* from the ground. The soldiers hammered wooden wedges into the ground around the base of the poles. They tested the stability of the poles by trying to shake and dislodge them. When they were satisfied the poles were secure, they retreated to the edge of the circle.

This had all been prearranged, I realized! Holes dug in the ground for the poles; wedges and hammers left for the soldiers. Props! Props for Duuhruhda's drama.

Without Duuhruhda as much as moving, Druce's man, Clou, threw back the canvass flap of the wagon and stood aside. Two of Bledigos' men approached the wagon, reached in and dragged something out. First feet, then legs, then a body. They were none too gentle about it. The man flew out from the rear of the wagon and hit the ground hard. The soldiers dragged him to his feet.

It was Malouuhnos' nephew, Malgounos mab Owenos.

"Duuhruhda is about to make the Venus throw," Troucillus commented.

Malgounos had not been treated gently since his arrest. He was naked from his waist up, dressed only in trousers; even his boots had been taken, his feet showing white in the grass. His upper body showed purple bruises, signs of rough treatment; there was a livid red bruise along his left cheekbone. His hands were bound before him.

Two other soldiers, carrying a thick, wooden pole some five *pedes* in length, approached the prisoner. The guards holding Malgounos drew his elbows back, his bound wrists pulling tightly against his belt buckle. The pole was slid through Malgounos elbows across the small of his back. Then all four soldiers, two on each end of the pole, lifted Malgounos onto his toes and dragged him into the circle.

The soldiers dragged Malgounos in front of Duuhruhda, just beyond the upright forks. They forced him down onto his knees; the man was so clapped out that he didn't seem to be able to raise his head to face the king.

I looked across the circle to where the Bear clan was assembled. Malgounos uncle, Malouuhnos, was standing at the edge. His face was as pale as the snow-caps of the great mountains on a cloudy day.

Duuhruhda was holding up his hand for silence. Then, "Malgounos mab Owenos! Warrior of five seasons! Leader of a hundred! Nephew of Malouuhnos mab Dermuhtos, *pobl'rix* of the Bear Clan! Here as my guest. Bound by the laws and tradition of hospitality!"

Duuhruhda waited a few heartbeats, then continued. "This man was arrested last night outside my *dun*! He was leading a group of rebel soldiers and acolytes of the black druids. Their purpose ... murder! They planned to murder a man who was also my guest! Protected by me and by the laws of our nation!"

At this point, Anionos mab Kamehros, the king's *barnuchel*, the senior justice of the Aineduai, came forward to the edge of the circle.

Duuhruhda, continued. "This man! Malgounos mab Owenos! Violated the law of Lugos who has dictated how we are to treat guests! He invited the wrath of the god against the nation when he threatened another protected under my hospitality! A *pendefig* of the Elvai! He planned to murder a man who was the emissary of the Caisar, who would certainly have avenged this crime on the nation in blood and fire! All this because he embraced the mad rantings of the priests of this Afalanos!"

"Does he plan to try and condemn the man here? Now?" I gasped.

All the king had to do was turn and face his chief justice, who was standing not three paces behind him, to prefer these charges. By the look on Anionos' face, the verdict against Malgounos was beyond doubt. The honor and crime price for threatening a *pendefig* protected by the king under the laws of hospitality were crippling! They would also fall on Malouuhnos mab Dermuhtos, as his uncle and clan chief.

And the forked stakes! Duuhruhda was threatening *crogan*, "hovering," a punishment similar to Roman crucifixion, except our people never carried it out to the death. It was only used in the most extreme cases. Even if the victim didn't die, he was often crippled. A warrior who could not use his arms was no longer a warrior. He would be sent out on the road to beg his bread from strangers. And, Duuhruhda was threatening to hang Malgounos here, in front of the five clans and the citizens of Bibracte.

"Wait for it! Troucillus whispered. "Wait for it!"

"Malouuhnos mab Dermuhtos!" Duuhruhda called. "Malouuhnos mab Dermuhtos! Come forward!"

Malouuhnos stepped into the council circle and approached the king. He stopped about two paces on Duuhruhda's right side, slightly between the king and his prisoner. Duuhruhda gestured his rival forward. He began talking into Malouuhnos' ear; the clan chief began nodding his head.

"The message is being delivered," Troucillus chuckled.

Finally, Malouuhnos nodded and stepped back from Duuhruhda. The king raised his hands for silence and began, "I, Duuhruhda mab Clethguuhno, *uucharix* of the Aineduai, hand over the prisoner, Malgounos mab Owenos, to his clan chief for punishment ..."

A deep rumbling erupted out of the crowd that surrounded us.

Duuhruhda raised his hands for silence. When the noise subsided, he pronounced, "I declare that Malgounos mab Owenos is banished from Bibracte and from the lands of the Wolf clan!"

A slightly more accepting rumble erupted from the crowd.

Duuhruhda gestured toward Malouuhnos to remove his nephew from the circle. Malouuhnos held back for a few heartbeats waiting for the king's troopers to remove the pole from behind Malgounos' back. None of the soldiers moved. So, Malouuhnos himself began to drag the pole from between his nephew's elbows. As he did, a few of his own household troops jogged across the circle to aid their chief. They soon had the pole removed, Malgounos on his feet between them; they dragged the man out of the circle back to where his clan had gathered. Malouuhnos followed behind them, straight backed, rigid.

As soon as Malouuhnos stepped out of the council circle, Duuhruhda turned and walked back to his clan. When the king departed, his troops pulled down the forked poles and carried them out of the circle, along with the prisoner's restraint, the hammers, and wedges.

"That was quite a show," I granted Troucillus.

"That was only act one," Troucillus agreed.

As soon as Duuhruhda resumed his seat, Anionos stepped into the circle. With his right hand, he raised his oaken staff, topped with the silver hand, fingers extended, palm open, the sign of peaceful deliberation. Anionos intoned, *"Mai cuhmooliat uh popl bellac uhn decrau ...* The assembly of the peoples now begins!"

Anionos no longer needed to announce his qualifications as barnuchel, but his assistant challenged, *"A oes unrhuhw un uhmginnull uhn i che hoon uhn herio awdurdod i barnuchel i benderfuhnu materion hin?* ... Does anyone assembled here challenge the authority of the barnuchel to decide these matters?" No one in the assembly answered, and Anionos took his seat within the circle.

Duuhruhda rose, removed his sword, and entered the circle facing Anionos. Anionos nodded and his assistant handed Duuhruhda the oaken "speaking staff." Duuhruhda turned to face the clans and beyond them the people assembled around the council circle. Duuhruhda raised the speaking staff in his right hand so all could see.

The king began, "I am Duuhruhda, son of Clethguuhno, *Pobl'rix*, clan leader of the *Wuhr Blath*, the Wolf clan, and *Uucharix*, tribal king of the Aineduai. I nominate as my *pendefig* ..."

"Wait for it," Troucillus hissed.

"... Morcant mab Cuhnetha, *pobl'rix*, clan leader of the *Wuhr Tuurch*, the Boar Clan."

"And so, act two begins," Troucillus chuckled.

After Duuhruhda made his nomination, there was silence around the circle. The king returned to his seat handing the speaking staff to Anionos' assistant as he stepped from the circle. Anionos waited more than a few heartbeats, then asked, "Are there more nominations?"

Nothing but silence. I saw Troucillus nodding with a small grin on his face.

Then, Anionos, "If there are no further candidates, I ask the delegations of the five clans to demonstrate their acceptance of Morcant mab Cuhnetha as *pendefig* of the nation!"

The delegations from Duuhruhda's Wolf Clan, Morcant's Boars, and Karadogos' Foxes stepped immediately into the circle. The nomination had technically carried. Any drama now lay with the reaction of the northern clans.

I looked across the circle to where Malouuhnos and his people stood. For a few heartbeats, there was no movement. Then, Malouuhnos stepped to the edge of the circle. He turned toward his ally, Bruhchamos, with a grim, slow, purposeful nod, and stepped into the circle. Bruhchamos and the Badger Clan followed suit.

The nomination had carried unanimously. Morcant was now *pendefig* of the Aineduai. The Roman alliance was safe!

I remember Caesar, in one of his informal lessons to me on leadership and negotiation, cautioned me about balancing long and short-term goals.

"You have to be careful, Gai. You may understand clearly that your objective is to drain a swamp but if, as our Egyptian friends say, you have a croc about to swallow you up, you have to drop everything and take care of that first, as if it were your only concern."

It was a cold night in late *Ianuarius*. We were drinking warm mulled wine huddled around a hearth in the *focus domus*, the private family quarters, of Caesar's villa south of Rome. This was where he had stashed the Macedonian and her brat, whom she had cheekily named Caesarion, well outside the scared precincts of the city where things such as an eastern mistress and an illegitimate child could be tolerated, or at least ignored. I was his *centurio ad manum*, detached from the army and in charge of security and babysitting. Cleopatra was off supervising the staff's changing the soiled linens of the future pharaoh of the two Egypts and putative dictator of Rome.

"The thing you got to be careful of is whether the short-term act excludes achieving the long-term goal. If it does, you just have to let that croc have his lunch. Of course, if the short-term thing could ruin you ... get you killed ... then you have to take care of it. Then, you must deal with the reptile as if killing him were your only concern. Once that's done, take stock and formulate a new plan. Remember, there are many roads that lead to Rome. If the one you're on is blocked, find another!"

At that point, the Macedonian burst into the room in a cloud of multicolored, flowing silks, tinkling of bangles and bracelets, and a cloud of jasmine and lilac perfume. She poured herself a cup of the warm wine, saying "*Tu' filius*, your son has finally settled down, *mi falco*. I don't think the Roman food the slaves are feeding him agrees with him!"

Cleo had taken to calling Caesar "My Falcon" in private. She claimed it was the powerful totem animal of the great Egyptian god of the sun, Horus.

Caesar thought it was a dig about the shape of his nose.

Knowing the Macedonian, it was probably both.

"Come! Join us, *Catula*," Caesar invited patting an open spot on his couch.

"Kitten" took a sip of the mulled wine and pulled a face. "I don't know how you can drink this stuff ... it's dreadful!"

By that time, the Macedonian's Latin was flawless; she could pass for someone who was born and raised on the Palatine. She always had a flair for languages. Many times, I have seen her entertaining her guests switching between the koine, Latin, Egyptian and even Parthian flawlessly. At her insistence, I had begun to teach her Gah'el. When

I asked her why she was interested in the language of a people she would never encounter, she'd just shrug and say something like, "You never know ... besides ... I'm bored."

She was saying, "Oh, Gai! Would you be a dear? Caesarion would love it if you'd give him a tuck in! You know how he dotes on you."

That was my signal that "Kitten" had something to discuss with her "Falcon" that was not for my ears.

Caesar gave me a slight nod and I left the room.

With Morcant's election, Troucillus felt quite content with himself. He had stabilized Duuhruhda's throne, protected the Roman alliance, and seemed to have put an end to the Afalanos nonsense.

What he couldn't possibly have known was that he also sowed the seeds of a greater revolt. When the *Vercingetorix*, the so-called great warrior king of the nations, rose in revolt against Caesar, the two northern clans of the Aedui would join him. I'm sure a part of Malouuhnos' motivation was to avenge the insult he had received that day at the hands of Caesar's agent, Troucillus.

But how was Troucillus to know? He clearly understood his immediate goal, but he had no idea what the long game was. None of us did. Not even Caesar. *Navem gubernare per noctem sine stellis*, as the Romans say; "we were steering a ship in a starless night." When the steersman does not know how to reach port, how can he plot a course?

Morcant stepped forward in front of Anionos. The barnuchel raised the six-strand golden torc of the *pendefig* of the nation. He handed the torc to Duuhruhda who had come forward. The king placed the torc around Morcant's neck. Morcant turned to face the center of the circle. It was now tradition that each of the clan chiefs come forward and embrace him. Karadogos did so immediately, pounding Morcant on the shoulder as he released his embrace and stepped back to allow the others to approach. Malouuhnos stood for a heartbeat near the edge of the circle scowling, then turned and strode out of the circle. Bruhchamos watched his ally depart. He looked over to where Morcant and Duuhruhda were standing; both were looking directly at him. Bruhchamos tossed a brusque nod in their direction, then followed Malouuhnos out of the circle.

"Best we could expect," Troucillus was commenting. "Now ... act three!"

Duuhruhda was holding up his arms to silence the crowd. Finally, Bledigos stepped forward, handed the king his sword, and shouted, "*Rando! Rando! Rando!* The king wishes to speak!"

When the crowd settled down, Duuhruhda raised his sword up in his right hand and began, "Clan chiefs! Warriors! My people! I have grave news affecting the nation!"

With the report of "grave news," everyone went silent.

"Our scouts and our allies report that a force of Bolgai, too large for our clans in the north to resist, have launched a raid into our territory!"

Now, Duuhruhda now had everyone's complete attention. I noticed he didn't mention that this "Belgian raid" was being led by his own brother, Deluuhnu.

Troucillus read my thoughts. "We discussed it last night," he whispered. "We agreed that Deluuhnu is still popular with certain segments of the people. We didn't want to distract their loyalty and resolve by the mention of his name."

Duuhruhda, "We believe the Bolgai will not be content with a few head of cattle and some slaves! They're objective is to attack Bibracte!"

A murmur across the crowd.

"Our allies, the Rhufeinai, have graciously offered to defend our town ..."

The murmur became a grumble.

"... but I have told them that Aineduai have always been able to defend themselves against any enemy ..."

Shouts of support from spots within the crowd. Druce's agents, I assumed.

"... our new *pendefig*, Morcant mab Cuhnetha, will ride forth this very day leading his personal *fintai* from the Boar Clan and leading the *fintai* of the *uucharix* of the nation to meet this threat ..."

The acclamation was general now.

"... he will join with the war bands of the northern clans, who are even now fighting a delaying action, and together they will destroy this enemy as the Aineduai have always destroyed their enemies!"

With the mention of the "northern clans," I looked over to Troucillus and raised my eyebrows. Troucillus just shook his head.

The crowd was cheering itself into a frenzy. In a way, it was a master stroke. A once divided nation now had a single, foreign enemy to hate.

I realized also that Duuhruhda's dismissal of Roman help got Labienus off the hook. His *turma* of Gallic cavalry from the Eleventh Legion was due to arrive this afternoon with mounts too exhausted to continue north. Now, Labienus could stand them down.

And, if Labienus stood the legions down, I assumed I would have some time to rest and recuperate from my own injuries.

I was wrong.

I saw Troucillus rise from his seat. Morcant was approaching us; Rhonwen was close in his wake.

"Congratulations, *pendefig*," Troucillus said in Gah'el.

"Thank you, *a pen*," Morcant answered. "I understand I have much to thank you for."

Troucillus shook his head, "It was nothing, *a pen* ... nothing at all."

"I am almost embarrassed to ask another favor of you, Troucille," Morcant said.

"Ask! And, if it is within my power to grant, it's yours, *a pen*," Troucillus offered.

Never make an open promise, Caesar had warned me many times. Unfortunately, Troucillus had not remembered that lesson.

"Arth, here," Morcant asked. "I'd like him to ride north with me as the eyes and ears of you and of the Caisar ... that is, if he's able."

I was about to ask Morcant if he had lost his mind. I could hardly stand up straight without groaning. Then, I saw Rhonwen. Her eyes were watching for my reaction, expressionless. I feared for her this was a test. If I begged off, would she think me weak? If I accepted, would she think me a *miles gloriosus*, a foolhardy, swaggering fool?

A seventeen-year-old boy does not have the maturity – or the *coleones* - to make a rational decision when he thinks impressing a girl is at stake. And, a seventeen-year-old boy is far too likely to favor *optio mascula* – the macho choice.

Before Troucillus could speak, I said, "I would be honored to ride at your side, *a pen*!"

XIV

Caput XIV De Iterinere Vehemente Per Montibus
Chapter 14. A Wild Ride Through the Hills

I have learned over the years that there is a vast difference between *saying* you'll do something and *actually* doing it. And bad promises made in haste usually lead to an almost immediate and overwhelming surge of regret.

No sooner were the words, "I would be honored to ride at your side, *a pen*!" past my lips, then I regretted the promise.

Sheer bravado, really!

I could hardly ride from Morcant's quarters to the Cattle Pasture on a gentle nag! Now, I was committed to a wild ride on a war horse through forests and hills chasing Belgae, rebel tribesmen, and mad druids!

All because I was trying to impress Rhonwen.

Why?

At seventeen years old, I hadn't a clue.

I just felt compelled.

Morcant was squeezing my shoulder, thanking me. Troucillus was looking at me as if I had lost my mind. Rhonwen just smirked and walked away.

I was *perfututus*! Totally screwed! Even worse, I had screwed myself.

As we walked back to our horses, Troucillus leaned into me and asked, "Are you sure you can do this?

I just shook my head. I wasn't even sure I could get back up onto my horse.

We left Bibracte during the ninth hour. Morcant was leading the equivalent of three *turmae* – about ten riders from his own men and eighty cavalry troopers from Duuhruhda's *fintai*. We also had a detachment of five warriors belonging to Malouuhnos' clan whose job was to "negotiate" with any of Malouuhnos' people who were riding with the Belgae. Malouuhnos and his ally, Bruhchamos, were "invited" to remain in Bibracte for their own safety as Duuhruhda's "guests" until the "crisis" was resolved. Clou and Pruhderos were also coming along for their boss, Druce.

Troucillus had managed to bring my horse, Clamriu, up from the camp of the Tenth Legion. She wasn't as docile as my gelding, but she and I were now a trained pair; she reacted immediately to my commands and leg pressure. I was as stiff as an Egyptian mummy. Spina had immobilized me from my hips to my chest by tightly wrapping my sore ribs in linen bandages. Fortunately, Clamriu was used to reacting to the pressure of my legs and knees; the use of my heels was at best an iffy proposition.

The war bands of the Gah'el are not organized as well as those of the Roman army; in fact, Roman officers considered them unruly mobs. The troopers were not "assigned" to an officer but tended to group themselves freely according to family relationships or into groups of friends. The good news was that warriors would not abandon family or friends on the battlefield. The other news was that once committed to battle, large formations were uncontrollable; they followed their friends wherever they led regardless of the tactical situation.

We rode out through the main gate and were soon passing Strabo's camp. The Romans had been informed of our coming, so there were no security formalities to speak of. I spied the mounts of the cavalry *turma* who had come in from the east. The troopers were walking their tired horses, so I assumed they had only recently arrived.

Further up the road, we encountered a group of mounted Roman engineers. I spied Strabo among them; like a good *mulus*, he was barely able to remain on the right side of his horse.

I broke out of the Gallic column and called out, "*Salve, centurio*! Greetings, sir!"

It took Strabo a few heartbeats to realize that a "shaggy wog" was speaking to him in Latin. Then, I saw recognition in his eyes, "Pagane? That is you, isn't it! Gone completely native, have we?"

"*Cum apud Gallos, ut Gallos*!" I shrugged. "When among the Gauls, be one."

Strabo nodded. "*Fortuna a'te rideat*! May Fortune smile on you! From what I hear, you may need it!"

When Strabo mentioned Fortuna, I rubbed my chainmail *lorica* where my medallion hung and mouthed the prayer, "*Fortuna memento me*! Fortune, remember me!" We had no idea what we were riding into up north.

I shrugged and answered "*Sic dictu fata*! As fate decrees! What can we expect down here, sir? We may have to pass back through in a hurry."

Strabo nodded. "Good point. In a rush, my men may not be able to tell good wogs from bad wogs. *Coleones Martis*! I could hardly recognize *you*! The challenge and password won't work, so let's do this ... have your people yell *canes quot*', 'four dogs'. That way my people will know you're friendlies."

The "four dogs"! A losing throw in knuckle bones! I hoped than wasn't an omen.

I nodded, "What can we expect moving south?"

"As soon as those long-haired Romans from the Eleventh rest their nags, I'll deploy them as a screen north of here. They're the guys you're mostly likely to contact first, so being wogs may work out to your advantage ... we're looking for a good place to deploy my cohort across this road ... a good choke point so the enemy can't turn my flank but not too far in case we have to leg it back to the *castrum* in a hurry."

I nodded and asked, "And, Labienus?"

Strabo ignored my informality about a senior officer. "The legate plans to establish a battle line with most of the Tenth on suitable ground east of Bibracte. It's the enemy's most likely axis of advance. He's going to scrape together a blocking force northwest of the town with his third-line cohorts and any auxiliaries he can scrape together ..."

"That's a bit thin," I inserted.

Strabo ignored my interruption and nodded. "The Ninth is assembling on the Arar. That should take two days. We decided not to bring them across piecemeal. So, they should be up with us in no more than four days. The Eighth is marching up from Lugdunum. Figure two days ... three at the most. So, whatever comes down from the north, we have to hold here three, maybe four days."

I nodded. Most of Morcant's column had passed me by on the road. "*Bona fortuna, centurio*! Good luck, sir!"

"*E'ti*!" Strabo answered as I was turning Clamriu. "You, too! And, Pagane!"

"Yes, sir?" I answered.

"When you get back down here, after this little boondoggle is over, we're going to have to do something about your military appearance," Strabo winked.

"*A'mperi'tu, centurio*," I answered in a parade-ground voice, "Yes, sir!"

I turned Clamriu's head and followed my column north.

We rode hard well into the first watch of the night. We halted a few miles southeast of the water gap which led into the lands of the Bear Clan where we expected to make contact with the Belgae and Deluuhnu's rebels.

When I say we halted, I meant exactly that.

This was no Roman-trained force organizing itself in a tight, defensible perimeter for the night. The column halted; word came down we were stopping for the night; troopers drifted off in small groups into the forests along the road. I was standing in the middle of the road still mounted on Clamriu, barely clear on what was happening, and already I could see fires glowing through the trees and men clustered around them, laughing, drinking beer, eating their rations, or just wrapping themselves in their blankets for the night.

Two riders appeared suddenly out of the gloom in front of me. Clou and Pruhderos.

"Here you are, Arth," Clou started. "We were afraid you had already faded into the woods with the rest of our little army."

I shook my head then realized they probably could see the gesture in the dark. "No ... not yet ... I was about to find Morcant ..."

"No point," Clou interrupted. "Our new *pendefig* is already in his blankets ... feel that wind? The hawk's out tonight."

Before I could respond, Clou continued, "It's gonna get cold ... may even see some snow flurries! Got an idea. Remember Ludnert? His place is just a few thousand paces up the road. I'd rather spend a cold night next to a warm fire drinking his beer than sleeping on rocks out here in the woods."

"You mean leave the column without permission ..." I started.

I stopped. I was thinking like a Roman soldier afraid to go ASP, *Abesse Sine Potestate*, Absent Without Authorization. Such an offense, in the face of an enemy, was punishable by death.

The Gah'el had no such concept. Gallic warriors didn't "enlist"; there was no *sacramentum* sworn to the king. They just joined a band and followed a chief into battle when they wanted. When they decided for whatever reason they had had enough, they just left.

No one would be calling our names for rollcall at dawn tomorrow. When Morcant decided it was time to go, word would be sent down the column, and the troop would just mount up and ride west. No one would care if there were a few less riders in the column.

I corrected myself, "... uhhh ... sure ... makes sense. I haven't felt my feet since the sun went down... a couple of miles, you say?"

"*Sha!*" Clou agreed. "Yeah! Let's get outta here before some of these other guys get the same idea."

I followed the two shadows of my friends down the road. Soon, we were beyond the lines of our campfires. I looked up through the overhanging trees until my aching shoulder and neck stopped me. The sky was so clear the stars didn't seem to flicker. The *Galaxia*, the *Via Lactea*, Road of Milk, as the Romans sometime call it, seemed a glowing cloud arching across the black firmament.

When I was a child, mama told me that the *via lactea*, was formed when Rhea Silvia was nursing her twins, Romulus and Remus. The boys' father, the god Mars, took Romulus to be suckled by his divine lover, Venus, so he would be endowed with godlike qualities. While she was doing this, Venus' husband, Vulcan, returned unexpectedly from his forge. Venus handed Romulus over to his father so quickly that some milk escaped from her breast, forming a milky path across the heavens.

Suddenly, Pruhderos was riding at my side. "Sky's clear as fountain water," he said. "Night's as clear as this can get cold. It'll be good sleeping under a roof next to Ludnert's fire."

"That it will," I agreed. "That it will."

"How's that shoulder of yours doing?" Pruhderos asked.

I rolled my right arm in its socket and felt pain shoot across my shoulders. "Could be worse," I hissed.

"Sure," Pruhderos chuckled, "You could be in the Land of Youth guzzling mead and bouncing a red maiden on your knee."

"And fighting over the hero's portion," I laughed. "It was a good thing you were there that night."

"It was a good thing you ducked," Pruhderos answered.

After a few heartbeats, I asked, "How we gonna find this place in the dark?"

"Ludnert is chartered by the king," Pruhderos explained. "He receives a stipend of five silver pieces every month from the royal treasury to run his place. So, by law, he has to hang a burning lantern on a white-washed post along the road all night so travelers can find his place in the dark."

I gave an affirmative grunt in response.

We rode the rest of the way in silence. Despite Pruhderos' assurance, there was no burning lantern. Clou spotted the place by picking out the silhouette of the roofline against the stars. As soon as we rode into the courtyard, dogs within the house started barking.

Then, we heard a man's voice yell, "Shut yer bloody gobs, the lot a ya!"

Clou was off his horse banging on the door, "Open up, Ludnert, ya lazy bastard! It's Clou and Pruhde! We even got young Arth with us."

The voice behind the door, "Keep yer bloody knickers tied!"

The sound of the bar being removed, then the door swung in and lantern light poured out. "Whatta ya doin' wanderin' around this time a night, Clou. Ya gave me a start."

"Where's your lantern, Ludnert? We almost rode passed your door," Clou said.

"Lantern? There's no one out on the road this close to Samon'win, except fools like you and your pals here ..."

Then, "Boy! ... Boy!"

A small boy approached from behind the door rubbing his eyes. "There y'are! Take care of these gentlemen's horses ... give 'em a good rub ... some barley!"

Then to us, "Get y'arses in here before we lose all the heat outta the house."

The boy brushed past us as we entered. Despite the cold, he was wearing no shoes.

When we were inside, Ludnert noticed the gear under our cloaks. "Chainmail ... swords ... so the rumors are true ..."

Clou put his helmet down on a table. "Let us get out of these rigs ... maybe some beer? Something to eat? We're famished."

Ludnert nodded, "Let me see what I can rustle up."

We helped each other out of our *loricae*. Taking that chainmail off my injured shoulders was one of the worst moments of my day. When Clou saw the bindings wrapped around my padded *subarmalis* jacket, he whistled through his teeth, "Still botherin' you, huh."

"Only when I breathe," I quipped and dropped into a chair with a long sigh.

Ludnert came in with a basket of rolls, a pitcher, and some cups. "Here! Start on this, boys. I'm heating up what's left of today's stew."

"Sure it's *today's* stew?" Pruhderos jibed pouring the beer.

I stuffed a roll into my mouth then realized my mouth was too full to drink any beer. I considered for a moment whether to chew my way through the dry bread or use my fingers to remove enough to make room for the beer. I went with the former, chewing and gagging until I could take a drink and wash the rest of the roll down.

Pruhderos was stoking up the fire, and soon I could feel the warmth leeching the cold out of my body. I moved a chair so I could get my feet up toward the fire, then drained my beer, belched, and poured another cup.

Ludnert came back in. "A little bit longer on the stew ... still lukewarm."

Ludnert plopped down onto a chair and poured himself a beer. "So, what brings you back up here this late in the season dressed for war?"

"We're riding with the *pendefig* ..." Clou started. When Ludnert's eyebrows went up, Clou realized he had gotten ahead of himself. "The nation has a new *pendefig* ... Morcant mab Cuhnetha ..." he stated.

"Morcant mab Cuhnetha?" Ludnert said. "Morcant mab Cuhnetha ... is that the grandson of the old king?"

"If you mean the one before Clethguuhno" Clou explained. "The one who dropped dead during the time of *Cluhfel uhr Almaen Faour*, the Great German War, then yes ... that's the one."

Ludnert whistled through his teeth. "A new *pendefig*, is it ... that still doesn't explain what yer doin' up here this time a year in chainmail and helmets."

Clou was just about to say something when Ludnert sniffed the air and said, "Hold that thought, Clou! I gotta tend to the stew."

As Ludnert bustled toward the kitchen, we poured the last of the beer. Pruhderos called out, "Would ya be bringin' us some more of this beer, Ludnert."

Ludnert's voice from the back, "Get it yer bloody self, Pruhde ... you know where the barrel is!"

Pruhderos got up, grabbed the pitcher, and muttered, "Good hospitality's a dyin' art these days."

The front door burst open and Ludnert's boy came in with a flood of cold air, "Yer horses're fed 'n' up fer the night, gents!"

"Good job!" Clou said and tossed the boy a brass coin.

Then from the back, Ludnert, "Come back here, boy, an' give me a hand!"

Pruhderos returned with an overflowing pitcher.

"Took ya long enough," Clou said. "Wha'd you do? Sample the entire stock?"

"Had to make sure it was up to standard," Pruhderos winked and filled our cups.

Our cups were half-way down when Ludnert and his boy brought in the food, bowls of steaming brown stew. "It's mutton in case yer wonderin'," Ludnert announced as he placed the bowls on the table.

We were too hungry to wonder; we dug right in.

I was half-way down the bowl before I came up for breath. Clou was asking Ludnert, "So, what's the news from the north?"

"Nothin' good," Ludnert was shaking his head. He had taken a seat between me and Pruhderos and was sampling his own brew. The boy was sitting off to the side with a small cup of beer.

"Malouuhnos' people have sealed the water gap, no one in, no one out," Ludnert continued after a long drink. "Still, word filters down."

"About?" Clou pressed.

"Things people've heard, not seen, mostly" Ludnert shook his head. "The neighboring tribes are raidin' ... the king's brother has come back ... even tales of Bolgai down from the north ... don't believe the half of it."

"The half of it's bad enough," Pruhderos inserted.

"You may not believe it, Ludnert, but it got your attention enough that you're not showing your lantern at night," Clou accused.

Ludnert nodded, "Can't be too careful these days ... they say they got black priests up north cuttin' the hearts outta people ... the old gods are comin' back at the Samon'win ... all me time here never heard such mad tales ... never!"

"Don't worry, old friend," Clou told him. "We're riding north with the *pendefig* to put things right."

In the warmth of the fire, my belly full and a few cups of beer in me, I began to nod. Clou spotted me.

"We'll be heading out in the morning," he told Ludnert. "Best we get some sleep."

Ludnert nodded. "I'll get ya some blankets."

Then, "Boy! Give me a hand cleaning up."

Despite my many aches and pains, I was asleep as soon as I wrapped myself in my blanket. The next thing I remember was waking up and seeing sunlight through the smoke hole. I bolted up throwing my legs off the table I was sleeping on. I immediately regretted it. Between my stiffened muscles, cracked ribs and bruised shoulders, my head exploded red with pain. "*Cac't! Cac't! Cac't,*" I cursed in Latin.

"You always this noisy when you wake up," I heard Pruhderos' voice from under a seeming pile of blankets on a table next to me.

"The sun's up," I hissed. "We missed movement."

Pruhderos' head popped out of his cocoon, "You're right about one thing ... it's morning! As far as the boys leaving us behind, I doubt that ... they're just starting to stomp the cold out of their feet and build their breakfast fires ... which reminds me, I could do with some breakfast myself."

Ludnert's door burst open and Clou came in, dressed but not armored. "About time you two decided to return to the land of the living! A troop of scouts just rode by toward the water gap. Don't know whether Morcant's going to wait here for them to get back or follow them into the gap. So, roll your arses out of those blankets. We got time to eat, then we got to get on the road."

Breakfast was beer, hot porridge and bread. The boy saddled our horses and we helped each other into our chainmail jackets. I was ducking into my baldric, when Ludnert noticed my sword. "Didn't know you Elvai took to wearin' those little *Rhufeinig* pig-stickers."

I was wearing my *gladius*, my short sword. With my stitched-up forearm and my injured shoulder, I couldn't imagine trying to swing a *spatha*, a cavalry saber, which I had tied down to my saddle.

I didn't know what to say for a heartbeat. Ludnert continued, "Unless you *are* one of those Rhufeinig gobshites ..."

"Insubres!" I blurted. "My tribe's the Insubres!"

"Insubres?" Ludnert pressed. "Never heard a that bunch?"

"We're from over the mountains ..." I started.

Before I could finish, Clou spoke up, "Arth here's working with us under the protection of *Mair Duhn Mawr*, 'The Big Guy'. Whether he scrapes his face like a *merc Rhufeinig*, a Roman girl, or has mustachio's that would make a boar fall in love with him, is none of your concern, Ludnert. Besides ..." Clou grinned, "... he's a friend of the *pendefig* ... may even be family someday if things work out with that red-haired cousin of his?" Clou winked.

I felt my cheeks flare up. Was there anything that Druce and his people didn't know?

We waited a few hundred paces down the road. The vanguard of Morcant's warband caught up with us during the second hour. Morcant was riding under three banners: the Red Dragon of the Aineduai, Duuhruhda's Wolf, and Morcant's own Boar. We fell in behind Morcant's command group and rode into the water gap.

By the fourth hour, we were nearing the pass that led to Malouuhnos' lands. We had encountered no warbands, neither Belgae, rebels from the Bear clan, nor the *fintai* of Deluuhnu mab Clethguuhno. There was no black smoke on the horizon and no packs of refugees along the road. The land seemed at peace and prepared for its long winter slumber.

Ahead, I spotted a detachment of scouts beating its way back toward us. Morcant called the column to a halt.

As the scouts approached, their leader called out, "Prisoners, *a pen*. We've captured some raiders!"

As the man pulled up in front of Morcant, the *pendefig* ordered, "Report! Are there enemy troops in the pass?"

"*Na, a pen!*" the man shook his head. "No, boss! The pass is clear! We have a prisoner! We're holding him in a farmstead just beyond the gap."

Morcant turned to Bledigos who was commanding the king's *fintai*, "I'm riding ahead. You bring the main body forward."

Then to his man, Trahernos, "You're with me. Bring the Boars with us."

As Trahernos gathered the riders from the Boar clan, Morcant ordered, "Standards! Stay with the main body!"

He nodded toward the scouts, and they rode north toward the pass. Trahernos finally gathered his men and followed a few dozen paces behind trying to catch up. Then, I heard Clou say, "We need to check this out!" And he was pounding down the road behind Trahernos' band with Pruhderos and I riding to catch up.

The farmstead was no more than a thousand paces beyond the gap. It was easy to identify; the yard was crowded with the cavalry mounts. We arrived on the heels of Trahernos troop.

Then, I noticed the two bodies sprawled in the dirt. They were warriors, not farmers. Each wore a *lorica* of hardened leather, cloth trousers that ended just below the knee, and leather boots. Both lay face down, side by side, in a pools of their own blood. They were not killed in a fight; both had been executed.

I heard the chief scout reporting to Morcant, "We kept one of the *moch* alive for you to talk to ... waste really ... can't understand a word of his grunting!"

Clou was examining the bodies, "Bolgai," he whispered to us.

"Where are the crofters?" Morcant was asking his scout.

"Not a sign, *a pen*," the man shrugged. "We think they got out ... probably hiding out in the woods."

"So, no one killed?" Morcant pressed.

"Not that we can see, *a pen*," the scout responded.

Morcant nodded and entered the cabin. We followed him in.

In the dappled light, we could see the prisoner, a Bolga by his costume. He was bound and squatting on the earthen floor. His bruised face betrayed the treatment he had received from his interrogators.

One of the scouts started, "Can't understand a bloody thing he's sayin' ..." Then the man spotted Morcant. "Sorry, lor'! Didn't see ya ..."

"Don't worry about it," Morcant said. "What've we got here!"

"Prisoner, lor'!" the man said. "Kept 'im alive so's you could talk to 'im ..."

"What's your name?" Morcant asked the man on the floor.

"*Ik begrip di net!*" the man shook his head.

Morcant shrugged his shoulders.

Clou asked, "Can I give it a try, *a pen*?"

Morcant nodded.

Clou asked, "*Binne io fan 'e Golbas volc?*"

The man immediately answered, "*Ya! Ya! Golbas volc bin ik!*"

"He's Bolga," Clou reported. "One of Golba's northern tribes. The Suessionai, I think."

Morcant nodded again. "Can you find out where his people are?"

Clou interrogated the prisoner for nearly a quarter of the hour. Finally, "He and his mates are alone, *a pen*. They were riding with a band of Bolgai down from the north, but the main body pulled out ... he doesn't know why. He and his mates decided to collect some food and loot before they followed ... your people surprised them asleep in the cabin."

Morcant said, "Ask him what they did with the people who live here. Did they kill them?"

"*Wair binne de boeren?*" Clou demanded. "*Hawe io se dedsie?*"

The prisoner vigorously shook his head. I caught the words, "*Nai! Nai! Nai!*" The rest was just gibberish.

"He says no, *a pen*" Clou translated. "The cabin was empty when he and his mates arrived yesterday. They just helped themselves to some food."

Morcant nodded, then asked his chief of scouts, "Did these *moch* burn the winter larder?"

"*Na, a pen*," the man answered. "Nothin's burned that we can see."

Morcant turned to walk out of the cabin.

The scout asked, "*A pen*! What do you want us to do with the prisoner?"

"Release him!" Morcant ordered.

"Release him?" the man questioned.

"Yes! Release him. No weapons, no horse, no food, no water!" Morcant ordered.

"He won't get five thousand paces up the road," Clou stated.

"Not my problem," Morcant said.

The main body was soon up with us. They had ridden hard through the gap, so we gave them time to rest the horses before moving north.

We rode up the main road. We hadn't gone three thousand paces when we encountered a troop of Malouuhnos' Bear clan. They didn't present any hostile gestures toward us. In fact, I recognized their leader as the officer who had tried to arrest us a few days earlier. I searched his band but could see no evidence of a black-clad druid.

The leader raised an empty right hand toward Morcant, "*A pen*! I am Tahernos mab Malagronos, leader of ten, warrior of five seasons, officer in the *fintai* of Malouuhnos mab Dermuhtos. I bid you welcome!"

"Greetings, Tahernos mab Malagronos," Morcant responded without raising his hand. "I am Morcant mab Cuhnetha, *Pendefig* of the Aineduai, *Pobl'rix*, of the Boar Clan. I have been sent here by our king, Duuhruhda mab Clethguuhno, to investigate reports of invasion, treason, and rebellion."

"There is no invasion, *a pen*," Tahernos started. "We have turned back the Bolgai ..."

Clou snorted when the man said that.

"... and the Bear clan remains loyal to the *uucharix*, the tribal king."

Morcant nodded and asked, "What do you know of the outlaw, Deluuhnu mab Clethguuhno, the king's brother?"

Trahernos's eyes widened a bit then shifted to the left. "I ... uh ... I have heard rumors of the king's brother ..."

"Where is he?" Morcant demanded.

"Where is he?" Trahernos repeated.

"Where is the king's brother?" Morcant demanded again.

"The king's brother ..." Trahernos started. "He ... uh ... I have heard that he has fled north ... north along the road leading to the lands of the Parisai."

Morcant nodded, then ordered. "Clou!"

My companion rode forward and joined Morcant. "Clou! Take ten from the king's *fintai* ... ride north ... find out if what this man is telling me is true!"

Clou nodded and yelled "Pruhde! You're with me." Then, ten names of troopers along the column. I got the distinct impression that Clou was expecting this and had selected his men in advance.

As Clou's *fintai* gathered, I joined it. Clou saw me and said, "Arth! You don't have to come along. Why don't you rest your injuries? We'll be back by tomorrow latest."

Something didn't smell right about all this. "I wouldn't miss this for the world," I told him.

Clou's lips compressed into a tight line across his face. He wasn't pleased. "Suit yourself! Make sure you keep up!"

We rode hard. And I barely kept up.

By the time we rode past the *Crugmawr*, the Great Mound, my ribs hurt so badly that I gave up worrying about it. I just loosened my knees and gave Clamriu her head. Like any good Roman horse, she refused to be left behind by a motley bunch of Gallic nags.

By the position of the sun, I estimated we were well into the seventh hour when the road wound its way down into a little valley. Clou halted the troop and conferred with Pruhderos. When I came up to them, I could see why. Below us, smoke from multiple fires curled up from among the trees.

Clou rode forward so he was clearly visible to anyone below. Then he waved his arm as if to signal. I saw a figure emerge from the trees, then it seemed to lean back toward the woods and call. Another figure emerged and the first figure pointed up to where Clou was waving. The second figure nodded and both men retreated back under the trees.

Clou waited.

Soon three fully armed men emerged leading horses. They mounted and rode toward Clou. As they did, Pruhderos joined his friend.

I hung back watching.

The three riders halted and ten paces below Clou. The leader yelled, "*Chruhdid*! Freedom!"

Clou responded, "*Ar guhfer uh genedlai*! For the nation!"

The rider nodded, then asked, "Who are you?"

"Catouallaunos mab Dubnogenos," Clou responded. "I come from Druce mab Cadmanos. I've brought the package!"

The rider nodded. He said something to one of his companions; then the man turned and rode back down the slope. When the man reached the bottom, he was joined by others from the wood.

Then, the leader said to Clou, "You are to follow me."

When Pruhderos made a movement to join Clou, the rider said, "Alone! That's the deal!"

Clou nodded and said, "Wait here, Pruhde. I'll be fine." Then he followed the two remaining riders down the slope.

As they descended, I rode up next to Pruhderos and said, "What the hell's going on?"

"Just wait, Arth," Pruhderos said. "Clou will explain everything when he gets back."

When Clou got to the bottom of the slope, he dismounted. A tall man emerged from the wood. I recognized him from Caesar's *principia*, the confrontation just before the battle with the Helvetii. Deluuhnu mab Clethguuhno!

Clou and Deluuhnu spoke for a bit. Then Clou turned, opened his saddlebag, and removed an object, a large bag. He handed the bag to Deluuhnu. They spoke a few more words, then Clou remounted and rode back toward us.

When he came up to our position he said, "We turn around and ride at least two thousand paces back down the road. That's the arrangement."

As we rode back down the trail, I sidled up next to Clou and hissed, "That was Deluuhnu mab Clethguuhno! The king's brother!"

"No need to whisper," Clou responded, "You were the only one in this bunch who didn't know what we're about."

"But ... but the mission was to capture him ..." I started.

"Capture him!" Clou snorted. "And then what? Bring him back to Bibracte? And, once in Bibracte, what do you think would happen?"

My head was starting to spin, "So, you just let him escape? And what was in that bag? Silver?"

Clou was quiet for a few heartbeats, then said, "It was to buy him off ... the king won't agree to his brother being killed!"

Clou could sense I still wasn't buying it, so he continued, "Don't worry about it, Arth. It was all part of the deal."

"The deal!" I exclaimed. "What deal ..."

"The deal that made Morcant *pendefig* ... the deal that kept your precious alliance intact ... that deal!" Clou explained.

"I ... I don't understand," I stammered.

Clou shrugged, "You weren't supposed to have found out. It's an arrangement cooked up between Druce, the king, Morcant and yes ... your friend, Troucillos. Druce understood that with the Caisar in the south, we couldn't afford a civil war in the north ... that would just encourage the Rhufeinai to move in and take over. So, the Bolgai were paid off and, except for those three dolts we ran into down near the water gap, they kept their part of the bargain ..."

"But Deluuhnu ..." I protested.

"We had to separate him from the northern clans, and we couldn't bring him back to Bibracte," Clou explained. "He's still popular with the people and with elements of the Wolf clan. Besides, that would force the Caisar's hand. What do you think would happen to Duuhruhda if the king handed his brother over to the Rhufeinai? Or what do you think would happen to the Aineduai if Duuhruhda refused? No! It's better this way. Deluuhnu just disappears into the north ... he has plenty of silver now to support himself."

"And Troucillos agreed to this?" I pressed.

"Agreed to it?" Clou snorted. "It was pretty much his and Druce's idea!"

"I ... I can hardly believe it!" I muttered.

"Well, believe it! You haven't seen everything yet," Clou hinted. "Not by a long shot."

Clou's comment about not having seen everything went by me. I was still reeling from what I then considered the duplicity a friend, Troucillus.

I was still naïve back then, a babe wandering through the labyrinths of duplicity. I have since seen worse, much worse. Gabi's betrayal and destruction of her former lover, Milo. Octavius' bribery of rebellious elements in Gaul to keep Antonius pinned down along the Padus. The Macedonian's offering up Antonius to Octavius to keep her throne. And, of course, there was her attempt to murdered me in order to ensure Caesarion's escape from Alexandria.

But I was only seventeen then, not at all experienced in *romanitas*, the "Roman game." As we rode south, I even wondered whether Rhonwen's attentions was part of the plan, meant only to distract me from discovering the truth.

By sundown we had reached the area of the *Crugmawr*, the Great Mound, the portal to the lower world where the black druids offered up their blood sacrifices to Afalanos. This time, however, the road was bustling with warriors and horses, the men who had followed Morcant up from Bibracte.

Clou asked one of the troopers, "Where's the *pendefig*."

"The boss?" the man responded. "He's back in the woods with Malouuhnos' bunch!" The man gestured with his head toward where I remembered the *Crugmawr* lay.

We dismounted. Pruhderos and another trooper supported me as I dropped down from my saddle. We followed Clou under the trees. I hoped we wouldn't have to climb to The Portal; the memory of the stone altar black with the blood of children was still fresh in my mind. As we walked under the trees, I smelled smoke. I looked up and could see the gray-white tendrils creeping along under the branches.

What can possibly be burning here? I wondered. *The forest?*

We found Morcant at the base of the mound, near where we had stashed our horses last time. He was nodding, being briefed by one of his men. Finally, he grunted "*Da! Da*! Good! Good! Take care of it!" He slapped the man on the shoulder and turned to Clou.

"Is it done?" he asked.

"Done, *a pen*," Clou answered. "He's riding north."

Morcant nodded, then noticed me.

"Does he know?" he asked Clou.

"About Del ..." Clou started, then realized he could be overheard. "... about what we did? Yes! He saw it."

Morcant nodded, then walked over to me. "Arth, I'm sorry for keeping you in the dark about ... about the men who rode north ... we thought it best to tell as few people as possible. Your role was to witness what we're doing here and report it to the Caisar."

"Witness what?" I challenged. "What's going on?"

"You didn't tell him?" Morcant asked Clou.

Clou shook his head, "No ... thought it was better coming from you."

Clou nodded, then to me, "We have destroyed the priests of Afalanos ... killed every last one of them ... burned their ... their 'monastery' ... Druce insisted and Troucillos agreed."

Now, I knew what the smoke was from. I nodded.

"I know you told us what they were doing up here," Morcant was saying. "But none of us were prepared for what we saw at The Portal ... that bloody altar ... I thought

I might have problems getting my men to kill *derwuhdai,* priests, but once they saw what these cursed druids were doing up there, I couldn't hold them back ..."

Morcant looked down and shook his head. I knew what images were going through his mind.

Then, "We freed three children they were holding ... that's something, anyway ... Tahernos' men recognized them and he promised to return them to their families ..."

Morcant's face was pale.

Finally, "We toppled their altar ... it was ... was polluted ... soiled ... this year the old ones will just have to find a different portal for their return to the middle lands."

XV

Caput XV Samon'Win
Chapter 15. Samon'Win

We reached Bibracte during the third hour of the day Romans call *Pridei Calandis Novembris*; for them, it's merely the last day of October. But the Gah'el call this the 29th day of Anagantio. Tonight, at midnight, the Aineduai would celebrate the Samon'win, marking the beginning of the month of Ogronnios, the season of cold and dark. The season of the dark ones.

I was in a black mood.

Despite the aches and pains of my injuries, I was wrapped deeply within myself. All the way back from the Great Mound, I had hardly spoken a word to Morcant, or to Clou and Pruhderos. At seventeen, I couldn't put a name to my behavior, but now that I'm a parent, I've seen it many times in my own children.

I was pouting.

I remember a few months back, my son, Gaiulus, was closeted in his room in the middle of the day when he should have been out playing with his friends. When I went to check on him, I found him sitting on his bed, his fists clenched, and his lower lip stuck out. I finally coaxed him into talking about what was bothering him.

He and one of his friends had gotten into an argument over who should be the "Caesar," as they call it, in one of their little soldier games. The friend had stomped off back home, swearing he'd never play with Gaiulus again. My little Gai came home, closeted himself in his room, and began to steep like a bundle of herbs in a pot of hot water.

I finally brought him out of it by telling him a Roman soldier never behaves this way. It's selfish! It betrays the comradery that exists between men. Especially a Roman officer, who must forego his own interests and desires in favor of his duty and the welfare of his men.

It worked for Gaiulus. But, as I'm writing this, I realize I lied to my son.

There I was, a double-pay *decurio praetorianus* riding down the road from a great victory as sullen as a girl who's been told her *stola* makes her look fat. I was shunning my friends and I wouldn't have been surprised if my lower were lip were stuck out like an eight-year-old whose best friend refuses to play wooden swords with him.

All because *my* friend, Troucillus, didn't share his secret plan with me.

I thought he saw me as his friend – an equal and a confidant. But he treated me like a tool, a somewhat untrustworthy tool.

My seventeen-year-old self-importance had taken a mighty blow.

Looking back at it now, I realize that what was really fueling my misery was Rhonwen. I believed all her flirting and her attention to me was meant only to distract me from discovering her cousin's plans. Now that the actors were off the stage in that little pantomime, I would be of no more interest to her than a mouse turd in the pantry.

I felt as if my heart had been ripped out.

Roman soldiers don't cry, my Gaiulus, never!

As we rode past Strabo's camp, I could see that the cohort had stood down. There was a lone sentry over the main gate, his cloak moving in the cool morning breeze. He watched impassively as we rode by. We presented no threat to him; just another mob of wogs riding down the road.

We entered Bibracte through the northern gate. I did see one of the guards from the town garrison pump his fist as Morcant rode through. That was a good sign. Deluuhnu, the king's brother, whom we had paid off to ride north, had been the commander of the garrison before his exile. The soldiers now seemed to accept Morcant as their new *pendefig*.

I decided to split off from the main body when we were parallel to Troucillus' quarters. I waved to Clou and Pruhderos, who acknowledged me with a nod, and rode across to Troucillus' roundhouse. I was able to slide down from my saddle without assistance and turned Clamriu over to the stable attendant. He informed me that Troucillus was at the king's *dun* awaiting our return with Duuhruhda and Druce.

Just as well, I thought. I wasn't ready to face Troucillus anyway.

There was a nice fire going in the main hall. Troucillus had taken all his *custodes*, his bodyguards, with him, so one of his attendants helped me out of my armor and equipment. As soon as I had unwrapped the bindings around my lower ribs, I took a deep breath to check my injured side. It felt better, but I still couldn't draw a full breath without pain. The effort almost caused me to cough. I suppressed it; I didn't want to find out whether my bruised side would tolerate that.

I rolled my right arm in its socket and pulled my elbow across my chest. There was still pain across my shoulders, but not as sharp as it had been.

I shed my padded *subarmalis* jacket and sat in a chair near the fire. My tunic chilled me, damp from sweating underneath my chainmail and padded jacket, so I threw my *subarmalis* over myself and pulled it up to my chin like a blanket. I felt a deep warmth wrapping my tired body.

That was the last think I remembered until I felt a hand on my shoulder shaking me back into consciousness. My eyes opened and I saw Pugnus standing over me.

"The boss is back," he announced. "He'd like to talk to you."

"Whah ... Where ... Where's he at?" I managed to stammer.

"In his office," Pugnus answered jerking his head in that direction. "Need a hand?"

"No ... fine ... I'm fine," I lied.

Pugnus stepped back. I realized someone had thrown a blanket over me. I peeled that and my padded jacket back and tried to lean forward to stand. My fist effort was a painful failure. Pugnus offered me a hand, but I shook my head.

I grabbed the sides of the chair and used my arms to get to my feet. The blanket and padded jacket fell to the floor as my injured shoulder reminded me that I may not yet be ready for any gymnastics. My limbs snapped like dry twigs in in a fire. Pugnus took half a step toward me in case I decided to fall flat on my face.

I held up a hand toward him while I waited a few heartbeats for the pain to recede and my vision to clear. Then I hissed, "I got it from here ... thanks ..."

My first couple of steps across the room weren't too competent. But my muscles finally managed to unknot themselves and soon I was walking with some semblance of competence. I got to Troucillus' door, knocked on the jamb and entered.

Troucillus looked up from his desk, "Gai! You look like you've just crawled out of a sarcophagus!"

I nodded and gave him a grunt. There was a vacant chair in the room, but I was afraid if I lowered myself into it, I'd never be able to get back up. So, instead, I placed my hands into the small of my back and stretched my head up toward the ceiling.

After no few snaps and cracks, I relaxed my back and assumed a reasonable parody of the position of attention. "You sent for me, *legate*?"

Troucillus' eyebrows raised, "*Legate*? You are being formal ... I imagine you're upset with me over the Deluuhnu thing?"

"No ... *sir*!" I shook my head. "I understand why you did it."

"But you're upset because I didn't tell you about it," Troucillus countered.

"It's not my place to question a senior officer," I responded.

Troucillus sighed and shook his head, "Please, Gai ... we don't have to do this ... I regret not having told you, but it was part of the deal I made with Druce and the king. The less people who knew, the less chance there'd be a leak ..."

"So!" I started, "I'm a security risk ..."

Troucillus raised his palm, "No ... not at all ... not as far as I'm concerned ... please ... not telling you was *not* my idea ... only Clou and his detail were supposed to know ... Morcant, of course, but no one else. It wasn't personal! It was just ... just ..."

"*Secretum*?" I suggested. "Security?"

"As good a word as any," Troucillus shrugged. "Listen, stop posing like a *mulus* on punishment parade and sit. You look like you're going to collapse."

I felt the anger leaching out of my chest. I didn't want to by angry with Troucillus. What was done, was done. I felt my muscles relax. I took the offered seat and sighed.

"Pugne!" Troucillus called.

Pugnus stuck his head in the door, "Yeah, boss?"

"Would you ask one of the servants to bring in some wine?" Troucillus requested.

"Sure thing, boss!" Pugnus nodded and left.

"I'm sorry," I told Troucillus. "I understand why you had to do what you did ..."

"Is something else bothering you?" Troucillus asked.

"No!" I lied.

Rhonwen, I thought.

"It's nothing ... just tired ... it's been a rough few days."

Troucillus nodded, "Then I may have some bad news for you."

My head jerked up. I envisioned saddling back up – full kit and weapons – and riding north again to clean up some new mess.

An attendant came in with the wine. We remained silent while he poured. Troucillus thanked him and he left.

Troucillus picked up his cup and offered it in my direction, "*Salut', mi amice*!"

"*Salut*!" I offered in return.

"We have a command performance," Troucillus began. "The king is hosting a feast this afternoon ... partially to celebrate Samon'Win, partially for Morcant's elevation, and partially for the 'pacification' of the north ... of course, naming no names ... we are 'commanded' to attend ... Morcant invited you by name."

I nodded.

Exactly what I need at the moment, I thought. *I was sure Rhonwen be sitting on the dais next to her cousin in all her glory reminding me of what a dupe she made of me.*

"Oh... and one more thing ..." Troucillus said, "We'll be celebrating Morcant's daughter ... we just received word that his wife Ula gave birth to a healthy girl! Morcant will proclaim her name tonight at the feast ... Gouenhouhvar ... Gouenhouhvar merc Morcant."

Gouenhouhvar, I thought. "*The White Fey*".

At Troucillus' *strong* recommendation, I headed toward the bath. The Gah'el were not accustomed to public bathing in those days. That little gift of *romanitas* was not yet appreciated among the nations. So, there were no bath houses in Bibracte. Instead, Troucillus house, like most well-appointed residences, had a bathing room adjacent to the kitchens.

When I arrived, his attendants had already poured heated water into one of the wooden tubs. I know I needed a good soak after almost three days on horseback up in the hills. But the indulgence of the hot water relaxing the muscles in my injured shoulder evoked a sigh of pleasure and relief from my lips. I rolled a towel and placed it behind my head, leaned back into the edge of the tub, and closed my eyes. There I remained for at least three additional buckets of heated water, my wounded arm propped along the edge of the tub.

I would have remained longer, but the memory of Rhonwen teasing me in the baths in her uncle's *dun* came back to me. Then, I looked at my arm and remembered who had stitched it for me. *Stop flinching, Arth! I've seen worse cuts on a careless cook!*

I wanted no more to do with the bath.

I sighed and rose from the steaming tub; I wrapped myself in towels. I noticed Troucillus' attendants had laid out fresh linens, a clean tunic, trousers, and socks. I toweled myself off and dressed. I discovered my boots had been cleaned, brushed, and oiled.

When I walked into the main room of the house, Pugnus was there waiting.

"Good to see ya, boss. I was beginning to think you'd drown in there," he greeted me. "The legate has already left. Your horse is saddled outside. So, as soon as you're ready, we're off!"

I nodded to him. I walked into the room I had been using and found my kit there. I decided my long sword would be best. I attached it to the baldric and threw it over my head and shoulder. I drew my belt around my waist securing the sword on my left side, like a warrior of the Gah'el. I noticed my *pugio* wasn't in its scabbard. Macro's training and a year in the army had taught me well that a soldier never goes out without his *pugio* hanging from his belt. I looked about and finally located it on my cot. Someone had run it over a whetstone and oiled it. I slid it home.

As we walked out the door, I grabbed the dark-green, woolen *sagum* Troucillus had given me. It felt fairly warm outside, but there was no telling how cold it might get once the sun went down. Clamriu was saddled and ready in the courtyard. I threw the cloak over the front saddle horns and was just about to launch myself into the saddle when I stopped. Was I ready for that jump?

Pugnus was immediately at my side, his hands cupped and his knees slightly bent. "Let me give you a hand up, boss," he suggested.

I nodded and placed my left foot in his cupped hands. He lifted me up onto Clamriu's back.

"*Grati', Pugne,*" I grunted.

"*Ni'l, capu',*" he answered. "Nothin', boss."

We rode south along the main road of the town toward Duuhruhda's dun. I noticed that the people had begun to string decorations for the festivities that night. Strips of cloth, some black, some white, hung over the road. Some of the people we passed had already begun to celebrate, cups in their hands, crooked grins on their faces.

Although the Samon'win was originally a solemn and somewhat ominous observation – the return of the "dark ones" from their six-month banishment in the underworld – no one took really took all that mythic, mumbo-jumbo very seriously anymore. The night of Samon'win was a time for celebration and mischief.

Folks would rub burnt cork or ash on their faces, so the "dark ones" would think they were one of theirs. The sense of anonymity - and the mead - released people from their normal sense of decorum and propriety. There was always a spike in the birth rate during June!

As we rode, we were offered cups of various brews and vintages – and no few offers of a kiss. It would be unthinkably rude to refuse! The ride was not a long one or Pugnus and I would not need a feasting hall to celebrate!

As we passed through the stone gates with its piles of dismembered stone heads, we were in a pleasant, somewhat bemused, holiday mood. We rode across the *lawnt* to the main doors of Duuhruhda's hall. Attendants took charge of our horses while the king's chamberlain welcomed us to the feast. As is the custom, we stacked our swords in an anteroom outside the feasting hall.

It was only the ninth hour, but most of the king's guests had already arrived. The mood in the hall was as festive as that in the town. The hall was filled with loud conversation, laughter, back slapping, and no little rough-housing and jostling among the young – and not so young - warriors. Men had their arms across ladies' shoulders; the ladies had their arms around the waists of putative lovers. Many of the guests had darkened their faces with ash. Many had brought their own skins of wine or mead; I even spotted a few pitchers of beer.

Pugnus led me to a table just below the dais where Troucillus' people had been seated. A place of honor. The nearer the kitchen, the sooner served!

The Gallic boys from the Eleventh had proven their training. *Semper parati bello*! Always prepared for combat! There were at least three large pitchers of beer already on our table. A brimming mug was thrust into my hand. A few slaps on the back, and I was seated.

The best part of the Samon'win was that it signaled the end of toil. All outside work was ended, the harvests were in, military campaigning ended. As long as there was enough food in the larder and enough firewood on the pile, there was nothing to do until the spring except find a warm spot near the fire and keep the beer cup full.

The honor party began to arrive on the dais! Everyone in the hall was on their feet cheering. Before Duuhruhda entered, Druce and Troucillus took their places - Druce to the left of the royal place and Troucillus at the foot of the table.

Then, Morcant entered. The hall went wild with ovation. Rhonwen accompanied him, since Ula was still back in the clan holdings with their newly born daughter. Rhonwen wore a long, form-fitting tunic of deep green; the tight bodice was embroidered in golden swirls. The sleeves were long and swirled out at the wrists. A wide, reddish-brown belt tightly circled her small waist; a *dagr* with a silver-wired handle hung on her right side. Despite the racket in the hall, I could hear the tinkling of bells sown to the end of her sleeves and to the hem of her skirts.

To this day, I have no memory of what Morcant wore; I had eyes only for Rhonwen.

She and Morcant took their places on the king's right. Morcant raised his hands to acknowledge his welcome. Rhonwen stared out into the hall with a slight smile. Although we were no more than three paces apart, she didn't see me.

I was no longer worthy of her notice.

Finally, Duuhruhda entered the hall with his wife. The volume of the cheering increased; fists pounded on tables. It had been a good year for the Aineduai. The crops had been plentiful. A major enemy had been defeated. A new *pendefig* elected. A civil war avoided.

Duuhruhda raised his arms out toward the hall acknowledging the ovation. I had never seen his wife before. I got the impression of a tall, thin, blonde woman. For me, her presence was as faded as a full moon in the daylight sky blanched to obscurity by Rhonwen, the sun.

Finally, the clamor in the hall died down. Duuhruhda made a final gesture of recognition and took his seat. A few heartbeats passed and his wife, Breeda merc Maccos of the Senones Troucillus later told me, rose and walked around the table. She took a golden chalice from one of the servants and presented it to the hall.

"Whom shall this cup serve?" she intoned the formula.

There were a few drunken cries in answer, "Duuhruhda the King!"; "Morcant!"; "Me!"

Breeda turned and presented the cup to her husband.

He shook his head and bowed.

Breeda then presented the cup to Morcant.

He rose, took the cup from her hands, presented it to the hall, and drank!

The hall went mad! "Morcant! Morcant! Morcant!" the chant started.

As the cries died down, Breeda took a large, deep platter of steaming meat from a servant; *uh duhgsul,* the deep platter holding the Hero's Portion.

Breeda intoned, "Whom shall this platter serve?"

This time there were no answers to that question

Again, she presented the platter to Duuhruhda; again, he declined.

She offered the platter to Morcant. He took it in both hands and presented it to the hall.

"Morcant! Morcant! Morcant!" thundered under the rafters!

The clamor was cut short. As soon as Morcant sat, dozens of servers rushed into the hall to serve the guests. To a hungry Gaul, feasting far outweighed praising!

Soon, we were all tucking into a generous feast. Slabs of pork; roasted fowl; steaming river fish; platters of turnips, red carrots, scallions, asparagus, leeks, eggs, cheeses. Baskets of bread, various nuts. And, most importantly, overflowing pitchers of beer and mead. We were even treated to the first pressing of this year's cider.

From where I was sitting, I couldn't stop myself from looking up at Rhonwen. She was seated next to a tall, dark warrior. Their heads were together. Whatever he was saying made her smile and nod.

Her clan had been restored as part of the deal with Duuhruhda. She was now desirable as a mate; she could represent valuable political alliances within and beyond the nation. I wondered briefly whether a political marriage was also another part of the deal I hadn't been told about.

Cac't, I thought. *You've got to stop this! You're driving yourself mad.*

I changed seats with a legionary sitting on the opposite side of the table. Now my back was to Rhonwen and whoever was the next object of her flirtations.

I decided the best cure for a broken heart was beer ... lots of it.

I was soon well on my way to a desired alcohol-induced oblivion. I decided that I would return to the *castrum* in the morning – or whenever my hangover ended. I would bury myself in soldiering; return to the windy plains of Troy with Dion; learn to speak the *koine*, as Caesar desired. Whatever it took to remain busy, distracted.

As we ate our way through most of the food and settled down to the serious drinking, Duuhruhda's *pruhduhd,* his bard, rose and intoned, "'*Rando!* '*Rando!* '*Rando!* ... Listen! Listen! Listen!"

The hall quieted down.

The *pruhduhd* rehearsed Duuhruhda's royal pedigree back to the god, Lugos. After a brief acclaim, the bard began to sing of the traditional Samon'win telling of the Battle of Taltinos, in which the Gah'el defeated the people of Dana and vanquished them from the middle lands.

> So they came out,
> The best warriors of Dana
> To the fields of Taltinos.
> There they fought one another,
> The Sons of the Gah'el
> Recalled the death of Iha
> And there was great anger on them
> They fell on the men of Dana to avenge him
> There a fierce battle was fought
> For a time neither side could prevail
> At the last the Gah'el broke through
> The army of Dana was put to flight
> There was great slaughter among them
> The Gah'el and drove them out of the place
> The three kings of Dana were killed in the route
> Their three queens abandoned them
> The white, the red and the black
> Andraste, the eagle
> Andarta, the hawk
> Catubodua the crow ...

At the mention of Catudodua's name, I noticed more than one warrior make the two-finger sign to ward off evil. I imagined some of them were tempted to spit toward the north, but remembered he was in the hall of the king.

> When the tribe of Dana saw their leaders were dead
> And their queens had abandoned them
> They fell back in great confusion
> The warriors of the Gah'el pursued them
> They followed the men of Dana so hotly
> That they were never able to assemble their army
> They had to own themselves beaten
> They had to give the green lands to the Gah'el
> Then Amerginos, son of the warrior, rose up
> Amerginios the wise, favorite of Lugos
> And he said to the people of Dana

We offer you this peace so our peoples will flourish
While Lugos' chariot is high in the sky
While the lands are green and verdant
From Aedrinios when warmth returns
To Anagantio when the leaves fall
The Gah'el shall rule the lands
But when Lugos goes to his rest
      From Ogronnios when the cold breath of the north is felt
To Elembiuios, the month of the red deer
      And the lands are brown and refuse to give up their fruits
Dana shall rule them
And the nations agreed to this compromise
As long as the nations honor the accord
Peace will last between the them
Then Amerginos mab Milour chanted this song,
    I am the wind across the plain
I am the wave of the sea
I am the bull of seven battles
I am the eagle on the rock
I am the flash of the sun
I am the most beautiful of plants
I am the strong wild boar
I am the salmon in the water
I am the lake in the plain
I am the word of knowledge
I am the head of the battle spear
I am the fire in the hearth
Who spreads light in the gathering on the hills?
Who can tell the ages of the moon?
Who can tell the place where the sun rests?

Throughout the hall, fists pounded tables in time with Amerginos' chant. When it ended, I reached out to take my cup but stopped as a hand fell onto my shoulder. I looked up behind me and found myself staring up into two orbs of green fire.

"So, Arth ... are you going to spend the entire evening ignoring me?"

Rhonwen!

Before I could answer, she continued, "Come ... walk out with me ... it's too beautiful an evening to spend under a roof!"

Without a thought, I stood up and began to follow her out of the hall. Then, I remembered I had left my *pugio* on the table. That was the mistake I made in Vesantio which caused me to face the *sicarius*, Bulla, with empty hands. I didn't think I'd need a blade to face Rhonwen, but I didn't need to make the same mistake twice. I wiped the blade on a towel and slipped it into the scabbard hanging from my belt.

I caught up with her as she was leaving the hall. She was right, the evening was too beautiful to remain inside. The western sky was streaked with deep yellow-gold and purple. The evening star, Venus, the Roman love goddess herself, was bright above the horizon, while the rest of heaven's candles were emerging through the darkling sky. Although it was the last evening of October, the night was still and warm.

Below us, candles and lamps marked houses and clusters of revelers out for the festival. The murmur of voices and laughter could be heard from the shadows below.

Rhonwen slipped her arm through mine, "Let's go down and join them, Arth."

We walked together arm in arm through the gate of the *dun*. The sentry, leaning on his spear, gave us a nod through the crooked grin of at least a pitcher of beer.

"*Buhdouch uhn fodous uh noson hon*," Rhonwen gave him the traditional Samon'win greeting, "Be fortunate this night!"

"And you, lady!" he responded with a wink.

Rhonwen was silent until we had walked a few paces down the hill. Then, she asked, "Why the long face, Arth?"

"What?" I responded. "Nothing ... it's nothing ... just tired ..."

Rhonwen sighed and squeezed my arm, "Please, Arth ... you look like a little boy whose puppy has run off ... you should be ... well, more festive ... cheerful, at least. Everything seems to have turned out the way you and Troucillos wanted. Your precious alliance is safe. Besides! It's the evening of Samon'win! The night when the rules don't apply ... a night when anything is possible ..."

I had no idea where she was going with this, so I remained silent.

She giggled and poked me in the side, "This isn't about *us*, is it?"

Us! She had engaged decisively but I had no counter. I think I made a choking sound.

"It is, isn't it!" she laughed. "You're jealous! Why? What have I done?"

Denial was my only viable defense. "I'm not jealous ..." I started.

"You *are*!" She countered pushing her shoulder into mine. "Was it Kunagnos ..."

When I didn't respond, she continued, "Kunagnos! The three-strander sitting next to me at the feast! Don't be silly, Arth! He's over thirty-five! Almost twice my age! He's married with a herd of kids! His oldest is joining the king's *fintai* next season as a shield bearer. You're jealous of Kunagnos! I can hardly believe it."

When I didn't respond, she continued, "If you're jealous, that means you have feelings for me ... doesn't it!"

She dug her finger into my side. "Come on! Admit it! You have feelings for me, don't you?"

She had stormed through my defenses. She had penetrated all the way to my third line, my forlorn hope.

Fortunately for me, she kept talking, "You men are hopeless at this! If Bronwen herself came down from the blue lands and threw herself at you, you'd stand there with that poker face of yours like you weren't at all interested."

Rhonwen seemed to be having most of the conversation with herself. I scrambled to reestablish my defenses.

We were down off the hill on the central road walking south toward the main gate of the town. There were few houses here, mostly parkland on both sides of the road as it descended toward the town walls. Groups of revelers and couples arm in arm passed us, their faces obscured with masks or blackened ash. They assumed we were out for the same reason as themselves.

Rhonwen seemed to have gotten over her celebration at exposing my "jealousy." In a calmer voice she asked, "Do you ever think about marriage, Arth?"

An attack from a different angle, I thought. "I'm a soldier ..." I began.

"That's no answer," she interrupted. "I think about marriage," she continued. "I am of the age ... and now that my cousin is *pendefig* ..."

It dawned on me then that this was the reason she invited me out, to break the news to me. "A political marriage!" I asserted. "Druce wants to marry you off to one of the clans ..."

"Druce!" she interrupted. "That ... that gnome! He's so ... so ... Roman! I'm a free woman of the Gah'el! No one's going to 'marry me off', Arth! No one! I'll make my own choice!"

She was silent for a few heartbeats, then continued, "But you are right ... a marriage has been proposed for me ... one my cousin, Morcant, and your friend, Troucillos, think a good idea ..."

Here it comes, I thought.

"Do you have a sweetheart back home?" Rhonwen suddenly asked me.

"A sweetheart," I gulped. A sweetheart. I thought of Gabi, the girl who tried to murder me twice; and Cynthia, my "wife for the night" in the Blue Door *lupinarium*.

"No ... I don't ... soldiers ..."

"Please, Arth! Enough of this 'I'm a soldier' stuff. Stop thinking like a Rhufeinos and more like a Gah'el ... our soldiers marry! What would *you* look for in a wife?"

"I ... I haven't given it much thought ... I guess she should be smart ... strong ..." I stammered.

"You make her sound like a well-trained war horse," Rhonwen sniffed. "Unlike you, I have given it some thought ... I'm a woman ... marriage means children, and children need security ... safety ... a home. Most men know how to ride, swing a sword, drink ... but they think like little boys ... no thought beyond the next fight ... the next drunken feast ... I will not marry a man like that."

"Then who?" I asked and immediately realized I didn't want to hear the answer.

"Then who?" she echoed. "I know exactly who."

We had reached a spot in the road from which we could see the torches burning on each side of the town gate below us. Off to the southeast, I could see the torches marking the ramparts of the Roman camp. We stood in the shadows, under the bare branches of trees overhanging the roadway. We weren't alone. Other couples were shrouded in the shadows taking advantage of the darkness.

Instead of answering my question, Rhonwen swung around to face me and asked, "Do you want to kiss me, Arth?"

"Yes!" I choked.

"Then what are you waiting for?" she leaned into me.

I leaned forward to kiss her. Suddenly she stiffened, started to pull away.

At first, I thought she had changed her mind.

Then, something hit me from behind. I stumbled forward, pushing Rhonwen back off the road.

I saw a shadowy figure recover itself in the road before me. I saw its arms go up over its head; a cry; it rushed toward me.

I drew my *pugio*. Without thinking, I executed a front thrust. My blade tore through flesh and cartilage where the throat meets the shoulders. I twisted the blade, withdrew, and recovered. The dark figure stood still for a heartbeat, staggered, and fell with a wet gargling sound. A short sword fell to the ground at my feet.

I moved forward to examine the figure. I was hit again from behind. A screaming fury seemed to climb up onto my back. I stood straight and flung my arms back. It fell off me. I felt a warm wetness on my right shoulder.

The dark figure recovered itself. I saw an arm go up, heard a shriek. Then, another shadow moved in from the right. I heard a thump and the fury fell onto the road.

The second shadow approached me. It was Rhonwen. Her *dagr* was out in her right hand. "Are you alright, Arth," she reached out with her left hand and touched my shoulder.

When she pulled her hand back, I could see her rubbing her fingers together, "You're hurt," she said.

She walked forward and called down to the gate below, "Guards! Guards! Come quickly! A king's guest has been attacked! Bring torches!"

I sat down in the road, my *pugio* still grasped in my right hand. Rhonwen walked back toward me sheathing her *dagr*. She checked my first attacker probing the body with her foot.

"That one's finished." she muttered.

The second figure lay in the middle of the roadway and moaned. "Hit her full in the face with the handle of my knife," Rhonwen said. "Felt like punching a stone." She flexed the fingers of her right hand a few times. "She'll be out for a while."

"Her?" I asked.

"Yes ... a woman." Rhonwen nodded.

Then, "One of your old girl friends trying to ruin our moment?" she chuckled.

The guards with torches were approaching us.

"Over here!" Rhonwen commanded. "I'm Rhonwen merc Gwen, cousin of the *pendefig*! This is Arth mab Secundos, guest of the king!"

One of the soldiers brought a torch over. In the light, Rhonwen examined my shoulder, "Not deep," she muttered. "A few stitches."

Then to the guard, "Let me have your scarf!"

The man surrendered his scarf and Rhonwen pressed it down on my shoulder. "Here, Arth, press down on this. And, put that knife away ... this fight's over."

She got up and examined the dead man. She had to rub the ash off his face, "Malouuhnos' black priest," she announced. "That clears up that mystery."

Then she and the guard walked over to the other figure recovering itself on the ground, "Ah ... the infamous Gourach merc Fetroda, daughter of the tomb ... tie her hands! The *pendefig* will want to talk to her!"

She returned to me. "Can you stand?"

I grunted in the affirmative and one of the guards helped me to my feet.

Rhonwen placed her fists on her hips and declared, "I've got to hand it to you, Arth mab Secundos ... going out courting with you is certainly not boring!"

Post Scriptum
Postscript

Looking over what I've written, I must admit that in those days I was a better soldier than a lover.

That's probably still true.

I still have the knife scar on my right shoulder. Rhonwen describes it as my "courting scar," and at times as her "first love bite."

The gate guards cleaned up the mess on the road and delivered the body and the witch to Duuhruhda. At Druce's suggestion, the king sent the body of the black druid to Labienus saying that this was the man who had murdered his soldier.

Labienus hung the naked body up on a training pole in the middle of the 10th Legion's *praetorium* campus. On it, he hung a sign,

Militem Romanum occidebam

Milite Romano occidebar

A Roman soldier I killed

By a Roman soldier I was killed.

The body remained there until the crows had had their fill. There was no more talk among the *muli* about the *Stryx* after that.

The poor crazed Morna, "Witch of the Tomb," disappeared into some druidical monastic community north of Bibracte. The Gah'el consider those whose minds are taken from them by the gods special. To do them harm would offend the gods.

Rhonwen did the stitching of my shoulder wound. She insisted, saying Spina's sewing skills weren't up to stitching storage sacks closed. Spina wisely chose not to argue the point.

I went back to the camp.

Labienus gave me some time to heal then put me to work. By that I mean, he turned me over to Tertius Piscius Malleus, "The Hammer" - *Centurio Primus Pilus* of the Tenth Legion, for winter training and conditioning. Malleus in turn assigned me to Strabo's cohort as a "supernumerary." Each morning, we made forced marches out into the boonies, *impedimenti*, with full pack. Then, in the afternoon, we worked out on training stakes with weighted, wooden swords and wicker shields.

I would need every bit of it. Caesar had ambitious plans against the Belgae for the coming campaign season.

When I wasn't getting my brains beaten out at the training stakes and practice scrums, I studied with Dion. I returned to the windy plains of Troy and learned how to speak the koine like an Alexandrian merchant.

Dion had become Ebrius' assistant in Labienus' *Principia*, which means he did most of Ebrius' work for him.

I saw little of Rhonwen that winter.

When Ula, Morcant's wife, came to Bibracte with their daughter, Gouenhouhvar, Rhonwen stayed on to help with the baby. I needed to know what she meant by her "courting" remark when we went for our ill-fated Samon'win stroll. But I had little time for visiting and she had little time for entertaining.

I felt that she had opened a space between us and was daring me to cross it. I had no idea how to approach her and less on what to say to her if I did. So, we settled into a quixotic stalemate for the rest of that winter; infatuation and confusion on my part, seeming indifference and disinterest on hers.

Now, this unattainable hope of my teenage infatuation warms her icy feet against my back on cold winter nights!

Our children are well and safe; we are at peace.

For that, I thank *Bona Fortuna*.

A Preview of
The Murdered Centurion
By
Ray Gleason
The First Book of
The Gaius Marius Mystery
Series

Journal of the Prefect of the Watch,
Mediolanum,
During the Consulships of the Imperator, Caesar, Son of the God, the Exalted
One, 8th Term, and Titus Statilius Taurus, 2nd Term
26 BCE

DIES I – A D XVII CALENDAE MAII
Day 1 – 15 April

If one were to ask what I hate most about getting old, it's sleep. Not sleeping itself, but the difficulty in sleeping.

When I was a youth in the legions, I could sleep deeply for an entire night on a pile of rocks. Now, well into my forty-ninth year, every night I feel like I'm taking a beating from my own mattress.

Any position I take in bed, I feel the aches of old injuries or the parts of my body that have been worn down by years of marching *impedimentus*, under full pack. I find the only position that's not all ache and agony is lying flat on my back ... which means I snore ... which means Rhonwen, my darlin' wife, plants a pointy elbow in my ribs to get me to stop.

Then, it's toss and turn ... on my back ... snore ... elbow ... repeat until the sun rises.

Some mornings, I feel like I've been beaten ... bruised ribs ... stiff joints ... limbs that just won't move.

Ah, dear gods, for one night of a twenty-year-old's sleep!

That is, when I get to spend an entire night in the sack, like the civilized, retired army officer and public official I'm supposed to be.

I am six months into a new career as the *Praefectus Urbanus Municipii Mediolani,* the Urban Prefect of the Enfranchised Town of Mediolanum.

Octavius, or the 'Exalted One' as he's known these days down in Rome, granted Roman citizenship to the former Gallic *oppidum* of Mediolanum. It was part of his program of extending *romanitas*, Roman culture, into the provinces. In order to ensure that his little experiment worked, he needed someone to be his 'eyes and ears' up here, as he put it. Hence, my appointment.

In the final campaign against Antonius, I was Octavius' *Praefectus Castrorum*, the tactical commander of his legions. Essentially, he and Agrippa decided what needed to be done, and I got the legions to do it.

When we finally got Antonius and his Macedonian tart safely tucked away in their tombs, Octavius demobilized most of the legions, both his and Antonius'. I took my retirement; Octavius gave me the golden ring of the *Ordo Equestris*, the Order of Knights, formalized my marriage to Rhonwen, granted citizenship to our children, and sent me on my way with enough sacks of silver to maintain my new lifestyle as a married Roman gentleman living in the provinces.

This was quite a change considering that right after Caesar was murdered, Octavius, in order to claim his right as Caesar's political heir, didn't know whom to kill first - me or Antonius. The night before Actium, when Octavius was deep in his cups - his way of preparing for battle - he told me that after Caesar was assassinated, I was higher on his wish-list than Brutus, Longinus, and the rest of the so-called *Liberatores*, but not quite as high as Antonius.

I sometimes feel sorry for Antonius. He was a bully, a braggard, a drunk, a hell of a fighter, and a good comrade. We first met in Gaul. He was a narrow striper on Caesar's staff, and I was junior officer in the old man's praetorian detail. But it was during the Vercingetorix campaign that Antonius came into his own as a leader, a fighter, and a drinker. He went into that campaign a drunken tribune and came out a drunken legate.

The *muli* worshipped Antonius. They would have followed him to the very gates of Dis' kingdom. His problem was that he didn't know what to do with himself once the fighting was over, except to drink, chase women, and dabble in politics, of which he was competent only in the first two. I believe that he would have been perfectly content to spend his life with a full beaker of wine and a good woman to warm his bed at night ... but then the Macedonian got her talons into him and pushed him into a confrontation he couldn't win.

By that time, Octavius had no further use for Antonius.

Fortunately, he still had a use for me and Agrippa. The *muli* couldn't stomach Octavius, so he had me between the soldiers and himself. And while Octavius couldn't plan a military campaign to defeat a mob of drunken Vestals rampaging through the forum, he had Marcus Agrippa Vipsanius for that. What was even better, neither Agrippa nor I had any political pedigree, so we could be of no real threat to his ambitions. We were his own personal triumvirate, but without any political baggage.

So, the three of us dealt with Antonius, and picked up the riches of *Aegyptus* for good measure. I retired and moved back to Mediolanum; Agrippa followed Octavius down to Rome; and Octavius became *Augustus*.

Now, although theoretically I report to the *triumviri* Octavius appointed to run Mediolanum, I send Octavius a confidential report each month detailing the gratitude of the people of Mediolanum for his generous gift of Roman citizenship; any indications of unrest or sedition among the 'natives' or among Antonius' veterans, whom he planted up here as a *colonia*; what broad stripers, senatorials, have passed through, or lingered, on their way between Rome and the northern provinces; and any rumors floating down here from Illyricum and the north.

Of course, I do this without the awareness of our urban *triumviri* ... they themselves are objects of Octavius' scrutiny, along with the gaggle of praetors, quaestors, and aediles they've appointed to run the town.

When I report to the *triumviri* for my weekly 'reviews,' I, of course, say nothing of this to them. Their interests are restricted to the cost of keeping the town safe, the number of runaway slaves reported, the number of runaway slaves apprehended, and the number of murders, muggings, fights, rapes, riots, robberies, drunk-and-disorderlies, public urinations, fire-code violations, fires ... all the *minutia* that keep our streets interesting after dark.

So, it is not at all surprising that someone is pounding on my door in the middle of the night. I hear it but am trying to convince myself it's part of a dream when Rhonwen's elbow hits its accustomed target.

"You going to do something about that?" she mumbles.

I manage to get enough body parts working to get both feet on the floor, which immediately reminds me that we are still in the middle of April, and the nights are as cold as a tax collector's heart.

I sniff the air. No sign of anything burning. *Good,* I think, *no fire ... at least no fire close to here.*

I rub my hands across my face to get the sleeper's cobwebs out of my eyes, then make a sound like an irritated horse with a bad cold.

"Where's Mustela?" I rumble. "Why isn't he taking care of it? ... it's his job for Hecate's sake."

"He's upstairs in his girlfriend's apartment," Rhonwen tells me in a tone that she usually reserves for merchants who can't get her change right.

"Girlfriend," I grunt. "I didn't know about any *girlfriend.*"

"Then *you're* the only one in the house!" Rhonwen dismisses me out of the depths of her pillow. "Even the girls figured it out weeks ago!"

I get to my feet and stretch toward the ceiling with my hands pushing in the small of my back. I hear the accustomed snaps and pops as my bones adjust back into place for my body to operate in the vertical. I throw on yesterday's tunic, still draped over the chair where I tossed it last night. For good measure, I unsheathe my *pugio* from my military belt hanging on the back of the chair. We live in a pretty good neighborhood, but you never know. Better a useless knife in your hand than an unexpected knife in your ribs. I then proceed to stumble about in the dark in my bare feet, and even though I should know where all the obstacles lie, my left foot finds one with a resounding crack.

When I make it to the inner door of our apartment, I see that the bar is still down. I also notice the curtain to Mustela's *cubiculum* is pulled back, the doorway like an entrance to a black cave gaping in the darkness ... more evidence that he is out of the apartment, off on some amorous expedition, as my darlin' wife claims and *everybody* knows.

I briefly register the thought that if this keeps up, I'll have to hire a regular porter ... some ex-legionary ... someone I can trust.

I lift the bar, stack it against the wall, then take the wooden key off a shelf next to the door. When I had the house built, I installed wooden locks in all the inner apartment doors, so that they could be locked when the bar was removed.

Dion, my children's tutor, had found a Greek manuscript that explained not only the principles of what he called 'tumblers,' but how to construct a lock that could be manipulated from both sides of a door. It took a Gallic artificer a bit of trial and error to get the mechanisms to work properly – they seemed to be especially susceptible to failure when Rhonwen was their target – but ultimately, I have a fairly reliable way of locking my doors from the outside.

I jiggle the tumblers with the key until they release, then push the door out into the connecting corridor. In the outer corridor the pounding sounds like the inside of a drum. I recognize the voice shouting for the door to be open. It's Crispus, 'Curly,' one of Antonius' ex-*muli*, who now serves as an optio of the watch in *Regio I*, the town forum and its immediate surroundings.

"Lay off the door!" I shout. The pounding stops and I lift the bar. "Move back," I say, as I push the thick oaken door out into the street.

I see Crispus standing back away from the door, his face illuminated by a torch held by someone standing behind the door. I'm just about to demand what's so shaggin' important that he has to wake me, my family, and half the neighborhood, when I hear one of the inner doors behind me slam open and bare foot-slaps rushing down the corridor.

The missing Mustela has finally materialized.

"What's up, *Capu*?" he calls, struggling with his tunic.

"*Beneventum ad terram viventum*," I greet him sarcastically, "Welcome to the land of the living ... I was just wondering when you would finally decide to join us."

I turn back to Crispus, "*Nuntia, Optio!*" I command, "Report!"

Crispus straightens a bit when he hears the military formula. "*Praefecte*! Sir! The tribune requests your presence in the forum, QC!"

"QC?" I repeat. "*Quam celerrime*? ASAP? What tribune are you talking about, optio?"

Crispus' eyes widen a bit at the question. I realize what a stupid question I just asked about a half a heartbeat before Crispus realizes that he's talking to a senior officer, so common sense and logic do not apply.

He responds, "The only sober tribune we got, sir! The Tribune Macro!"

Macro and I go way back to the days when I was a farm boy with dirt behind my ears. I had a bad case of puppy love for a senator's daughter who was possessed by all the Furies of the underworld. Macro is a good ten years older than I am, so whatever has gotten him out of Rufia's bed in the middle of a cold April night must be important.

"*Bene*," I nod. "Leave that torch in a sconce and come on into the house."

"It will take me just a little while to get ready," I say as we walk down the corridor. "It's a cold night. Do you boys need anything warm to drink while you're waiting?"

As I'm reaching for my key, I hear a muffled chorus of "*nolo ... gratias ... no ... thanks.*" Then Mustela cuts in, "It won't take me long to get my kit together, *Capu'.*"

"You don't need to go," I say absently, jiggling my key in the door.

Then, I realize what a mistake I have just made. Mustela was my personal servant when I was Octavius' *praefectus castrorum.* His job was to keep my kit straight, my quarters clean, and me fed; so, of course, the slang term in the legions for his job was *uxor,* the boss's 'wife.'

But more than that, Mustela was also my *geminus,* my 'battle brother.' On the battlefield, it was his job to protect my open side, to relieve me when I was too tired to hold my shield up, and to make sure that I came back from the fight in one piece. No *geminus* worth his daily salt would ever abandon his companion; such a thing was shameful. That's why in the legions we refer to a good and trusted battle companion as '*me'umbra,*' 'my shadow.' He's always with me.

I finally jiggle the door open. "Sorry, *me'umbra* ... I wasn't thinking ... it's too cold and too late at night ... kiss your lady goodnight and get back down here *QC* ... we travel light ... belt, *pugio* ... a sturdy pair of *bracae,* and a good woolen *sagum* with a hood should be handy on a night like this ... I don't know how long this will take."

Mustela issues an affirmative snort as he heads up the stairs to his girlfriend's apartment. I'm forgiven, but he heard me say it.

When I finally get into the apartment, I see Rhonwen has the lamps lit. As she suddenly appears, I turn to my men and hiss, "Keep it quiet ... the children are sleeping."

"You are welcome into our home," she intones a Latinized version of the traditional Gah'el welcome.

Being Romans, neither man knows the response, "The blessings of the gods on you and all in this place." Both stop, incline their heads toward Rhonwen and mutter something sounding like, "*Matrona* ... Missus!" Then, Crispus' torch man, Somnus, so called because he has never been seen to move quickly, actually knuckles his forehead.

Rhonwen has been dealing with Romans long enough not to be concerned by their not understanding the protocol of entry. She continues, "I have prepared some warm *mulsum* to take away the edge of a cold night. Isolta is bringing it from the kitchen. Please, enter and be comfortable."

Rhonwen is observing the custom of our people. She is obligated to offer hospitality to guests, regardless of the dark hour and their unexpected appearance. That is exactly how our gods test our piety.

The guests, if they were Gah'el, would also understand that it's irreverent and boorish to refuse such offered hospitality. In the old tales, it's the way in which wars got started.

But being Romans, they haven't a clue. So, I anticipate both men refusing, out of some Roman sense of decorum ... they realize they are standing in the middle of their boss's house after getting his wife and him out of bed at the-gods-only-know what part of a cold, black April night.

I quickly deflect their potential refusal in a manner Romans understand, "That is *not* a request, gentlemen. Come in, sit down, enjoy the wine."

Then, I tell them, "I'll be back before the candle can burn down an *uncia*, and we'll be off."

As I'm leaving the room, I see Rhonwen trying to get my *vigiles* to sit. They treat my chairs as if they are somewhat dangerous, forbidding things, not to be trusted. Isolta, Rhonwen's maid, arrives from the kitchens with a tray carrying six steaming mugs.

I'm sure Rhonwen will sort it. She'd have made a damn fine *decanus* in any legion I served.

In our room, I slip my *pugio* back in its sheath. It's the same one Macro gave me on my sixteenth birthday, and like me, a bit worn down over the years. It's one of the few survivors from those days when my dreams were of becoming a fabulously rich and urbane wine merchant married to the beautiful daughter of a Roman Senator.

How the gods must have pissed themselves laughing over that!

I pull my tunic slightly over my head and sniff at the sleeves. It's one of my old military tunics, faded legionary red, with long winter sleeves sewn on. It passes the sniff test, so I decide I'll keep it.

I let the tunic slide back down over my shoulders and reach into my clothing chest for a pair of woolen socks and Gallic *bracae*. The problem with dressing this time of year is that you don't know whether to dress for the morning, when the ice is as hard as stone on the pavement, or for the afternoon, when the dandelions are poking their heads out from between the cobbles.

I'm old, so the priority of staying warm ends debate on that dilemma.

I'm about to pull on a pair of old army boots when I remember Rhonwen's rule about our wooden floors, hobnails, and my not having a home-cooked meal for a month. So, I decide I'll carry the boots out to the door.

I shove the end of my tunic down into the *bracae* and secure the cords. Then, I strap my military belt around my waist. I check where the buckle fastens; my life since leaving the military can be measured by the 'buckle-slippage' around my waist.

I remember that my heavy winter *sagum* is still hanging on a peg near the front door where I hung it last night. I pick up the boots and am heading out the door when I stop short.

"*Cac't!*" I utter aloud ... *I should wear a scarf for extra warmth,* I think to myself. Aquila, the north wind, blows right across the forum in April.

I go back into our *cubiculum* and rout through my clothing chest looking for my *sudarium*. Then, I remember, it's hanging up with my cloak.

"*Cac't!*" I say yet again, then head out to our *atrium* and rejoin my little midnight *comitatus*.

When I reach the *atrium*, there's quite a little party going on. Not only is Rhonwen entertaining Crispus and Somnus, but Mustela has made it back downstairs with his girlfriend, Merope.

I don't believe for a second that Merope is a real Greek. She speaks Latin, and only Latin, with an accent ripe of Roman *Subura*, the slums. But Rufia put her up with us and paid a generous rental - part of her Blue-Door-*Lupinarium* retirement plan, I imagine. My original connection to Rufia was through my friend, Macro, and through the fact that she saved my bacon many years ago when some hitters came up from Rome looking to do me.

But Merope and I have a history too, an encounter, really, that I'd rather never have to explain to Rhonwen. So, if Merope wants to be a mysterious Greek who speaks slum Latin, it's alright with me.

Then, I spy my middle daughter, Maria Minor, or Edana, 'Little Terror,' as she's known among the *familia Insubreca*. She is cozied into Isolta's side, hoping not to be noticed, but her flaming red hair's a dead giveaway.

"*Filia!*" I call to her in Latin, just to make sure she knows I'm being 'official.' "Daughter! Get back to bed!"

"But Daaah!" she whines back in Gah'el, to make sure I know she's not buying the Roman *paterfamilias* routine. "I can't sleep! There's so much noise out here!"

Before I can respond, Rhonwen intervenes. "*Coniunx!*" she says in Latin, to let me know she's being 'official.' "Husband! I'll put her right back into bed as soon as you men go on your way."

I'm about to object when my hard-won wisdom regarding family life - or how things get done in my house - intervenes. Don't start a fight you cannot win.

Just to save a little face, I say, "*Bene, Coniunx!* Alright, wife! You have *my* permission."

I'm sure I'll pay for that one sometime soon.

"As soon as I get my boots on, we'll be off," I say to the men. Then, I see they all have their boots *off*. Obviously, Gallic hospitality does not extend to scratching wooden floors with Roman hobnails.

"*Eamus,*" I correct myself, "Let's go, then! There are benches outside to put boots on."

As I'm leaving the apartment, I hear Rhonwen announce in Latin, "I will clean everything up, *O Coniunx*, and put *your* daughter back into her bed." This is accompanied by a muted chorus of feminine snickering.

Recognizing her tone, I accept that I will pay dearly - and repeatedly - for my *coniunx* comment.

When we get outside, I lead my party southwest down the *Clivus Fontium*, the Street of Fountains. It's not the most direct route to the forum, But being a wide street, it's the safest at this time of night. Not that I expect a mugger to attack a party of four burly men with torches, three of whom are carrying clubs. But as I have already learned in this job, assuming any intelligence on the part of a criminal is not well advised.

I have been told that the *Clivus Fontium* traces the *fossum et vallum*, the ditch and wall, of the old legionary *castrum* from the days of Scipio the Bald. After the conquest of the Insubres, the *castrum* served as the center of the *colonia* established for Scipio's veterans. The Street of Fountains used to lead to the water point for the old camp, which has long since disappeared.

We soon intersect the *Via Praetoria*, one of the main streets of town. We turn left, entering the forum from the northwest. I immediately spot torches clustered in front of the old *Aedes Veneris*, Temple of Venus, which now also serves as the center of worship for *Divus Iulius*, the deified Iulius Caesar.

I immediately feel a slight wave of anxiety.

We just had a major Roman dog-and-pony show at this site to install a new statue of Caesar's heir, our *Augustus*, Gaius Iulius Caesar *Divi Filius, Imperator*. Of course, we all had to turn out for the installation - the *triumviri*; the town praetors, questors and aediles; and all the knights and leading citizens. It was a sea of glistening white togas, broad and narrow purple stripes, and bare white legs. That day, the sun never broke through the clouds and there was a stiff breeze from the mountains to the north. At one point, snow flurries were whipping across the forum on the wings of the *Aquila*, the north wind. By the time all the speeches and posturings were over, all our local nobs were blue around the lips, and their knees were shaking so bad I'm surprised their balls didn't fall off.

I dressed up in my parade uniform. At Rhonwen's insistence, I didn't wear my Gallic chainmail *lorica*, festooned with my *phalerae*, my battle decorations. Instead, I wore my gilded plate armor; 'snob plates' we used to call them in the legions because only pompous idiots would trust their lives to them in combat. I wouldn't compromise on my torcs, especially the five-strand golden torc of a Sequani chief that my friend, Athauhnu had given me after Bibracte. Of course, trying to look somewhat like a good Roman, I was bare legged too. After the ceremony, I couldn't feel my toes for hours.

Representing Octavius, Tiberius Claudius Nero, one of Livia Drusilla's brats, came up from Rome for the ceremony. In all fairness, he wasn't a bad sort. He sought me out at the feast that followed the installation. He was curious about army life, legionary tactics, and what the terrain was like on the northern borders and along the *Rhenus*. He was especially curious about Caesar ... how did he make decisions? ... how did he interact with the men? ... He said that his father, Augustus, was going to start him out on his political career in Rome this November as soon as he turned sixteen. But Tiberius felt the only worthwhile and noble profession for a Roman was in the military. His mother, Livia Drusilla, discouraged such ideas. She insisted his 'destiny' lay elsewhere.

I told him that *I* had joined the legions at sixteen, but I did not share why. I was about to share some anecdotes about Caesar when my cousin, Lucius Helvetius Naso, one of our *triumviri*, swept Tiberius up to keep him circulating.

As Tiberius plunged back into the crowd, I noticed that he was being closely shepherded by his security detail: three huge Germanic-looking thugs, who were obviously concealing weapons under their tunics. I had heard that Octavius had continued the practice of Caesar, his 'father,' of maintaining a troop of private bodyguards recruited from the Germanic tribes along the *Rhenus.*

Ironic, I thought, *I spend half my life helping Caesar push those Kraut bastards out of the imperium and now they live in a palace on the Palatine!*

Di rident ... the gods laugh!

As I join the vigiles clustered in front of Venus' temple, I immediately spy the cause of this midnight commotion. A corpse is laid out right in front of Octavius' new statue.

My friend Macro separates himself from the cluster of *vigiles* flocked together around the torches for warmth. Dion says men age according to their predominant element: water men become fat; earth men become slow and lazy; fire men become irascible; and air men grow thin. If this is true, Macro's predominant element is air; he does not look like he gained an *uncia* in body weight since we first met almost thirty years ago. He still has the limp and the scar down the left side of his face from his days chasing Mithridates through the boondocks of Pontus and Armenia.

"Sorry for getting you out of your nice warm bed on a cold night like this, Gai," he quips, "but I thought you'd better see this."

"Just a killing?" I challenge.

Macro shrugs. "Maybe, but someone dumped the body of a citizen right under the Brat's marble nose."

I grimace. During the wars, Macro developed a bad habit of mimicking Antonius and referring to Octavius as *puerulus Caesaris,* 'Caesar's brat.'

"Not out here, old friend," I caution him. "Statues have ears. A citizen, you say ... show me the body!"

Macro nods and leads me back through the cluster of *vigiles,* who part before us like the sea did for the escaping Egyptian slaves in an old eastern miracle myth. Right where the four main roads of the town intersect, a highly-polished, granite plinth - black, blank, and about ten *pedes* in height – was raised long ago to mark the spot. Since it stands directly outside the shrine of *Divus Iulius,* the forum wags began to refer to it as 'Caesar's last erection.' There, at the base of the plinth, its back against the pedestal and facing the newly installed statue of the *Augustus,* is the body of a man.

"Have you summoned Spina?" I ask Macro.

"What's the point?" he shrugs. "We know what killed him."

I call for a torch and squat down for a closer look. As I do, one of my knees makes a snapping sound like the breaking of a dry twig. When the torch arrives, my first impressions of the body are the half-open, staring, brown eyes; gray stubble on the chin; and the sallow, gray-yellow color of the face. I look lower and see a reddish-black rent in the tunic, right below the sternum.

I point, "That what killed him?"

Macro nods, "A *percussus* ... basic military stabbing blow ... it's perfect ... in at a slightly upward angle ... slight push left and right ... twist and out ... we haven't turned the body over, but that wound alone would have done for him ... whoever did this had some training.”

“And a soldier's *pugio*,” I add. “One of Antonius' veterans from the *colonia*, you think?”

“Possible,” Macro agrees. “That'd explain dumping the body right under the Bra ... I mean, Octavius' marble nose ... and I think our victim here's ex-military, too.”

I look again at the victim's head. The hair is short, like a military cut. “Why ex-military?” I ask.

Macro uses a stick to lift the corpse's right sleeve; he's careful not to be contaminated by the body, whose *lemur* might be hovering nearby. There I see the tattooed head of a bull and the numerals ‘VII.’

“That's the Seventh Legion,” he says. “By the age of this guy, he might have served with us up in Gaul.”

Macro let that settle in, then says, “And, look at this!”

Macro uses his stick again to indicate something on the corpse's forehead. At first, I see just a red mark. Then, it resolves itself into a symbol.

“What in the names of the three Furies is that?” I say to no one in particular.

Macro answers me anyway, “Don't know, Gai ... me and the boys think it looks a bit like a cross.”

“A cross?” I question. “Why would someone paint a cross on the forehead of a dead citizen? Citizens can't be crucified ... only slaves and foreign criminals. What was used? Is it the victim's blood?”

“Probably,” Macro agrees. “Don't see a murderer carrying around a little pot of red paint ... about the cross, no idea ... unless it's an insult ... or maybe the murderer's signing his work.”

“We have a few of Toni's boys on the force,” I point out. “Any of them recognize this guy?”

“Not so far,” Macro answers. “Maybe one of the day-shift guys can. You want me to rouse them?”

“No ... let them get their sleep ... but we're not going to leave this stiff lying out here,” I say. “We got to have this place cleaned up by sunrise. We have a guy that can draw portraits, right? One of the slaves? Get him to draw a picture of this guy's face ... maybe we can find out who this is."

Macro calls over to the dark mass of vigiles hanging about behind us. "Hey! Sexte! Run back to the house and rout out Scriba ... the one who draws the pictures ... bring him back out here ... make sure he brings some charcoal and papyrus with him."

"Sure thing, boss," I hear a voice shoot back from the crowd.

As Sextus runs off on his mission, I say, "Let's turn this guy and see what we have."

Macro summons two of our slaves to move the body. Romans believe that slaves are below the notice of evil spirits, so contamination is not a problem with them. They roll the corpse, but it maintains the same posture it had leaning against the plinth.

"Note that the body is fully stiff," I instruct. "Spina can fix the time of death knowing that."

Macro and I examine the body, but we can find no other wounds. Then, Macro remarks, "No blood ... if he were killed here there'd be a pool of it."

"So, he was killed somewhere else and dumped here?" I ask.

"That'd be my guess," Macro confirms.

"Then, we should have a blood trail," I say. "Let's sweep the area ... get these *vigiles* on line ... no more than three *pedes,* single arm's length, between each man ... centered on where we found the body ... start a good ten paces back from this spot and sweep right across for another ten ... then again at a right angle ... pick up everything that isn't growing here ... but especially look for a blood trail ... have the duty *optio* supervise it."

"Basic legionary police call," Macro quips. "Noses to the ground ... arses and elbows in the air."

"You got it," I agree. "Pick up everything but find me that blood trail."